PERL

The Awakening

MELISSA FLESHER

Cover design and illustrations by: Melissa Flesher
Map designs by: Erik Flesher
Printed in the United States of America

LOVE AND GRATITUDE

*For my son Noah, my nieces Cora and Elena,
my nephews Oliver, Sebastian and Johnny,
and all the children who will inherit this world.*

*A special thanks to my parents Roger and Diana,
and my brother Nick and his wife Katherine, and my
brother Chris and his wife Jennie.*

*To my moon, my co-creator in this world,
my husband Erik.*

*To those with imaginative hearts
that hear the songs in nature,
connecting us to all life on Earth.*

Greetings,

I am the Mapmaker of all living things ~
every leaf, every feather, I speak softly in nature
and in the quiet pockets of a silent mind.
Listen close, I have a secret ~
As you take a deep breath from the air we all share,
look up at the open night sky,
watch as a new star is being born,
and feel the energy of our oneness.

This book has found and chosen you.

~ Ever

1 OCEAN TREASURE

On a tranquil dawn, the polluted waters off the shores of Mont Michel were unnaturally still. Waves were barely at a ripple, and the seagulls, normally a noisy bunch, were quiet, not one squawking for their breakfast. Breaking the morning silence like an angry clap of thunder, a great blue whale *(Balaenoptera Musculus)* burst from the water. Her powerful two-hundred-ton body breeched up nearly thirty feet before splashing back down in a spray of white foam. Against all reason, she made her way towards the shore, flopping heavily onto the soft sandy beach. As the sun perched on the horizon, the only sounds heard around the island were the whale's deep, low moans and tail slapping up and down against the shallow surf.

A small group of monks, emptying fishing crates from the previous night's catch, spotted the whale and ran to her. The first monk slid to a halt next to the enormous creature.

"I don't believe my eyes! A blue whale! I thought they'd gone extinct?"

Another answered, "no, last I heard there were at least thirty or so still swimming in these waters." He tenderly patted her giant fin. "Come, we had better act fast. Run and fetch Brother Ximu."

In the Brothers of the Quill order, one-hundred-two-year-old Ximu was the eldest and wisest. His wire-rimmed circular spectacles magnified the playful twinkle in his deep-set eyes, while his mustache ends curled upwards, gave him a cheerful air. Ximu bounded down the beach, making a beeline for the whale, his long white beard billowing over his shoulder, sandals kicking up plumes of sand. His round belly swayed to and fro as he shambled toward the commotion. Under each freckled arm he carried a plank of driftwood, both as long as dolphins. Following closely behind the old monk was a hooded stampede of his fellow brothers, all clutching boards and shovels, scampering to see the rare sight lying on the shore.

They all came to a bumbling halt next to the colossal mammal. Without a word, they went to work, pushing and prodding, attempting to wedge the boards underneath her enormous one-hundred-foot-long body. The morning was already warm, and the monks, in their heavy robes, were soon drenched in sweat. They tried pitching the whale back and forth, but she wouldn't move. In fact, it seemed to them as if she was resisting, pushing back against the monks with her remaining strength.

As the monks struggled to move the whale, she suddenly let out a long deep "eeeuuugghhhh…" Her eyes widened, then peered down towards her crustacean-covered belly. There, attached to her side, was the largest barnacle *(Coronula Diadema)*, the men had ever seen.

"Maybe that's the cause of her pain?" exclaimed one of the hooded holy men. Pulling a shelling knife from his satchel, he began prying around the barnacled growth, then howled in horror, "oh dear mother of Ever!" he exclaimed. All within earshot gasped.

"Watch your tongue, Victr! What could bring you to use Ever's name in vain?" Ximu corrected him, tightening the rope belt around his waist.

Victr rubbed his wrinkled brow. "I, I, I…" he stammered in disbelief, "it has…an eye." He slowly backed away, while the others huddled in for a closer look.

From inside the dark, crusty barnacle, there were indeed two pale green, sparkling eyes staring back at them. A tiny hand reached out and gripped the edge of the barnacle.

"A baby," muttered Ximu. "Impossible."

The brothers looked at one another in amazement. As if prompted, they kneeled together, and began chanting in unison. In a hushed whisper, the monks repeated softly, "The Prophecy…The Prophecy…The Prophecy."

The whale's cries grew more intense, echoing off the shale cliff walls. Brother Victr, ever the anxious one, stopped chanting and looked around nervously. He stood up and swiftly detached the barnacle, the newborn still snug inside. "Ximu, we should go. If this whale gets any louder, she'll wake all of Mont Michel!"

Agreeing, Ximu gently took the baby out of the barnacle and gestured to the monks with a hurried wave of his arm. "Go. All of you. Swiftly now, and not a word of this. No one can know. Praise be…Ever has chosen us." Ximu paused to look at the child and fell instantly in love. "Hello, little treasure. My, what a bumblebee belly you have! It appears as though someone's been fed well." Ximu smiled at her; she gave a gassy grin back. "Oh, and such marvelous hair! Why it's like a dandelion puff ready to be wished upon." Her thick crop of black hair was so fuzzy, it kept popping out of Ximu's robe. He nestled the baby safely into the nook of his arm, hoping to avoid any gawkers peering at them from the dozens of ramshackle huts scattered along the beach.

Victr's panic was intensifying. "Take the child. I'll stay behind. Surely the Slaughterman is already on his way." He gazed up affectionately at the great mammal, who had ceased her moaning and fallen silent. "I don't think she's long for this world. She won't budge."

Ximu placed a gentle hand on the whale's broad side, saying a quiet prayer for the dying beast. The miraculous blue whale had sacrificed herself for the child. Knowing this was her purpose, she accepted her fate with grace. As she let out her last low, heaving breath, the baby girl, quiet until now, began to wail.

"Hush, hush little one," Ximu cooed softly.

Several monks formed a protective circle around them. They walked in a brown-hooded huddle up the beach, chanting louder to muffle the cries and distract any onlookers, "ohmmmm…ohmmmm…"

The monks squeezed together as they shuffled up a narrow sandy pathway, eventually reaching the oak door of their root cellar home. The infant continued to cry. Tears streamed down her plump, dark cherry cheeks. Some of the baby's teardrops, though, drifted to the ground, and where each drip met Mont Michel's rich, fertile soil, a tiny spout immediately sprang up.

Once safely inside, the monks quickly pulled the heavy door closed behind them, none of them taking notice of the twisting line of bright green leaves now running from the beach to their cellar door.

Line IV, Verse XI (The Prophecy):
And from the depths of the ocean from which life sprang,
so shall the treasure be found.
— *The Awakening*

2 TRUE NATURE

Papa Ximu yelled to Perl's room from down the hallway, "Bumblebee, you must wear your boots when climbing the steps for deliveries, and no arguments!"

Perl hated to wear her boots. They were too hot, too tight, and kept her from feeling the earth beneath her feet and the sand between her chubby brown toes, but Papa Ximu insisted she wear them while making her deliveries.

There were two thousand and ten steps to the summit of Mont Michel, where, like an enormous, glistening crown, sat the Golden Palace, home of the powerful Graves family. Perl, now twelve years old, knew the exact number of steps by heart, having counted them in her head over and over again each day for the last several years.

"I know every rock on this island, and I don't need boots to climb," Perl mumbled to herself, trying to locate her lily pad galoshes hiding somewhere within her very cluttered bedroom.

Nearly every inch of floor space in her small room was carpeted with sketches of plants, animals and other nature drawings. Scattered amongst these doodles were origami birds and insects, carefully folded from leaves Perl had discovered while on her daily walks. There was also an odd collection of twigs, rocks, berries, and other random bits of wildlife.

"Ahh, there you are, Mr. Magnifying Glass. I've been looking for you." She held the lens up to her eye and continued scanning her floor, slowly and deliberately, until stopping abruptly on a pair of green vine laces poking out from underneath some papers. "Ha, ha, you thought you could escape me!" Like a tiger, Perl pounced on her boots, swinging them over her shoulder as she headed down to the kitchen for breakfast.

The smell of warm apples and cinnamon filled the cozy room. As she sat down at their large wooden table, Perl held her boots up to Ximu like a hunter displaying her prey. "I have retrieved the bandits as requested! Their punishment will be life in the dungeon!" she cried, dropping her boots onto the dirt floor beside her.

Ximu placed a large bowl of steaming apple porridge in front of her, and Perl dug in immediately. Picking up Perl's boots, Ximu placed them into her lap. "Yes, brave one," he teased her, "you have made the island safe once again, but I am certain their torture will be having to stay on your stinky feet for an entire day."

"I think my prize should be getting to take the sailboat out after chores," Perl giggled, "I won't go past Trash Island. Cross my heart, Papa. Please!"

"I'm sorry, but the answer is still no. There are dangers beyond our shores, and it's just not safe for a girl your age." Ximu leaned back against the counter and took a sip of piping hot tea.

Wearing boots was annoying, but what really irked Perl was being told she was too young for something. Whenever she'd ask Ximu about the dangers, he'd quickly distract her with one of his many stories.

Ximu dipped a cranberry biscuit into his cup and took a bite. "Have I ever told you why acorns wear hats?"

"Ughh, yes, like five hundred times." Perl scooped a spoonful of apple porridge, reciting with her mouth full. "It's called a cupule, and it protects the delicate embryo inside the kernel, yet only about one in every ten thousand ever successfully sprouts. But did you know, Papa Smarty-pants, that the Druids believed eating acorns would help them see the future?" Perl scooped another bite. "Also, acorns are good luck charms."

Ximu knew that it didn't take much to get her curious mind going, especially when it had anything to do with nature.

"All right then, Acorn Master, how about you tell me why crabs walk sideways?" That got Perl's attention.

"Because long ago, crabs were sandcastle guards and they had to march along the walls sideways to keep watch." As she said this, Perl wielded her spoon like a tiny sword, blocking, dodging and weaving.

Ximu laughed. "I was going to say that's how they move the fastest, but I think I like your theory better."

Perl loved living with the monks. Their underground root cellar was home, and together they worked the gardens, pickling vegetables, preparing, storing and providing food to the residents of Mont Michel. The monks did most of the fishing, but when it came to scaling and deboning the enormous piles of cod *(Gadus morhua)*, grouper *(Epinephenlinae)*, and salmon *(Salmo salar)*, Perl was as skilled as the monks. The Brothers of the Quill were her teachers, her friends, and the only family she'd ever known.

Perl adored each and every monk wholeheartedly, although Papa Ximu was, and always would be, her favorite. He looked after her like an over-protective father from the very first time their eyes met.

However Perl felt about the monks, the locals of Mont Michel had other opinions. Despite the fact that the monks brought them fresh fish and vegetables, the majority of the islanders kept their distance. They viewed the monks as leathery-skinned, fish-odored codgers; throwbacks from a bygone age, and a little too mysterious for their own good.

Little did the islanders realize, Mont Michel had once been a spiritual mecca. In centuries past, the monks who resided there were revered. Around the world, those in search of enlightenment would make a pilgrimage to the sacred island, seeking advice from the divine Brothers of the Quill. In fact, many years ago, the monks once lived within the shimmering gates of the Golden Palace itself. Back then, the entire island was a paradise, rich with colorful exotic flowers, towering trees and wildlife of every kind imaginable. As the years passed, however, the Palace was eventually purchased by a wealthy oil baron by the name of Rutherford Graves, who didn't care for the Brotherhood's curious ways, so he offered them a deal. Graves would allow the monks to live peacefully in the root cellars at the bottom of the island; in exchange, they could keep their fishing nets and gardens, as long as they delivered fresh produce and seafood to the Palace and upper tiers. The Brotherhood agreed, and while they continue to deliver goods to the wealthy, the monks have also done their best to make sure as many islanders as possible receive food.

Today Mont Michel is still the center of the universe, not as a spiritual mecca, but as the most powerful capitalist nation in the world. Now a fast-paced and tech-driven society, most of its citizens choose to escape into virtual, augmented realities rather than look to the monks for guidance, or the natural surroundings for inspiration. Spiritual awakening and personal reflection have taken a back seat to self-indulgence, wastefulness, and greed.

Perl, finishing up the last bite of her porridge, tried one more time to convince Ximu. "Papa, are you sure I can't go out on the boat? Just a really, really short trip? Please?" she pleaded, batting her bright green eyes, although she already knew what the answer would be.

"No, Perl. That's enough. No." Ximu walked over to the sink and began scouring the stack of dirty dishes.

For as long as Perl could remember, it seemed like Papa Ximu was always telling her no. No to climbing barefoot to investigate the puffins' (Fratercula) cliffside nests. No to snorkeling the reef for triggerfish (Balistidea). No to searching the caves of Trash Island for bats (Chiroptera). When asked why she couldn't do these things, the old monk's answer was always more or less the same, "It is dangerous out there." When she would press him, he would only say, "We need to keep you safe, Perl. You are special." Perl didn't really understand what Ximu meant by that. Why was she so special? She cleaned the fish, folded laundry, and hauled the baskets of food up the stairs, just like all the other servants who worked with the monks. Was Papa talking about her vision? Her "Gift from Ever," as he called it? Sure, it might've made her a little different, but why did Ximu and the other monks protect her like she was made of glass? She'd had this gift her whole life, and nothing bad had ever happened. And, she was twelve now. She understood that there were good people and bad people in the world. The monks had cautioned her about the evils in the world since she was able to walk, and Perl herself has witnessed it firsthand.

Perl looked at Ximu, sighing heavily. She carried her empty bowl to the sink and stacked it with the others, then walked over and pulled her brown robe off the wall hook; it was a smaller version of the robes the monks wore. Perl headed out the door without saying a word.

The Gift from Ever, as Ximu called it, was unique indeed. It further solidified to the monks that Perl was the Chosen One. This extraordinary ability allowed Perl to look at someone and see their "essence," as it was referred to by the monks, rather than their human form. Seeing a person's essence was like seeing who they were at their core; it was their spiritual identity, revealing their true self. To Perl, the essence would appear in the form of some sort of creature, but mostly as animals. Perl could alternate between seeing both a person's human form or their essence. If she chose to, she could view the citizens of Mont Michel as an endless menagerie of bears (Ursidae), foxes (Vulpes vulpes), giraffes (Giraffe), dolphins (Delphinus), warthogs (Phacochoerus africans), armadillos (Dasypodidae), zebras (Equus quagga), flamingos (Phoenicopterus), cheetahs (Acinonyx jubatus), snakes (Serpentes), grasshoppers (Melanoplus), gophers (Geomyidae), moose (Alces alces), or any other type of furry, scaly, swimming, crawling, winged, horned, or feathered creature imaginable; whatever that person's true essence revealed.

At birth, Perl could only see a person's essence, never their human form. In fact, for many years she thought she was the only human in all of Mont Michel. Even her dear, sweet monks were never humans in Perl's eyes. She always saw them as very large and quite spectacular spiders (Pholcidae), shambling to and fro, their eight spindly legs moving furiously under their thick brown robes. As a toddler, Perl loved to engage with the locals on the daily walks she took with Ximu around the island. "Aren't my spiders adorable?" she'd ask anyone passing by. "They're so cute and cuddly! Don't you love all their eyes?" Already leery of the strange monks, the islanders would walk quickly past the two of them, shaking their heads and whispering to one another. Perl would ask them innocently, "What? You don't like spiders?"

"Remember, Perl, only you can see us as spiders," Ximu would remind the small girl. "The rest of the world sees our human form, but your vision of us is accurate, my precious one, for we are very much like spiders. We are often misunderstood, and as you have seen, people tend to avoid us if possible. That said, we are on Earth for the good of the world, to help maintain the balance of nature, each in our own way, my little Bee."

Around age seven, Perl's Gift evolved; it was the year she saw another human for the first time. While at the docks learning how to gather the fishing nets with her Papa Ximu, Perl heard a loud stomping noise approaching. She looked up and saw a massive rhinoceros (Rhinocerotidae) headed their way. He was carrying crates of fish that obstructed his view as he clomped down the wooden planks. Not noticing either of them, he stumbled over Ximu. The rhinoceros staggered and then stopped abruptly, his eyes narrowing angrily. "Watch where yer goin', you ol' fool!" Perl watched with growing unease as the rhino's giant foot came crashing down on Ximu's spider claw. At that moment, Perl was stunned to see Ximu's spider essence flash out of her mind, and for a brief moment, she saw him as a man for the first time in her life. Perl screamed. Panicked, she looked up at the rhino and saw he had also changed. An angry, sweaty, stubble-faced man stared down at her. "What are you looking at?" he bellowed.

"Y-you…you're a…" Perl mumbled, unable to think straight. Ximu, sensing the girl's confusion, scooped Perl up and hurried back to their cellar home. Gently sitting her down on the kitchen counter, he did his best to calm her.

"It's okay, Sweet Bee, I'm here. Are you alright?" He pulled back her hood, revealing her bounty of frizzy black hair. She looked back at Ximu, her piercing green eyes wet with tears.

Perl was in hysterics. "Where did all your legs go, Papa? And all your eyes? And that mean rhino! He was human! A mean, ugly human! I saw it! But now you're back to your spider self!"

Ximu wiped her tears with his sleeve, speaking softly. "Try not to be afraid, Perl. You merely saw me, and the dockworker, in our Earthly human state. It's okay, this is completely normal."

"But why now?" Perl asked.

"I don't know for certain, but perhaps the confusion and distress of the situation back there caught you so off-guard that it momentarily jarred your vision. You've never witnessed someone acting unkind like that before. However..." he reached down, rubbing his sore foot, "this also tells me two things. One, that it could be possible for you to see both the human form and the essence of people, and two, that you are growing up. Probably faster than Papa is ready for, but try and embrace it as a blessing, my dear. As you get older, I believe you will begin to learn the purpose of your gift."

Perl, from morning to night, continued to practice controlling her vision, switching her focus back and forth from human form to essence with anyone who happened to cross her path. When others saw a boy on the beach playing with a ball, Perl saw a seal (Pinnipedia), balancing the ball on his snout. Peering through a hole in a fence one afternoon, Perl spotted a woman with a crying baby in one arm, a wicker basket in the other, hanging laundry out to dry. Looking deeper, Perl would see a nimble octopus (Octopoda), holding clothespins, folding sheets, and calming her baby, all with her skillful set of tentacles. As time went on, Perl began to gain control of her ability and could decide how she wanted to view the world. Seeing the essences of people was fun and exciting, but some of them scared her, leaving her shaken.

One time while in her favorite garden, Perl passed an old woman. As she looked back, the woman had turned into a hideous hunched-over vulture, her black, crooked beak scraping angrily at her wing. The more Perl ventured out around the island, it seemed to her as though she saw more and more bad essences, and fewer good, so she chose not to look, opting instead to view only human forms. One person in particular on the island whose essence Perl never wanted to see was the one they called Slaughterman, a mysterious loner who worked the butchering barns and was rumored to live deep inside a cave on nearby Trash Island. The mere thought of him gave Perl the willies, and she imagined his essence would be something terrible, like a rabid, fanged mole rat, or a blob fish full of maggots. Perl never wanted to be anywhere near Slaughterman if she could help it.

The one and only exception Perl made when it came to using her Gift was with her beloved spider-monks. In her eyes, the monks were perfect in every way—kind-hearted, caring, loving souls. She had seen them as spiders as a baby, and she would always choose to see them that way; eight-legged, fuzzy, and wonderful through and through.

Now at age twelve, word had traveled around the docks about Perl's odd visions. People stayed clear of "the strange monk girl," just as they did the monks. They thought she was bizarre because she was often seen humming to plants, or talking to bugs. Of course, the plants and bugs never talked back, but that didn't stop Perl from wishing them well, or saying hello. No one else on the island seemed to care about nature. They didn't understand why Perl was always picking up flower petals, shells, and other bits of nature she found along the ground, stashing them inside her robe. "What does she do with all those dirty twigs and berries?" they'd scoff. "Nonsense! Utter nonsense!" They were oblivious to nature's magic, their eyes instead locked on their tech devices, satellite skin implants, or immersed in simulation pods.

As if Perl's odd behavior wasn't enough, the locals didn't understand why she carried a ratty journal everywhere. In this new age, all communication and information gathering was achieved through holographic mind projections, optical interaction sensors, and virtual visits to the communal thought and memory vaults located on the island. Nobody had books anymore, let alone a pencil or paper. Perl didn't care. She was never seen without her sketchbook. It was where she captured all of her thoughts, visions, and studies of nature. She loved the feel of it in her hands; soft, woven fibers with a birch bark cover, carefully stitched together with honeysuckle vines.

From time to time, Perl caught the island folk gossiping about her when she was out sketching. She would overhear them speaking in hushed tones. "I heard she's an illegitimate child of Count Graves, sent away from the Palace to live in the cellars," or, "She's the daughter of a Virtual Fantasy club worker." No one seemed to know who her real parents were. Perl most of all.

3 FORCEFIELD

Ever since the day they discovered Perl hidden inside the barnacle *(Coronula Diadema)* on the great blue whale *(Balaenoptera Musculus)*, the Brothers of the Quill have recited the sacred chant from their ancient text, The Awakening, to protect the Chosen One.

To summon the monks across the island, an enormous bronze bell, known as the Evensong, was forged and erected in the courtyard outside the root cellar. Three times a day, its deep chime would reverberate around Mont Michel, prompting the monks to begin their ritualistic chant. The bell itself was a true work of art; its polished surface intricately engraved with a large praying mantis, surrounded by an interwoven pattern of decorative fern leaves and elegant swans. The bell's clapper was curved like the sliver of a crescent moon. At its tip was a star-shaped head that struck the sides of the bell at dawn, midday and dusk.

The monks' chant began with arms outstretched, palms toward the sky. They would then lower their arms in front of them, palms facing Mother Earth, and end by crossing their hands over their hearts to honor the spirit that dwells within.

Verse XXI : The Bulwark Chant

"Loammm" (be thankful for the fertile soil)
"Doreaaash" (be thankful for the Gift of Ever, given freely from the sea)
"Ummmeverrr Artemmm Infintummm" (give praise to the Artist of All Things)

The Brothers of the Quill were an ancient and mysterious order. Unbeknownst to others on the island, the Brothers possessed an ability besides providing fresh fish and vegetables for the local residents. The monks had an acute awareness of the hidden, mystical forces of nature. Through their collective daily chanting, they had invoked a powerful protective ring around Mont Michel which kept any violent storms from reaching the island.

Brother Ximu was quick to remind the monks about the importance of the chants, but the Brotherhood knew and understood their responsibility. They said their chants daily, without fail, mindful of what could happen should the ritual be disrupted. Having done so for twelve years now, it had given the island's surrounding waters an unnatural stillness, the waves always crashing miles from the shore.

As could be expected, none on Mont Michel were even aware of the protective barrier. The locals, although agreeing it was curious, never really questioned why the seas were always so calm, or why a serious storm had not approached their coastline in years. "We're just lucky, that's all," they would boast. Had any of them noticed, they would have realized an odd coincidence; the bad weather had immediately ceased twelve years ago, right at the time a new baby arrived on the island.

The Brothers had always done everything within their power to keep a close watch on Perl, however difficult that might have been at times. Since she could crawl, Perl was drawn to the magic of the natural world, endlessly fascinated by what lived on the land, in the sea, and in the skies above. The monks, always happy to nurture Perl's love of nature, took turns reading and re-reading to Perl for years, sharing stories and facts from every wildlife book they had in their dusty old library. Perl, in turn, was like a sponge. The science of how each living thing was designed perfectly to connect and work together in the natural world delighted her to no end. As Perl got a little older and more fleet of foot, it became harder and harder for the elderly monks to keep up with the energetic girl.

"Where has she gone now?" was an often-repeated phrase among the tired monks. If they took eyes off of her for a second, she was gone, darting under bushes and digging up the soil to see where earthworms *(Lumbricus terrestris)* lived, or hopping onto the backs of giant turtles *(Testudines)* for ride in the garden. Sometimes she would be found huddled inside a damp, hollowed-out log with her trusty sketchbook. There she would be drawing a cluster of spongy mushrooms, taking meticulous notes about them. The monks would always say, "the winds whisper to Perl, and the plants grow for Perl."

That was true, but it was the lure of the vast, salty sea above all else that hypnotized Perl. When the monks invariably lost sight of her, many times they could follow her bare footprints down the sandy path from their root cellar door to the beach. There they would find Perl, staring longingly out at the open sea, sometimes appearing to be in conversation.

Like clockwork, the monks continued their daily Bulwark Chant. The waters surrounding Mont Michel remained calm and Perl, other than the occasional scraped knee, was safe with her spider-monks. Recently, though, for reasons he could not explain, Ximu could not shake a growing sense of unease. Normally upbeat, more and more the monk could be seen pacing around during the day, a concerned look etched on his face.

"Brother Ximu, what troubles you?" his fellow monks asked.

"Oh, just a bit under the weather," Ximu would reply, not wanting to trouble them.

At night, his sense of dread would increase tenfold. Ximu would stay awake into the wee hours. Sitting in his hand-carved rocking chair, he would page through stacks of ancient texts, until eventually nodding off in front of the fire. Dark days turned to dismal weeks as Ximu continued to fret. He desperately searched for a reason for his deepening worry, unable to shake the notion that a darkness was closing in.

One night after dinner, Ximu grabbed his favorite pipe and strolled down to the beach to get a glimpse of the ocean. Having gone just far enough to get the tops of his feet wet, he stopped and peered out, closed his eyes and listened to the crashing of the far-off waves. He took a puff of his pipe and blew out a circle of blue smoke. From behind him, he heard a voice.

"Brother Ximu, I apologize for disturbing you," said the man, "but if I may be blunt, you continue to mope and sulk, and we...that is, I...am beginning to worry."

Ximu closed his eyes and chuckled. "You, Victr? Worry? What a surprise."

Victr ignored him. "Is there something you're not telling us? Is it about Perl?"

Ximu opened his eyes and glanced back at his fellow monk. The deep creases in Victr's forehead wrinkled even more as he saw the look on Ximu's face.

"I honestly don't know," Ximu replied. "I only feel that something is not right. A shadow is drawing near."

"But we are reciting the chants. Perl is happy, she is safe," Victr responded, noticing Ximu turn once again to look out over the horizon. "Do you sense something...out there?" Victr asked, scanning the ocean, as if hoping to find the answer himself.

Ximu said nothing as he searched the inky black waters for a sign.

"Dear Ever! That's the tenth basket of king crab to come up dead this week!" said Brother Simon, cranking the metal cage open and dumping the contents onto the deck of their battered old fishing boat.

The monk with him, a sinewy, sunburnt older monk named Brother Kirkwood, scanned the horizon with a telescope as the lifeless crabs *(Lithodidae)* spilled over his boots. "I've got a bad feeling, in my bones," he muttered, surveying the seascape.

Brother Simon nodded. "And I smell something rotten on the winds. We'd better get back and report this to Ximu." The two monks tied up their lines, grabbed their oars, and quickly paddled back to shore.

4 DARKNESS STIRS

From the dark depths an inhuman voice whispered; cold, pitiless.

"My power growsss…Humankind weakensss…
As I poison their mindsss…they poison the seasss…
Sssoon…only darknesss."

It paused.

"Sheee is near…protected…..no matter…sheee will sssuffer…"

5 SECRET POCKETS

The morning Evensong bell sounded, signaling the servants to make their way to the root cellar pantry. Two by two they lined up by the dozens, ready to fetch the baskets for their deliveries. Every day, the servants carry orders of fresh fish and produce around the island of Mont Michel, traveling anywhere from the bottom burrows, to the mid-partments, to the very tip-top of the island, where the Golden Palace stood.

Perl skipped into her usual spot beside Regor. "Morning, partner," she greeted him as she squatted down, plucking a few leaves of clover and stashing it inside her robe. "Hey, did you know that kangaroos lick their arms to stay cool?"

Regor snickered. "Heh-heh, no, I definitely didn't."

Regor, a lanky, middle-aged man with a scruffy salt-and-pepper goatee, paired up with Perl as often as he could. It made the days more interesting as the two enjoyed each other's company immensely. They were a pair of odd birds for sure, but the gangly man and the willowy, quick-witted girl were as tight as two peas in a pod. Regor had a nervous laugh, and Perl would try anything to get his giggle going.

"Regor...why do you suppose antlers chose to grow on deer heads, and not on humans?"

"I, uh...heh-heh...I'm not quite sure how to answer that, Perl, heh-heh," Regor chuckled. Although he didn't always understand the girl, he adored her, and she him.

After a short wait the two reached the front of the line, where a host of monks gathered. They quickly handed out the bundles they had painstakingly prepared, each carefully tagged as to where it should go on the island.

Perl and Regor took their baskets from Brother Sebastian, one of the younger monks of the Brotherhood.

Brother Sebastian smiled at the girl. "You two be careful today," he said, winking.

Perl flipped over the note that was attached to one of their baskets with a twisting vine.

"We get to go to the Palace today," Perl elbowed Regor. "Ready to do some climbing?" The simple man gave a nod, giggling.

It was still early; the last glaze of morning dew was burning off the grass, and Perl could already sense it was going to be a hot day. The two set off under the topiary arch, following the cobblestone pathway that took them to the stone steps leading up the mountain.

Every day as the two made their rounds, Regor would watch with a curious fascination as Perl gathered up bits of nature along the way, tucking them into her hooded robe. She had sewn lots of tiny pockets inside the lining to keep all of her newfound delights, along with her most prized treasure, her sketchbook. At each home they stopped at, Perl would leave a little something extra next to the delivery— a snail shell, a flower bud on the cusp of blooming, a leaf with a particularly intricate pattern—anything she felt might brighten that person's day.

"Why do you leave those weeds at peoples' houses?" Regor asked, interrupting Perl as she hummed a tune.

"Hmm-hmm...hm? Obviously, I want them to see the magic," she replied, "and by the way...what's wrong with weeds? They're beautiful, too!" The girl resumed her humming as the two continued their ascent up Mont Michel's steep, winding steps.

Regor giggled. "Magic? What in Ever's name are you talking about, silly one?"

Perl, always five steps ahead of the spindly-legged man, both literally and figuratively, looked back at him and glared. "The magic of nature, Regor. I mean, they live on this island with beautiful nature all around them, but they never bother to leave their houses! They're always plugged in to their pods or obsessed with their tech gadgets. People don't seem to notice what's right outside their own doors! So, if they won't visit the outdoors, the outdoors will visit them." She cracked a proud smile.

Regor smiled back at the girl, leaning on one knee. "Well, you're persistent, I'll give you that, and I agree, they're much too wrapped up in their devices...especially when it comes to fawning all over those Graves twins."

The sun grew hotter and the two of them, now up many hundreds of steps, paused to take in the view out over the ocean. "Up here, the other islands look like the backs of turtles, don't you think?" Perl asked.

Regor, of course, just giggled. High above, skyscrapers loomed over them like dark sentinels, guarding the top of the island. Through a thick yellow haze, the electric glow of endless office lights, holographic 3D displays, and neon billboards flashed and flickered like a grim carnival.

Perl broke off a bit of a cranberry cracker, handing half to Regor. "From what I've heard, the twins' father is not very nice. Do you think he keeps them locked up there in that tower?" She said, pointing up at the colossal Golden Palace.

Regor brushed cracker crumbs from his goatee. "The Count's pretty rotten, that much I know. But I think he does love his daughters...maybe even as much as he loves himself!" Pleased with his cleverness, the lanky man broke into a laughing fit , falling onto his backside.

Perl shook her head and smiled at her buddy, "you're ridiculous, you know that?" She craned her head back, squinting up through the sun and haze at the towering Palace, wondering what secrets lay behind those giant walls.

Zell Graves, known as "The Count," was the current ruler of Mont Michel. He, the eighth generation of Graves men to rule, resided in the Golden Palace along with his wife, Sarr, and their twin girls, Ivry and Mik. As head of both the Oceanic Council and the Worldwide Waterways Committee, as well as the proprietor of the only large-scale, state-of-the-art aquatic ionizer, Graves controlled and regulated nearly all of the world's freshwater. For years, he'd taken full advantage of his coveted position when wheeling and dealing with other governments, always making sure they understood who was in charge. *"Without water, you will surely need Graves,"* was the Count's favorite saying. In fact, he loved the quote so much, he had it plastered everywhere around Mont Michel, even etching it on the jewel-encrusted platinum gate that guarded the entrance to the Palace.

At the bottom tier of the island, the working classes had limited resources. Peasants, fisherman and farmers struggled daily. This didn't bother Graves one bit; his only goal was to consolidate power. "The world will answer to the might of Mont Michel," he boasted, "but most of all, they will answer to *me*...I am the source and the very center of the world's survival."

The world Count Graves governed was mostly one of struggle and desperation; of "haves" and "have nots." Years of warming atmospheric temperatures, rising sea levels, food shortages, and massive flooding had forced much of the remaining population to seek refuge on a dwindling number of islands. Endless wars had battered the globe, leaving behind tainted water supplies, radioactive waste, and disease. Those who could not reach an island, or chose to remain where they were, burrowed underground. There, they carved out gigantic labyrinthian cities in hopes of survival. All of the sufferings of the outer world had little effect on The Count and his family, who lived a life of extreme luxury, safely protected in their golden castle in the sky.

Having reached the mid-partments, Perl and Regor came to a home belonging to a single father of three young, pasty-skinned boys. The door was open.

"Hello?" Perl called, announcing their presence as they cautiously slipped inside, baskets in hand. The father wasn't home, but his sons were there. The boys were pressed together on a couch, their faces glued to their tech devices, none of them bothering to look up. "I said, *hello there!*" Perl waved her hand in front of one the boys. He swatted at her hand like it was a pesky fly. The blue glow of his game cast an eerie teal light on his face. Perl thought he looked like a robot.

"Leave their stuff, Perl. Let's keep going," Regor urged.

Perl left a sprig of lavender on the counter next to their bag of turnips. Most of the residents brushed her gifts into the trash. Occasionally, however, on a return delivery, Perl would spot one of her flowers in a vase, or a leaf stuck to a window. *"One person at a time,"* she'd think to herself with a smile.

Regor and Perl left the boys with the glazed-over eyes, continuing their deliveries. Bounding up a long stretch of steps, Perl realized she'd gotten too far ahead of Regor, so she stopped to wait. As he slowly approached, Perl decided to use her Gift. She stared at the skinny man, revealing his true essence as he ambled up the steps, huffing and puffing. Perl already knew what Regor's essence was, but it cracked her up every time she did it.

"Keep up, goat-feet!" Perl yelled back at Regor.

In Perl's eyes, Regor was now a knobby-kneed, furry-footed goat. He raised his fuzzy brow and quickened his pace, clomping up the steps until finally reaching Perl.

"Bah! Why do you call me that? Is it because you know it bugs me?" Regor gave her a slight kick with his hoof.

Perl snickered, "it's not my fault," she teased. "That's who you are, goaty-goat!" She hopped on her tiptoes to the next set of steps.

Regor paused, slightly smiling, stroking his bristly goatee. "Heh-heh. Guess it is kind of funny."

The two continued to make their rounds, dropping off delivery after delivery. The sun now burned high in the sky. Before long they had reached the Palace, the last stop of their day. Perl didn't see Regor's goat essence anymore, but was still giggling about it. She continued to lightly tease him as the two stood on a patio in front of a large service door made of pure gold. A sign above the door read, *"Deliveries. Ring Bell Once."*

Perl was about to press the doorbell when the golden door swung wide, nearly knocking her backwards off the patio.

"Late again, I see! Give it here!" a burly man in a towering white chef's hat shouted at them.

The red-faced cook grabbed the basket from Perl's arms, tugging her small frame forward across the threshold. She stumbled onto the cold marble floor. The cook glared down, seeing dusty footprints across the newly waxed tiles. As always, Perl had kicked off her lily pad boots as soon as Ximu had left for his morning chants.

"Out, you dirty urchin!" the cook hollered, his face turning a deeper shade of red, "out!" The door slammed shut.

"So, you plan on giving *him* some of your magic?" Regor giggled, pulling a handful of leaves off a nearby tree and waving them in Perl's face.

"Maybe," Perl shot back, unfazed by his teasing. "I'll get my chance in a couple of days! I've been chosen to attend the twins' birthday ball." She pulled a titanium coin stamped with the Graves family crest from her pocket and flipped it with her thumb.

"What? You got picked?" Regor caught the coin midair and examined it closely. "Why didn't you tell me?"

"Well, I didn't want to hurt your feelings since I knew The Countess didn't pick you." Perl took the coin from Regor, tucking it safely back inside a pocket.

"That's okay, Perl...no one wants an old goat ruining their party," Regor elbowed Perl. "Besides, I'm happy for you. You'll have tons of good stories and we'll finally know what really goes on inside that place. I mean, you will tell me...right?" He gave her a big smile.

Perl looked at him. Slowly, she started to see his goat form again. "Duh. You'll be the first," Perl laughed, "goaty-goat-goat!"

Perl zipped past Regor, down the stony steps. She disappeared around a bend, the giggling, gangly man chasing after her.

It was a hot, hazy, record breaking June 11th, two days before the biggest event in recent history; the Graves twin's birthday ball. Ivry and Mik were turning eighteen, and it was promised to be a celebration for the ages. Pictures of the twins were everywhere on the island. Dozens of marble and gold sculptures of them were erected around the Palace walls. Decorative banners hung in every street and alleyway. A 200-foot high glowing holograph of the twins rotated above the Graves Fountain in the city's main plaza.

Indeed, the eyes of the world would be on Mont Michel, even more so than on a typical day. The birthday ball would draw the wealthiest and most powerful aristocrats from around the globe. Tickets were VIP only and no one wanted to miss the rare opportunity to hobnob with their fellow elite. Potential male suitors would be sailing in to try and win the twins' hands in marriage.

According to Countess Sarr, who was never at a loss for words when it came to her precious daughters, it would be the "glitziest, grandest, and the most unforgettable gala to ever take place anywhere, ever."

Sarr had hand-selected every servant, not wanting any "undesirables" to "taint the festivities." Because Perl was small, she had been deemed acceptable by The Countess. The day of the selection, the Countess had pointed at her, "yes, that one," she wiggled her silk-gloved finger at Perl, "the tiny, fluffy squirrel girl there. She can move about quickly and unnoticed. She'll do."

While the upper tiers of Mont Michel prepared their lavish costumes, the citizens at the bottom of the island got to work. Fishermen hauled in their catches at a breakneck pace. Hired hands harvested grapes, cherries, oranges, bananas, nuts, and an abundance of vegetables, filling basket after basket. Trash pickers, normally a rare sight, cleaned garbage off the beach, shipping it over to nearby Trash Island. Everyone prepared, from painters and tree-trimmers, to street sweepers and even the monks. They cleaned and readied the island for the throngs of visitors soon to come.

6 SEEING SPOTS

Crashing through the subterranean pantry doors to the root cellar's kitchen, Perl burst in like a wild animal. She bounced across the dirt floor, leaping on to the broad, muscular back of Victr, the Brothers of the Quill's head cook. As usual, Victr was hunched over an open stove, his knotty knuckled hands stirring a giant kettle of kelp and carrot stew.

"Ah, Perl, my jumping beetle! You have returned from your adventure. What say you?!"

"I have climbed the mighty cliffs, destroyed the dragon, and brought you it's glorious scales." Perl bowed and placed a handful of pink flower petals into the monk's big, meaty hands.

Brother Victr raised his eyebrows, closely examining the petals, the wrinkles on his forehead deepening. Aside from his masterful culinary skills, Victr was nicknamed "Brother Worrywart" for his never-ending fretting. Having lost all but a ring of hair around his shiny bald crown, the monk never met a topic he couldn't worry about. From big things—"If we don't do something about the polluted oceans, all will be lost!", to the tiniest of issues—"Oh, I do hope I closed the lid tightly on those canned beets!" The monk was sweet and funny, every bit a gentle giant, but he chose to view every moment in life as an opportunity for rumination. Of his many concerns, the safety of little Perl was at the top of his list.

"Well done, mighty beetle!" Victr played along, "well done, indeed. Your reward for slaying such a foul beast will be to help me set the table for supper."

"Boo! Hiss!" Perl moaned, swooping one side of her robe dramatically over her head. She spun in a circle, trying to disappear from her chores.

"No time to hide, brave warrior," Victr pointed with his spoon, "your next quest is to venture into yonder crawl space and fetch me the molasses."

"Molasses? Yum!" Perl licked her lips as she pulled off her robe and hung it on a small wooden wall hook with her name carved on it. "What's it for?"

"It's for making ale for the ball. Not for young dragon-slaying beetles."

"Fine," Perl huffed, "but only because I am an honorable warrior."

Grabbing a candle off of the top of a barrel, Perl opened an oval door next to the kitchen sink. She headed down a narrow, sloping passageway until she came to a second door. Perl pulled the handle, a quick shiver ran through her body, "brrr." It was always colder this far down, and needed to be to keep the food properly preserved. The room was filled with rows upon rows of jars and cans, all meticulously labeled.

Holding up the candle, Perl ran her finger along the shelves. "Apples, beans, beets, carrots, shrimp brine, honey, ah...molasses." She unscrewed the lid and dipped her pinky finger into the sticky delight. "Just a tiny taste...mmm..."

"Perl!", Victr's booming voice echoed down the tunnel as if he was sensing what was happening, "Hurry up, Beetle! Spit spot!"

She closed the lid. "Coming, Victr the Victorious!"

Perl hustled back and finished setting the table, as sweet and savory aromas filled the cozy dining room. She took her seat, looking on as her beloved spider-monks gathered around the table to eat. All except one.

"Where is Ximu?" asked Brother Johnathan, a short, squatty monk known for his healthy appetite and lack of patience.

"We are to start without him," Victr informed the room, "he is tending to some important business."

"Important business? What kind of business?" The others began to murmur.

Victr's brow furrowed. Grabbing a piping hot cornmeal biscuit from the basket, he quickly passed it to his left. "Uh, Perl...tell everyone about the dragon you battled today," Victr grinned forcibly, trying not to reveal his concern. "But first, why don't you sing us the Grateful Song?" He motioned for the group to hold hands around the table.

Perl, although visibly pondering the whereabouts of Ximu, was always ready to perform. She stood up from her chair and watched as the monks held spider claws and bowed their fuzzy spider heads. She began to sing softly.

"We thank you sun, soil, roots and rains,
We thank you for growing, giving and nurturing our veins,
We thank you for today, tomorrow, from our happy humble shores,
We thank you Ever, for ever, ever more."

Heads went up and the stew went down faster than an eel swims. Perl entertained the monks with her imaginary tale of bravery while they slurped and sponged up broth with their biscuits.

"Okay, off to the tub with you, little warrior," Victr chimed. "The guards won't let you pass through the palace gates unless you are sparkling like a starfish." He licked his bowl clean and stood up from the table, eager to end the night without having to answer any questions about Ximu.

The monks, full from the meal, either wandered into the library to read or stepped outside for a stroll. None asked again about their elder Brother; Ximu would be home soon enough.

Perl didn't have to be told twice to get in the tub; she loved relaxing in the hot water, although the washing part she could take or leave. The water was her sanctuary. It made her feel at peace.

Like most of the lower residents of Mont Michel, the monks had to use saltwater from the sea to bathe, relying on the underground lava streams to heat the pipes. Only the Golden Palace, and those few who could pay for it, received fresh water for bathing.

This didn't bother Perl in the least. She loved the salty ocean water, its buoyancy, and its frothy sea foam. Most of all, she loved to slip completely under the water, letting the world go silent. Now submerged, Perl could only hear the beat of her heart, *bump-bump...bump-bump*, as the bubbles popping inside her ears. This is where she felt most at home. Perl closed her eyes just as the sound of the root cellar's heavy front door banged shut. *"Papa must be back,"* she thought. She began to hum.

As she lingered below the surface of the warm water, singing softly, she heard another sound; a deep, low *hummmm...hummmm...hummmm*. The notes seemed to mimic Perl. She stopped and listened, her head still submerged but her eyes wide open, trying to locate the source of the sound. The deep melodic tones thrummed on, growing louder. It seemed as though the humming was coming directly through the pipes, reverberating through the tub, right into Perl's body. She listened closely, focusing all of her attention. *"That sound,"* she thought, *"it's so familiar."* All at once she understood it, clear as day.

"Whales!" she thought, *"and they're singing!"* Perl closed her eyes again and concentrated. An image began to materialize in her mind; a dozen bowhead whales *(Balaena mysticetus)* had gathered near the moonlit shores of Mont Michel. Perl could not only visualize them swimming in circles, but she could also understand them. Their lyrics were coming to her; slowly at first, then so clearly that Perl began to repeat their melody, word for word.

"Hommmme Hommmme,
Every day I take a breath and hold it tight,
hoping you see me, but you float on by,
as the rough tides topple, we need your light,
still you don't seem to care
this is our Earth,
the home we all share.
There's still magic to believe,
some love that binds us,
just promise not to leave,
I need you to breathe~
Please come home.
Hommmme, Hommmmme"

Perl sat up with a jerk, splashing water onto the floor. Rubbing her eyes, she reached for a towel, but not before noticing her arms.

"What the—?!" She stared in disbelief. "My arms…there's spots on my arms!"

Perl could feel her heart pounding. She caught a glimpse of her knees poking out of the water; more small clusters of glowing spots were forming.

She dunked her head under and came back up. She blinked, hoping she imagined it, but the white, marble-sized lights were still there, glowing through her amber brown skin. Perl grabbed a sponge, trying to scrub them off, but it was no use.

"Papa! Papa! Papa!" She shouted as she hopped out of the tub, throwing her nightshirt on over her wet body, "Papaaa!"

Ximu burst into the room, tightening his robe belt around his full belly, "what is it, Bumble? What? Tell me!"

One look at the girl and he didn't need to ask again. On her dark cheeks, small glowing dots pulsed. Perl held up her arms to show him. She watched Ximu as he blinked his many black eyes at her, "it…it's going to be okay, Sweet Bee."

"What's happening to me, Papa?! I'm glowing…and the whales…I heard them singing…they want me to come home!" She started to hyperventilate, "I…I can't breathe! Papa…I…I…"

"Sit, sit. Put your head between your knees." Perl dropped down onto a wooden stool shaped like a mushroom that she had used to reach the bathroom sink when she was little. She watched as her Papa Spider quickly found a brown paper bag. "Here, breathe slowly into this." He put three of his arms around her shoulders and held the bag up to her mouth. "In. Out. In. Out. There. Breathe now. Breathe."

Eventually, Perl began to calm down. "Papa, I heard the whales…I, I, know what they want…"

"Slow down. Breathe, Sweet Bee," Ximu returned the bag to her mouth. "Did you know that whales are one of the few mammals that don't breathe involuntarily? They have to think about every breath that they take."

The old monk's soothing voice relaxed Perl, and just like that, the strange spots started to fade. Her skin returned to its bronze hue. She and Ximu locked eyes.

"We have much to talk about," he said, crumpling the paper bag into a ball and tossing it into the trash.

Moments later, Perl had put on a warm, dry gown and climbed into her comfy, quilted bed. Ximu sat on the edge, pulling the blankets up. Perl looked anxiously at her Papa Spider, "so, spill. I know you know something you're not telling me."

Ximu sighed heavily, curling his white mustache. "Perl, you are very special. There is no one in the world like you."

25

"Yes, you tell me that all the time. But what do you really mean, Papa? What were those spots?" She pulled the covers tight under her chin.

"It is called bioluminescence. The reason you have this incredible gift is no doubt because of your father."

"My father?" Perl sat up. "You know him?"

"I know *of* him. From what I learned earlier today, he was a Light Protector of the ocean, and was bioluminescent. When we found you as a baby, you were swaddled inside a barnacle, attached to the side of a great blue whale."

Perl's eyes widened, then squinted as she gave him a look of disbelief. "Stop it. I don't want one of your stories right now. I want the truth, Papa."

"This is the truth, my child, as incredible as it may sound. You, my little treasure, came to us from the sea," he said as he walked over to a painting of a bear hanging on her wall. "Bioluminescence can act as a warning when danger is near, or as a beacon, helping you to harmonize and connect with nature." He lifted the frame off the wall; behind the painting was a hollowed-out space.

Perl leaned forward, a look of puzzled surprise on her face, "hey, how long has that been there?"

"Furthermore, this gift is a sign," the monk continued, "it tells me you are ready."

Ximu reached in and pulled out a large object, protected in layers of fine silk cloth. Perl eagerly watched as he carefully unwrapped it. Pulling back the last layer of fabric, Ximu held in his arms a highly polished barnacle *(Coronula Diadema),* and placed it on the bed in front of her.

"What is this?"

"This is the barnacle we found you in."

Perl's mouth fell open.

Ximu continued, "in the ancient Book of The Awakening, there is a particular passage known as The Prophecy; it foretold of a Divine Protector who would come from the ocean's depths, where life on Earth began."

Perl was listening, but also inspecting the extraordinary barnacle, running her hands over the swirling pattern of silver-blues and deep purples.

"It is said that a Chosen One will shine a light from where no light shines to awaken the world, turning the tides of evil, and restoring the balance of nature." He took a long breath, "Perl, I believe that you are the one that is spoken of in The Prophecy. I've kept the barnacle hidden here for all these years, waiting to show you when the time was right."

"What are you talking about, Papa? I'm just a girl. I'm not some protector. And evil? What kind of evil? You're starting to scare me," she said, pushing the shell back towards him.

"You know the essences that you see aren't just your imagination. They are real." He stroked her cheek, but Perl pulled away, wanting more answers.

"I understand that. But how can I hear the whales? And now glowing spots?"

He took her hand. "You are growing up, and if I've deciphered The Prophecy's words correctly, your gifts will increase as you age. Only you can see the true essences of humans." Perl squeezed Ximu's furry spider paw, nodding softly. She felt tears welling up.

"And that, my child, is a good thing, a true gift. But there are also many dark things in this world, and perhaps you may have seen evidence of that already." Ximu paused, pulling his spectacles off to wipe his brow, "and though it saddens me to say, I fear the darkness is winning." The old monk went into the bathroom and came back with a cup of water. He sat back down on the bed, the girl rolling towards him as the mattress sunk.

"What do you mean, darkness is winning?" Perl asked, blinking the tears away.

"The scales of life have tipped out of the light, away from goodness. Because of this, nature is suffering. Just like the whale's song you heard tonight. They're crying out for help, and it is all of our jobs to come to their aid. Not only just the whales, but their home as well." He handed her the cup, "I know this is a lot to take in, my Bumble."

"Understatement of the universe," she joked, taking a sip.

Ximu squeezed her hand and stood. "Come. I want to show you something else."

Perl slipped out of bed, following the monk down the candlelit hallway. They passed the door to Ximu's room, stopping in front of a small locked door. It was an irregular shape, half the size of the other doors, and one that Perl had always been curious about. He pulled out a tiny brass key and carefully unlocked the heavy latch, and the two ducked inside. Ximu lit a kerosene lantern, illuminating the room.

Covering the walls of the large round chamber, from floor to ceiling, were spider webs; not musty, dusty cobwebs like the ones she had to sweep up. These were beautiful, intricately laced webs, decorated throughout with an assemblage of flower petals, spiraling vines, honeycombs, and shimmering dewdrops. Baubles, trinkets and treasures were thoughtfully stitched into the glistening webbed tapestry.

"Wow," Perl gasped, "did you make this, Papa?"

"I had some help."

"And what's that?" A strange spectacle in the center of the room caught her attention.

Surrounded by a clear pool of water rose a marble pedestal, nearly ten feet tall, sculpted in the shape of two arms rising up from the ground, palms

27

open. Hovering in the air above the hands were thirteen bubbles.

"This, my child, is the scale of the universe, Globus Natura. It oversees the balance of nature across the entire Earth and its atmosphere. For centuries, the Brothers of the Quill have been entrusted to oversee it." Ximu spoke softly, solemnly, "the center orb, the large one there, monitors the Milky Way galaxy." He gestured to a bubble the size of a watermelon; swirling inside was a night sky, filled with millions of tiny stars. There were six spherical bubbles rotating around the Galaxy Orb, and six more spinning outside of those.

"It's beautiful, but how does it work?" Perl moved closer for a better look.

"Each orb contains one element of nature. If balanced, they revolve on a continuous axis, like this one here," Ximu gestured to a spinning, sand-filled bubble, "or that one, the Air Orb."

Perl was on her tiptoes. "It looks like a captured cloud inside."

The monk moved around the Globus Natura. "Yes, and this is the Fire Orb," Ximu pointed to a spinning red flame flickering inside an apple-sized orb.

Perl blinked in amazement, "look! This one is filled with flowers, and that one has seeds! Oo, crystals! And does that one have dirt inside of it?" She took mental notes, eager to add drawings of all of them in her sketchbook. "But what's in that one? I've never seen anything like it."

"That is the Genesis Orb," Ximu spoke softly, "and those are microscopic organisms. They are the things that make up life."

The rotating bubbles cast shiny rainbows of color around the circular room, bouncing and sparkling off the lace webs.

"They're so delicate," Perl leaned against Ximu, feeling almost hypnotized by the beauty.

Ximu put his hand on her shoulder, "as is the balance of nature. When the universe is off kilter, when the darkness pulls too strongly against the light, the bubbles slow, their insides falter, and they may even slip out of their natural orbit. See how the Water Orb wobbles?" Unlike the others, it was not a perfect sphere, but misshapen. The water inside sloshed around as it orbited erratically.

"So, there's something harming the Earth's water?"

"It appears that way," Ximu replied.

Perl felt overwhelmed. Papa had told her so much. Despite the wonder of everything she was seeing and hearing, she was tired. She tried to stifle a yawn, but Ximu noticed.

"I think there's been enough excitement for today, Bee. Off to bed."

"But I'm not tired."

Ximu gave her a look.

"Okay, but could I sleep in here tonight?" Perl suggested.

He spun her toward the doorway. "Perhaps another night."

Back in Perl's bedroom, Ximu took the barnacle from her bed and carefully placed it on her dresser. He tucked her in tightly and kissed her cheek. "We will talk more in the morning. Try and rest now." He backed away quietly and blew out the wall sconce. "I love you," he whispered as he closed the heart-shaped door to her room.

Perl immediately shot up in bed. *"Rest?! How am I supposed to rest after that?"* She reached over and lit the beeswax candle next to her bed. "Oh, guess what? You're some kind of ocean light thingy, and here's a secret room that controls the universe, night-night, sleep tight." Perl mocked. Swinging her head down to peek under her bed, she addressed an origami dog, "and what about this darkness that's out there? Papa grazed over that pretty quickly, didn't he?"

Sitting back up, Perl fluffed her pillow, grabbed her sketchbook from the nightstand and scanned the room. Her eyes stopped on the barnacle. She stared at it, recalling Ximu's story about her and the whale...and her father. Licking her finger, she turned to a fresh page and scrawled, *"Who am I?"*

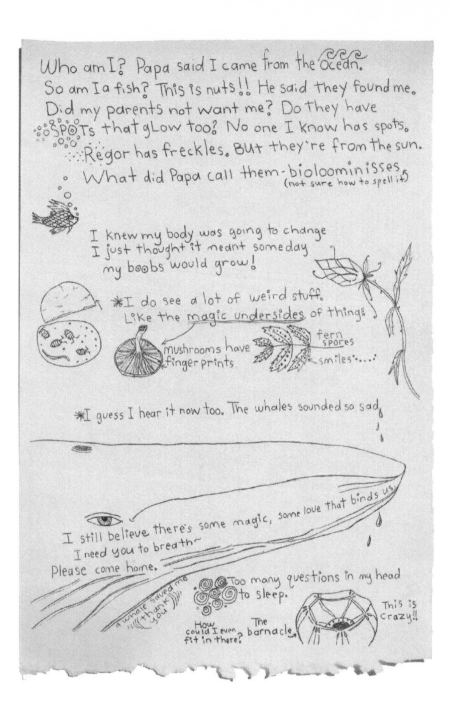

Who am I? Papa said I came from the Ocean.
So am I a fish? This is nuts!! He said they found me.
Did my parents not want me? Do they have
SPOTs that gLow too? No one I know has spots.
Regor has freckles. BUt they're from the sun.
What did Papa call them - bioloominisses
(not sure how to spell it)

I knew my body was going to change
I just thought it meant someday
my boobs would grow!

✳ I do see a lot of weird stuff.
Like the magic undersides of things.

mushrooms have
finger prints

fern
spores

smiles

✳ I guess I hear it now too. The whales sounded so sad

I still believe there's some magic, some love that binds us.
I need you to breath~
Please come home.

Too many questions in my head
to sleep.

a whale saved me
thank you!

How
could I even
fit in there?

The
barnacle

This is
crazy!!

30

7 ORCHID

Perl fumbled with the latch leading to the garden, still tired and reeling from her sleepless night. Her freshly washed hair was poofed out three times its normal size, the hood on her cloak unable to contain the mass of dark curls as the morning breeze tossed them back and forth. She had her gloves on, her trusty shears out, and went about collecting fresh berries and flowers for the upcoming ball. By midmorning, the warm rays of the sun had poked through the trees, bathing the entire garden in a pinkish yellow hue. A hummingbird flitted nearby, hanging in midair next to Perl, its wings a blur. Normally, she'd say hello, but today she was preoccupied. Perl was halfway down the row of bright orange poppies when Ximu slipped through the gate, wearing his veiled beekeeper's hat.

"Papa!" Perl ran to him, wrapping her arms around the jolly monk. Lifting the netting from his face, Ximu gave her a quick peck on the top of her head.

"Did you sleep well, my Bumble?" he asked.

"Not really. I have so many questions," she said, relinquishing her bear hug.

Ximu handed her a piece of dulse, a red seaweed that was one of Perl's favorite snacks. She gobbled it up in one bite, not having eaten breakfast.

"All will be revealed in time, but first let us call Hadza." Ximu whistled a little tune.

"Look, there she is!" Perl pointed up to a birch tree. Perched on the end of a spindly branch sat a tiny yellow-winged honeyguide bird *(Indicatoridae)*.

"Good day, Hadza, do show us the way." On Ximu's command, the adorable little bird swooped down the path, mimicking the same song that was used to call her. She chirped louder and louder as she glided down the path.

Perl chased the bird, "warm...warmer...hot...hotter...you're on fire, Hadza! Annnd...eureka...bees!"

Of course, they all knew the way to the hives, but this was a favorite game of theirs. Ximu began to pump smoke around the entrance of the hive with a metal canister. The bees *(Apis mellifera)* scattered, buzzing as if to say, "how dare you?" There was something about the bees' low buzz that calmed Perl. Ximu broke off a small part of the honeycomb, just enough for the day.

Honey was a rare commodity on Mont Michel, harvested for just the select few that could afford it. Perl understood this, but still scooped three fingers worth straight from the hive, quickly licking it off her fingers before

Papa took notice.

"Do you know the difference between you and this fellow?" Ximu held up his thick glove with a small bee sitting on the top of his finger.

"Yeah, he gets to have all the honey he wants." Perl's tongue searched her chin for any remaining drop of sticky sweetness.

"No, my little ocean gem, the bee is motivated by its instincts. You, on the other hand, are motivated by your desire for sweets." Ximu peered over his glasses, raising an eyebrow. He gave her a bop on the top of her head.

"Hey!" she giggled.

"Hurry along and finish up your pruning." Ximu closed the canvas pouch holding the honeycomb.

"But I thought we were gonna talk about last night! The evil that's out there, and my father, and the biolu-lu..." she paused. "There's still so much I need to know." She examined her arms, looking for spots.

"Yes, we will, later. We're having a very special guest to dinner that I want you to meet. I know you still have many questions, and tonight some will be answered. For now, there's still too much to get done if we're going to be ready for the twins' ball by tomorrow."

"Fine." Perl grabbed her shears and leisurely walked over to a hydrangea bush, clipping a few flowers half-heartedly. The heat of the afternoon sun, now directly overhead, beat down on the back of her neck.

As if on cue, the midday Evensong bell sounded. Within minutes, the chants from the Brothers Quill could be heard across the island. Perl absentmindedly picked and placed the flowers in her basket. Lost in thought, she didn't notice that Ximu hadn't joined in on the chanting.

Perl dragged her feet sluggishly, "Papa, can you at least tell me about the whales?"

"Not now, Bumble," Ximu said, collecting the rest of his supplies, "don't you need to get up to the palace soon?"

Perl dramatically tossed her head back, feigning exasperation. "Yesss."

"Oh, and remember to gather Belladonna for the Countess." Ximu tipped his netted hat towards her as he closed the gate. "Move along, little Bee. Don't be late." Ximu turned and headed back up the dusty path. Perl spotted Hadza swooping down, eager to follow the cheerful monk. The two disappeared around a corner, whistling a song together.

"Hm...a mystery guest," Perl thought as she picked blueberries. She popped a few in her mouth and sang, "One for them, two for me, one for them, two for—"

"...and one for mee?" came a tiny voice.

Perl straightened up quickly and looked around, "who said that?"

"Down here," squeaked the voice.

It was an orchid. Dark purple in color, like a bruise. Perl couldn't believe her eyes or her ears.

"Did you just talk?" She set her basket down and slowly crouched close to the flower, bewildered, "say something else."

"I'm so hungry."

Shocked to hear the orchid speak again, Perl stammered, "oh, uh...here," she held out a blueberry.

"Closer."

"You're so beautiful," Perl, charmed by the mystical flower, didn't see the spots on her knees beginning to glow.

"Closer, dear. I can't quite reach."

Perl held the juicy berry up to it. Instantly, the orchid's petals curled into a snarl. It rose up like a viper, striking Perl's thumb with fangs as sharp as thorns.

"Ouch!" She stumbled back, knocking over her basket, "you bit me!"

"Mmm...delicious. Much sweeter than any berry."

The orchid *(Ochidaceae)* swallowed Perl's blood. It flowed through the flower, coursing down the plant's stems before traveling deep into the ground below. The small but potent stream of blood continued branching out, moving from root to root, beyond the garden perimeter. It twisted and turned until it made its way to the edge of a cliff overlooking the water. A single droplet of ruby red blood bubbled up to the surface, then fell into the briny sea. From beyond the darkest depths, an ancient soulless entity awoke from its slumber, tasting Perl's blood.

"The chhhiiilld..."

Rising slowly from the earth's bowels, the creature was at first nothing more than a polluted, oily cloud; a hideous mass of contaminated filth. As it lifted itself upwards, the shadow began to take on a ghastly shape. Barbed fins sprouted from its torso, twisting and wriggling in the murky water. Black sludge and mucus-colored algae oozed from the folds of its rough, scarred carcass. A grotesque tongue poked through endless rows of needle-like teeth, searching the waters for another taste of the sweet, vital fluid. The enormous beast inhaled deeply, filling the scaly sacks of its hulking frame, swelling out to a monstrous size. Schools of fish swimming near the beast instantly died. It was a nightmare, come to life.

"The chhhiiilld..."

Frantic, Perl scooped up the basket and ran down the hill. Her tiny legs churned so fast that she nearly tumbled head over heels. Seeds, petals, and feathers dropped out of the pockets of her flapping robe, leaving a trail of treasures in her wake.

"What was that? I've never seen anything so horrible!" Perl's thoughts raced, as the flower's creepy, smirking face flashed in her mind. She sprinted past a clock tower as it chimed, momentarily slowing Perl's stride. She looked up and frowned. "Shoot! I'm never gonna make it to the palace in time!"

At that moment, Brother Victr rounded the corner, pushing a wheelbarrow full of fresh fish. His pleasant demeanor quickly changed to worry when he saw Perl. She ran to him, hastily dumping her garden basket and tools on top of his morning's catch.

"And what's all this?" Victr halted the barrow, his brow furrowing.

"A really important favor that I promise I won't forget?!" Perl batted her shiny green eyes. "Pretty please, Victr, take my stuff to the pantry for me?!"

"Fine, but you're helping me clean these later," Victr replied, but Perl was already down the path, climbing the cliffside steps two at a time.

8 URIEL

Perl, sweaty and out of breath, reached the back entrances of the Palace. Next to a door marked, *"Maid Services"* was a circular screen.

"Do you have a coin?" A sharp voice was heard on the intercom. Perl pulled out her titanium coin, holding it up to the screen. A tiny laser scanned the Graves family crest. There was a buzzing sound, and the door flew open.

"It's about time!" An extremely slender woman with a very severe top bun came to the door. For just an instant, Perl stared at her and saw the woman's essence—a long-necked and slightly perturbed crane *(Gruidae)*.

"This way!" she squawked, dragging Perl in, pinching her shoulder as she guided her down the hallway. The impatient woman showed Perl a wheeled cart of cleaning supplies and slapped a map into her hands. "Only, I repeat, only, go into your assigned rooms."

Perl looked down at the map; several of the numbers had been highlighted in orange. "Yes, ma'am. Thank you, ma'am." Perl tied a white apron tightly around the outside of her robe.

The crane-woman shook her long wing in Perl's face. "Don't talk. Don't dawdle. Don't stray from the map." She tapped her watch. "Return your cart by three o'clock. Now, go! The elevator's that way!"

"Sheesh. Nice meeting you, too," Perl mumbled as the woman reverted back to her human form. Perl tried to get her bearings, then started down the long, mirrored hallway with her cart. *"The Palace. I'm actually inside."* She looked around at the lush surroundings.

The Palace was abuzz. Dozens of servants were hustling through the halls, busily sweeping, dusting, and straightening. There was no end to the number of golden statues, silver utensils, and crystal chandeliers that needed polishing.

"Everything must shine! Do you hear me? Shine!" Countess Sarr spit-shouted directly into the ear of a small man on his knees, buffing the paw of an enormous golden lion *(Panthera leo)* statue whose head was a spitting image of none other than the patriarch, Count Zell Graves. Each of the four Graves' family members were represented
by a statue. Countess Sarr, had her head immortalized on a statuesque flamingo *(Phoenicopterus)*, while the twin princesses, Ivry and Mik, were two fragile fawns *(Cervidae)*. The four strange-looking statues stood on imposing marble pedestals, nearly ten feet tall, staring down at anyone passing underneath their judgmental gaze.

Perl pushed her cart past The Countess, who was too busy berating another staff member to pay any attention to her. She quickly passed by the Graves' sculptures, hurried to the elevators, and pushed the grand ballroom button. Perl stared at the shiny, glistening button, wondering if it was a real diamond. A shrill voice echoed behind her.

"My darlings! Come to me, my babies!" Countess Sarr called from the foot of the long, winding staircase, having just sent yet another cleaning person away in tears.

From the top of the stairs, Ivry and Mik Graves nonchalantly sashayed around the corner. As the Countess babbled on, neither girl bothered to look up, both feverishly tapped away on their arms, checking their social media feeds. Running from the twins' wrists to their elbows were identical flowering vine designs dotted with red rosebuds. What at first looked like tattoos was actually state-of-the-art sensory-ink. Only a few people in the world could afford this brand-new technology, so of course Mik and Ivry had it. Through the transmitting ink, the twins could send and receive messages, take and upload photos, and most importantly, engage with their millions of adoring fans. The latest craze was acquiring "Wannabes" on the most popular social network of the day, *Narcissi*.

Satisfied with their latest fan numbers, the twins finally looked up from their arms. "Yes, Mother," they chimed in unison.

"My darling girls, you need to have your final dress fittings. Gaspard will be at your door at one o'clock sharp. Look. At. Me. When. I. Am. Speaking!"

Re-checking her arm, Mik heckled her sister. "Ha, I just got one more Wannabe than you!" she teased.

Sarr scratched her four-inch, sharpened fingernails down an onyx stairway spindle. "Babies! Did you hear me?"

"Yes, Mother." The girls posed, flipping their lush red hair back in unison, then spun around and disappeared back into their room.

Ivry and Mik Graves were the last living natural redheads; The Count and Countess had seen to that. Once their split-fetus had been genetically engineered, Count Graves had all of the remaining red-haired designer genes and DNA strands destroyed, along with the labs they were created in. The few existing redheads remaining on Earth simply...disappeared.

Being the only daughters of the wealthiest plutocrats in the world made them the subjects of constant fascination. *Narcissi* caught fire at every move they made, with even the smallest bit of news garnering massive buzz. The twins loved being adored by millions, and they loved each other very much as well. However, the limelight kept them in fierce competition.

The sound of a harp softly strummed, and the elevator doors opened.

"Finally!" Perl mumbled under her breath as she hurried in. As the doors shut, Perl watched The Countess pick up where she left off, screaming at another servant.

"I don't see why we have to dress alike tomorrow of all the days," protested Mik, the more unpleasant of the two.

The twins and their designer, Gaspard, stood in their cavernous bedroom closet. Numerous crystal chandeliers hung from the high arched ceiling; the walls were painted a bright cherry red and embellished with floral patterns dusted in gold leaf. The girls stared at themselves in ornate mirrors while the thin wispy man, looking utterly frustrated, scurried underfoot like a scared puppy.

"You must both wear zee emerald green," declared Gaspard, the girls' tailor and French fashion guru. "Zee Countess Sarr will be in zee red coral fish tank gown, and you will need to pop off of her, no?" he insisted, pinning Ivry's hem as she squirmed.

"Fine, but I get to wear this one. She gets the smaller one." Mik put on a gorgeous towering headdress, lavished with giant emerald encrusted beetles, exotic tropical flowers, and matching peacock feathers.

"Oui, zat one is for you! Zee praying mantis one goes better on Ivry, oui?" Gaspard nodded, as he adjusted a beetle wing on Mik's dress.

Mik shot a wincing glare at her sister in the mirror. She had always been jealous of the fact that Ivry had been named Ivry. It was because she had exactly one fewer freckle than Mik did. Mik hated the freckle and complained all the time to her mother to have it removed. "But how will I ever tell you two apart, darling?" Sarr would laugh. Despite any differences the two might have, they needed each other.

Mik reached over and grabbed her sister around the waist. "Lean in, Twinny, let's post our fitting fab-moment." The girls robotically went cheek to cheek. Puckering their lips like a pair of fish, Mik pressed the camera sensor embedded in her wrist. The shot went viral within seconds, the image instantly projected onto the full-screen wall inside their bedroom. They watched as the adoration of their virtual fanbase poured in.

Countess Sarr appeared in the doorway, blinking and rubbing her eyes. She felt her way along the wall and into the girls' dressing closet. Their spacious wardrobe was the size of most mid-apartment homes; it housed their endless growing collection of priceless couture.

Hearing the girls' giggling, The Countess called out, "girls? Where are you, my babies?" Sarr blindly moved her hands across the backs of chairs, along tables, and through rows of clothes, until she was able to reach out and grab one of their arms.

"Mother, seriously, when are you going to quit that deadly nightshade? You're going to go blind," Ivry squeezed her mother's hand.

"Don't call it that, it's Belladonna," Sarr corrected her. "I have trouble focusing sometimes. Not to worry, my darlings."

Sarr kept a vial of the plant extract on a massive hollowed-out ring around her middle finger at all times. Placing one drop into each of her eyes abnormally dilated the pupils, and made her appear wide-eyed and innocent, or so she believed. The Countess was always experimenting with the latest, youth-promising potions, desperately trying to keep up with the growing beauty of her twin daughters.

Sarr smiled coyly, "well, I just thought you might like to know that I just heard from satellites eight, fifty and two hundred, and they've all confirmed that Prince Névenoé will officially be attending! I mean, in case either of you care."

"Yes!" screamed the twins, jumping up and down in their pinned, insect-encrusted ball gowns.

Still tending to the dresses, Gaspard pricked his finger, "oh my Ever!" He fell backwards, catching a bowl full of shiny twenty-four carat gold beetles before it tipped off the dressing platform, "You girls will be zee death of me!"

"Room 144, check...*and* lilacs, check." Just like with her deliveries, Perl left a gift of nature in each room she cleaned. Room 160 received a neatly stacked pile of acorns in a crystal bowl. A single seagull feather was left in a tall marble vase in room 164. Perl paused; she could hear the twins down the hallway, shrieking in delight. Her curiosity getting the better of her, Perl ventured toward their room, inching quietly along the velvet-covered walls before stopping next to the open doorway.

Perl peered inside. There was no sign of the girls, but the first thing she noticed were the gorgeous floor-to-ceiling windows; the view of the ocean was breathtaking. "Whoa."

Perl had only seen the view this high up from the back steps of the Palace, the one that faced the garbage and farming islands. From here, the seas were crystal clear and blue as could be. Perl couldn't believe there wasn't any trash floating on the surface.

"Okay...a quick look around, and then I get out of here," Perl thought, tiptoeing into the room.

The twins had matching red canopy beds with red poppy sheets that cascaded down to the white marble tiles. A holographic portrait of each sister hovered above her own headboard. Perl ran her hand across the bed, feeling the luxurious silk fabric. *This must be like sleeping on a cloud."*

A pair of albino snow leopard skin rugs lay at the foot of each bed. On top slept twin robotic chihuahuas. *"What the—?"* Perl stepped quietly around them as their internal cooling systems buzzed softly.

She began humming as she strolled through the gaudy, gymnasium-sized room, stopping in front of a glass pod on the wall fully stocked with drinks and desserts of every kind. "Hmm...yes bring me my freshly squeezed orange juice and honey toast, extra honey. Oo! Then I'll have a swim," she said, noticing the infinity pool at the far end of the room.

Hundreds of elegant perfume bottles, sparkling jewelry boxes, and gem-encrusted trinkets lined the shelves of a colossal curio cabinet. Sun rays from a ceiling skylight hit the treasures, casting tiny rainbows onto Perl's face. A blue diamond butterfly hairpin caught her eye; she picked it up. "Wow."

Perl was startled as a small drone flew into the room, buzzing overhead. She ducked, watching as the bird-shaped drone picked up two hairbrushes with its claws and disappeared through an arched doorway. She heard the twins' voices approaching, and suddenly realized she'd wandered too far inside and couldn't get out without them seeing her.

"*Shoot!*" Perl quickly crouched down behind an enormous chair in the shape of a swan, adorned with real feathers.

Mik entered the room first, brushing her long red hair, taunting her sister as she twirled like a ballerina, "Princess Mik Névenoé! What a splendid ring that has to it!"

Ivry followed, holding her hairbrush to her mouth like a microphone, "Princess *Ivry* Névenoé is more like it!"

"Sorry, sister, but—" Mik paused, noticing their bedroom door was open.

"But what?" Ivry asked, seeing her sister's face.

Mik motioned towards the door. Both saw the cleaning cart that propped it open. "Is someone in here?" she whispered.

"The staff know better than to clean while we're in here." Ivry tiptoed over to her sleeping chihuahua and pressed her thumb into its collar. Recognizing its owner's fingerprint, it woke and sprang to its paws.

Mik did the same. "Search!" she commanded.

Both robot dogs began sniffing along virtual gaming tables, under makeup vanity chairs, and around several large video pillars broadcasting the photos from the twins' dress fitting, until stopping in front of the pair of high-backed swan chairs. "Grrrrr!"

"What is it, girl?" Mik stepped closer.

Perl held her breath, stifling a sneeze as the soft down feathers tickled her nose.

"Maybe we should call the guards?" Ivry suggested.

"*Ah-choo!*" Perl couldn't hold it in another second.

The twins screamed in unison. Clutching one another, they jumped up onto a nearby couch.

Perl sat up, realizing her cover had been blown. Seeing only the top of her brown hood peeking over the swan chair, Mik and Ivry screamed again. "Attack! Attack!" The dogs went berserk, barking and snarling.

"Ow! Down! Down!" Perl high-stepped out from behind the chair as they nipped at her feet.

Realizing it was just a young girl, the twins breathed a sigh of relief. They heckled Perl as she ran for the door. "Ha! Ha! You'd better run!" Ivry said. "We're gonna have you arrested!" Mik shouted.

Perl looked back, "I'm sorry! I just wanted to see the ocean! It's so clean on this side!"

"Clean?" repeated Mik, looking at Ivry. "Get back to *your cleaning* and get out of our room!"

"Yeah!" Ivry threw a rabbit fur pillow at the door, just as Perl closed it with a bang.

"Hahaha!" The twins snorted, rolling in their seats. "What a weirdo," Mik added.

Sarr peeked her head out of the closet, squinting. "What's going on out here, you two?"

"Nothing, Mother."

Perl stepped on to the back of her cleaning cart, pushing it with her foot like a scooter. Hearing the echoes of the twins' laughter, she kicked the ground to go faster, coming to a crashing halt at the elevator. As Perl was about to hit the button, she realized she was still holding the butterfly hairpin.

"Oh no," Perl quickly stashed the pin inside one of her robe pockets. "Well, I'm not going back there. No way. I'll just have to try and return it tomorrow during the ball." It was nearly three o'clock. Her shift was ending, so she quietly returned the cart and slipped out the service door.

Perl was almost home when she turned a corner and came across an old man sitting on a step near the bottom burrows. He was holding a sign that read 'Help Me'. Perl reached into her robe pocket and handed him what remained of the blueberries she had stashed for herself. As her fingertips touched the homeless man's rough, hardened hand, she shifted her vision to see his essence. She was shocked to see him transform into a beautiful rainbow.

"Beautiful," she mouthed; the misty, colorful essence was unlike any she'd ever seen.

"A gift, for a gift," the old man said, tapping Perl's arm with a folded note.

Perl took the note, tucking it into her robe. "Thank you." Continuing on her way, Perl looked back, watching the man's colorful essence fade.

As Perl reached the last set of steps near the shoreline, she stopped. Glancing out at the sea, she took a deep breath in and the smell of salt filled her nose. She was eager to find out who Papa's special dinner guest was tonight, but the lure of the ocean was too strong to pass up, especially after the day she'd had.

"Maybe just a quick dip."

This part of the beach was always empty in the evening. No one ever swam there because of all the garbage in the water, but Perl didn't mind.

She removed her pants and tossed her robe onto the sand. The old man's note popped out of her pocket, as if wanting to be read. Perl sat down and recited it to the ocean.

"I quench the willow
in the raspberry field
where children run free~
in and around the shade tree,
picking ruby gems,
climbing wooden boards
nailed to the side~
so they may go higher
and higher to see.
I am the rain."

"I'll keep you someplace special," she thought, tucking the poem safely into a deep back pocket of her robe.

The waves crashed at her feet as she swam out in nothing but her undies and a gray tank top.

"Weird, the tide is so rough today. I've never seen it like this."

Plastic bottles, lids, and bags of all sorts clung to Perl's body. Closing her eyes and spreading out her arms, she floated, as her thoughts turned back to the Golden Palace and the twins. They were lucky to have so much. She thought about the homeless man. How sad he was; how unfair it all seemed.

"Papa said, *"the scales of life are tipped."* Was this what he was talking about?" As Perl contemplated what it all could mean, she started to softly sing a line of the whale's song, *"there's still magic to believe, some love that binds us, just promise not to leave."*

Perl closed her eyes and listened. The only sounds were the waves, crashing over and over again like clockwork. A larger wave washed over the top of her, stirring her from her peace.

"Oh, shoot! I gotta get home!" Perl swam back and gathered her clothes, putting them on as she ran, her thick head of hair bouncing with each step. It seemed like she was running everywhere she went today. Goose bumps prickled up on her arms and legs from the chilly air on her wet skin.

When she reached the root cellar, Perl tore through the mossy front door like a tornado. She looked for Ximu or any of her spider-monks, but there wasn't a soul around. The dining room had been prepared for a meal;

the large table had been covered in a beautiful embroidered tablecloth, beeswax candles had been lit, and sweet honeysuckle leaves had been placed in each water glass.

Perl heard the hum of voices coming from the library. It sounded like they were arguing. She slipped down the hallway. Peering between the bookshelves, Perl saw several spider-monks standing around a woman. The woman was so tall her head nearly grazed the ceiling; her cropped hair was the color of crystal blue water shimmering in the sunlight.

"Who among us broke the chant? Who?" Victr pounded on the table. He scanned his brothers. "Look out there! A fierce tide has returned. Our defenses have been compromised. Someone broke the Bulwark Chant…Who was it?" He turned, the creases in his already furrowed brow deepening.

"It was I," Ximu said, walking to the center of the room. The monks gasped in disbelief.

Victr turned to him sharply. "Great Ever, Ximu, why? You've made Perl vulnerable! The poor girl is not ready for what darkness may come!"

"Darkness?" Perl thought, *"what's going on?"*

Ximu spoke softly, "you are wrong, old friend. Perl has heard the whale's song. Have you not seen how she takes note? Her bio-light has shown itself. Her gifts are revealing themselves. She is ready."

Brother Basil, always the voice of reason, tried to calm the room. "Peace, brothers. Uriel would not have come if Perl was not—"

The tall, stoic woman, until now silent, interrupted; her ethereal voice immediately commanded attention. "Let us have the girl speak on her own behalf." Uriel stared into the shadows, directly into Perl's eyes. "Come out young one."

Perl was suddenly very aware of the puddle of water she was standing in, as all eyes turned to her. Licking the sea salt from her bottom lip, she stepped out from behind the old, musty bookcase. "Hi." She walked in and stood next to Papa Ximu. Perl looked up at the Amazonian woman, trying to process the otherworldly vision.

The statuesque figure was dressed head to toe in gilded heavy armor, her arms wrapped in silver chainmail sleeves. A dazzling floor length cape of translucent lavender flowed behind her, sparkling against her ebony skin. Tiny purple and yellow flowers seemed to be growing right out of the cloth, as if the cloak itself were alive. Strapped over her shoulder attached by a green vine was a gittern; the medieval wooden guitar adorned with ornate botanicals and carved cherub faces. Perhaps oddest of all was the giant leopard moth *(Hypercompe Scribonia)* that permanently hovered over the Being's left eye, remaining in place no matter where the woman moved.

Perl swallowed. "What are you?" Light laughter broke the tension in the room.

The Being looked into Perl's face with her one piercing violet eye. "My name is Uriel, young one. I am a Divine Protector from the Light Realm. I've been watching over you since birth." She extended her long thin hand out to the girl.

As they shook, Perl felt a jolt of energy, and the most indescribable feeling of joy. It ran through her entire body, leaving her foolishly grinning from ear to ear.

Ximu ushered the group into the kitchen, "come, let us eat and talk more of your adventure to come."

Perl ran to the iron kettle. The monks formed a line, as she ladled out hot cabbage and potato stew, with mounds of crispy fried agave worms on the side. Uriel held up her bowl; it was small in her large hands.

"It smells delicious."

Perl said proudly, "Papa says cooking is like my hair. You work with what you've got."

"Excellent advice." Uriel took a seat with the other monks. "Come and sit," she said, patting the wooden chair beside her.

Perl spooned out a bowl for herself and squeezed in beside Uriel. "So, um, where's the Light Realm?" The monks' idle chatter stopped as they listened closely.

"I'll try to put this as simply as possible. There are three realms encircling your Earth, invisible to human eyes. There is the Light Realm, the Half-Light Realm, and the Dark Realm. The Light Realm is where Ever reigns. Divine Protectors, Light Creatures, and humans of pure heart that have passed on exist there peacefully." Uriel pushed a stray curl out of Perl's eye. "The Half-Light Realm is where we battle evil entities that seek to blind the human race to the true magic of nature."

Perl interrupted, "True magic? Like when I heard the whales?"

Uriel nodded. "They are hurting."

Perl took a spoonful of stew; the hot soup felt good in her belly. "Why don't people see this?"

"Keep eating, you'll need your strength," Uriel pushed the rest of her fried worms onto Perl's plate. "The Darkness blinds them. It exploits human desires. It preys on their fears, manipulates their free will."

Basil, normally shy by nature, stood up and placed his hands on the table. "This is why the oceans are suffering!"

Uriel replied, "yes, Brother Basil, and it is why I've come to collect your Perl."

Perl panicked. "Me? Why me? Victr is right. I don't know anything. I've never been off the island. You must be wrong."

Uriel stood, towering over the group as she cast a long shadow across the length of the table. "I am not wrong!" The timbre of her voice caused the bowls of soup to wobble and spill. Everyone at the table shrank down into their chairs as Uriel continued, her voice softening. "I promised your father that I would always watch over you."

Perl sat up quickly, "you know my father?"

Uriel did not answer. She knew everything about Perl; where she came from, who her parents were, her abilities, but now was not the time to share that information. Instead, she addressed the room.

"Brothers of the Quill, you have done well nurturing and protecting the child. But the orchid's bite has alerted the Darkness of Perl's presence. More spies will be lurking."

Perl looked at the bite mark on her thumb, now turning purple. *"How could she possibly know about that?"*

"I will return in two Earth days, when the moon waxes full. Perl will not be safe here for much longer. The Dark One will stop at nothing."

Basil cleared his throat, "what should we do now, Protector?"

"Go about as you were. Perform your daily tasks. Resume your chants. Do not worry." With that last comment, all eyes turned to Victr.

"I'll...I'll do my best," the monk replied, wringing his hands.

Uriel placed her hand on Victr's shoulder. "Stay together and stay strong. I will take Perl to Venusto. There she will begin her Light Realm Seeker training."

Ximu smiled to himself. Perl, unsure of what was happening, said nothing.

Uriel clasped her hands together and closed her eyes. All at once, a brilliant violet light filled the room. Squinting, the monks looked up and Uriel was gone, leaving behind sparkling dust particles floating in the air.

The monks jumped up, bursting into conversation, "The Prophecy is real!", "It will be fulfilled!", "An actual Divine Light Protector, in our cellar!", "Glory be to Ever!"

Victr groaned, "I still say Perl needs more time to mature."

Perl squeezed through the crowded room of robes and long hairy spider legs, working her way to Ximu.

Ximu shouted over the monks, "back to work, good brothers! There's food to be prepped and ale jugs to be filled. You heard Uriel, the Palace Ball is still tomorrow, and we'll be expected to be of service."

The monks cleared the room. Perl tugged on his rope belt.

"Papa, how did she know all of that about me? What's Seeker training? She knows who my father is? What's going on? Who is the Dark One?"

Ximu placed his furry claw on Perl's head. "Breathe, little Bee. In. Out."

"I'm not sure I wanna go to Benusto." She flipped her hood up, covering her eyes.

The kindly monk chuckled as he pulled her hood back, "it is pronounced Venusto, and it is a great honor. You will learn your purpose there. I have taught you all that I can. It is in the hands of the almighty Ever now."

She twirled his belt rope around her wrist. "Are you going with me?"

Ximu looked down at her as he pulled her close to his side. "I'm afraid I cannot. I must remain here. The Brotherhood needs me."

"But I need you! I don't want to go! I don't have a purpose!" Perl ducked under Ximu's arm and ran towards her room.

He yelled after her, "Bumble, wait! It's going to be—"

She ran down the hallway and turned a corner, smacking headfirst into Victr.

"Hey, hey, there you are. We still have fish to scale. A promise is a promise, remember?"

The pair sat over a smelly compost pit. Victr chopped off the fish heads. Perl held them by the tails, scraping off scales.

"I don't know how people can eat fish or any meat for that matter. They have lives, ya' know?"

Victr tossed a head into the hole filled with decaying scraps. "Yes, and so do cabbages and agave worms, but you gobbled them up without thinking twice about it," he chuckled.

Perl shot him a sarcastic look. "That's different."

"Is it? All life is precious. All life has meaning. We should only take what we need and give back to the Earth what we can. That's how we keep balance."

Perl put down her knife. "I heard you back there. You don't think I'm ready for whatever this thing is. Heck, *I* don't think I'm ready!"

Victr sighed, "no, it's just that...well, I worry a lot. Too much, the brothers say. But when it comes to you," the monk wrapped his arm around the girl, "I don't believe there is such a thing as too much worry. But I see how strong you've become, and I'm so proud of you."

Perl rested her head on his shoulder.

The large monk reached over and picked up another fish. "It's always been one of my shortcomings. I tend to not trust my gut instincts, doubting what I feel to be true. But alas, I am human, and I am working on it."

Perl looked up at the spider-monk, his dark eyes teary. Victr looked down at Perl's tiny frame snuggled in against him.

"I love you, my little warrior."

She squeezed his arm tightly, "I love you too."

9 SLY FOX

The morning sky was flawless, as if Uriel's celestial gown had swept across the sky, blanketing the island in a canvas of lavender. The ocean breeze was warm, a few cottony clouds drifted lazily over the island. It was a picture-perfect day for a party.

"Let me see!" Mik yanked the binoculars from her sister; a gift from their father from a few years ago. The binoculars were handmade using a taxidermy owl head, its large eyes removed to form the lenses.

Ivry pointed. "There! To the right of that giant monk bell!"

Mik whined, "Where? I don't see them!"

"Just beyond the casinos. Hundreds of them. How can you not see? Are you sampling mother's nightshade?"

Mik adjusted the binoculars. "Very funny. Oh, wait, I see them! Yachts, baby! My people have come!"

"Uh, don't you mean, *our* people?" Ivry corrected her.

Mik tossed the spyglasses into the air. She grabbed Ivry's hands and spun her in a circle. "Weee! It's happening!" They fell onto the canopy bed laughing.

"Time for our massages," Ivry sat up. "Mani-pedis. Hair and makeup."

"Let's hit the juice and oxygen bar first!" Mik suggested. They snapped a pic, toasting with their coconut water and dragon fruit kombucha drinks held high. The caption read, *"Holla! It's our birthday! Party at the Palace!"* In an instant, three million comments wished them happy birthday.

Despite her incredible evening and a long night of filling her journal, Perl was up early, ready to take on the day. The excitement and allure of the twins' birthday ball had her running on pure adrenaline. She, Regor, and the other servants would be making many trips today, up and down, pantry to Palace, hauling king oysters, caviar, crab, lobster, sea urchin, and countless other delicacies. Large shipping vessels carrying exotic fare from around the globe were arriving.

Like the servants, the monks were also busy, gathering and unpacking the seemingly endless amounts of crates being delivered. Palace guards were on hand to assist the monks, although it seemed to the Brotherhood that they were there less to help and more to intimidate the help.

Prying open a large oak crate with a crowbar, Victr's brow crinkled as he viewed its contents. "What is this?! Baby eel? Manatee? Shark? Dolphin? Oh, my Ever!" Several other monks gathered around to see. Victr's face reddened. "Who ordered these?! I will not prepare dishes from endangered species!"

A heavily armored guard approached the monk. "Orders from the Palace! And you *will* make them, or you'll see the inside of a cold, dark dungeon!"

Victr furled his wrinkled brow, shooting daggers at the thick-necked guard. "And what atrocity is in *that one*?!" Victr pointed to a large box that was intentionally set aside. Unlike the stacks of cardboard and wooden crates, this one looked more like a gift, elaborately wrapped in shimmering purple cloth and tied up with a delicate silver chain.

Count Graves had ordered a special meal of bluefin tuna *(Thunnus orientalis)* for the twins to share as their special birthday entrée. It was said to be the very last of its kind left on Earth. Priceless.

The guard rubbed his gloved hand over the box. "This here is special. It's for the princesses, so you better take extra good care with this one, or else." He squeezed the stock of his gun and bared his yellow teeth, chuckling as he stomped away.

Victr wanted to protest, but then thought better of it. "Alright brothers, I know this will be a difficult day. Heads down and let's get to work." The other monks nodded silently, continuing to stock the kitchen.

Neither Perl, nor her delivery partner Regor had time to think about what they were carting up that day. They were far too busy with all the excitement going on.

"I've never seen so many people outside," Perl exclaimed.

"And mid-apartment crowds mingling with the rich, no less!" Regor giggled.

Locals lined the streets, crowded shoulder to shoulder, trying to catch a glimpse of the arriving elite. Behemoth six-story yachts were pulling into ports, pushing aside and damaging small fishing boats. Satellite towers sprang up like mushrooms, and paparazzi drones filled the skies. Like an enormous beehive, the island of Mont Michel had come alive.

Midway up the two thousand steps, Perl stopped to let Regor catch up. She looked down at the gangly man's feet and smiled. "Keep up, Goat-foot!" she teased. The pair were on their final delivery. Perl had to head home to bathe, then turn right back around and return to the Golden Palace for server duty.

Regor huffed and puffed, "I'm dying. Say goodbye to Pie-Pie for me." Next to Perl, Regor's beloved tuxedo cat, Pie-Pie, was his best friend.

Perl lifted a bundle of heavy titanium conch shells from the skinny servant's stack of boxes. "Oh, Goaty, let me help you."

Sweat dripped from Regor's forehead. "Thank you. You are an Eversend."

Perl secured the bundle to her waist belt. "Don't even get me started on that subject."

"What subject? Whaddya mean?" Regor had started back up the steps when he turned, a look of confusion on his face.

Perl pushed past him. "Oh nothing. I just have to leave Mont Michel to go with a Divine Protector to some 'light' place and learn how to fight some sort of evil monster, that's all."

Regor giggled. "Come again?"

"It's a long story." Perl quickened her pace.

"Why did you wait until now to say anything?"

Perl pulled her hood up. "I really don't wanna talk about it, Regor. Papa and Uriel and all the monks think I'm someone I'm not."

Regor played along, thinking this was another one of Perl's fantastical stories, "I see. Who exactly do they think you are, my mysterious friend? Heh-heh."

"I don't know, but they say I'm the answer to some ancient prophecy to save the oceans. Because I can see and feel things others can't. All around me. In the plants, in the ocean. I never should have told anyone. Now Papa and Uriel want me to leave the island, and..."

Regor pulled her hood back slightly. "And, you're afraid? You?"

"Yeah? So what." Perl yanked her hood down tighter.

Regor let out a nervous giggle, ducking down as several drones buzzed over their heads.

"Perl, if Brother Ximu thinks it's something you should do, you should probably do it, right? I mean, he's the smartest man on the island."

Perl whispered, "smartest *spider*."

"Hm, what was that?"

"Nothing. Let's hurry up so you can get home and give Pie-Pie his catnip."

Perl purposely avoided Ximu. She was still upset, not able to shake the feeling that he was abandoning her by letting her go with Uriel to this Venusto place alone. She cleaned up quickly, slipping out of the root cellar unseen. Perl had another reason she wanted to get back to the Palace early. She had a very special gift that she wanted to leave for the twins, one that she would have to smuggle in.

As she walked back up the long flight of zig-zag stairs for her final time that evening, Perl looked out at the parade of boats docked at the various ports around Mont Michel. She passed people as they cheered and waved at the scores of arriving guests. Perl saw that a few of the children were holding the nature treasures she had left in their homes. Little hands waved long colorful feathers, tropical flowers, berry branches, and even shells. Perl smiled as she rounded the mid-apartment cliff steps and headed up towards the elite dwelling pods, a renewed pep in her step.

Perl was met at the servant entrance by the same sinewy crane-women from the day before, only this time she was dressed in a bright white pant suit and matching cape. She had a big grin on her face, but Perl couldn't tell if it was genuine or if her extremely tight bun was just pulling her skin back.

"You can change out of your robe in there." Handing Perl a plain beige box, she pointed to a long room filled with rows of lockers. Perl read the woman's name tag: *Ms. Kind.*

"Hardly," she thought.

"Meet me back here in ten minutes. Not eleven. Not twelve. Ten minutes." The crane-like woman gestured to a set of swinging kitchen doors.

"Yes, ma'am."

"And the coin!" Perl reluctantly gave Ms. Kind her titanium coin, wishing she could have kept it.

"Yes, ma'am."

Perl found a locker and set the box down on a nearby bench. Opening it, a wave of panic washed over her. She stared down at a crisp, starched white uniform.

"I didn't know I was going to have to wear a costume! Now how am I going to sneak you guys in?" She pulled a water-filled vial from her robe pocket and placed it carefully beside her on the bench. Staring back at her were two matching, fuchsia-colored seahorses *(Hippocampus).*

Perl put on the stiff outfit. It had a white fur collar and gold shell buttons that ran the entire length. The skirt was uncomfortably short. Perl yanked on it, trying to pull it down as far as it would stretch. A white fox tail was attached to the back of it, but that did little to cover Perl up or make her feel any less uneasy. The last item in the box was a fox-head hat. It looked real, but she couldn't tell for sure.

"Do I really have to wear this?" Perl thought, pulling out the furry headpiece. She worried about transporting her seahorses safely, but then had an idea. She made a bun with her massive hair, tying it up with a vine she had in her robe. She nestled the vial of seahorses into the bun and used the fox hat to hold it all down.

"There." As she was about to head out the door, Perl stopped. "Shoot! The hairpin! I gotta take that back to the twins' room." Opening the locker, Perl reached into her robe and pulled out the blue diamond butterfly pin. Not wanting to upset the vial, she tucked the hairpin into her sock.

"Monk-girl, where are you!?" Ms. Kind swung open the door.

"Yes, ma'am. Coming, ma'am." Slamming the locker shut, Perl slipped on the fur boots. She hurried past Ms. Kind, who suspiciously eyed the fox hat resting high upon Perl's mound of hair.

49

Perl fell into line with thirty other young girls, all dressed as white foxes. They were all holding trays that displayed the Graves family crest of two crossed swords, flanked by a pair of leaping dolphins wearing crowns.

Ms. Kind squawked orders, "okay, listen up, ladies! You are to replenish your trays here." There was a long buffet table, filled with the appetizers Perl had helped to deliver all morning, only now they looked much fancier.

The crane-woman snapped her fingers. "Wear your gloves at all times. You are not, I repeat, not, to remove your gloves for any reason. As she spoke, Ms. Kind's assistants began handing out pairs of gloves to all the girls. The white silken gloves were elbow length, with long glittery fingernails sewn into the tips.

"As if this outfit isn't strange enough, right?" Perl whispered to the girl next to her, recognizing her from the lower apartments. The girl lived with her baby brother and mom, and occasionally helped Victr weave fishing baskets. Perl made a pretend clawing motion with the tips of her gloves.

"Rowrrr!" she growled. The girl stifled a giggle.

"Keep your veils pulled down over your faces, your heads bowed, and your trays up at all times! And no funny business today! Do you understand?" Ms. Kind poked her pointed beak-like nose into Perl's face. "You are not guests here. You are staff, meant to be invisible. Service starts in two minutes. Stand straight, fill your trays, then veils down. Now, go!"

Perl had never stood so rigid. Not because of Ms. Kind's command, but because she was trying to keep the seahorses from spilling out. The foxes filed into the grand hall; trays held high. The mirrored hallway was filled wall to wall with guests. Perl squinted to see where she was going. The thin, translucent veil she wore clipped to the front of the fox hat restricted her vision; her view of the festivities would be through a cloudy haze. *"Great,"* she sighed.

At one of the bars, Count Graves was already busy hobnobbing. "King Coppice! How are you?" A heavyset man with two prosthetic stallion legs clomped up and swung his arm around The Count.

"Zell, you old tycoon, where has the time gone?"

"Indeed! I still can't believe my little Red Gems are eighteen," Graves smiled.

King Coppice took a crab puff from a tray and swallowed it in one bite. "It seems like only yesterday the twins were out riding fawns, while we shot ducks at the wetlands chateau. Those were the days!"

"Ah, they do grow up too fast. But not us, we haven't changed a bit. Well, *I haven't*, at least!" The Count teased, pointing down at the King's metallic horse legs.

"Pretty nice, eh? They were a fortune, but you know I…goodness, truffles!" The portly King swiped a couple off Perl's tray, scarfing them down.

Perl didn't look up, but she could see that the Count was wearing shark skin boots with studded shark teeth running up the backs. Perl started to walk away, but the King stopped her, grabbing four more sea turtle truffles off her tray. "Mm, fantastic spread! Sarr has great taste...in food anyway!" He slapped Graves on the back and trotted off, chasing down another server with hors d'oeuvres.

It was all quite lavish, from what Perl could discern through her annoying veil. At first, she thought, *"am I seeing their essences?"* But after a while she realized these were all just elaborate, outlandish costumes, ones she was dying to get a better look at. There were couture fashions from around the globe. Bronze armadillo scaled skirts banged into her shins, beaded zebra tails brushed against her, and something that looked like a neon crocodile tail slithered over her fox fur boots.

"Mm! Is this harp seal shish kabob? Dee-lish!" A woman wearing bright orange feathered gloves took the last bite from her tray.

"Did she just say harp seal?" Perl thought to herself, *"nah, couldn't be."*

As Perl went to refill her tray, she lifted her veil slightly, peering around. *"No Ms. Kind in sight. Now's my chance."* Setting her empty tray on the counter, she quickly crept up the service staircase at the back of the kitchen. Halfway up, Perl paused to look out a large circular window. The glass inside was magnifying glass, so looking though it was like peering through a telescope. Perl gazed down at the fishing docks, then paused.

"Slaughterman? What's he doing?" she pressed her face to the glass.

In one of the ports, the shadowy figure stood on a box-shaped pontoon boat loaded full of large metal tubs. Filled to the brim of each were bloody sharks *(Carcharodon carcharias)*. Their fins had been cut off, but they were clearly still alive, flopping around in the tubs. Working methodically and without sentiment, the man dumped them back into the ocean, the waters turning red. At the sight of this, Perl felt her stomach turn.

"He's killing them!" she gasped. Perl thought of the time she saw the Slaughterman pushing baby calves into the butcher room, because The Count preferred to eat veal. She shuddered. *"Why? Why would he cut off their fins?"* Perl recalled hearing rumors about Slaughterman performing strange experiments on nearby Trash Island. She quickly turned away from the window, making a mad dash up to the penthouse suite, her insides doing flip-flops.

Everyone was downstairs except for the twins, who were waiting to make their grand entrance. Perl unlatched the door ever so quietly, slipping into their enormous bedroom. Mik and Ivry were on the far side of the room, sitting at their matching crystal vanities, prepping.

Mik dabbed on a spot of lip gloss. "He's not here yet. There's no point in going down if the Prince isn't here to see me."

"Or me. How do you know he's not here?" Ivry said, as she blotted her lips on a floral, embroidered, silk hanky, tossing it into the trash.

"Oh, I have my spies," Mik tapped on her rose vine tattoo. A tiny holographic image projected a roving bird's-eye view of Mont Michel. Mik had ordered dozens of drones to scan the shoreline, tracking all incoming vessels.

Stealthily, Perl removed the vial of seahorses from her hair. Holding them up carefully in one hand, she crawled across the floor to the snow leopard carpet and hid under Ivry's canopy bed.

Suddenly, a loud whirring sound was heard outside. The noise rattled every window in the penthouse. Mik jumped up. "He's here!"

"Gee, ya' think?" Ivry covered her ears.

Hovering outside like a colossal alien spacecraft was Prince Névenoé's AirB&B-copter, with rooftop modular pools, neuro-escape spa, Mars vapor lounge, 60D concert stage, and fifty of the most luxuriously decorated estate rooms in the world. The massive turbines made a deafening roar; nearby trees bent and cracked from the sheer ferocity of the fan's gusts.

"Well, I hope it's sound proof inside." Ivry slowly removed her hands from her ears.

Mik twirled in her beetle-encrusted ball gown. "Of course it is, silly, and soon it'll be mine, all mine!" She held out her hand to Ivry, tapping her ring finger.

"Or mine," Ivry retorted, slapping Mik's hand away with a smile.

Their governess, Ruby, chirped as she appeared at the door. "Places, girls!" A dazzling blonde, buxom woman, she wore a low-cut snakeskin top with a long chinchilla fur skirt. "Come quickly, angels. Time to shine."

"We know!" they sang in unison.

Ruby gushed, "Oh, don't you both look like fresh cut emeralds in your gowns. Now remember, shoulders back, smile...and no alcohol."

The sisters stepped around Ruby's chinchilla train and out into the chaotic hallway. A group of paparazzi in pearly-white plastic jumpsuits clambered around the girls snapping pics. The twins had hired them to capture every second of the day to upload to their adoring fans on *Narcissi*.

Mik flipped her red hair. "Remember to shoot me from my left side only." This was the side that did not show her extra freckle.

Each member of the paparazzi wore a pair of camera goggles, the lens extending in and out as they focused, blinking to activate the shot. They shouted directions to the twins.

"Look here, ladies!"

"Big smiles!"

"One more! Beautiful!"

Like a swarm of hornets, the girls and their chatty clicking entourage moved down the long corridor and out of sight.

The coast was clear. Perl slipped out from under the canopy and set her fox hat on the bed, turning it around so it wasn't staring at her. She gently placed the vial with the seahorses on a marble night table between the two beds. Stuck to the side of the tube with a dab of molasses was a small packet of brine shrimp, and a note:

"For Mik & Ivry. Please name us. We require four shrimp daily and lots of love. Thank You & Happy Birthday! Your Secret Admirer."

Perl took a moment to make sure everything was in place, then grabbed her fox headpiece and walked down the hallway in the opposite direction of the chaos, back down the servant's staircase.

10 UNVEILING

The twins stood waiting at the top of a winding staircase. The railing was shaped like a long black eel spiraling down, its head staring ominously at every guest. As the lights dimmed, a thin, bald man wearing a floor-length red leather gown and matching four-inch heels, tapped lightly on a tiny microphone that jutted out from his forehead like an antenna.

"Queens and kings, duchesses and dukes, princesses and princes! I give you, our ladies of honor, Mik and Ivry Graves!"

The twins, hand in hand, curtsied together. A spotlight hit the two, lighting up their cherry red hair like a bonfire. Crystal chandeliers lowered, and the girls' exotic headdresses sparkled, casting a rainbow of twinkling lights around the ballroom. The guests applauded, marveling at the dazzling spectacle.

"I see him!" Ivry muttered to her sister through grinning teeth.

Near an extravagant fountain where pure silver mercury flowed, Prince Névenoé, decked out in a lavish peacock-feathered tuxedo, posed next to a woman who looked like a giant pink pufferfish *(Tetraodontidae)*. Pinpricks of neon light flickered at the ends of her pointy spines.

"Let the celebration begin!" Feedback from the announcer's mic screeched.

"Ready?" Ivry squeezed her sister hand.

"Let's do this!" As they strutted confidently down the serpent steps, a thousand tiger swallowtail butterflies *(Papiliondae)* were released. A symphony of electric harps began to play. Cameras flashed, and within seconds, fashion designers worldwide were sketching the twin's brilliant beetled gowns, soon to be turned into knockoff apparel.

Count Graves' footman, a weasely man named Snive, eased over to The Count and whispered in his ear, "sir, the oil spill has been contained."

"And the protestors?" Graves asked.

"There was a slight altercation but it's been handled, sir."

"Good work."

Snive bowed and backed away. "Thank you, sir."

The ballroom was abuzz; a mix of laughter, clinking glasses, and the rhythmic beat of the amplified harps filling the air.

"I'm missing it!" Perl hurried down the winding steps, running past the magnified window, not daring to sneak another peek.

Perl adjusted her fox hat and swiped a tray of shot glasses filled with squid ink before causally sauntering out into the cocktail party. Butterflies were flying everywhere. One landed on her shoe.

"Hi, lil' tiger. Isn't this heavenly?" It batted its wings and took off.

As she wandered through the crowd, Ms. Kind's shrill voice cut through the air like shattering glass.

"Foxes, prepare for dinner service!" The crane-woman flitted through the room, corralling the servants back into the kitchen.

Countess Sarr opened the enormous stained-glass doors leading to the banquet hall. She was then escorted up onto a gaudy glass pedestal, where she gestured to the crowd.

"Please be seated, one and all."

Determined to outshine her daughters, Sarr wore an eye-popping spectacle of a gown. Its lacy bodice was made from four-thousand-year-old coral, cut fresh from the island's reef. The entire lower half of the dress was a water-filled globe, complete with live flameback angelfish *(Centropyge aurantonotus)*. Balanced on her head was an aquamarine colored wig, fashioned into the shape of an 18th century tall ship, the sails flying the family's crest. In a room full of outlandish ensembles, hers truly stood out.

"Girls...my darling girls! Come take your seats."

The banquet table was a giant round aquarium, bottom lit by hundreds of glowing jellyfish *(Pelagia noctiluca)*. The twins sat side by side on a double-seated throne shaped like a giant clam shell. Mik pushed Ivry aside, beating her to the spot next to Prince Névenoé.

"Get a close-up of me with the Prince," she commanded her paparazzi.

Snap. Snap. Tabloid columnists gobbled up the gossip. Mik's relationship status changed to *"Possible Future Princess of the Europa Islands."*

Ms. Kind ushered in the fox-servants. "Alright. Veils down, and don't spill." Their job was now to keep the drinks flowing.

Many of the dishes were already plated at the table. Some appeared to be moving, bubbling, and smoking. Pink, purple, and tangerine clouds drifted above the feast. Count Graves stood, his shark-fin cloak cascading to the floor. He twisted his gold, tentacle mustache, the one he always wore pierced through his nose. The guests grew quiet.

"Thank you all for coming to our most...humble abode." The crowd laughed. "A toast. First, to my lovely wife, Sarr. Darling, you have outdone yourself this time."

The Countess smiled, her dilated eyes squinting to see her husband.

Ivry nudged her mother's arm, whispering, "cheers, mother."

Countess Sarr raised her glass. "And to you, my pet!"

Glasses clinked. Perl moved down the long row of diners, rapidly filling goblets. As she got to the twins' throne, Mik held her glass below the table. She signaled to Perl to fill her cup with alcohol.

Perl shook her head, "I'm not supposed to. Ms. Kind said adults only."

Mik glared at her. "And I'm not supposed to tell anyone you were snooping in my room yesterday, right? Now fill it, to the top."

Perl did as she was told.

"And keep 'em coming."

The Count raised his glass again. "And to my angels. My sweet, perfect angels, Ivry and Mik! Happy eighteenth birthday! May your every wish come true!"

Clink. Clink. Clink. The table came alive with cheers and praise. Mik downed her drink as the room settled into idle chitchat.

"The rebel burrowers are growing. We'll need to cut off supplies to the north and south poles."

"Baroness Von Rutherford wore the same holographic gown to my niece's Imperial Court Ball. Unthinkable."

The steady hum of conversation filled the hall as the patrons devoured their exotic meals.

An hour into the feast, a loud drumroll silenced the crowd. Four gourmet chefs carried out a wobbling bubble on a giant silver tray. The guests looked on as they proudly placed the dish in front of the twins, bowing humbly.

One of them, a towering chef with large mutton chops, cleared his throat, "Princesses Ivry and Mik, we present to you the bluefin tuna, a rare delight indeed." The chef handed a small purple box to the girls. Mik grabbed it first. Inside was a long pin. The chef bowed, "your honor, my lady."

Mik giggled. Pulling out the pin, she closed her eyes, and popped the iridescent bubble. It burst into a fizz of little water droplets, revealing the carefully prepared delicacy within. The table of diners marveled at the dish.

Mik clapped with delight. "Oh, Father, it looks delicious!"

The Count twisted his mustache, "yes, well, it was in captivity, but anything for my captivating angels."

The rare fish was cut into two perfect halves and garnished with lilacs. The twins split their meal, as they always did, daintily nibbling while flirting with the Prince.

Ivry leaned over, batting her eyelashes. "Prince, tell us more about your rhinoceros racetrack."

Mik pushed Ivry back into her seat. "Yes, it seems so dangerous."

Prince Névenoé puffed out his chest. "Separating the baby rhinos from their mothers and training them from birth is the key to establishing dominance."

Mik licked her fingertips and leaned in closer. "You're so brave."

The Prince beamed. "Well, I don't jockey the rhinos myself, but viewing the races from my private hover-loge can get pretty crazy."

The girls laughed loudly, each of them trying to outdo the other, as the gluttonous feast went on into the night.

Perl's arms were sore from hours of pouring drinks. A man with a solid copper aardvark nose pulled on her white tail.

"Hey, foxy-fox! More ale!" He yelled, belching loudly.

At the unexpected yank on her tail, Perl turned sharply. As her tray slipped from her hands, glasses crashed to the floor. Ms. Kind was there in a flash with a mop.

"Get back to the kitchen," she glared at Perl.

Perl pulled back her veil, "I'm so sorry."

Frantically sopping up the spill, Ms. Kind gritted her teeth. "Go!"

Backing away, Perl noticed a number of guests had stopped to see the commotion, Count Graves one of them. She looked at The Count and saw something dark perched on his shoulder. She locked eyes with it. It was a small winged creature, ugly, impish. It was crouched with its knobby knees pressed to its chest. It was whispering something in The Count's ear, its black tongue flicking as it wrung its spindly paws together. Strangely, Graves didn't seem to see it. Perl then noticed what he was wearing; a long black cloak, with rows of real shark fins stitched along the length of it.

"The fins." Perl remembered Slaughterman and a heavy lump formed in her throat.

Draped around The Count's neck was an icon starfish *(Inconaster ilongimanus)*. Running down the left side of his partially shaved head was a crisscross of thin wire filaments. Before Perl could even process what she was looking at, the winged creature looked right at her and hissed like an angry feral cat. Perl screamed and ran through the kitchen door, unsure of what she'd just seen. Needing some air, she ducked out of an exit door that led to a patio. Perl pulled off her fox hat, breathing in the cool night air.

"What the heck was that thing? How did The Count not see it on his shoulder?" she wondered.

Perl tried to calm herself, taking slow breaths as she looked out over the carved stone railing. She saw the protestors in their usual spot, floating in boats in the dirty polluted waters.

"There's so many of them today." After a few minutes, Perl regained her composure, put her hat back on, and straightened her tail. "Okay. Okay. I can do this. I gotta get back to work."

Several hundred activists had gathered close to shore, growing louder and increasing in number as the night progressed. Some of the larger boats had giant catapults mounted on them. Stacked next to the primitive but imposing weapons were piles of boulders the size of watermelons.

"On my mark!" A sunbaked woman in a retro 'There is No Planet-B' t-shirt yelled out. "Take aim…fire!" Twenty rocks took to the sky.

Inside the main dining hall, the meal was winding down and dessert was about to be served. Suddenly, through the floor-to-ceiling stained glass window came a deafening crash. People screamed, jumping up from the table, some running out of the room. A massive boulder bounced and scraped across the marble floor, stopping at the feet of none other than Count Graves. He looked down and saw that there was a message tied to it with plastic trash rings— *"Murderer! Stop the senseless killing and polluting of the oceans!"*

Even more unsettling was what was strapped to the rock; a lifeless, finless sand shark *(Odontaspididae)*. The room of onlookers gasped. One man fainted. Without missing a beat, Graves quickly unsnapped his cloak and covered up the unsightly spectacle. He clapped his hands, forcing a big phony grin.

"And that, ladies and gentlemen, is our signal to begin the dance!" The Count lied as he breathed. "Head to the ballroom! The cocktail and oxygen bars are open!" He made a gesture, and like that, dozens of stewards appeared to escort the shaken guests out of the hall.

Graves pressed a sensor along his temple, "Snive. Snive. Get in—" Before he could finish, the loyal footman was at his side. The Count sneered at his lackey, "you said this was handled."

"Yes sir, it was. It will be," Snive stammered as he nervously tapped a sensor embedded in his wrist.

Graves lifted the cloak, exposing the rock and the bloody shark. "Do whatever it takes. I want them out of my bay. Now. And get rid of this."

Snive marched away, speaking into the mic on his arm, "I need ten gunmen in the tower, pronto. And don't alarm the guests. Silencers on."

In mere seconds, ten sharpshooters, dressed in all black, fell into formation outside of the Palace's upper deck.

"No casualties. We don't want to start a riot," Snive commanded. The men aimed their scopes at the protestors' signs.

"Fire at will."

As the bullets whizzed by their heads and pelted holes in the wooden placards, the protesters dropped their signs and took cover.

"They're shooting at us!"

"Move back!"

"You monsters!"

A stray bullet grazed a teenage boy across his cheek, just missing his eye.

"Gretar!" A woman screamed.

The boy fell to the deck, crawling to the woman. "I'm...I'm okay. Get us out of here!"

Immediately upon re-entering the ballroom, Perl was struck with a wave of sound. The dance floor was packed with people. She pressed the fox hat against her ears, feeling her heart thumping in her chest from the deejay's heavy bass. Hiding behind the stage curtains, she spotted Countess Sarr dripping two nightshade drops into each eye before stepping out into the spotlight. The Countess raised her arm, and the music cut out.

"Girls! My babies! It's time to cut your cake!" she announced into a floating microphone, as an enormous cake was wheeled out. The dessert was twenty feet high, nearly five hundred pounds, and decorated to look like Mont Michel. At the top of the cake were busts of the twins. The crowd pressed in for a closer look.

"On the count of three. One. Two…" Sarr squinted, trying to make out her daughters, "three!"

The twins cut into the gargantuan cake together, their knife a pointed bill of a blue marlin *(Makaira nigricans)*. A strobe-flash of lights and clicks went off as the paparazzi swarmed.

As the cake was distributed, the deejay started back up, and the floor was soon vibrating once again. Perl knew she was supposed to be working, but she had never heard music like this before. Her hips swayed and her head bounced to the hypnotic beat. She danced with the curtain, twisting it around her tightly and then unwinding again. The booming sound of a cannon firing over the speakers caught her attention. Perl poked her head out.

"Bah! This stupid thing." Perl lifted her veil. No longer a blur of colors and lights, the room came into focus. Perl blinked, taking it in. At first glance, it was breathtaking. Tiger swallowtails fluttered in the laser strobe lights. Women in glorious gowns danced with men in marvelous attire. It was like some kind of candy-colored dream. As she looked closer, though, the scene suddenly became much clearer.

"No. Oh, no."

Perl watched in horror as the butterflies started dropping to the ground, the thick smoke in the air too much for them. People were laughing, spilling drinks. They danced wildly, unaware that they were stepping on them. Bloody wings ripped and stuck to the ale-soaked floor.

"No! Stop!" Perl looked away. A middle-aged woman danced with a live parrot *(Psittaciformes)* strapped to her head, violently bouncing the poor bird back and forth. A man viciously swung a chameleon *(Chamaeleonidae)* around the room on a chain, the reptile body dipped in silver. Two young women were laughing, showing off the severed rabbit ears they each wore.

Everywhere Perl looked, animals were being hurt, or killed. Plants and flowers were being trampled. The guests seemed not to care at all. They drank, and smoked, abusing everything in sight.

"Oh, Ever! This is horrible!" Perl hid her face in the curtain, sensing something crawling on her leg. She looked down, and there was The Count's nasty winged creature. It hissed at her, baring its pointy yellow teeth. Perl screamed, kicking it off her leg. The tiny beast hissed again, then flew off.

Perl jumped off the stage, trying to push her way through the screaming, gyrating crowd. The smoke burnt her nose and drinks spilled on her as she was jostled this way and that, looking for a way out, but there were too many bodies pressing in on her. Perl could see the butterflies, mangled and bloody on the floor, the birds squawking for help. She covered her ears, trying to shut out the cries of pain all around her. She bumped into a woman wearing a fishbowl bra; there was a crack in the glass and all the water had drained out. Two bulging-eyed goldfish *(Carassius auratus)* stared at her, gasping for breath.

"They can't breathe!" Perl yelled at the woman over the clamor.

"Ah, yes, do fetch me another cocktail!" The shrill woman waved her empty glass in Perl's face.

Angry now, Perl pushed hard through the crowd, seeing more and more horrors along the way. She saw a teenage girl with a sapphire ostrich (Struthio camelus) egg purse passed out in a garden of roses, the flowers crushed. A boy with sewn-on eagle *(Haliaeetus albicilla)* wings and a real toucan (Ramphastidae) beak, blissfully ate his cake out of a hollowed-out tortoise *(Testudinidae)* shell. A large, sweaty man in a leopard-skinned jumpsuit was rolling on the floor, oblivious to the fact that he was squishing a tiny chinchilla *(Chinchilla Lanigera)* beneath him.

Perl felt nauseous. Her head was spinning. She stumbled through the twisted mass of bodies, running smack dab into the twins. Mik and Ivry were dancing with Prince Névenoé, each clutching one of his arms.

The Prince boasted, "girls, girls, there's enough of me for two. Perhaps I'll marry you both."

The twins giggled, clinging to him like a pair of sucker fish. Perl watched as Mik turned and retched. Vomit splattered down the back of an enormous man with a severed elephant *(Loxodonta africana)* trunk hinged to his face. He didn't even notice. Mik wiped her mouth on the elephant man's coattails and kept on dancing. She recognized Perl and yelled.

"Hey, you! You! Sshneaky girl!" her voice slurred between hiccups. "You'd better shtay outta my room!"

Perl suddenly remembered the butterfly pin still in her sock. She had forgotten to leave it when she dropped off the seahorses.

"Hey, I yam tokkin to you!" Mik slurred, "Hey wasson your cheeks? You got spots!" Perl pulled her veil down and ran.

"Gebback here!" Mik yelled, as paparazzi cameras flashed.

The Prince grabbed her, pinching the inebriated girl's chin. "What's wrong, my cherry blossom?"

Mik hiccupped, clumsily flipping her red hair out of her face. "My hero," she slurred before dropping to the ground in a heap. Ivry reached down and helped her up.

Perl made her way back to the locker room. "I'm getting out of here."

She tore off her uniform, throwing the fox head into the trashcan. Putting on her robe, she made a beeline for the Palace's exit.

"They're murderers, all of them," Perl cried. She tore down the steps, and as her tears hit the walkway, green leaves sprouted up.

Perl was nearly home when she looked toward the beach. She saw a group of the protesters huddled around a bonfire, deep in conversation. Perl hesitated, then decided she wanted to know more about them.

A woman turned and looked at Perl. "You okay, honey? Come, join us."

"Thanks," Perl said shyly, wiping the tears away with her sleeve.

A teenage boy with a bandage around his head motioned her over. "I'm Gretar. Looks like you could use a warm fire."

"Hi. I'm Perl." She stepped into the circle. They seemed as tired and worn down as she was. A girl offered her a small wooden bowl of nuts and berries. Starving, Perl gobbled them up and plopped down on the sand, exhausted. She sat quietly, listening to the group for almost a half hour as they argued and debated about what their next steps would be. The warmth of the crackling fire made Perl sleepy. It was getting late and she knew Ximu would be waiting up.

Perl stood. "Sorry to interrupt, but I gotta go. Thanks for the snacks. You've all been so nice." Tears welled up as she thought again about the ball.

Gretar stood up. "Hey, it's okay...things are gonna get better." He wiped her cheek.

Perl sniffed, "I hope so." Turning, she trudged up the beach toward the root cellar.

Gretar watched Perl walk away. He then looked down at his hand, rubbing the girl's tears between his fingers. A dizzy euphoria rushed over him and his thoughts of anger and revenge melted away. He stumbled backwards and a woman grabbed him before he fell into the fire.

"Gretar, are you okay? What's wrong?"

He collapsed onto the ground, a peaceful expression on his face. "Th-there...has to be a better way."

As the morning sun broke through the horizon, the last party guests pulled away from the docks, the boats knifing through the trash-filled waters.

Ivry, in her canopy bed, rolled over to face her sister. "I'm not feeling so good."

Mik peeked at her sister from under her rabbit fur sleep mask. "Shhh...not so loud."

Ivry sat up on her elbows, adjusting her bangs back with butterfly hair clip. "I told you not to drink so much."

"Little Miss Perfect," Mik mocked her sister. "Ugh, my head is throbbing."

"My head doesn't hurt, but my stomach is killing me!" Ivry said, rubbing her midsection.

"Mine hurts a little. Probably a good thing I hurled."

"You got sick? When?" Ivry asked.

"It doesn't matter, just go back to sleep." Mik pulled her fur mask back over her eyes.

Seeing her sister's red tangles hanging in her face, Ivry asked, "hey, where's your pin?"

The twins had worn their matching blue diamond butterfly hairpins to bed each night without fail, ever since Grandma Graves had gifted them with the heirlooms on their tenth birthday.

"I dunno," Mik mumbled.

"Wait. Do you think that servant girl took it?"

"Who cares? Please, shut up."

"*You* should care. I'm going to call security."

"Fine, *you* do that."

Ivry rolled over. "Fine, I will…later. Right now, my stomach hurts too much to move."

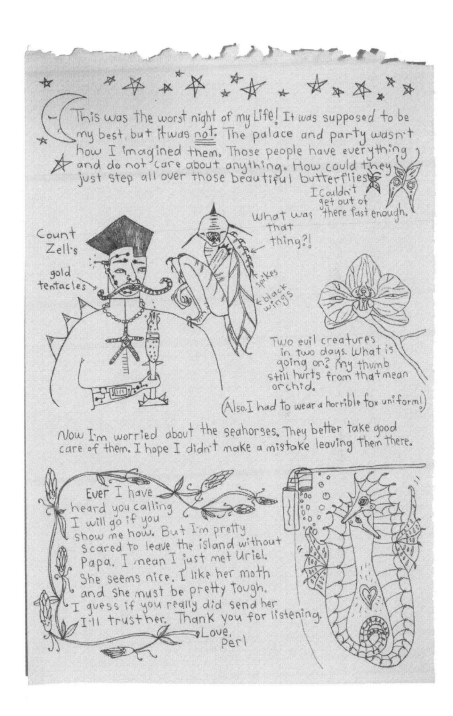

This was the worst night of my Life! It was supposed to be my best, but it was not. The palace and party wasn't how I imagined them. Those people have everything and do not care about anything. How could they just step all over those beautiful butterflies?

I couldn't get out of there fast enough.

What was that thing?!

Count Zell's

gold tentacles

spikes

black wings

Two evil creatures in two days. What is going on? My thumb still hurts from that mean orchid.

(Also, I had to wear a horrible fox uniform!)

Now I'm worried about the seahorses. They better take good care of them. I hope I didn't make a mistake leaving them there.

Ever I have heard you calling I will go if you show me how. But I'm pretty scared to leave the island without Papa. I mean I just met Uriel. She seems nice. I like her moth and she must be pretty tough. I guess if you really did send her I'll trust her. Thank you for listening.

Love,
Perl

63

11 BALLOONING

Perl had spent the rest of the night sketching and writing in her journal. As the night sky gave way to the faint pink and yellow traces of morning, the girl's eyelids were just beginning to grow heavy. Perl closed her eyes, succumbing to the sleepiness, when, like a flash of lightning, her bedroom door flew open. A bright purple glow filled her small room as a soft voice called out, "time for worms, little bird."

Perl squinted as the radiant light dissipated, leaving behind a faint lavender hue, "Uriel?"

Her protector stood over Perl, her tall frame casting a striking silhouette. "Yes. Wash up and meet me in the library."

"What time is it? I'm so tired," Perl pulled the blankets up over her head.

"It is time for you to wake!" The bed shook on its posts as Uriel's voice reverberated like a thunderclap.

Perl pulled her covers down, swinging her legs over the edge of the bed. "Okay, okay, I'm up!" Rubbing her eyes, she looked over, but the Light Being disappeared as quickly as she entered.

Ximu and Uriel were talking in hushed tones in the corner of the library when Perl entered. Stacks of ancient texts were piled up floor to ceiling. Perl loved old books; their smell, their yellowing pages, and their timeworn bindings. On the library's ceiling was a charming fresco of a forest landscape. As a toddler, Perl used to lay on her back and stare up at the painting, pretending to live inside of it, hopping with the rabbits and climbing the trees with the squirrels.

Ximu waved Perl over. "Good morning, my little social butterfly. I didn't hear you come in last night. How was the ball?"

Perl shrugged. Her eyes were dark and puffy.

"Hmm…are you okay, Bumble?"

"I'm not a bumble," she mumbled under her breath, pulling her hood up.

Uriel was removing books from the shelf. With a wave of her hand, the books would levitate in the air and land neatly in a perfect stack on the table.

Seeing this woke Perl up instantly. "How are you doing that?"

"Telekinesis," Uriel said.

Behind the empty bookshelf was a round door. About six feet in diameter, it had an ornately carved pattern of geometric shapes in the center, with rays like the sun emanating out from it.

"Behold, the Ravine Trapdoor," Uriel exclaimed, "after the spider of the same name."

Perl looked at Ximu, "all the times we've been in here! How come you've never shown me this?"

Ximu smiled at her. "Everything happens in divine order."

"Phragmosis..." at Uriel's command, the heavy door rolled sideways into a pocket in the wall, revealing a dark passageway. Uriel looked down at Perl. "Shall we go?"

"A secret tunnel," Perl tugged on Ximu's robe. Her heart began to race.

The three of them lit kerosene lamps and ventured in. Uriel, with a wave of her hand, sealed the door behind them, the muffled sound of the books re-shelving themselves. As they walked, Ximu lifted his light up to the ceiling, revealing ancient writings scrawled along every inch of it.

"Those are prayers," Ximu said, "centuries ago, the Brothers of the Quill dug these secret tunnels."

"Why?" Perl reached over, taking hold of Ximu's spider-claw as they continued through the labyrinth.

Uriel added, "the monks worked with the Divine Protectors of Water, Land, and Air, to keep the balance in nature. Perl, I hear you've recently learned about the Globus Natura?"

Perl nodded.

"Many courageous Brothers have been laid to rest here," Uriel pointed at stone tombs lining the walls. The crypts were decorated with amethysts, garnets and emeralds.

Perl leaned in for a closer look. "A lot of the people were wearing gems like these at the ball last night. Some of the animals were decorated with them too. They looked like they were being tortured," she swallowed hard.

Ximu gave Perl a concerned look, crinkling his spider brow, "that doesn't sound like a joyful celebration."

"It was awful." She squeezed his fuzzy claw tighter.

"This way," Uriel indicated. She ducked though a narrow opening, heading down a side tunnel, the portly monk and petite girl following close behind. The passageway was narrow with twists and turns. They moved slower, navigating their way through until they saw a faint glow ahead.

"We're almost there, just a little farther," said Uriel.

As they got closer, the light grew brighter. The tunnel widened, and soon the three found themselves in the middle of a glistening crystal cave; the heat inside was stifling.

"Wow!" Perl uttered, her voice echoing.

Ximu agreed, "truly beautiful...Ever's handiwork, indeed."

Uriel leaned against the wall. "Isn't it magnificent? They're selenite crystals. Brother Ximu, I'm afraid you'll have to go back up and wait for us in the passageway. Human beings can only survive down here for a few minutes."

Ximu wiped his brow. "Yes, perhaps that is wise."

Perl looked confused. "I need to go, too, right?"

"No Perl. You're fine."

"Whew, it is hot in here." Perl pulled her heavy hood back.

Everything in the room sparkled. The floor they stood on was made of faceted crystalline blocks. Huge crystal beams jutted out from the walls and ceiling like enormous shards of glass. Observing more closely, Perl saw that each of the larger crystals encased something inside of them. The objects were hard to make out through the blurry ice, but they looked like chests.

"Treasure chests," Perl thought, *"this really is an adventure...Wait'll I tell Victr!"*

"Come," Uriel motioned for Perl to join her beside a beam, nearly eight feet long. A long box floated inside of it. "Monodon Monoceros!"

In an instant, tiny fissures formed on the top of the glasslike stone; it fractured more and more until it burst into powder.

"How did you do that?" Perl said in amazement.

"All will open with the right words," Uriel reached in and pulled out the chest, placing it gently on a crystal slab in front of her. "These are gifts from your father...go ahead."

Perl closed her eyes, concentrating. "Open sesame!"

"A noble attempt," Uriel laughed, lifting the lid. She reached in, pulling out an elegant spiral sword. It was about three and a half feet long and the color of bone.

"A weapon? From Papa?" Perl asked, confused.

"Not Ximu. Your biological father, Noaa. He was a Light Realm Protector, like me. He safeguarded the oceans."

"Was a protector? Is he alive?"

"He lost his life battling Malblud, defending you and your mother, Dianna."

"Papa never told me he was dead," Perl sat staring at the intricate sword; she wasn't sure what to feel— Sad? Angry? Should she mourn the loss of someone she'd never really known? She tried to wrap her head around it.

"What about my mother...is she alive?"

"Yes."

"Can I see her?"

"I'm afraid not at this time."

"Why did she abandon me?"

"It has to be this way. It's safer for you both. Dianna knew she could trust the whale to bring you to this island, where the brothers have cared for and protected you."

"So I really did ride a whale," Perl mused.

From the chest, Uriel pulled out a small wooden instrument shaped like a sea turtle, handing it to Perl. "This is a kalimba. I know that you hear the music in nature that others do not. This will come in handy."

The instrument Perl held was a turtle shell containing seven metal tuning pieces like a tiny piano. She plinked one of them with her thumb; a beautiful single note vibrated off of the crystal cave walls. A smile flashed on her face.

"I love it."

The last item Uriel pulled from the chest was a small backpack made of finely woven bamboo fibers, dyed turquoise, with spotted junonia shells for buttons.

"It's beautiful," Perl twirled a button in her fingers. "So, who is this Malblud?"

"Don't speak his name. He is a fallen Light Protector, cast down to the Dark Realm for opposing the Law of Ever. He is the very definition of evil."

"Where is Mal—"

Uriel held up a finger to silence Perl. She turned toward the cave's opening, her pointed ears perking up. "We need to get going."

Uriel strapped the backpack on Perl, placing the kalimba inside. A scabbard stitched onto the right side of the backpack perfectly held the sword in place. Perl took comfort from Uriel's presence, and by the fact that she had been so honest with her.

Uriel placed the box back into the crystal beam. "Perhaps one day you will reunite with your mother, but as long as Malblud and his parasites exist, neither of you are safe."

As they hurried out of the cave, Perl stopped. "Uriel...do I...look like her?"

Uriel put her hand under Perl's chin; her dark, frizzy coils framing her tawny oval face. "We can talk more on our trip...but yes, you do have her hair."

Usually more of an annoyance, Perl now felt proud of her unruly curls.

The two met up with Ximu, who looked worried. Perl noticed the two of them were unusually quiet, their pace quickening on their way back through the catacombs. By the time they reached the library and closed the ravine trapdoor, every hair on Ximu's spidery head was standing on end.

"Papa, you look like you saw a ghost," Perl giggled.

Ximu and Uriel turned and faced Perl; their faces were deadly serious.

"It's time. The Dark One is close. We need to get to the pier." Ximu started toward the door, leaving Perl to catch up.

"What? Right now?" Perl asked, trailing after him.

"Move! We must hurry!" The girl had never seen Papa move so fast; his eight spidery legs a blur. Uriel strode past Perl as well, one of her long steps matching ten of hers.

"Wait up, you guys!" Perl yelled, now growing uneasy.

Brother Victr was tying up crab cages on the beach, when Ximu, Uriel and Perl sprinted by.

"Whoa! Where's the fire, Brother?" shouted Victr. He didn't need to hear the answer, as his spidery hairs, and the hairs of his brothers, were now standing on end as well; trouble was near.

"It's time for them to go!" Ximu shouted half out of breath, pointing out to the dock.

"Don't I even get a goodbye hug?" Victr chased after them.

Perl froze in her tracks and turned back, "Victr!"

"No time! Please, come on!" Yelled Ximu.

Perl grabbed Victr's spider-claw and they ran to the end of the creaky, wooden dock, "Victr, I'm scared."

The large monk peered down at the girl. It suddenly occurred to him how much bigger she had gotten, "I was wrong, Perl. You are ready. You can do this. Be brave, my little warrior, and don't worry, okay?" Victr smiled, his wrinkled brow softening, eyes tearing up.

She looked up at him, squeezing the large monk's claw tighter, "I will. Don't worry about me."

"Perl, say your goodbyes! We must leave the island!" Uriel commanded.

Ximu went to Perl and got down on one knee. He looked at the frightened girl, her face reflected in his eight gentle eyes.

"Remember to listen to your heart, Bee. Destiny has many paths, but where you go is up to you." He placed an arm on each of her shoulders. "You are an artist, use your Gifts from Ever, and always remember that you are beyond enough." Tears started to well up in Perl's eyes. Ximu hugged her as he leaned in close to whisper, "Honeybee, don't let a page of your book go untouched. Fill it with your adventures. Tell your story."

Perl reached inside her robe, a look of panic crossing her face. "My sketchbook! I have to go back!"

She started to make a move to run, when Uriel gently took hold of her hood, "I'm sorry, but we cannot go back. Only forward."

"No! No! I need it! I can't go without it, Papa please! I'll run faster than a rabbit!" Perl turned to run.

Ximu held her arm, "I'm sorry, Perl. There's no time. You must go." She knew he was serious; he never called her by her name.

"How are we going to leave? There's no boat!" Perl stared out over the dock; foamy waves dotted the choppy sea.

"We're going to fly." Uriel took Perl's hand, drawing her away from Ximu.

"Fly? How?"

"With a little help from your Spider Papa," Uriel answered, placing her hand on Ximu's forehead. Closing her one good eye, she began to glow a brilliant lavender light and chant, "true essence of Ever, come to our aid in this hour of need." She repeated the mantra over and over again, until slowly, Ximu transformed into an actual man-sized spider; not just to Perl, but for all to see.

Victr stumbled backwards. "Great Ever…it's a…you're a real…"

Perl cheered, "a spider, of course! You finally see it, too, Victr?"

"You always said we were spiders, but this, this is…magic."

Uriel directed, "help us, Ximu. The shape-shift is only temporary."

Ximu's body tilted towards the sky, and with a graceful motion, began producing silk strands, his many legs furiously sculpting the fine silk thread. In minutes, a giant web-like balloon was taking shape. Perl couldn't believe her eyes as he moved with speed and purpose. Before long, a massive parachute sat at the far end of the dock. Attached to the balloon was a woven basket.

"Quickly, now. Get in." Still attached, Ximu stepped back, releasing the webbed creation.

Perl ran and hugged the monk tightly. Ximu squeezed her, then took a pouch of dulse treats from his pocket and handed it to her. "Uriel will watch over you as she always has."

The portly monk glanced out at the rumbling sea, cocking his head as if listening for something, his spider hairs prickling. Although the wind was calm, they spotted a large storm cloud rolling in quickly, casting a dark shadow over the water; a sour odor permeated the air. From above came a faint buzzing sound.

"Whisper Wisps!" Uriel yelled out to the group.

Victr looked up and gasped. From the cloud, a dozen flying imps descended upon them. The yellow-eyed creatures snarled, baring their black, razor sharp teeth as their wings beat frantically.

Perl screamed, "it's the thing I saw on Count Graves shoulder!"

Uriel scooped her up and ran to the balloon. Victr pulled out his fishing knives. One of the foul beasts dove at Perl, trying to tear at her with its claws. Victr threw a knife at it, picking it out of the air mid-flight, sticking it to one of the wooden posts anchoring the dock. The thing let out a hideous screech.

Uriel hoisted Perl up into the basket of the balloon and climbed in after her.

"I love you, Papa!" Perl held out both arms.

Swatting the nasty beasts away, Ximu leaned in for a last hug. "You are the why of all my smiles. Fly, little Honeybee, fly!"

With tears running down his fuzzy face, Ximu gave the web-chute a jerk up and down, filling it with air.

"Get them out of here, Ximu!" Victr, fifty years Ximu's junior, was fighting off the other hideous Wisps with unbridled fury. He plucked one out of the air, throwing it on the ground, crushing it with his sandal. It squealed and burst, spraying dark green blood across the wooden planks. Another one he swatted at, ripping off a wing.

With one last wafting wave, the balloon filled, a breeze picked up, and Perl and Uriel were airborne, floating out over the choppy waters.

"I love you!" Ximu shouted as Perl hung over the side of the sleigh, arms still outstretched.

Perl pointed and screamed, "look out!"

Ximu turned, his instincts heightened. A small horde of Wisps were coming at him. In a flash, he shot a wide net across the dock, capturing the buzzing, angry beasts in flight. The Whisper Wisps struggled, but the more they moved, the more they became tangled in the sticky webbing.

The waves grew rougher; the old pier started to sway. Just as Ximu and Victr started to flee, a giant wave crashed over the dock, knocking the two monks off their feet. Wave after wave pounded over them. Fearful they'd be swept into the water, they clung desperately to the slippery planks and each other. Ximu reached out, grabbing hold of one of the wooden piles. The waters around them began to turn black. A deep groan bellowed from below, the sound cutting through the deafening roar of the ocean. The boards creaked, beginning to give way.

"Run, Brother!"

The monks half-ran, half-crawled, slipping and staggering on the wet planks. Just as they reached the beach, the rickety pier collapsed; or rather, it was dragged under. A slew of slimy black tentacles had wrapped themselves around the old wooden structure, pulling the entire structure down as if it were matchsticks.

From out of the oily water, the monks heard a deep, gurgling voice.

"...*Venussto*..."

The voice faded away; the sky cleared and the waves calmed. The storm ended as quickly as it began. Bits and pieces of shattered wood buoyed on the water's surface.

On the beach, the monks lay on their backs, coughing and wheezing.

"By Ever's grace, what was that?" Victr stared at Ximu, still trying to process that his fellow monk was now a giant spider.

Ximu said nothing. With his spindly arms, he wiped his glasses, forcing himself upright with a deep groan. He shook the sand off his wet robe and reached down to help Victr up.

"...our Perl is gone," Victr's voice cracked.

Ximu pulled the large monk up. "Yes, but she is safe, brother."

Under the midday sun, the two trudged home along the beach, Victr stopping to pick up his crab cages.

"We must tell the brotherhood everything," Ximu announced.

Victr looked up. Despite all he had witnessed, he allowed himself a smile; Ximu had reverted back into his human form.

"Agreed," said Victr, "but you tell them, Brother…they'll never believe it coming from me."

12 PALO SANTO

The air was crisp. Uriel pulled her floral cloak over Perl's lap. Perl watched as her island grew smaller and smaller the higher up they climbed. Soon it was no more than a green dot, eventually disappearing altogether. Perl felt a sinking feeling in the pit in her stomach. Uriel tried to reassure her.

"Papa and Victr will be fine. Never underestimate the power of an old *Pholcidae*," she said, tapping Perl's knee.

"What's a *Pholcidae?*" Perl scratched her head.

"A spider. We prefer to use the mystical names for life in the Light Realm. You'll see. But first, we have to make a quick detour." Uriel pulled the reins abruptly to the left, turning the great balloon. Perl fell back against the seat with a thud.

"How about a little warning?!"

In the far distance, Uriel pointed to a pair of clouds in the shape of two swans. The swans faced one another, their necks forming a heart between them. "Ah, there it is."

"Those clouds?" Perl asked.

"Not just clouds, directions. Whereas humans enjoy identifying shapes and animals in the clouds for their amusement, we use them as location markers, like on a map. In this case, those clouds are leading us to Palo Santo," Uriel flicked the reins.

"Palo who?"

"Palo Santo is a Master Garden Nurse. Her responsibility is to tend to all that grows."

Not a breeze stirred, yet the spiderweb balloon continued its ascent. Perl leaned against the side of the sleigh. "How are we still floating? There's no breeze keeping us up."

"We're flying through the light of electric fields. The earth's upper atmosphere has a positive charge." Perl blinked, watching Uriel's mouth move, but she was suddenly having trouble focusing. Perhaps because of the altitude or the lack of sleep from the night before, a wave of fatigue took hold of her. She closed her eyes as Uriel continued explaining the science of their flight.

"...while the ground has a negative charge...providing the web with lift," Uriel paused, seeing that Perl had fallen asleep, her backpack propped under her head.

After allowing her to rest a bit, Uriel cleared her throat loudly, "ahem!"

A string of drool snapped from Perl's lower lip as she sat up, an imprint of her sword's handle pressed into her cheek.

"Where are we?" Rubbing her jaw, she looked around and saw nothing but big, white, fluffy clouds all around her. The chilly air gave her goose bumps.

"We're nearly there. You drifted off for a bit."

"Ow. My face hurts." She reached around and pulled the sword from its sheath. "I must've been leaning on this."

"That weapon is made from the strongest material on Earth. Stronger than spider silk."

Perl held it up, "what kind of material?"

"It's edge and handle are comprised of limpet teeth from *Patella Vulgata*."

Perl tilted her head at Uriel. "English, please?"

Uriel grinned, "sea snail's teeth. The spiral blade is also a tooth, removed from a brave and noble *Monodon Monoceros*."

"Wasn't that what you said in the crystal cave?"

"Yes, it was sealed with the narwhal name to honor the brave warrior. He went by the name Dum Spiro Spero, meaning, *"While I breathe, I hope."* He lost his life in the Great Barrier Reef Battle, fighting alongside your father in the Half Light Realm. The sword you hold is a tribute to the sacrifice Spero made in the fight against evil." Uriel solemnly clasped her hands and brought them to her chin; she closed her eyes, giving thanks to the fallen comrade.

Perl inspected the blade; on one side of the tusk, there was a row of thousands of tiny needles. "Are these teeth?" She started to run her fingers along the edge.

"Ah-ah, careful. Yes…extremely sharp snail teeth. Also, this is just the tip of the narwhal tusk. It was shortened so you could properly wield it."

"How long was it before?" Perl spun it in her palm.

"Close to ten feet. You know, every good sword needs to be given a name."

Perl closed her eyes, thinking, "Fortis."

Uriel nodded. "A proper name, indeed. Do you know the meaning of that word?"

"No, not really. I just heard it in my head, why?"

"Fortis means to be brave in the face of fear."

Perl waved the sword around wildly in the air. Uriel held her wrist. "Easy, you'll need some training first."

"Before I can be a Light Warrior, like you?"

"That's right," Uriel laughed. With the lightest touch of her finger, she guided the tip of Perl's sword up, past her shoulder, pointing the sword outward. "Behold, our destination."

Perl squinted through the sun glare. There, between two swan-shaped clouds, floated a glistening greenhouse, its many windows sparkling like diamonds. Hundreds of birds circled around the magnificent building, while two enormous silver weeping willow trees flanked it on either side.

"Hold on, we're going in," announced Uriel, steering the balloon full steam ahead. Uriel swung the massive balloon around, banking left as they wound their way down toward the greenhouse entrance. Once close to it, Perl realized how gigantic the building was.

"How is this floating in the sky?" she marveled, gazing up the colossal glass building.

Uriel gently brought the balloon to a halt in front of two enormous doors.

"I do hope she has some tea on." Uriel swung open the sleigh's door, stepping confidently onto a platform made of clouds. Seeing her get out, Perl shrieked, thinking Uriel was about to fall to her death, but remarkably, the puffy white vapor held her.

"Ready?" Uriel asked.

Perl took a deep breath, closed her eyes, and placed a tentative foot onto the cloud. It felt soft and cool under her feet, like an entire floor covered in down pillows, "I don't believe it! I'm standing on a cloud!"

"Come, we have a schedule to keep."

"We do?" Perl asked, tapping her toe to make sure it was solid.

"Yes. Seeker training begins in one Earth day."

The two walked across the clouds like stepping stones. At the entrance, a doormat read, *Please Wipe Your Feet.* Two large golden-yellow broom plants in clay pots sitting on either side of the doormat bent over and dusted off the tops of their shoes.

"Did you see that?" Perl stepped on and off a few more times; each time the flowers swept off her shoes. She giggled.

Uriel pushed through the set of doors. A rush of warm air met them, followed by the sweet, perfumy fragrance of flowers. A sign hanging from a vine read, *"Do Not Feed the Plants, No Matter How Much They Beg."*

"Beg?" thought Perl, stepping into the palatial glass nursery.

She recognized many of the plants and flowers from her library's botanical books and from years of wandering through Mont Michel's gardens. Only here, everything was on a grand scale. Grapes looked like watermelons. Hanging fern baskets were as wide as sailboats. A single bluebell flower was as big as Perl; she could crawl inside it and take a nap if she wanted.

Uriel headed down the greenhouse's main walkway, pointing out various flowers to Perl, only to realize she was walking alone. She turned back to see Perl chatting with a giant Venus flytrap.

"No, I'm sorry I don't have any flies. Yes, I think squirrels are silly, too." Perl reached into her robe and pinched off a piece of dulse leaf, tossing it into the mouth of the imposing plant. She pulled her hand out of the way in time before the carnivore snapped its jaws shut. "Hey, easy now."

"Ut-ut! No feeding!" Uriel waved for Perl to come walk with her.

"Sorry. He asked so nicely." Perl had a quick flashback to the day in the garden, when that orchid bit her. She recalled its ugly, snarling teeth snapping repeatedly, and its voice…so wicked sounding.

The two continued their exploration through the exotic paradise in the sky, the sound of Uriel's heavy chainmail clinking with each stride. They entered a spacious, oval-shaped room, brimming with even more oversized varieties of plant life. Exotic fruit trees, vibrant blossoms of every shape and color, meandering vines, and a patchwork of grasses, shrubs, herbs, moss, and other horticultural artistry filled the space.

In the center of the room, a breathtaking bonsai tree sprung from the middle of a bubbling fountain pool filled with rainbow-striped fish. Near the fountain, a charming table for three was set, the steam still rising from freshly poured tea. In the middle of the table sat the stump of an oak tree, hand-carved to resemble a miniature fairy house. Tiny triangle sandwiches, strawberry scones and lemon pastries were neatly arranged on plates. Throughout the room, dozens of bunnies hopped to and fro, chasing one another and nibbling on leafy morsels.

Perl picked up a butterscotch-colored bunny. "Hello, little one." She rubbed its furry softness against her cheek. Six other rabbits closed in around her legs, waiting for their turn to be cuddled.

All at once, a warm yellow light filled the room, and the soft fluttering of wings could be heard.

"She's here," Uriel smiled.

Perl put down the bunny and looked over to a vine-covered archway, where a swarm of iridescent hummingbirds in the unmistakable figure of a woman drifted into the room. The birds parted but remained hovering over the woman's head like a halo.

"Palo," Uriel said warmly, "so good to see you again."

Palo Santo, the Master Garden Nurse of the Light Realm, had gentle, sky blue eyes deeply set into a cherubic face, her soft, full cheeks stained like strawberries. Her hair was a bouquet of tropical flowers, green moss, and blossoming vines that fell gracefully to her milky white shoulders. A large straw sunbonnet tied around her neck hung casually down her back, while her lustrous dress resembled a silken garden; interlacing patterns of flowers and bees, berries and butterflies were embroidered throughout, the gown cascaded down to her bare feet. The hummingbirds moved in a tight group with every step Palo took, poking their beaks into the sprigs of petunias, lilacs, and roses she had in her hair.

"Uriel, lovely as ever," Palo said, as the two statuesque women embraced. Perl suddenly felt very small.

Palo pulled out a hand-woven wicker chair from the table. "Just in time for tea. Come sit. And this must be Perl." She set a large watering can in the shape of a swan next to the fountain. The can instantly began refilling by dipping its beak into the water.

Perl was surprised Palo Santo knew her name. "I love your hair, uh...Miss Santo."

"And I yours. Go on, help yourself," Palo insisted.

Perl sat down at the table and took a bite of a strawberry treat. The flavor of the berries burst inside her mouth, like nothing she'd ever tasted.

"This one has quite a sweet tooth," Uriel tipped her cup at Perl, sipping her tea.

"And she has her father's glow," Palo Santo ran a finger up Perl's arm. Her bioluminescent spots lit up, following her touch. Perl saw that the tips of Palo's fingers were grass stained.

The Master Garden Nurse placed a potted plant on the table. "I'd like to introduce you to *Mimosa Pudica*. Shake hands." The bashful plant uncurled its leaves and shyly took hold of Perl's hand.

"And you are of your mother's seed. *Mimosa* is very cautious. She only warms to those with a pure heart."

Perl reached for a second pastry, "do you know where my mother is?"

Palo eyed Uriel, who shook her head without Perl noticing.

"That I do not know." Without batting an eye, Palo reached over, crushing the *Mimosa Pudica* plant into the pot with her hand. The plant curled in on itself, as Perl watched in shock.

"No! Stop that!" Perl tried to move Palo's hand.

Palo Santo kept her hand pressed down. "What I do know, however, is that there's no one like you, Perl. Your essence is one with both the natural world and the spiritual realm. The art of each commands your attention."

Palo released her hand. The plant quivered, then slowly sat up, its bright green leaves stretching for the light. "Never underestimate, never take for granted, the soul of a living thing, nor its will to survive. Nature is beautiful, but powerful."

The leaf wrapped around Perl's pinkie. The Garden Nurse peered into the girl's piercing green eyes. Perl looked around, feeling more than a little uncomfortable by the woman's stare.

"Your roots are strong," Palo leaned back in her chair, holding her gaze, "you are Dianna's child. Her heart gave beat to yours. She let you go to give you what you needed in order to thrive." Palo patted the *Mimosa* plant on its pink, flowery head.

"Walk with me," Palo stood, waving her hands over her head, sending the hummingbirds flitting away. The three of them strolled down a glass corridor lined with the largest flowers Perl had ever seen.

"Ew! What's that smell?" she plugged her nose, gagging.

76

Palo pulled her sunbonnet on, "*Rafflesia Arnoldii.* Corpse flowers, just blooming today."

Perl talked without breathing in, "they're disgusting."

Palo stopped. "Careful, child. All words matter. Plants, flowers, every living thing in nature has feelings, too." She opened a door to what appeared to be a laboratory. Perl stepped through quickly to escape the vile stench.

Inside, rows of floor-to-ceiling shelves packed with jars, vessels, and vases held an endless assortment of plant specimens. On the walls were an array of charts, graphs, and anatomical drawings of hundreds of animals Perl had never seen. She smiled; this reminded her of her room back home; lovingly filled with the studies of nature.

Palo started pouring a bubbling gray liquid into a hollowed-out coconut shell while stirring in various herbs.

"Now, let us have a look." She waved her hand over the leopard moth that fluttered above Uriel's eye. "That's a good *Hypercompe Scribonia.*" The moth fluttered away, revealing an empty socket, the wound just beginning to scar over.

Perl tried to watch, but Uriel turned her head away from the girl. The Garden Nurse dipped her pinkie into the potion, placing a few drops into Uriel's eye socket.

"There now, that should help with the healing and pain." Palo welcomed the moth back into place.

Perl was about to ask what had happened to Uriel's eye when she heard a tapping sound. She looked around and noticed that inside a nearby terrarium, a strange mushroom was knocking at the glass. Intrigued, Perl walked over to examine it more closely. The mushroom seemed like it wanted to say something. Perl had seen plenty of mushrooms and other fungi in her day, but nothing like this one.

"Your mushroom cap looks a lot like a brain." Perl paused, "I wonder if that's where the phrase 'put on your thinking cap' came from?" Perl tapped on the glass; the mushroom began gesturing for her to open the lid.

As she reached for the latch, Palo Santo called out to her, "don't lift that dome! Bad *Gyromitra!*" The mushroom shrunk back. "He's a false morel. A poisonous fellow. He knows he's not allowed out. Not until he apologizes."

Perl backed away. As she did, she noticed Uriel take a glass vial from the table and slip it inside in her cloak.

"Did Uriel just steal something?" Perl thought.

"Okay, it's time for us to be off." Uriel and Palo headed towards the door. Perl picked up one of the bunnies, cradling it in her arms.

Palo took the rabbit from her by the scruff of its neck. "I'm afraid the hare must stay with me. You'll be seeing plenty of new furry friends where you're headed."

As they climbed back into the sleigh, Palo Santo handed Perl a folded napkin filled with lemon scones. "For the ride, daughter of Dianna. I'll see you again, when need be."

Perl beamed, "thank you! Oh, and tell *Rafflesia* I'm sorry for saying she was stinky."

Palo smiled, "it is not untrue, but the flower will be made happy by your kind words."

Uriel waved the reins of the web, "Palo, my dear friend, would you mind giving us a little boost?"

Palo Santo blew a gust of wind, filling the parachute. The balloon was off and flying again. Perl looked back; there was no sign of the greenhouse, only puffy white swans. Uriel looked over at Perl as she stuffed a lemon scone into her mouth.

"Did it occur to you that perhaps Palo meant those to be shared?"

Speaking with a full mouth, Perl had already devoured half of the scones, "you waawone?"

Uriel laughed, "that's quite alright."

"Look over there, that cloud looks like a bear!" Perl said, pointing with her scone. Off to their right, only a few hundred yards away, a cloud in the shape of a grizzly bear drifted through the sky.

"You have a keen eye. That's our next stop."

Uriel guided the balloon towards the bear's face. Its mouth opened wide and they flew inside.

"Where are we going?"

"Venusto! Hold tight!"

The misty clouds gave way to a cave opening, with a white river flowing into it. They landed on the surface, a spray of frothy white water splashing up on either side of the carriage. The balloon slowed, floating effortlessly along. Uriel released the reins, letting the current carry them through the belly of the mountain.

Perl looked over the edge, "the water looks like milk!"

She popped the last lemon scone into her mouth, marveling at the creamy silver water. As Perl's eyes adjusted to the dark cave, she couldn't believe what she was seeing; images of strange and wonderful animals, scrawled in crude black outlines, appeared along the walls. As if noticing their boat go by, the drawings came to life, galloping alongside them.

"Do you see that, Uriel? They're chasing us!" Perl leaned out to get a better look.

"Yes, sit, sit! Papa should have given us a seatbelt," Uriel pulled Perl back.

As the two drifted away from the animals, continuing their journey down the river-under-the-mountain, other caves opened up on either side of them. From those caverns, other boats emerged, joining Perl and Uriel.

The vessels were unlike anything Perl had even seen.

"That one has a hull made of red rose petals! And look, a giant floating acorn with windows! Is that a ship? It looks like a bee's nest!"

Perl noticed that all them were based on nature—some were made of woven palm fronds, others constructed of birch bark, starfish, or antlers. There was a giant chambered nautilus with three dozen white oars sticking out of it, a glowing ship made entirely of fireflies, and a boat with bird wings that flapped as it sped past them—each floating vessel more magnificent than the next.

"Are they all going to Venusto, too?"

"Yes. Some as Seekers, like you...others, for more advanced training."

Uriel reached into her cloak, removing a small pair of dark goggles. "We're nearing the entryway. Put these on."

"What for?"

"Your eyes will need time to adjust to the light."

Perl strapped on the goggles. "Uriel, these are pitch black. I can't see a thing." She started to pull them off; Uriel stopped her.

"It's just for a little while. Patience."

Perl crinkled her nose. "If you say so, but I want to see stuff."

Uriel laughed, "you'll see," she flicked the reigns, adding air to the balloon, "oh, you'll see."

In total darkness, Perl fell back onto the seat to wait as they increased speed, swept along by the mighty current.

13 VENUSTO

Perl opened her eyes wide, desperately trying to see anything through the goggles. Her veiled vision did not last long; farther down the river, a tiny circle of intense light appeared.

"Hey, Uriel! I think I see the sun."

"We're approaching."

As they got closer, Perl had to squint as the dot of light widened. Even with the goggles on, she shielded her eyes from the intense glow. All at once, the darkness fell away, and a powerful white light filled Perl's entire field of vision. She closed her eyes and held her hands up.

"Uriel, what's happening? This light is blinding me!"

"Hold on just a little longer. It will subside."

After a few seconds, the whiteness softened to a dim red behind Perl's eyelids. Curiosity getting the better of her, Perl opened one eye ever so slightly. They were floating on an enormous alabaster lake; a rainbow of dazzling, luminescent colors shimmered off of it.

"Wow! It's like being inside a kaleidoscope!"

As they sailed along the crystalline waters, Perl's vision adapted, and she began to take in her surroundings. The lake itself was massive, filled with hundreds of other boats. It appeared to be circular, the coastline wrapping around it on three sides. The island itself was lush and tropical-looking, yet it sparkled like a polished gem in the sunlight, reminding Perl of Palo Santo's greenhouse. Perl lifted her goggles for a better peek, only to be hit with a fierce blast of light.

"Ah!" She quickly yanked the goggles back down.

Uriel tightened the strap behind Perl's head. "Not yet. Leave them on a little longer."

Blinking her eyes to clear up the spots, the first thing to catch Perl's eye was an extraordinary cloud formation in the shape of a woman from the shoulders up. Her long arms stretched out at her sides as if welcoming all visitors to paradise, and the balanced pose she struck reminded Perl of a scale. Floating above each of the woman's open palms were smaller clouds that kept changing shape. Perl watched as the white puffs morphed into apples, then fish, then rabbits, then fern leaves, then snakes, and so on, image after image. Rising up through the cloud-woman and blooming out of the top of her head like a grand headdress was a tree the size of which Perl couldn't believe was real. Hundreds of times larger than any tree she had ever seen, it towered above everything else on the island. The massive trunk and branches were decorated in multicolored rings and stretched on forever, disappearing up into the skies above.

Perl noticed poking up here and there around the island were giant animal sculptures that looked to be carved directly out of the ground. Near the shore, Perl could make out an elk up on its hind legs, brandishing a sword, and a chameleon curled up with a book. She got a sense of their scale by looking at the clusters of palm trees growing off of them; compared to the enormous sculptures, they were no more than tiny sprouts. Farther off in the distance, Perl saw dozens of other silhouetted creatures. She spotted a hawk, a bear, an elephant, while others she couldn't quite make out, the dazzling glow of light from the island making it difficult to see clearly.

"How are you feeling now?" Uriel watched Perl's head swivel like a meerkat on the lookout.

"Each thing I see is more beautiful than the next! I…I…can't believe my eyes!"

Uriel held her hand over the ivory water; out leapt a creature, squealing with delight. It had the head and body of a dolphin but with antlers, like a deer. Perl gazed speechless as the creature bobbed in and out of the milky water. The porpoise was completely translucent, like wet glass. All of its internal organs were a bright neon orange. Uriel touched it lightly on the nose. It squealed again, then swam off.

"What was that?"

"Our welcoming committee."

Perl skimmed her hand along the water's surface as another dolphin-deer swam to her. Perl felt its warm, slick skin. "Nice to meet you." It gave a cheerful squeak and dove below. As they got closer to shore, Perl realized they'd been followed by a large pod of the translucent Beings, who now swam up ahead of them. They sprang out of the water onto the dry land, walking upright into the thick brush.

Perl tugged on Uriel's arm, "did you see that? They grew legs…and then…I mean how?"

"I know it's a lot to take in, but try to be…" Uriel looked down at Perl. Smiling back up at her with her infectious, toothy grin, the girl was practically hopping out of her seat. "Never mind. Just be yourself."

They maneuvered their craft past and around dozens of other boats in the harbor, angling towards a massive lily pad which served as Venusto's docking platform. Boats of all shapes and sizes were jockeying around one another, while the clamor of horns, whistles and spirited conversations filled the air. They found an open spot between a gondola carved out of ice and a sailboat with black scalloped sails. Studying the sails closer, Perl noticed they were actually giant bats, perched on the masts. One of the bats looked over at her and gave out a friendly screech before flying off.

"Hello there," Perl waved.

She turned her attention to the bustling wharf. If the boats were unbelievable, the collection of eclectic Beings moving about were a sight to behold. Some had wings, horns, tails, scales, or feathers. Others seemed to be made of stone, or wood, or seaweed, or vines. There were some that simply defied explanation. All of this thrilled Perl, who gazed in awe at the creatures.

"Who are they?"

"Like you, they are all here to train. But they are not like you. They are solely of the Light Realm. None of these Beings have human genes, Perl. None but you."

Just then, an eight-foot tall Being stepped out from the bat-winged boat. Its long, sinewy body was a twisted assortment of tree branches, while its head was a misshapen mound of mud with hundreds of pink, brown, and green mushrooms growing out of it. It gave a slight nod in their direction.

Giddy with excitement, Perl wiped the steam off her goggles. "This. Is. Amazing!"

Out of the ice gondola came a massive Being with the head of an emperor penguin and the body of a polar bear. Upon seeing Uriel, it bowed, greeting her, *"Chakunta var dey lune."*

Uriel nodded back, *"patoo chee nah."*

"What language was that?" Perl asked.

"It's Articali. Just like your vision, simply wait a moment. Your mind will adjust, and you'll be able to understand all of Venusto's languages," Uriel said, opening the webbed door of their basket. "Shall we?"

Perl took a deep breath and stepped onto the lily pad dock, trying not to stare too much at the otherworldly Beings. Many arrived by boat, but some flew in from the sky, or simply swam up out of the water. Though it was crowded, the traffic flowed orderly as the Beings made their way to their designated locations. Where the wharf met the island, it split into three distinct pathways, each one decorated with a beautiful floral archway. The path to the left had a sign reading *'Greenheart'*, the center led to *'Callowhorn'*, and the sign leading arrivals to the right was *'Natatory.'*

Perl focused on one of the Beings, wrinkling her brow. "That's weird. I can't see anyone's essence."

Uriel shook her head, "and you won't. Light Realm Beings exist in their pure form. What you see is what we all see." Uriel put her arm around the small girl; the chainmail she wore felt heavy on Perl's shoulders.

From under the Callowhorn sign, a ten-foot tall green grasshopper with a wrinkly old man's face appeared.

Uriel gave a nod toward the grasshopper-man, who wore a tall black stovepipe hat. She squeezed Perl. "Time to begin, little one."

"Who is that?" Perl whispered.

"Come, let's line up."

Perl glanced as a number of other trainees began gathering around the grasshopper. Her vision was still a bit fuzzy through the goggles, but she thought one boy looked like a dark bird, another a monkey, and definitely one was some type of lizard.

The grasshopper-man did a quick count, "…seven, eight, nine…good! Everyone is here, here!" He tipped his hat, "I am Olliv, Olliv. Two L's, one V. I will be your guide, guide."

"I understand him," thought Perl.

Olliv bowed deeply, "Protector Uriel, Uriel." The rest of the group followed suit, bowing to the ancient warrior, a few of them whispering to one another. Perl beamed; she felt honored to be with Uriel. The insect-man rubbed his hind leg against his wing, vibrating it to make a low, pleasant sound, like a bow strumming a cello.

"Welcome to Venusto, Venusto!" With a dramatic flair, he held aloft a small baton with a yellow buttercup flower on the end, "Seekers-to-be, be. Follow me, me." He spun and headed through the floral Callowhorn archway.

Grandmaster Olliv had overseen Seeker Orientation since the dawn of time. Charged with getting the trainees situated, re-acquainted, and transported to and from their lessons, it was a joyful responsibility, one that Olliv relished with each new class that arrived. The system of coaching and educating recruits had been in place for centuries; not much had changed, and they preferred it that way. It was a necessary process, one created in order for the trainees of the Light Realm to fully understand how to keep all of nature in balance and protect it against the evils of the Dark Realm.

Perl and the rest of the new arrivals formed a line behind Olliv as he led them away from the jumbled collection of bizarre boats and mass of magical Beings.

"Follow, follow!" Olliv commanded, strolling down the path quite gracefully for a giant six-legged grasshopper. As the group scampered after him, Perl noticed she was the only student whose mentor had stayed with the group; the rest had remained back at the dock.

Olliv sang out, waving his buttercup baton into the air, "Seekers! You are here to discover, discover, the art of life, life! You may feel small, but together you have much to offer, offer. Listen to the voice inside you. Choose wisely, wisely. Think carefully, carefully. The ordinary is quite extraordinary!"

As they walked, Perl nudged Uriel over and over again, pointing out the astonishing spectacles all around her.

"Look up! I don't believe it!"

A school of yellow mantra rays with aquamarine spots passed over their heads. Perl giggled as a tall, stoic oak tree lumbered past them, smoking a long, curled pipe. It was like a dream. Seeing peoples' essence was one thing; this was truly unimaginable. Everywhere she looked, Perl saw the beauty and magic of nature in its greatest manifestation.

"Try to pay attention, Perl," Uriel said, attempting to be stern, yet secretly delighted to see Venusto through Perl's eyes.

"It's incredible! I love it here already!" Perl stepped closer to better hear Olliv.

"First, we will get you all settled in, in. Get your uniforms…get re-acquainted."

The group followed Grandmaster Olliv until they reached a clearing, where three large nests the size of houses stood. Perl noticed other clusters of nests in the area; it looked like an enormous campground.

"Students, say hello to your new homes, homes. The Bowerbirds have made your living quarters, quarters."

Each of the units were carefully woven together with sticks. At each nest, a host of black birds were busy making paths of cobalt blue pebbles, leading up to their front doors.

Olliv stopped at the first nest, "Air Seekers, this one is yours, yes, yes. You will be sharing, groups of three, three."

The Air lodging was a large funnel-shaped hut with an enormous pair of bird wings protruding from either side. Above the door, three of the recruits' names had been engraved onto a sign: *Corvax, Nan, Lyre.* Three Seekers broke off from the group, chatting as they made their way inside. Perl looked at them—there was the muscular boy from earlier covered in pitch-black feathers, a thin, insect-like creature with gorgeous butterfly wings, and a birdlike girl with a long, wispy tail-feather that curled above her head. Still wearing her goggles, things remained a bit blurry.

"Land Seekers, you are here, here."

The middle nest was fashioned into a large pinecone, with three more names etched on a sign: *Tars, Flax, Javan.* Perl watched as three of them— The monkey-like creature, another that was reptilian in nature, and a third that Perl couldn't identify—got together. The last boy was tall with long dark hair that hung in his eyes, a wide flat nose, and covered in short brown fur. The three boys strolled into their nest, slapping each other on the backs like they'd known each other forever.

The remaining group moved to the last nest, where a towering structure in the shape of a water droplet stood.

"Water Seekers here, drip, drip."

Perl, Opis, Bear were inscribed on the sign.

"Look, Uriel, I'm a Water Seeker! Come on!" Perl pulled off her boots, so she could feel the smooth pebble pathway under her feet. Taking Uriel's hand, she ushered the statuesque woman hastily up the path ahead of the other two.

"Yes, don't be shy. Approach, approach. Get changed, and come when you hear my call, call." As he said this, Olliv played a few quick notes on his legs as a little reminder, "Master Yew will be along shortly to finish orientation, then I will return and see you all to supper, supper."

Upon entering the roomy living quarters, Perl noticed their names were also spelled out with tiny sticks at the end of each bed, the bunks stacked three high. Folded neatly on each pillow was a new outfit made of a shiny material.

"I have the top bunk!" Perl climbed up, spun around, and was now looking eye to eye with Uriel, her dirty feet dangling off the bed.

"I did as well, eons ago. That's lucky, you know."

"You were a Seeker?" Perl asked. She took off her backpack and flipped off her robe, letting it drop to the floor. She slipped on the new iridescent shirt and pants; they were cool to the touch, and weighed next to nothing.

"Everyone starts out as a Seeker."

"They do? So, when can I be a Divine Protector, like you?"

Uriel laughed. "One day at a time. It takes serious training, not to mention, superior skills...to be like me." She reached over, pulling Perl's goggles off.

Perl blinked; things were still extremely bright. She smiled, marveling at the impressive woman; her tall, muscular frame cloaked in shining, battle-ready armor; she looked every bit like an elite warrior.

Uriel walked over to the far wall, where an old faded map the size of a bed sheet was stretched.

"Is that all of Venusto?" Perl asked. She recognized on the map the mountain river they had sailed on, as well as the lily pad dock, but there was so much more to explore. Uriel pointed to a vast stretch of land that lay to the east of the dock.

"Where we are now is called Callowhorn. After you complete Seeker training here, you'll advance to Seer training on the island of Greenheart," she pointed to a nearby island shaped like a heart. "After Greenheart, you will study Awakener training at Natatory," Uriel motioned south of Callowhorn to a mountain range that appeared to be floating above the water.

"How long is all this training going to take?"

"If all goes well, approximately one year for each level."

"A year??"

"Perl, time in Venusto is difficult to explain; it is more of an abstract idea. But in terms of time, as you understand it, a week here is roughly one day back on Mont Michel."

"Wow. A whole year." Perl sighed heavily; patience was never her strong suit. At that moment, the door swung open, and her roommates walked in. One was a slender girl with bright, translucent skin and glowing tentacles for hair; the other, a large, roly-poly boy with numerous sets of arms who looked like a great big caterpillar. The girl sashayed up to Perl.

"You must be Perl. I'm Opis. Nice to meet you."

"Hi." Perl slid off the bunk bed and held out her hand; the girl shook it daintily. Her hand felt strange, like a glove filled with gelatin. Perl noticed that Opis' skin was translucent; inside her hand, an interwoven network of bright blue and silver muscle, nerves, and cartilage could be seen. Up close, Perl was struck by the girl's bright blue eyes. Her long hair, green and pink tentacles that hung past her shoulders, sparked and wiggled like electrical wires. Perl could even hear them making tiny zapping and crackling noises. The boy bounded over to Perl, nearly knocking the waif-like girl over.

"Hello, I'm Bear, at your service," he mumbled, holding out numerous hands for her to shake. The boy had a sweet, round face, with deep-set black eyes, and a short head of sandy brown hair that looked as though it had never met a comb.

"Uh, hello," Perl said, picking out one of his eight hands to shake as she tried to take in the lumpy, wormlike creature standing before her. Bear's mouth was slathered in sticky goo.

"In case you're wondering, I'm not a caterpillar, or a slug, or a worm. I'm a tardigrade. Want a jam roll?" He held up a handful of gelatinous treats, green mucus-like syrup dripping from his stubby fingers.

"Thanks, but I just had a bunch of lemon cakes," Perl said, patting her stomach, trying not to be rude.

"Suit yourself," Bear puckered his lips, sucking the gooey slime balls into his mouth with a loud slurping sound.

"Disgusting," Opis muttered.

Perl smiled awkwardly. Her eyes caught a slight glint from her new top. "This cloth is really strange. One minute I think it's blue, then it's white, then silver, then, well...I'm not sure. I don't have a word for it."

"It's Harmony, silly," Opis was quick to learn things, and even quicker to educate others.

"Harmony? That's a color?" Perl asked.

"Of course. Seekers wear Harmony, Seers wear Humor, and Awakeners wear the color Hope. I mean, I don't mean to be insensitive, but how is it that you don't know your colors? How new *are* you?"

At that moment, Uriel, who'd been quietly watching from the shadows, strode over, her heavy chainmail rattling. "Good afternoon, Seekers."

Opis stammered, "Protector Uriel, I apologize. I, that is, we...didn't see you there."

"I wasn't wanting to be seen," Uriel said, a cunning smile crossing her lips.

The three students looked up at the dark, statuesque woman; she commanded attention.

"This is Perl's very first time to Venusto, and the start of her training at

Callowhorn. As fellow Water Seekers, I trust you both will look after her."

"Yes, of course," Opis glanced at Perl. "Is…is she the one? The homo sapien hybrid?"

Perl shot Opis a bewildered look.

Seeing Perl's face, Opis backtracked. "It's just that, we've heard stories about—"

Uriel cut her off. "As I said, you will look after her…with kindness." Uriel voice intensified, "like all of you, Perl is here to learn. I am merely here as her guardian." As she spoke, her dark violet eye bore into the two students like a laser.

"We'll look after her, right, Bear?" Opis elbowed the boy.

"I uh, yes…with my life!" Bear nodded.

Uriel's eye softened, "excellent. Then we're all in agreement."

Perl didn't like being called a hybrid, but her mind was full of questions. "How many times have you guys been here?" she asked.

Bear burped, then proudly puffed out his flabby torso. "Well, being a tardigrade, able to withstand almost any environment, from boiling to freezing, it's pretty tough to kill me. I've probably been through Venusto, oh, let's see now…only about three hundred cycles."

"Bragger," Opis crossed her arms.

Perl stammered, "*Only* three hundred? Are you kidding me? That's impossible. You're messing with me, right?"

"Ever's honest truth," Bear said, pointing a thumb at Opis, "but this one, she's died, what? Almost a thousand cycles, right?" Opis rolled her eyes. Bear chuckled. "Ah, she's just jealous. Makes sense, her being a *Turritopsis dohrnii.*"

Perl shot an inquisitive glance to Uriel, who translated, "jellyfish."

"Get it? Jealous? Jelly-fish?" Bear grabbed Opis, hugging her with a few arms, ruffling her tentacle-hair with a few others. "We've roomed together close to two hundred times, her and I!"

"Two hundred and twenty-three, but who's counting?" Opis put a hand in Bear's face, playfully pushing him away.

Perl scratched her frizzy head. "You've…died? Over and over?" Her mind was reeling. "So, if you're both that old, then how come you look so young?"

Opis pulled her snake-like hair up into a big ponytail. "A fresh start needs a fresh form," she said, letting her tentacles fall through her fingers. "Every time we meet our demise in the Half-Light Realm, we return to train again, retaining whispers of our previous cycle. We must re-learn once more. It's the way of the Light Realm. The battle is eternal, and so are we."

Perl was all ears now. "So, you two are like Uriel? Divine Protectors?"

Opis glanced up at Uriel respectfully.

Bear chuckled, "hardly! Protector Uriel has never died. *Never!* Plus, it takes thousands of years to become a Protector of the Light Realm."

Perl raised her brows, "so, who are you fighting exactly? Do you have weapons? How do you—"

Uriel spoke up, "I think that's enough for now. I have things to attend to here in Callowhorn, so if you two would give us a moment." Bear and Opis bowed.

Uriel directed Bear and Opis towards the door. Perl shrugged. She had so many questions, and she'd only just scratched the surface.

"Later, Perl!" Bear quipped, popping another glob treat in his mouth. As the door closed behind them, Perl turned to Uriel.

"You die over and over again? And fight battles? What is all this?"

"All your questions will be answered, Perl. I promise."

"Opis called me a hybrid, why?"

Uriel placed a hand on Perl's shoulder. "Take no offense. Opis is referring to you being half human and half Light Realm Protector. Bear and Opis are both kindhearted Beings. They've just never met anyone like you."

"They've never met anyone like *me*? What about *me*? I'm new, too! I'm just this little nobody in this big, strange place…up in the clouds, no less! I don't have a freaking clue what's going on!"

Perl believed Uriel when she said that Opis and Bear were kind, but she also recalled her years on Mont Michel, and the way people on the island had viewed her. She had always felt like an outsider, the odd one, the "strange girl," and now here in this otherworld far away from home, it seemed that nothing had changed.

Perl picked her robe up off of the floor and flung it onto a nearby chair. Seeds inside her pockets scattered across the grass floor. Uriel bent down and picked up one of them. She held it between two fingers, eyeing it closely.

"Perl, look at this seed. If we were to dismiss it for its size, that would be a great dishonor. If planted and cared for properly, this seed will grow into a towering, beautiful creation. It will produce fruit to feed a generation of families. Like you, it was made perfectly, for its given purpose. It has everything it needs to become its greatest self, all within this tiny shell. So never doubt what you are made of. You are capable of the unimaginable."

"You really believe that?" Perl picked up a seed, inspecting it.

"I do," Uriel reassured her, "now close your eyes. I have a gift for you." Perl's ears perked up, as Uriel placed the seed on the bed.

"Hold out your hands." Uriel pulled a book from inside her cloak, resting it gently in Perl's open palms. "Okay, you can look."

"A new sketchbook!" Perl was elated.

Written on the cover in shimmering opalescent ink were the words, *Perl's Wisdoms.*

"I love it." Perl opened it and ran her fingertips across the pages, "the paper is so smooth." There were no wood pulp bumps or flecks like the handmade pages of her old journal. "It's too nice to draw on."

"Nonsense," Uriel handed her a wooden pencil with a tiny carved figure of a girl riding a whale on the top of it. "For you, whale rider."

"It's the best gift I've ever received. Thank you." Perl flipped to the front inside cover. There was an inscription: *Never stop seeing the magic. Love, Uriel*

Perl slipped the book into her backpack, slinging it over one shoulder.

"So, what now?" Perl asked, "should we go look around?"

"I can stay long enough for you to meet your fellow Seekers, but after that, I must go. I have matters to attend to here."

"Wait, you're *leaving* leaving?"

"Just for a while. You'll be in very good hands here. Listen to your guides, they are very wise."

Perl hugged the great warrior, Uriel's armor cold against her bare arms. "Stay the night?"

"I can't, but I will send you *Hypercompe Scribonia* messages from time to time."

Perl looked up at Uriel, confused. Uriel pointed to the moth fluttering over her eye.

"Moths. My leopard moths will always find your light. When you see them, you'll know they're from me." She winked at the girl, "chin up, little one. It's going to be amazing, as will you."

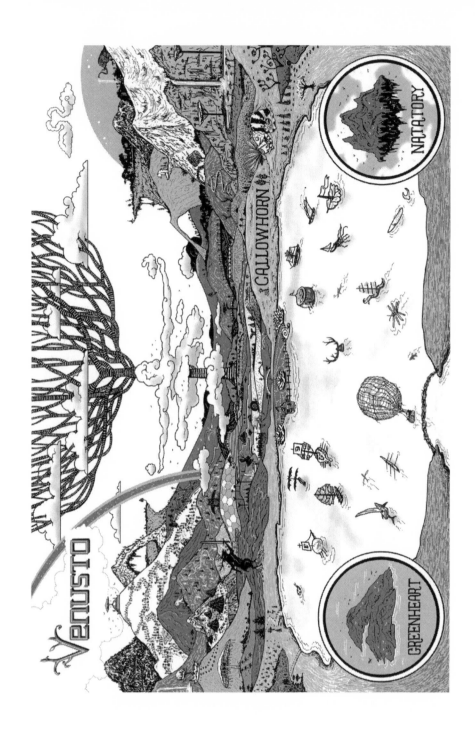

14 DEEP ROOTS

Bear and Opis closed the door behind them, giving Uriel and Perl a moment of privacy, only to be confronted by the other six Seekers who were eavesdropping outside.

"Why is Uriel here?" Corvax was in Bear's face, the black crow feathers on top of his head standing at attention.

"Yes! Tell us! This is so exciting!" Nan fluttered her butterfly wings, lifting her up off the ground for a moment.

"Well hello, friends," Bear giggled, suddenly surrounded by his peers.

"Uriel hasn't been to Venusto since she sponsored Noaa," Tars blinked nervously, his large bulbous eyes like two oranges, "that was centuries ago!" The monkey-boy twirled his long, curlicue tail through his thin, leathery fingers.

Opis parted the crowd, marching up the pebble pathway. "We have been...chosen."

This announcement only brought more questions.

"For what?" Lyre chirped, her beak snapping.

"Is it the Earth Prophecy?" Flax, the salamander, chased after Opis, his yellow and orange speckled arm raised high, waiting for the tentacled girl to acknowledge him.

"Isn't The Prophecy a myth?" Javan said, nearly tripping over his feet as he spun to follow Opis. The shy platypus-boy was more comfortable in water than on dry land, where he tended to be a bit clumsy.

"She has a name, Javan. It's Perl," Bear said protectively.

Opis turned, her long pink electrified strands twirled like an amusement park ride. "It's no myth."

The chatter swelled once more.

"Why are we the chosen ones?", "What else did Uriel say?", "That was her?", "She's so tiny!", "What's she like?"

From out of nowhere, a gust of wind hit the group, knocking all of them to the ground. Even Bear fell, folding in his eight arms as he toppled backwards.

"What was tha—", before the large tardigrade could finish, he noticed Uriel had stepped out of the nest.

"Now that I have your attention, I believe proper introductions are in order. Circle around, by your element...I'd like you all to meet Perl, of the island of Mont Michel...Earth."

At Uriel's command, the Seekers sprang to attention and closed in around the small girl. Perl stood awkwardly beside her guardian with her backpack on, the handle of her sword, Fortis, poking up over her shoulder. The light outside the nest was still extremely bright to Perl. She squinted as their faces slowly came into focus.

"Air, proceed," Uriel said, placing her hand on Perl's back, nudging her to take a step forward.

"Hello! I'm Nan! So very pleased to meet you!" said the butterfly-girl, hovering effortlessly above the ground. Her white and gold crystalline wings flapped gently, the antenna on top of her bulbous, fuzzy head bounced as she smiled sweetly. She had dark, almond-shaped eyes, a long proboscis nose that curled under in a spiral, and wore a Harmony gown, with six spindly copper arms and legs poking out.

"Your wings are lovely," Perl smiled back, seeing her face reflected in Nan's wide set eyes.

"Your wings are lovely," repeated the bird-girl covered in blue and yellow feathers next to Nan. Her voice sounded exactly like Perl's. "I'm Lyre. I'm a mimic." She did a little curtsy, tipping her plumed head down in a short, jerky movement. Perl saw Lyre had matching flecks of color that came down her forehead, forming a V-shape point at the tip of her nose. She walked upright with arms and legs covered in soft down, a pair of wings were tucked behind her under a Harmony cloak. Lyre's most stunning feature was a great motley plume of tail feathers that rose up into a swirling question mark over her head. As she spoke, her tail bobbed playfully.

"Yes, Lyre's pretty entertaining. She can copycat anything from a warthog's call to a newborn kitten softly cooing." The tall, older-looking crow-boy with jet black feathers stepped forward matter-of-factly. "I'm Corvax. Puzzles, riddles, strategy…those are my specialty. There isn't a problem I can't solve."

"Except how to relax," Bear joked.

Corvax gave the roly-poly boy a steely glare. Perl looked up at Corvax; he had a dark hooked beak of a nose, with cool gray eyes that reinforced his serious temperament. The feathers on his head swept up and back on one side like a mohawk, the other side shaved. Beneath his Harmony clothing, smaller black feathers covered his muscular arms and legs. Corvax stepped back into line, giving Perl a look that made her feel a little uneasy.

"Um…nice to meet the you," Perl said shyly.

"Land Seekers, acquaint yourselves. Tars, why don't you go first?" Uriel nodded to the monkey-boy.

"Uh, yes, I'm Tars." Nervous in the presence of Uriel, he stammered, running his fingers through his short, spiky hair, "I…I can see in the dark…and, Oh! I once spotted a Venompus a mile across the desert in the dead of night, Ever's truth!" He blinked, his large eyes the size and color of oranges.

Perl thought Tars seemed even more anxious than her. "What's a Venompus?"

"Oh, they're nasty critters! Tiny. They release a toxic pus. If it gets on a plant, it kills it instantly." Tars placed his paw on the back of a lizard-boy next to him, pushing him forward. "Anyway, this is my boy, Flax. I'm sure he's got a question or ten for you."

Flax turned to Tars, sticking out his unbelievably long pink tongue at his friend. "I do have a few questions. For one, what's *your* Ever-given gift, Perl?"

"Um, well, I have bioluminescence, and I see people's essences, and I can hear…um, I'm actually still figuring them all out really." She paused, seeing every eye on her, and suddenly wished she had on her old robe so she could pull up her hood and disappear.

"Those are magnificent gifts!" Flax replied, "I have energy to burn, as long as the sun shines, that is." Flax held up his spotted arms. "I have solar powered skin."

"That's really interesting." Perl was feeling overwhelmed, but mostly it was exciting to discover that there were others like her.

Flax spun back into place, elbowing the third Land Seeker. The boy with a thick, unruly head of hair and a prominent nose waddled forward. Under his Harmony clothing, Perl saw a coat of short, fine, chestnut brown hair.

"Hi, I'm Javan, I have electrolocation," he said softly; his bangs hung low over one eye.

Perl didn't know what that was. She smiled politely at the boy, who was staring down at his boots.

Uriel cut in, "you've already met your Water roommates, Bear and Opis, so Perl…welcome to your family of nine."

"Family." Perl liked the sound of that.

"Yes, and like family, you will all watch over one another," answered Uriel.

"Sure, and also like family, everyone has a say. No matter how annoying they can be at times," Bear chucked a gooey tart at Tars.

"Not cool, Bear!" The monkey-boy shouted, brushing the glob off of his new shirt with a swipe of his tail.

Bear giggled, "what? That's the glue that holds a family together!" Nan fluttered her wings, giggling. Corvax shook his head.

"Alright, Callowhorn Seekers, Master Yew will be here momentarily to complete your orientation. I will see you all again. Perl, a moment alone, please?"

The eight Beings said goodbye to Uriel as she and Perl walked to the end of the cobalt pathway. The Seekers began chatting and joking with one another, like best friends back from summer vacation. Perl looked over at them, feeling a bit left out.

"When will you be back?" She asked.

"Sooner than you think, little one," Uriel held Perl's face in her hand. "Remember, I will always have my eye on you. As I said before, my moths will find you, so watch for my messages. Be brave. Listen to your heart."

They hugged one last time, and Perl watched as her guardian and balloon-mate rounded the corner and disappeared, her faint lavender glow going with her. Perl, feeling very alone, wandered back over to the group, overhearing a bit of their conversation.

"So, how'd you die this time, Flax?" the butterfly-girl, Nan, asked.

The salamander-boy wrung his hands. "Well, Nan, it's getting worse out there, isn't it? I lost a fight at the Fornia coastline. The air there is virtually unbreathable." Flax pushed his sleeves up, exposing his glassy amphibian skin. "We're losing more and more battles in the Half-Light...I fear it will not be *half* light much longer...the darkness is gaining ground."

"Stay hopeful, Flax." Nan descended softly, touching the tips of her toes to the ground, then springing back up, light as a feather.

"I am. I'm hopeful the Light Realm, and our skills on the battlefield, will prevail."

At that moment, the low strum of a cello could be heard. It was Grandmaster Olliv, rubbing his leg against his wings. The group looked over and he tipped his hat to them, then approached.

"Seekers, line up, up." He walked down the line, smiling at each of them. Olliv stopped at Flax, tapping him lightly on his moist, smooth head with his buttercup baton. "You, Flax, are correct to have hope. However, the Light Realm alone cannot achieve victory. No, no." He then projected louder, so the whole group could hear him, "humans must play a part, as you all know, know. It is our purpose to awaken them to the magic of nature, nature."

Flax mumbled, "what's left of it."

Perl had slipped into line with the others. At Flax's comment, she shot him a look of concern.

"Yes, *Ambystoma maculatuma,* what is left, is quite correct, correct. And that is precisely why you are here, here." Olliv tapped Flax twice more on his slick head. "Now bow please, as we welcome Master Yew."

Olliv touched his baton to the ground where the cobalt pathways met. Every Seeker bowed their head except for Perl, who watched as the blue pebbles below her feet began to tremble. The soil gave way, and a tree rose up before them. It was three stories high and as wide as a hippo. The trunk of the enormous tree split down the middle, revealing its hollow center. A yellow vapor came from the large crevice, swirling around like a tornado in slow motion as it began to take on a shape. Lemon yellow feathers appeared in the golden mist, quickly multiplying as the spinning increased. Perl watched, transfixed by what she was seeing. A large, pear-shaped entity materialized, floating in front of them. It was nearly ten feet tall and had no recognizable face, just a pair of intense tiger eyes that gleamed brightly through a head of thick, tangerine hair that flickered like a campfire. Its body was covered head to toe in layers of fluffy yellow plumage that danced in the breeze. Perl didn't know if it was male or female, but it was quite extraordinary.

"Seekers, I am Yew. The past is forgotten. All is anew. Gather round." The guide spoke, its breathy voice was calm, restrained, almost hypnotic.

The group lifted their heads and formed a circle around their instructor. Perl followed their actions, not knowing what she should be doing.

"Why exist?"

No one said a word at first, then Opis spoke up, "to protect the Earth."

"From?"

Corvax crowed over Opis before she could speak again, "the evils of the Dark Realm."

Perl thought to herself, "*okay. Now maybe I'll get some answers.*"

Slowly, Yew raised its arms, and the ground trembled once again. All around Perl and the others, roots poked through the dirt, crawling up and taking hold of each of their ankles, twisting and turning as they serpentined up their legs.

"Hey, that tickles," Perl giggled, as the roots weaved in and round her bare feet, wrapping up to her knees. *"I should've put on those new boots."*

The shy one, Javan, was beside Perl, wobbling, trying to keep his balance. As he was about to fall backwards, he grabbed hold of Perl's hand. She was surprised to feel his fingers were webbed. *"He's like a duck,"* she thought.

"Oh, sorry," Javan apologized.

"That's okay, I got you." Perl gave him a tug.

The furry brown boy righted himself, quickly letting go of her hand. He went back to staring at his boots.

Perl glanced around at the others in the circle; feet, paws, and claws were all bound in the giant tangled mass of tree roots. Yew hovered in the center, spinning slowly. As the Being turned its back to Perl, she saw an impressive longbow strapped over its shoulder.

"Roots are the hosts for the living…animals, minerals, plants all rely on them…to anchor the land, to breath the air, and to be nourished by the water. Each new Seeker class entering Callowhorn is put into groups of nine. Three of air, three of land, and three of water."

Perl looked out over the campground's rolling hills. The other Seeker groups had gathered in front of their nests and were receiving a welcome by a different, yet no less remarkable, Being.

Yew, noticing Perl's attention had wandered, increased its tone, *"this* nine is unique."

Perl felt the tiger eyes on her and focused, shifting her weight from side to side, as Yew continued.

"The number nine represents a divine symmetry, the perfect harmony of spirit, nature, and science. You are a circle. Each of value. Just like a grove, with its elaborate root system, you will learn to link your abilities for the greater good."

The Being paused in front of Opis. "Your ancestry nourishes both the Light Realm and the Earth. Death and rebirth remind us not only of the infinite power of nature, but to live fully between the doorways of those worlds."

Yew spun to face Corvax once again. "The Dark Realm's evil is omnipresent. What then, is your purpose?"

Corvax jumped at the chance to solve the riddle. "To fight it and defeat it, proving Ever is the one true enduring entity."

Yew's tiger eyes flickered. The tree roots tightened their grip around the Seekers' legs.

The crow-boy, thinking he was wrong, changed his answer. "No, um…we must stand united in our circle…to help future generations," Corvax squawked. The winds picked up, causing the group to sway like trees before a storm.

The boy grew frustrated. "…By keeping the balance between the Light and the Dark?" The roots relinquished their hold on the group.

"A Seeker's purpose is just that, to seek." Yew turned to Perl. "A Seeker's goal is to find the opportunities that will enlighten the human race of their oneness with nature." The Being continued rotating, eyeing each Seeker. "With this new cycle back into the Realm of Light, you eight are unlike any other group that's ever been. The eight of you have been brought together for a purpose…"

"Eight?" Perl thought, *"but there's nine of us."*

The Being locked its bright eyes on Perl. "And these eight shall be your guides, Perl, to help you grow and flourish." Yew floated back towards the huge tree it had emerged from. "You nine are vital to Earth's survival."

Yellow and orange vapors began streaming out of Yew's hair and feathers, swirling and engulfing the Being. The misty golden cloud seeped back into the tree which then sank into the ground, leaving behind a patch of green grass with a single daffodil sticking up. The roots wriggled back into the dirt, leaving a few rings around Perl's ankles and a scratch on her left foot.

"Well that was definitely…*anew.*" Lyre mimicked Yew's monotone voice perfectly, as the others laughed.

Corvax plucked the flower from the ground. "Always looking after the humans. Here you go, rare Flower." He handed Perl the daffodil and marched down the hill.

"What's his problem?" Perl asked.

Bear put an arm around Perl's shoulder, "don't mind him, he's just used to always being right about everything. Corvax can be little headstrong, but he's a good leader…only don't tell him I said so."

"I won't," Perl tucked the flower behind her ear.

Grandmaster Olliv's song chirped from the bottom of the hillside. "Time to hydrate, and nourish, nourish! Follow me to the Dragon, Dragon!" He waved his buttercup baton.

"Finally, I'm starving!" Bear ran on all eight arms and legs, rumbling past everyone.

"Did he say *dragon?*" Perl fell to the back of the line, moving quietly behind the others. Looking up ahead, she caught a glimpse of Javan peering back at her. He smiled, combing his fingers through his thick bangs. Perl smiled back, finding a newfound pep in her step.

On their way to the dining area, Perl glanced around at the gorgeous views. She spotted a falls, only instead of water, an endless flow of pastel flower petals cascaded down from the rock formations above them, spilling into a glorious rainbow-colored lagoon. The flowers branched out into a number of floral streams that twisted and turned, flowing throughout Callowhorn; it was breathtaking. Perl bent down and scooped up a handful of the soft velvety petals.

"Oh, duh. I'm not wearing my robe." With no pockets for hiding treasures, she let the petals fall through her fingers. Perl's thoughts turned to home; she wondered what Victr was cooking for supper back at the root cellar. She pictured Papa leading them in the Grateful Song as the spider-monks dug into their meals. The sound of Olliv's voice brought her back to the present.

"And we're here, here. Seekers, after you've eaten, just follow the path back, back to your bungalows. I will wake you with the morning sun, sun. Make sure to get a good night's sleep. Big day tomorrow, tomorrow!"

Perl breathed in the delicious smells— fresh bread, savory cheeses, earthy mushrooms, sweet honey, and fresh tomatoes. She realized how hungry she was, the rich aromas making her mouth water.

A large floral archway in the shape of a fire-breathing dragon greeted the diners into the park. Hanging under the arch was a sign:

~Welcome to Dragon Maw~

Below that, there was a quote:

97

If home is where your heart is, keep it open for unexpected guests. ~*Tryfon*

An even smaller sign hung below that:

Remember to push in your toadstools!

Perl filed through the gate with the rest of the bustling crowd. The smells were stronger now, and her stomach growled loudly. Spread out before her was an enormous dining garden, walled in by rows of lush green poplar trees. The park was packed full of the most fantastic Beings she had ever seen.

Everyone seemed to know each other. There was the flutter and buzz of wings, the screech and squawk of birds, the bark, bellow, and roar of large beasts, and an ongoing symphony of whoops, whistles, grunts, growls, and other curious sounds mingling about. The dining tables were *Dracena Cinnabari* trees, sculpted to varying heights to accommodate the many walks of life in Venusto.

Losing sight of her Seekers, Perl meandered around the park, looking for a spot to sit. Passing by table after table, Perl could hear some of the creatures whispering.

"Is that her, the Earth child?", "She's younger than I thought she'd be.", "Noaa died for her, you know."

Perl, feeling eyes on her, turned to leave, when Javan appeared. He peered down his dark brown snout at her. "I smelled your mortal blood coursing through your muscle tissues."

"Huh?" Perl stepped back.

"Oh, sorry, I do that sometimes. My electrolocation…like a platypus. I was, uh, sensing you," he said, his cheeks darkening.

"Sensing me?"

Javan brushed his long bangs aside. "Yeah, I can't always control it. My nose, I mean. Being back in Venusto, it sorta has a mind of its own."

"Back home I had to learn to control my visions, so I get it."

"I can tell you have human genes. You know, there's never been a human in Venusto."

"So I've heard, but like, never?" She asked.

"Not in all of the eternity that I've known, anyway."

"What do you mean, *your* eternity?"

"Oh, I've cycled more that I care to say. I can be a bit clumsy, as you might have noticed. Not a great trait to have in battle."

Javan's bangs fell into his face again; he jerked his head, tossing his hair out of the way.

"You wanna eat with me?"

Perl couldn't hide a big toothy grin. "Yes."

The two found a tree-table off in a corner; it was a bit small, but they managed to balance on the tiny toadstools.

"I was told I had to come to Venusto," Perl said, squeezing her knees up under the table.

"Had to? I didn't know that." Javan looked a bit surprised.

A beautiful albino lioness, her mane made up of multi-colored butterflies, placed two piping hot soufflés in front of them.

"What's in this?" Perl asked. She didn't really care, though; the smell was heavenly.

Javan shrugged, picking up his fork, "Honestly? I didn't think humans were even allowed in Venu—" He stopped himself, "uh, what I mean is, I think it's great that you're here."

Without warning, Bear plopped down next to Perl. "Ah, I've been looking for you!"

"Well, you found us," Javan replied.

"No, I was talking to your soufflés," Bear joked, dipping a finger in the boy's dish.

"Hey, get your own," Javan shoved Bear's arm away.

Perl took a bite of the golden puff-pastry. It was flaky, creamy, savory, salty and then suddenly sweet. It melted in her mouth, the flavors erupting on her tongue. "This is…delicious," she closed her eyes, savoring each bite.

The two boys looked at one another and smiled. Perl didn't come up for a breath, devouring the entire dish, licking it clean; her spider-monks would have been proud.

"You missed a spot," Bear chuckled.

"That was, by far, the best thing I've ever eaten, and I don't even know what it was!"

Javan brushed a few crumbs from his furry arm. "Just wait for dessert."

"There's more?"

The Light Beings nearby were snapping twigs off their tree-table and dipping them into their drinks.

"Are they breaking that table?" Perl asked.

"These are *Dracena Cinnabari*. Dragon blood trees. They're good for the ol' tum-tum," Bear rubbed his stomach, holding out a small branch for Perl to try.

Just then, the whole dining area was flooded with a kaleidoscope of color, the source coming from a small flower garden located at the front of the park. Everyone paused, turning their attention to a tall, glowing figure.

Perl tapped Javan. "Is that…*Ever?*"

"Close. That is Tryfon." Javan straightened his posture.

Perl remembered the quote on the sign at the gate. "Tryfon?"

"The Divine Master of Venusto," Javan bowed his head.

Tryfon radiated warmth and sweetness. As the Divine Master came closer, Perl suddenly felt like she was in one of Papa's hugs; safe, happy, and loved. Tryfon's skin was teaming with life, changing constantly like a chameleon. One minute it resembled ocean coral, the next it was moss, then sand, then honeycomb. His long beard of wildflowers dragged on the ground behind him.

"Whoa...Regor's never gonna believe this," Perl thought, transfixed.

The mystic's head had three faces. The center one was ancient, human. On either side of it were two faces that transformed in sync with his skin, going from a furry lion, to a leathery bat, to a feathered owl, to a rough-skinned rhino, and on and on. Tryfon held a large white walking stick, carved into a totem pole of hundreds of animals.

"Welcome back." His voice was soothing yet exotic, like the sound of nature itself. The park was utterly silent.

"Familiar faces, I see," Tryfon nodded to a few tables.

A Being covered in monarch chrysalises nodded back, "Your Grace."

The residents of Venusto paid their respects as Master Tryfon made his way through the park.

An elder Awakener, a milkweed pod Being, shook its head, releasing seeds. "Praise to all Nature."

A Seer resembling a lynx held its paws together as it bowed to the Divine Master.

Tryfon smiled. "Use your time in Venusto wisely. Seek. See. Awaken. Be open to the refined beauty of a simple blade of grass, a drop of rain, a speck of pollen. Find perfection in the imperfections." The Master came to Perl's table and knelt down. The entire garden looked on. "For when it rains..." he touched the top of her bare foot where the roots had scratched her, "...it falls on all." The wound healed instantly.

As he stood, Perl saw that he had three sets of glorious wings; a pair above his head, a pair at his sides, and two more that lay across the front of his legs.

Tryfon gestured to the crowd, "all of you are given magnificent gifts, with a collective power to change and heal the world."

Perl looked up at him, "excuse me...why am I here?"

The tables within earshot gave an audible gasp.

Tryfon reached down, holding her cheek in his large, soft hand. "You are the flame to those who ask the same."

Perl became lost in his brown, green and gold flecked eyes; genuine peace and love washed over her. Tryfon continued down the rows of tables, touching the heads, wings, and furry manes of the seated Beings. Upon reaching the front gates of Dragon Maw, he turned, facing the group once more. "Hope is on the horizon. Let humankind know that they are loved." Tryfon vanished, his rainbow of twinkling light cascading with him. Some of the Beings wiped away tears.

Bear leaned over to Perl, "the Divine Master touched you. You've been blessed."

Perl walked back to the barrow nests ahead of Bear and Javan, needing some alone time to process everything she had seen on just this first day. Climbing up into her feather down bed, she pulled out the journal Uriel had given her and began writing and sketching feverishly. After many hours, exhausted, Perl finally put away her book. Rolling on her side, she spotted the tiny seed that Uriel had placed there.

She picked it up, holding it gently between two fingers. "I guess you *should* grow to your full potential, shouldn't you?" Careful not to wake the others, Perl hopped off the bed and tiptoed outside.

"This looks like a good spot." Perl knelt down and dug a small hole, dropping the seed in. She filled it, tamping the dirt down with her foot. "Goodnight, little friend. Sweet dreams."

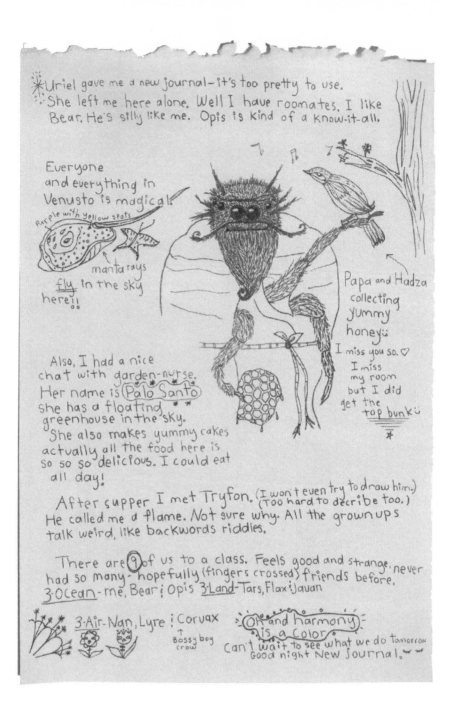

※ Uriel gave me a new journal—it's too pretty to use.
∴ She left me here alone. Well I have roomates, I like
Bear. He's silly like me. Opis is kind of a know-it-all.

Everyone
and everything in
Venusto is magical!

Purple with yellow spots

manta rays
fly in the sky
here!!

Papa and Hadza
collecting
yummy
honey..

I miss you so. ♡
I miss
my room
but I did
get the
top bunk..

Also, I had a nice
chat with garden-nurse.
Her name is (Palo Santo)
She has a floating
greenhouse in the sky.
  She also makes yummy cakes
actually all the food here is
so so so delicious. I could eat
all day!

  After supper I met Tryfon. (I won't even try to draw him.)
(Too hard to decribe too.)
He called me a flame. Not sure why. All the grownups
talk weird, like backwords riddles.

  There are ⑨ of us to a class. Feels good and strange, never
had so many—hopefully (fingers crossed) friends before.
3-Ocean—me, Bear ; Opis 3-Land—Tars, Flax ; Javan

3-Air-Nan, Lyre ; Corvax
↑
Bossy boy
crow

Oh and harmony
is a color
Can't wait to see what we do tomorrow
Good night New Journal. ﹏ ﹏

102

15 KALIMBA

Bright sun streamed in through Perl's window, waking her from a deep slumber. She sat up and stretched, taking in a deep breath. The morning was fresh and warm, with a hint of dew on the grass. Perl stretched. A smell of Spring was in the air.

The others were already awake and outside waiting for Olliv. The grasshopper-man came around the bend pulling a triple-decker wicker basket on wheels.

"Rise and shine, Seekers. This way, way."

Perl laced up her new Harmony boots and ran to catch the group.

"Good morning, sleepy head," Bear teased.

Perl fluffed her hair and adjusted her backpack straps. "Where are we going? What's in the baskets?"

"Morning meditation, and fingers crossed, breakfast!"

"Oh, okay." Perl thought of her spider-monks back home meditating in their candlelit chapel.

They headed down a path of crunchy silver gravel past Dragon Maw, the landscape of rolling hills flattening out into tranquil pastures. Olliv stopped in front of a patch of land bordered by lilac bushes, giving a quick whistle as he unlatched the buckle on the top basket. Two chipmunks wearing little knitted hats poked their heads out, giving a quick chirp, announcing their presence. Moving efficiently, the woodland critters delivered warm biscuits to each Seeker, popping back and forth from the basket to each student. After the biscuits were handed out, the chipmunks offered everyone a flower petal cup filled with sweet tea.

"Thank you," Perl took the tiny cup gingerly. "Mmm, honey." As she sipped the last drop of tea, the flower cup withered in her hand. Perl let the petals fall to the ground, and noticed that as they landed, new plants began to grow. "Magic," she whispered to herself.

Olliv fluttered his wings vigorously, the buzzing sound getting everyone's attention. "Form a circle, circle. Every other, please...Air, Land, Water, and so on, so on. Lace hands, hands."

The group slowly fell into a loose circle, clumsily taking hold of each other's hands. Nan sidled up to Perl. "Good morning! You look lovely today."

"You too," Perl smiled, taking hold of the butterfly-girl's dainty hand. She turned and there was Javan. He gave a quick nod, flipping his hair back. Perl blushed a bit as he reached his webbed hand over, taking hers.

Olliv spoke, "excellent, excellent. Each morning we shall begin here and in this very manner, manner." The grasshopper made a dramatic gesture with his flower baton, panning over the field. "Daybreak is for lessons, lessons. Afternoons are for battle training, training." He bowed deeply, puffing on his pipe. "I will return for you when your training is completed, completed. That is all I have for you this morning, so I bid you all good luck, luck."

With that, Olliv wheeled the cart away, the chipmunks riding on his shoulders. The cute little rodents gave a wave goodbye to the group.

Perl thought it felt a little weird to be holding hands with people she'd just met, and kind of nice at the same time. From behind the lilac bushes, great clouds of dust rose up as the sound of galloping hooves approached. Tearing around the edge of the tall bushes came a magnificent herd of horses. Once they got closer, Perl saw that the horses all had enormous ram horns. The lead horse, powdery white with a blue mane and tail, was carrying a rider.

"Whoa, whoa." A deep voice eased the beast to a stop, pulling gently on the reins. The rest of the creatures slowed, stamping their hooves and clearing the dust from their nostrils with a series of loud snorts. Dismounting gracefully, the tall, imposing figure strode confidently into the center of their circle. Perl looked up in awe at the captivating Being; it was like an ancient alien statue come to life. Fanning out on the front of its head—as part of its head, in fact—were seven perfectly formed wings, pure white, each wing containing three silver eyes. The wings covered its entire face, leaving only chiseled cheekbones and its mouth visible. Its bare torso was porpoise-like; bluish-silver in tone and smooth like wet glass. It wore a long, pleated wrap tied around its waist. The dusty pack of horses whinnied loudly, knocking their mighty horns against one another playfully.

"I am Bodhi. Light Protector Guide. Salutations." Standing in the very middle of the group, the figure turned and bowed deeply four times. When it faced Perl, she stood wide-eyed. Javan gently nudged her; she took the hint, bowing stiffly.

"Here, with me, you will begin your meditative training. You will learn to listen to the natural world. Become one with it."

In a slow, controlled movement, Bodhi lifted its hands up to the sky, then outward, then clasped them together as if in prayer. It reminded Perl of the monks' chant back home.

"Rest." The Light Protector eased itself gently to the ground, crossing its legs. The students did the same. Bear grunted a bit as he forced his numerous legs to cross. Tars giggled at his friend.

"Let us begin." Bodhi closed its eyes.

Perl watched and repeated as the others placed their hands on their knees.

"Close your eyes. Bring your attention to my voice. Feel the pressure of your body on the ground. If worry tugs at you, return to my voice. Shall we begin?"

"Yes, Master Bodhi," they said as one, Perl mouthed along, unsure of what to do.

"Focus. Deep breath. Slow. In through your nose. Take in the fragrance of the lilacs around you. Hold it there. Exhale slowly out of your mouth. Be still. Feel the soft breeze on your face. Inhale again. Let it fill your lungs. In. Out. In. Out. Open your mind's eye. Before you is a cloud. It grows purple as it swells. Rain is imminent. Rain cleanses the spirit. Makes all things green. A fresh start."

Perl peeked. Tars, Nan, Corvax, and the entire group was focused, their eyes closed. The Guide sat, tranquil and stoic as a marble sculpture. Perl quickly shut her eyes before Bodhi noticed. The Guide continued, its voice peaceful and composed.

"A quiet mind hears clearly the faintest voice. All of life speaks a language. Grow silent to harmonize with it. To serve it well, one must understand it. Commune with it. Listen now."

As if on cue, the gentle patter of rain began falling, splashing against the lilac leaves, one drop at a time. "Each water droplet has a message. Listen. What do they say?" Bodhi's voice faded. The only sound was the soft pitter-patter of raindrops lightly tapping the leaves around them.

...drip, drop. drip drip, drop. drip, drop. drip, drip, drop...

Perl opened her eyes, remembering the kalimba in her backpack from her father's treasure chest, and Uriel's words when she gave it to her, *'I know that you hear the music in life that others do not.'*

As the rest meditated, Perl quietly retrieved the small turtle-shaped instrument and began to plink the metal bars, trying to match the beat of the raindrops. The hypnotic sound of the kalimba synchronized with the rain, and within minutes, a calmness settled over Perl. She drifted deep inside herself, like she would back home in her tub, listening to her heartbeat.

...drip, drop. drip drip, drop. drip, drop. drip, drip, drop...

Perl soon heard more than just the rain falling. There was a distinct pattern to the drops, a rhythm. The rain was singing! Perl began to quietly sing along.

'I quench the willow
in the raspberry field
where children run free~
in and around the shade tree,
picking ruby gems,
climbing wooden boards,

nailed to the side~
so they may go higher
and higher to see.
I am the rain."

"You are the one known as Perl?" Bodhi's voice echoed around her, bringing her back to the present.

When she opened her eyes, the other eight Seekers were all looking at her. As quickly as the showers had started, they stopped, and a pleasant petrichor smell filled the air. The Guide smiled at her.

"You have found the words, Perl. You have listened to nature's song. Well done." Bodhi closed its eyes, nodding at Perl.

Bear was surprised, his mouth hanging open. Tar's tail was twitching.

"That was lovely. How did that song come to you?" Javan asked.

"I dunno," Perl shrugged, a shy grin on her face, "just heard it." She thought for a minute, *"Why is that song so familiar? Wait, I remember! The homeless man...it was his poem."*

Corvax crossed his arms. "Where did you get that?" His black feathery hair was standing up like a mohawk.

Perl looked down at her kalimba, the sunlight gleaming off its shellacked surface. Inside of the instrument was an engraved message: *"Dianna, my moon, my love, my eternity. Noaa."* She hugged the turtle instrument, realizing it must have been a gift from her father to her mother.

"What was once a connection of two souls," Bodhi looked at Perl, "now becomes a connection of three."

Corvax complained, "isn't that cheating, using an instrument?"

Bear bellowed, "Cor, stop being a jumble-gut!"

Bodhi's powdery white hand went up; everyone fell quiet. "Rest."

Bodhi closed all of its eyes; from the ground rose a miniature apple orchard. The tops of the trees were only a few feet tall. The exquisite Being rose, strolling down one of the rows, plucking juicy apples and placing them in a small basket. Bodhi turned to the crow-boy.

"Corvax, if allowed to choose apples, are you not pleased with the bounty you select?"

Corvax shrugged, "I guess so."

"But should you look back down the rows from which you've been, do you not see dozens of perfect apples not chosen?"

"Yes, I suppose," Corvax agreed.

"There are many ways to get the ripest fruit from the same path. No one way is the right way, if all yield happiness." Bodhi plucked a red, shining apple and tossed it to one of the nearby horses, who caught it mid-air, gobbling it up.

The Guide raised its hands again, circling them over the rows of trees. At once, the trees bent, rippled, and faded, churning into a whirlwind of leaves, apples, branches and dirt. A new scene appeared before them, in miniature form again; a duck pond lined with tall grass and pussy willows.

"Ever. Master painter. Endless canvases of unimaginable environments. Each carefully created to bring joy. To all, for all." Bodhi waved his hands over the small pond; the scene now changing to an arctic landscape. A small icy blue glacier formed, surrounded by dark green waters. Tiny seals slid across the floating chunks of glistening ice. "The world is a palette of blended colors. You too, must grow together. Blend your talents."

Flax raised his glistening amphibian hand. Bodhi nodded at him.

"Um, yes, Tryfon spoke of there being a hope. On, uh…on the horizon. What did he mean?"

Bodhi waved one hand over the glacier and it melted into the tiny sea. "It is all there. On Earth. Humankind must want to see it. Tell its story. All must become one. They must awaken their collective consciousness."

Flax tilted his head, "but will they awaken?"

"Water has spoken," Bodhi bowed to Perl, "quench their thirst. Let them rise to see."

Suddenly feeling very self-conscious, Perl smiled awkwardly. She was struggling to make sense of all of this.

"Flax, don't you see? *We* are the art as well," Opis chimed in, "we need to be…"

Perl spoke up, "a collage." Opis looked at Perl, surprised.

"Yes. That's what I was going to say," Opis retorted. "A collage…pulling all of our gifts together."

Bodhi whistled for the horses. On command, they trotted into formation, making even rows of three in front of the class.

"Very good, but for today let us be in the moment. Choose a companion." He passed around a silver bucket filled with dandy brushes. One by one, they each picked out a brush and stood next to a horse.

"Brush. Back. Neck. Mane. Tail. Nose. In that order. Think of nothing else. Only brush." The Seekers began brushing.

"Be mindful. Remove all thoughts. Let them disappear as you brush. There is no past. No future. Only this moment."

As Perl stroked the beautiful horse, her mind started to relax. She stopped thinking and simply focused on brushing. The spots running down her arm began to glow and her filly whinnied, enjoying the massage. Perl looked closely at the horse's fine coat, noticing the subtle flecks of brown, tan and white on its back.

"It really does look like a painting up close," she thought.

Bodhi walked up to Perl. "There is beauty in the whole of things, but only in drawing closer does one see the magic in the details."

The Light Being walked away as Perl held the horse's curved horn in her hand, feeling every bump and ridge. With one last stroke of the soft brush down its long nose, Perl locked eyes with the magnificent creature. "Thank you," they both said, without saying a word.

A light melody floated on the breeze towards the meditation meadow, where the Seekers waited to be picked up. Olliv, strumming his legs like a virtuoso, soon appeared, riding on a snail the size of a bus. The grasshopper-man sat up front in a seat near the snail's head, gripping a pair of reigns to help guide the sluggish creature.

"Our time together has evaporated like the morning rain." Bodhi held out the bucket for them to drop their brushes in. "Until our spirits cross again. Listen for life's language. Be an artful collage."

The snail slid to a stop along its mucus trail. Olliv rolled out a rope ladder from the top of its shell. "All aboard. Up, up. Time to feast, feast!"

The group climbed up, finding quite the surprise once they came aboard. Built on top of the snail's hard shell was a tent; inside was a quaint dining area. A round table draped in Harmony cloth sat in the middle, with nine chairs neatly arranged around it. There were nine place settings, each one complete with a wooden cup and bowl, and a Harmony napkin, carefully rolled up and tied with a vine. The hungry Seekers quickly grabbed a seat, eager to dig into their lunch. Plumes of steam rose from each bowl, where a mound of mossy gel wiggled like jelly.

"Alright, alright. Off we go *Gastropoda*!" With a tap of Olliv's buttercup baton, the snail grunted, and ever so slowly started up again, contracting the muscles in its foot to propel itself forward.

Everyone dug in, eating with their hands. Perl nudged Bear seated next to her. "What's this weird stuff?" She pointed at the squishy lump of turquoise blue goo in front of her.

"It's your favorite food!" he sang, before shoveling two fistfuls of vivid yellow moss into his mouth.

Perl scrunched up her nose, "I doubt it. Looks like a mound of disgusting goop to me."

She'd eaten her share of seaweed back home, but this stuff looked inedible. Everyone else was happily gobbling it up, though.

Bear pinched off a piece of moss and held it up to Perl's face, mimicking Bodhi, "whaaat is your faaavorite thing to eat for luuunch? Imagine it in your miiind and you will taste it on your tooongue." He popped the spongy bite into his mouth. "Mmm-mm, mushroom goulash!"

Perl picked up a clump, carefully examining it. Bear, as always, spoke with his mouth full, yellow moss squishing between his teeth.

"Go on, try it. Looks can be deceiving."

Perl closed her eyes and thought of Victr's carrot and potato potpie. She smiled, picturing the monk rushing around the kitchen, his food-stained apron tied around the outside of his brown robe. She took a tiny bite of the blue moss. The roasted yummy flavor of gravy filled her mouth, transporting her back home. Perl tasted the savory carrots, the earthy potatoes. She happily swallowed and was going in for another bite when she overheard a conversation. Corvax and Lyre were whispering. Perl thought she heard her name mentioned.

Lyre leaned in, speaking in a hushed tone, "a kalimba song won't be enough against…Malblud."

Corvax peered over at Perl, whispering back, "I trust Uriel, but even she isn't infallible."

Perl was straining to listen when Javan threw a bit of moss at her, lodging it in her hair. "Hey, who did that?"

"Thought you'd like to try my banana squash porridge," Javan laughed.

"Have some of my carrots, why don't ya?!" Perl heaved a ball of moss back, only it ricocheted off of Javan, splattering Nan and Opis. Both girls screamed, instantly grabbing fistfuls of their lunch, ready to retaliate. It wasn't long before an all-out food fight was happening on the back of the giant snail.

"Eat up!" Yelled Flax, flicking orange lumps of goo at Perl.

"You look hungry!" Tars lobbed a purple glob at Corvax, just missing him as he ducked.

"Get down, Nan!" screamed Lyre, as a thud of pink splashed on her Harmony top.

All nine of them, even the usually serious Corvax, were giggling uncontrollably, pelting one another with their lunches. Soon the whole group was coated in a smorgasbord of rainbow-colored goop.

Perl held her face, rolling back in her seat, "my cheeks hurt from laughing."

"Master Bodhi would be pleased," Bear licked his lips, "this is an artful collage, indeed! And tasty!"

Olliv, hearing the ruckus, uttered down to the snail, "they are playing together, together. This is a good sign, sign." He turned and shouted back towards the students, "since you're finished eating, hold tight, tight!" Snapping the bridle with a loud crack, he shouted, "show 'em what you've got, ol' girl! Hyaa! Hyaa!"

The snail picked up speed, sailing like a ship on a gust of wind. In the back, bowls, spoons, and napkins went flying. Opis, light as a feather, nearly flew out of the back of the tent before Bear pulled her back into her seat. The nine Seekers held on to each other as the snail sped along, leaving a trail of gooey slime in its wake.

16 WATTLES

The farther up the trail the snail traveled, the more mountainous the terrain became. The Seekers rolled back the tent flaps to take in the scenery. They passed through a long, covered bridge with a sign nearby reading *Callowhorn Combat Fields*. Once on the other side, they were greeted to a bright patchwork of green, yellow, and orange grasslands, the area surrounded on all sides by heavily forested mountains.

Perl leaned out for a better look. Several Seeker training sessions were already underway in a few of the fields. One team was attempting to lasso a centipede nearly forty feet long. Another class was scaling up a gigantic pyramid of mushrooms. Farther away, geysers of neon-yellow liquid shot into the sky, as Seekers tried desperately to balance on top of the spouts.

Bear leaned out beside Perl, his chubby tardigrade face beaming at her.

"Pretty cool, huh?"

"This is amazing! I can't wait to get started," Perl was giddy with excitement.

Olliv halted the snail alongside a blue grassy patch. "Brrreak, *Gastropoda!* Break, break!" Everyone hit the floor as the snail came to an abrupt stop, letting out a bubbly belch for good measure.

The nine sticky, goo-covered Seekers exited their ride, where they were met by a burly fellow, his voice like a clap of thunder.

"Well, well, well! What a mess Ever has brought before me today! Ha!" A great muscular Light Protector with the head of a bison stomped toward them, his heavy armor clanging as he lumbered through the muddy grass. "Ah, I see you've partaken in some conviviality! Excellent!" As he spoke, red-billed oxpecker birds flew in and out of his scraggly, matted beard.

Olliv tipped his stovepipe hat. "Seekers, salute your Callowhorn Combat Guide, Master Kamani, Kamani."

The nine stumbled into a makeshift line. Some bowing, others saluting. Bear clapped.

"Ha! Good! But let us have a look here!" Kamani trudged up to Javan first, placing a heavy hoof on his head, rumpling his hair, "electrolocation! A fine platypus, indeed!"

Brushing by Nan's wings, Kamani bellowed, "antifreeze in your blood! Good! You will come in very handy!"

An oxpecker fluttered out of Kamani's beard and pecked at Tar's monkey ears. "Ha! Night-vision! Outstanding!"

Perl was holding her ears. *"Why is he so loud?"* She winced. Kamani was shouting every word.

Flax, as usual, had his hand up.

"Yes, you! Solar-powered salamander!"

"Will I get a weapon this cycle? Something fierce, like a crossbow?" Flax asked enthusiastically.

"Perhaps, we shall see!" Kamani moved down the line.

"Ooo, a mimic!" Kamani said to Lyre.

"Ooo, a mimic!" Lyre repeated back to him in his booming voice.

"Haha! Marvelous!"

Kamani bowed to Corvax. "The tough, resourceful crow! Always thinking!" Corvax returned the bow.

Continuing his assessment, Kamani paused at the translucent girl with tentacle hair. "What a surprise, Opis the ancient!" he said, tongue-in-cheek.

Opis flipped a lock of hair out of her face. "Nice to see you too…again."

Kamani went in for a hug. "Water Bear, adaptable one! You're back so soon?!"

"I know! But the oceans are a mess these days, even for me!" Bear yelled back, trying to be as loud as his Combat Guide. The two were old friends.

Kamani placed his hooves on hips and stared down at Perl. "Ah, bioluminescent mortal! I heard you were coming! Welcome!"

Overwhelmed from the loud bison, Perl stumbled, tripping over one of Bear's feet and landing on her butt.

"Apologies!" Kamani held out his hoof. As Perl grabbed it, one of his birds tried to nest in her hair. Kamani pulled Perl to her feet, snatching the tiny bird and placing it back into his beard. "Ha! This is going to be a most miraculous team! Let us begin!"

The massive bison warrior began stomping the ground, churning up dust with his thundering hooves. The air grew thick around them, and within minutes, Perl and the others found themselves lost in a brown haze. Kamani continued pounding the ground, laughing all the while. Perl and the others covered their mouths.

"I can't see a thing!" Flax shouted.

"Is this some kind of joke?" choked Lyre, flapping her wings to try to blow the dust away.

Everyone was coughing and trying to catch their breath. Kamani stopped; a dense cloud of soot hung in the air like a dirty blanket.

"Ha! Hard to see now, isn't it?!" Kamani yelled out to the group; he sounded far away. "Tricky to navigate, yes?!"

Perl took a few steps, unsure of where she was going, and ran smack into Bear.

"Is this part of our training?" she asked.

Bear shrugged, spitting out soot. "I guess so, how's that *sand*-wich tasting?"

Like a veil lifting, the smoke began to dissipate. Silhouettes slowly materialized.

"One, twothree…fourfivesix…seven…eight." Perl counted off her fellow Seekers. They looked around as the last of the dust faded.

The patchwork fields had disappeared; now they were standing in front of a small pond. On its banks, yellow wattle plants grew in bunches between the trees, circling the water like a golden halo. Across the water was a log cabin. A young boy sat along the pond's edge, silently casting out his fishing line and reeling it back in, over and over. Oddly, the boy seemed to pay no attention to the group.

"Can he see us?" Perl asked.

"Although we are on Earth, he cannot! We are in the Half-Light Realm, the plane where Earth and the Light Realm intersect!"

Perl ran her hand along the bark of a nearby tree; it felt like any on Mont Michel.

Kamani climbed up onto an enormous boulder. "It is here that Seekers, Seers and Awakeners work to maintain the balance of nature, but even more importantly, we come here to waken the human race to the wonders they have been given!"

"What's today's wonder, Master K?" Bear asked.

"Symbiotic relationships!" Kamani barked, "some are a win-win, like my oxpecker birds! They keep me tick-free and chirp to alarm me of danger! I in turn provide them shelter, protection, and a warm home to raise their young! Nature binds many species! For better or worse, it keeps the balance!"

Perl swung her backpack around, pulling out her journal. She started to write "*symbiotic relationships,*" when a thick cloud of mist rolled in low over the lagoon, casting a dark shadow across the pages; a cool breeze picked up. Kamani jumped down from the rock. The cloud sank lower, hovering just a few feet above the pond's glassy surface.

"Corvax!" The crow-boy perked up upon hearing his name. "What do you see, Seeker?" Kamani shouted over to the boy.

Corvax closed an eye, his vision was stronger with one. "Wattle plants." He scanned the terrain. "Autumn winds blow the treetops." He looked at the pond. "I see *Anguilliforms.*"

Perl mouthed to Bear, "*Anguilliforms?*"

"Eels," he replied.

Kamani pointed to the mist. "Yes…what else?"

Corvax squinted. Inside the mist he saw thousands of tiny flying insect-like predators. His eye widened. "Bacillus Devourers, lots of them. They'll kill the wattle plants unless we do something about it."

"Good! Now form a plan!" Kamani moved back along the tree line, giving Corvax and the others room to work.

Corvax turned to his new Seeker family. "What else do we know about wattle plants?"

Opis was about to enlighten the group, but Nan spoke up first, "the wattle plant is home to a grub that tastes like candy to *Anguilliformes*. In the fall, the petals from the wattle flower drop off and land on the water's surface. Seeing this, the eel then come up to feed on the grubs."

Tars swung on a nearby branch. "Making it the ideal time for the boy to fish for eel!"

"Okay, so the Devourers are trying to choke off the human's food supply. We need to destroy these things." Corvax drew a quick sketch on the ground with a stick. "First, let's corral them into a tighter swarm. Nan and Lyre, can you do that?" The two girls nodded.

"Then a nice shock from your lovely hair," Corvax pointed at Opis, "should be enough to take care of them."

"What about the eels?" Bear asked, "won't they be hiding?"

Corvax waved his stick. "You, Javan, Tars and Perl will hit the water. Swim down to the bottom, stir up the eels. Let them know the grubs are waiting on the surface. It will be dark so use Tars' night vision and Perl's luminescence to find them. Okay, let's move!"

Bear reached over, putting a handful of flowers into his pocket. Nan and Lyre took to the air, fanning the mist, forcing the Devourers together into a buzzing dark horde.

"Okay, now!" Nan yelled down to Opis.

Opis waded out into the water up to her shoulders. She stretched her tentacles up, grazing the bottom of the gloomy dark cloud. Opis squeezed her fists tightly; electric bolts shot up through her hair. The *Bacillus Devourers* screeched with each shock Opis deployed. Some dropped dead into the water, others scattered.

Flax yelled, "it's working!"

"Now, the four of you! Swim down! Find the eels!" Corvax shouted orders.

Tars held Perl's hand, "I'll lead. You light it up."

"I'm not sure I can. It just kind of happens. I can't control my bioluminescence."

Bear held her other hand. "Brush the pony."

"What? How is that going to help?" Perl asked.

Bear held up four arms, pretending to brush up and down. "Quiet your mind. I saw you glowing as you brushed your horse earlier today."

Perl closed her eyes and thought of the whale's song, the night in the tub back home. Her arms prickled.

"You're doing it!" Bear cheered.

She opened her eyes to see her spots illuminated. "I didn't know I could do that."

Tars tugged at her. "Great! Let's go!"

Perl continued to hum in her head as the four of them swam down in search of eels. *"Hmm, hmm, hmm, every day I take a breath and hold it tight, hmm, hmm, hoping you see me, but you float on by..."*

The murky water would have been impossible to see through had it not been for Tars and Perl. Tars pointed at a bunch of tall reeds of dark green seaweed, swaying back and forth. "Eels! There!"

To her surprise, Perl heard Tars' voice in her head, even though he hadn't opened his mouth.

Bear pulled the wattle flowers from his pocket. "Grub time!" He released the petals, watching them drift up to the surface.

"I heard him, too," Perl thought. Somehow, they were communicating telepathically to her!

"There's something else down here." Javan's sixth sense was kicking in; his nose began to twitch. "Something big." His panic made Perl's bioluminescence glow brighter.

A cold-blooded and pitiless creature slithered out of the muddy bottom. Its head was a giant water moccasin, four feet in diameter; its body, a tangled mass of serpents. It floated up out of the gloom, a phantom in the shadows. It came at the Seekers, a ghost in the water.

"Look out!" Javan shouted in his head, but it was too late.

Within seconds, Bear's neck was wrapped in snakes, his limbs bound. The serpents squeezed tightly, immobilizing the large boy. Bear pulled, trying to break free, but the creature was powerful. With one subdued, the goblin searched for the girl.

Up above, with the Devourers scattered, the eels surfaced and began feeding on the tasty flower grubs. The Seekers on the shore celebrated.

"We did it!"

"Yes!"

"Nice plan, Corvax!"

Kamani pointed to the boy on the shore. "He's caught one!"

The boy reeled in his fishing line, an eel dangling from the hook. "Dad! Dad! Come quick!" The boy's father came running.

"What is it?" He looked at his son's hook. "Wow! We're gonna eat like kings tonight!"

The boy beamed with pride. He and his dad noticed that the eels were eating the wattle's petals.

"It's probably a good idea if we plant more of those yellow flowers for next year," the boy said.

"Good idea," the father replied, "but right now, let's get inside. Look at that sky. Storm's coming."

The boy's father gathered up the fishing gear, and he and his son headed back towards the cabin, blissfully unaware of the assistance of the Seekers.

"Where are they?" Nan called out from the shore, resting her delicate wings.

"They should have come up right after the eels!" Lyre swooped over the water for a look. "All I see is a faint glow near the bottom, but it's too murky to see."

Bubbles breached the water's surface. Corvax was about to jump into the lake, when Kamani blocked him with his arm. "Hold!"

"But something's not right!" he tried to push past Kamani, but the husky bison held him firmly.

"Hold!"

Corvax stepped back, frustrated. He peered into the water, trying to see something, anything.

Below the surface, the water was thick with mud; Tars' pupils were fully dilated. "It's too hard to see. Perl, can you glow any brighter?"

Perl couldn't find Tars, but she heard him. Recalling Papa Ximu's words; *bioluminescence can act as a warning when danger is near.* Perl illuminated as brightly as she could. A ghastly form appeared just feet away from her, its fangs bared. Perl saw Bear floating helplessly, slimy black snakes lassoed around him. Bear stared at her, a look of pure fear in his eyes. Perl put her hands over her mouth, holding in a scream. Her whole body went full supernova, glowing with an intensity she'd never seen or felt before. Now it was the goblin's turn to be afraid. It hissed and flinched, shrinking away from Perl's radiance.

Bear, seeing an opportunity, grabbed any snake he could get a hold of and pulled with what little strength he had left.

With the help of Perl's beaming light, Javan spotted Bear. A snake was curled around the roly-poly's neck; he was starting to turn blue. Bear had managed to tear a few of the snakes off the serpent, revealing its white belly.

Without hesitation Javan took aim and fired his weapon. A venomous spur shot from his hip, whizzing through the murkiness like a torpedo, striking its mark. The monster grabbed its midsection, letting out a muffled cry. The snakes around Bear's neck loosened as they clawed at the embedded spur, trying to pull it out. It writhed in pain as thick, black slime bubbled from its abdomen.

"Swim!" Tars snatched Perl's hand and Javan grabbed hold of Bear as the four frantically paddled to the surface.

Above ground, the others saw a light emerging from the dark pond.

"There! Across the pond!" Lyre pointed to the foursome climbing out onto the grassy bank.

"What was that thing, Javan?" Perl dropped to the ground. "Was…was that part of our training?"

"I don't know…and no, that's not supposed to be there."

"What did you shoot at it?"

"Poison darts," he said, tapping his hips, "just one of the many advantages of being a platypus."

She watched as the water beaded up and rolled off of him. "And you're hardly wet."

Javan opened his fingers, revealing webbing. "Semiaquatic, remember?" He leaned back onto a pile of rocks to catch his breath. They smiled at each other as Kamani and the rest of the Seekers ran over.

Immediately, the bison's massive head was right in Perl's face. "What did you see?"

Perl had covered her ears, but realized Kamani wasn't yelling; he was quiet, his tone serious. She looked over at Bear; he was rubbing his neck, now streaked with dark purple bruises.

"Something evil," Perl replied, "it had snakes for arms."

Bear swallowed, his voice thin and raspy, "never seen anything like that in Seeker combat training. It came straight out of the bottom of the lake."

"Malblud," Corvax uttered, getting the other's attention, "it's sending its minions after her, isn't it, Kamani?" He gestured to Perl.

The large bison straightened. "The girl is not to blame." He turned his back to the group, looking out over the gloomy pond. Kamani knew he had to get word of this strange occurrence to Uriel right away. "Circle up! Around me! Time to go!"

With a series of resounding ground pounds, the group was back at Callowhorn, standing in a circle at the very same spot as before, only now there was a tree in the center that wasn't there when they had left. Kamani pulled something off one of the branches.

"The black walnut!" Perl muffled her ears again as the Battle Guide's voice rose, "secretes a poison from its roots! Killing the trees that try to grow around it!" As he spoke, the healthy blue grass they stood on dried up, turning a lifeless brown under their feet. "The damage is done, and the walnut lives on, unharmed, but alone!" He raised an eyebrow at Corvax.

Opis elbowed the crow-boy, but she didn't need to; Corvax understood Kamani's message was directed at him.

As Olliv and his snail slowly pulled up, the group waited in silence, too drained for conversation. They boarded without word, slipping into the seats around the table. A large bowl of blueberries sat in the middle.

"Alas, our time is done, until the next battle!" Kamani shouted up to them. He then climbed halfway up the ladder, where he whispered something to Olliv.

The grasshopper-man nodded back. "I will be sure she gets the message, message."

It was a long, quiet ride back as the snail headed home, rocking gently as it moved along the trail. Their eyes grew heavy as the sun dipped lazily below the purple horizon. Unknowingly, Perl's head drifted over onto Javan's shoulder. Within minutes, she was fast asleep.

She dreamt of the root cellar and the monks' smiling faces. She saw Ximu in the garden chasing Hadza as they whistled a tune together at the beehives. Ximu was collecting the day's honey when guards from the Palace took him. Ximu winced as an angry guard tied his spidery arms behind his back.

"No...no," Perl mumbled.

She saw Ivry, pale and thin, and Mik by her side, sobbing. Count Graves and Countess Sarr looked on from the twin's bedroom doorway. The Count turned into a giant Whisper Wisp. "He will suffer for this!" He screeched out. Sarr burst into tears, her eyes growing larger and larger and larger until they popped like bubbles.

Perl twisted, talking in her sleep, "No! It's Malblud."

The guards threw Ximu into a dungeon; rats scurried around him. The ocean around Mont Michel went pitch black; whales floated up, pale and bloated. The oil began oozing into Ximu's cell, filling the chamber. He scratched and crawled, trying to climb up the walls, his spider legs slipping over and over again.

"Papa!" Perl was screaming in her sleep.

Javan, who had also dozed off, sprang up and nudged her. "Hey, wake up."

"What's going on?" Opis sat up, rubbing her eyes.

Javan noticed her arms were glowing. He shook her. "Perl!"

Startled, Perl woke with a jolt. "They took Papa! He wouldn't hurt a fly." She had tears in her eyes.

"It's okay," Bear held Perl's hand, "it was just a dream."

"No! I was there! It wasn't a dream!"

Javan placed his hand on top of hers. "I'm sure he's fine. Don't worry," he assured her.

"Keep it down, would ya? Some of us are trying to sleep." Tars, his head on the table, rolled over to the other side. A long strand of slobber went with him.

"I have to go back. Can't this snail go any faster?" Perl stood up, yelling up towards Olliv.

Javan pulled her back down. "Whoa! No one's going anywhere. We'll help you figure this out."

"Papa needs my help now! You don't get it!"

Javan put a hand on her shoulder. "Perl, I promise you. We will do whatever you need."

Bear bobbed his head in agreement, grinning. "We will."

Javan turned Perl towards him. "You aren't alone, Perl. We're a family

117

now."

"Yeah, Perl," Bear chimed in, "how about a few blueberries, they always make me feel better?" As the roly-poly boy grabbed the bowl, sliding it in front of Perl, a large leopard moth fluttered into the tent.

Perl looked at the gorgeous moth; it was ivory with black spots. "*Hypercompe Scribonia.*"

Bear leaned in. "Look, there's a little bird design on one wing, and it looks like a bee on the other."

Perl slowly moved closer to the moth, holding her breath, trying not to startle it. "It makes me think of Hadza."

Javan whispered, "who?"

"Our honey guide bird from back home."

"It came right to you," Javan said.

"It must be from Uriel. She said I'd know her messenger when I saw it."

The moth fluttered its wings faster, releasing puffs of white, crystalline powder. As the tiny particles danced in the air, a message slowly materialized. Perl, Bear, Javan, and Opis stared on in amazement, while the others slept. Javan read the words aloud.

My Precious Perl,
I saw your first steps. Heard your first song. You are where you need to be. Sometimes we must go adventuring to learn why home is home. Pour your heart onto the pages.
Love, Uriel

As soon as Javan uttered Uriel's name, the particles dissipated, the message and the moth vanishing before their eyes.

He turned to Perl. "Ya' see? Uriel is taking care of things. You just got here, and there's still so much more to learn. When the time is right, we will face any troubles back home. Promise."

Bear squeezed the both of them with a big four-armed hug. "Together."

Opis spoke up, "and Perl, don't confuse what you see in dreams with what's real. The Dark Realm can send its parasites anywhere, including into your dreams."

"I know what's real, and I know what I saw," Perl mumbled, "and it wasn't my imagination." Perl turned to Bear and Javan. "I'm fine. Thanks. Go back to sleep."

"Okay," Bear said, "but you should still try those blueberries."

The three closed their eyes, Bear snoring almost immediately. Perl reached into her backpack and took out her journal. She pulled her knees to her chest, balancing the book there.

"Okay, Uriel," she thought to herself, *"I'll give this a chance."*

She started writing as the giant snail chugged along, a dark silhouette against the blood orange sky.

Callowhorn Seekers

Corvax
*always has a plan
~not sure if he likes me?

Nan
sweet but tough

Lyre
amazing mimic

Flax
solar power

Javan
elecrolocation
has darts and dimples

Tars
night vision

Opis
*nice roomate~
very smart and
I like her tentacle hair!

Bear
gooey inside and out!

(And me!)
This is my new family of nine.
We're learning to work together.
Still can't believe I'm here.
ⓟ

17 A MONT OF LIES

After the ball, the story of the Graves twins falling ill had leaked. No one knew for sure how, but Countess Sarr became so irate, she fired the entire penthouse staff. Theories began to surface about a disease, or a mysterious island virus. Others believed Prince Névenoé did something to them the night of the party. When news got out that Ivry was by far the sicker of the two, many started to accuse Mik, saying she was trying to do her sister in so she could reign as the one and only redhead in all the world.

"This has to stop!" Count Graves threw his drink at the projection on his bedroom wall. The screen froze on the headline, *"Graves Twins Abducted by Aliens?"*

"Snive, get a press conference ready!" Graves barked into his headset, get me more toxicologists! Get me a veal steak! And get all of this red crap out of my sight!" He kicked a plush heart across the room, the words *'Our hearts are with U!'* stitched onto it.

"Yes, my liege, right away."

The Redhots, as Mik and Ivry's mega fanbase called themselves, started sending gifts to the Palace as soon as word got out that the twins were sick. Every gift sent came in pairs; red teddy bears, red roses, red candy, red robes and slippers, even small animals like baby chicks and hamsters were sent to the Palace, the poor creatures dyed red. It was a flood of gifts and messages, so much that it had to be hauled over to Trash Island daily. Locals joked, many of them referring to it as "Redhot Island."

Redhots had also started making pilgrimages to Mont Michel. By the thousands they came, their hair dyed red, wearing t-shirts with messages reading, *"Save the Twins!"* and *"Mik and Ivry, Long Live Our Red Princesses!"* Scores of fans drifted near the shores in boats right alongside the environmental protesters, who had their own signs for the Palace: *"Clean the Oceans!"*, *"Save the Planet!"*, *'The Earth is Not Your Garbage Dump!'* Dozens of roaming drones buzzed about the island capturing the ongoing fights between the groups, and every night the news would report the latest developments, complete with dazzling graphics and dynamic musical scores. It was a circus, and the Palace was the Big Top.

Watching her seahorses swim about in their massive new tank was one of the only things that made Ivry forget about the gnawing pain in her stomach. She lightly tapped on the glass. "Oh, Star and Moon, when will I get better?"

The girls had named their sea pets as the note that was left with them had requested. Ivry pressed her palm against the glass. Moon swam over to her.

"Oh, I wish I could shrink down to your size and swim with you. I would get a tiny saddle and ride with you off into the sunset," Ivry mused.

Mik looked over at Governess Ruby, whispering, "I think the new meds are messing with her mind." Both kept a close bedside vigil over Ivry.

It was not lost on Ruby that Mik was not as ill as her sister. Their entire life, the twins had shared everything. If one of them came down with a cold, within days, the other would catch it. When pressed, Mik did come clean to her nanny, telling her about drinking the night of the ball and throwing up her dinner. Ruby promised not to tell Mik's parents about the drinking. In exchange, Mik would run her own baths, and turn down her own bed for the rest of the year. Mik agreed, although not without some complaining. Ruby had been the twins' nanny since they were babies. She cared for them like they were her own daughters, something Countess Sarr was ill-equipped to do.

Mik wasn't the only Graves family member good at deception; her father was a master liar. When it came to spinning a tale, The Count was relentless, repeating a lie longer and louder than any dictator on Earth. Graves wore down entire nations with his speeches, going on and on until the whole world had no choice but to give in and agree to his usually preposterous demands.

The Graves press conference took place on the glass bottom balcony of the Palace.

"Here me, my daughters' loyal Redhots!" The world was all ears as The Count bellowed, "my sweet, sweet darling daughters are fine. Fantastic! Gloriously healthy!"

Hordes of reporters packed in tightly. Drones buzzed like flies, clicking off pic after pic.

A woman in a triple-decker red wig yelled over the crowd, "the twins haven't shared anything in *forever!*"

"Yes, it's been three whole hours," a man clutching a photo of the twins added. "What are they doing now?"

With a mild wave of his hands, Count Graves settled the crowd. "The ball was an unbelievable achievement! A great success! The hugest event of their young lives!" He nonchalantly pushed a button at his temple, whispering, "Snive, get the girls prepped for a photo shoot."

Snive heard the order and instantly sprinted up the stairs.

Countess Sarr joined her husband on stage. She took his arm and gently nudged him out of the spotlight. She tapped on the gold floating microphone with her four-inch long platinum fingernail. "Hello, World! I can assure you that my babies have never been better. They are safe and resting comfortably, just as my loving husband says...isn't that right, darling?"

"Absolutely." The Count pushed Sarr to the side to regain his position, front and center. "And we'd like to reiterate that there is no need for gifts. Please stop sending them. Mik and Ivry are very thankful for all of your love and support. But they are so unnecessary." A smattering of boos was heard.

A small group of protestors, the ones who usually congregated in their boats around Mont Michel, had pushed their way into the press circle. Gretar, the teenage activist who'd been shot the night of the ball, shouted over Graves, "it's the water quality! It's poisoning the fish! Even your own daughters are not immune to the danger! A danger that you've allowed to happen!"

The Count signaled again to Snive, "how did these protesters get up here? I thought these malcontents had been roped off. Remove them, but do it discreetly. I don't want some scene playing out on the nightly news."

A reporter for the New Globe spoke up, "what is the latest water safety reading? Is it dangerous?"

Count Graves gripped the podium with both hands. "It's clean! Cleaner than last month, actually! The water is safe! Very, very safe! The fish are plentiful, and delicious as ever!" He ran a hand through his hair, trying to maintain his composure, then pointed in the vicinity of Gretar. "That young man's claims are full of falsities and stupid nonsensical myths!"

Several more news reporters shouted questions. "What about the oil?", "When will the latest spill be contained?", "Will you have the water tested?"

Graves ignored them all. "All questions will be answered! As head of the Oceanic Council and of the Worldwide Waterways Committee, I of course, will be the first to know anything, and will happily pass any information on to you. Now if you'll excuse us, my beautiful wife and I have lunch plans with our darling twins."

Sarr gripped The Count's arm, batting her severely dilated eyes. "Have a swimmingly superb day, one and all!"

As Gretar and a few of the other activists were being roughly escorted away from the balcony by Snive and his guards, the commotion had caught the attention of some reporters.

"The oceans are toxic! The quality readings are false! Graves lies!" Gretar shouted.

"What proof do you have?" A reporter in a short plastic skirt held her hand up to his face, a tiny microphone imbedded in her wrist.

Gretar leaned in. "Scientists from around the globe have done their own tests on the water, and they've all agreed. The WWC is covering up the truth, all in an attempt to make the rich richer!"

Another protester added, "overfishing is endangering more species than ever before! Driving many to extinction! It has to stop!"

"Not to mention their sick, elitist games. Hunting helpless sea life for sport! Is this what humanity has come to?!" Gretar shouted.

"What's happening to our water?", "What's Graves hiding?", "We demand to know the truth!" The crowd grew louder, less concerned with the twins, and more interested in what the protesters had to say.

"Okay, okay, move it. Show's over." Snive and his huge palace guards shoved Gretar and the other protesters down the steps, far less discreetly than Graves had hoped.

Several drones were capturing the protesters' claims when the excitement was quickly overshadowed as a fifty-foot tall hologram of the Graves family appeared above the crowd. The twins were in bed together with their red hair done up in messy buns, wearing nightgowns with gold starfish and lace trim. An enormous crystal bowl of shrimp cocktail sat in front them. Flanking the two girls were their parents, giant fake smiles plastered on their faces. The Count was propping Ivry's weak body up to a sitting position with one arm, while toasting with a piece of shrimp with the other. The picture was captioned, *To all of our devoted Redhots out there! We treasure you more than all the fish in the sea! Kisses, Mik & Ivry.*

At the bottom of the island, The Brothers of the Quill had called an emergency meeting of their own, gathering in the underground chapel. Illuminating the room were hundreds of handmade candles, shaped into a variety of animals. The day after Perl had left for Venusto, Victr collected all of her works of art and hung them up in the chapel, as well as in the kitchen, the dining room and down the hallways of the root cellar. The monks missed Perl's adventurous stories and her sweet smiling face. Seeing her artwork made them feel better and gave them hope.

Brother Basil stood at the front of the chapel behind an old wooden pulpit carved from a peach tree. "Yes, it is true. They have arrested Ximu."

Cries of disbelief filled room. "But why?", "They have no right!", "This is ludicrous!"

Basil went on, "a woman saw the palace guards handcuff him while he was in the garden."

"We must go get him!"

To quiet the room, Basil rang a set of chimes, clearing his throat, "Ximu was taken to the dungeon on Trash Island. The guards told her the tuna we served to the twins was tainted. They are accusing Ximu of attempting to poison the girls."

"Impossible!", "A false accusation if ever there was one!", "The tuna was not even from our nets!" The monks shouted.

Brother Jonathan added, "this is all because we broke the chant!"

Basil rang the chimes again. "Brothers, brothers." He stepped out from behind the pulpit. "Now listen. First, we will do our best to free Brother Ximu. Of course, we know he is innocent, and second..." he hesitated, crossing his arms, "...our chants needed to be broken...to fulfill The Prophecy."

The room fell silent, the only sound the soft *"taptiptap"* of wax dripping onto the stone floor. Basil continued. "Brother Ximu and I had a conversation. He confided in me at the time that he had spoken with Uriel when she visited us, and they agreed that what he needed to do was...necessary."

A brother asked, "necessary? Opening ourselves up— nay, the world, to darkness? How could that be necessary?" More muttering echoed around the chapel.

"Brothers, Ximu and I, and Victr as well, have been studying and reexamining the Globus Natura. They are most definitely off their normal rotations, specifically the Water Orb. It is crucial that we pull together and pray for the oceans. Uriel told us in no uncertain terms that we are to continue as we always have. We will chant, we will feed those who are hungry, and we will resume our responsibilities as Brothers of the Quill. That is all for now. Go in peace to serve Ever."

At that, the room erupted into a buzz of conversation, some asking questions, others arguing, while many began praying loudly, asking for Ever's favor in this time of crisis.

Moments earlier, Regor had come to the root cellar looking for Perl, when he heard the monks' raised voices. He slipped into the chapel and found an open pew in the back, overhearing some of the monks' discussion. He had his cat Pie-Pie tucked under his arm.

"Um, excuse me, brothers, heh-heh...but does anyone know where Perl has run off to? She hasn't shown up for her deliveries," his voice muffled under the loud chatter.

The monks ignored the awkward, gangly man. Regor tapped the shoulder of the monk seated in front of him, but the monk, deep in prayer, didn't turn around. Regor whispered, "excuse me, Brother Johnathan, do you know where Perl is?"

Brother Jonathan leaned over and whispered into the ear of the brother seated next to him, who in turn whispered to the next monk, all the way down the pew.

Regor kept talking to no one in particular, "she was telling me one of her silly stories about being magical and leaving the island, but everyone knows that's just Perl being Perl, right?" he giggled, "That girl's got some imagination. I didn't really think too much about it at the time, heh-heh."

Brother Kirkwood slid into the pew beside Regor, scooting him down the bench.

"Brother, did she really leave the island? Is she okay?" Regor asked the monk.

Kirkwood put his arm around Regor's shoulder. "Perl is fine. She is very special, as you know. Not only to us, but to the world. Come with me, Regor," Kirkwood gestured at Pie-Pie, "and bring your companion. I know you and Perl are close. I will explain everything, but not a word of this to anyone."

Regor followed Kirkwood out of the chapel and down to the kitchen, where they shared Perl's journey over a steaming hot mug of ginger root tea with cinnamon.

While the monks were having their debate in the chapel, Brother Victr had quietly snuck away to Mont Michel's main dock, and was now pushing off in a small rowboat, water up to his knees. Not a star shone in the pitch-black sky as he rowed across to Trash Island. He navigated the boat through the polluted waters, the harsh smell of chemicals burning his nose the closer he got to the aptly named isle. Twenty minutes later, Victr docked among the piles of litter. Gathering up his robe, he scrambled over mounds of garbage, most of it discarded gifts for the twins. Victr found the path that led to the dungeon. He approached the guard on duty outside the old cinder block building.

"Who goes there?" The guard held up a fiber optic torch, searching the darkness.

"Good evening, fine sire," Victr said as politely as he could.

"What are you doing here, monk?" The large armed man barked, dropping his free hand down to his pistol.

"I am requesting a short chat with someone you are currently holding...my brother, Ximu. I only ask but a brief chat, no one need know. Here my friend, surely you are thirsty?" Victr reached in his satchel feeling around, before pulling out a small flask of ale. He waved it at the guard.

The husky man grunted, yanking the flask out of Victr's hand, "eh, maybe. What else ya' got, old man?"

Victr searched the bag. "Let's see...ah, here! Some delicious dried bacon sticks from the finest hogs. Count Graves choice cuts, if I'm not mistaken?"

The guard tried to grab the processed snacks, but Victr pulled them away quickly. "Just five minutes is all I require?"

Grabbing the sticks of bacon like a hungry bear, he stepped aside from the dungeon door. "You've got five minutes, not a second more," he growled, unlocking the main door and handing Victr his torch. "Be quick about it."

Holding the torch high, Victr pushed open the heavy stone door leading to the jail cells. The stench was unbearable. Holding his robe over his nose, he called out, "Ximu?" Victr peeked into a small barred window on one of the doors, seeing a pile of human bones. He heard chains rattle farther down the corridor, and hurried towards the sound.

"Brother, it's me, Victr." The monk pressed his face against the dirty bars of the window; a shadowy figure was huddled in the corner. "Ximu, is that you?"

A weak, brittle voice answered, "yes. I'm here."

"Oh Ximu, I should be the one in this cell, not you. I allowed the fish to be served that day." Victr held up the torch, squinting.

Ximu shuffled as close to the door as he could; one foot was chained to the wall behind him. "You are the only jail keeper of your life, Brother Victr. Even a prisoner is free to choose their own thoughts. Do not blame yourself. It was the Dark One's doing. All is how it should be." Ximu let out a raspy barking cough, trying to clear his throat.

Victr clutched the bars. "This is not how it should be!" He saw rats' gleaming yellow eyes in the corners of the cell.

"Go with peace, Brother Victr. Try not to worry. Stay in a loving mindset. No person can take that gift from you or any of us."

Victr pulled sliced apples from his bag, and a loaf of dried bread. "Here, it's not much, but it's sustenance." He shoved the food through the rusty bars.

"Thank you." From the shadows, Ximu's dirty, bloody hand reached out. He took the food as another coughing fit took him. Victr heard some of the apples hit the floor as the rats scurried to steal a snack.

"I will get you out of here, somehow. Stay strong in Ever." Victr held the torch up, seeing Ximu's sickly, pale face. A sadness and worry like none he'd ever felt overtook him. The monks' eyes met. "Goodbye, Brother."

Much like the multitude of lies circulating around Mont Michel, the darkness in the water was also spreading. Along the coastline, the coral reef was dying, its bright pinks, yellows, and reds all draining to a bleak, ashy gray.

Next to Mont Michel, sat a smaller island that housed the large hydroelectric plant. It was mainly uninhabited, but for the dozen or so locals in charge of overseeing the plant's daily operations. Looming from high atop one of the water towers, a figure crouched in the shadows, its form unrecognizable. From a distance, it appeared as a giant gargoyle, pressed against the skeletal frame of the tower. The creature's many pus-filled cysts oozed black liquid down its sides, shining like oil against the full moon.

"...alll will sssufferrr...shheee willl diiee...an eye for an eye..."

Whisper Wisps circled in the air around the abomination's head like flies, ringing their tiny clawed hands and hissing. The gruesome beast reached down, plucking a handful of lampreys off its cold, clammy flesh. It

126

held the funnel-like eels out in front of it, watching as their mouthfuls of sharp teeth opened and closed, hungry for another bite. It squeezed them in its powerful claw as the lampreys squealed and squirmed.

"...go...ssshe escaped once...not again...sssearch the Half Light Realm...fiiind me the girl..."

The nightmarish creature tossed the lamprey into the sea below. A mass of clouds rolled in, drawing a dark curtain over the face of the moon.

18 QUILLS AND QUANTAA

Dawn's chorus of mourning doves filled the air; Venusto's early wake up call. Perl sprang out of bed, the birds' song a mental boost, like Papa Ximu after his first cup of tea.

"Good morning, fellow Water Seekers!"

She felt more refreshed than she had in weeks. Bear was already up, studying the map, his round face pressed close to the wall. Opis sat on her bed, braiding her tentacles. Bear spun around, sniffing the air like a bloodhound.

"You smell that? Breakfast!" He tore out the front door, leaving Perl and Opis staring blankly at one another.

"He never met a meal he didn't like," Opis smiled.

The two followed Bear as the yummy aroma drew the other Seekers out of their Bowerbird nests. The giant snail was parked out front, lazily munching on grass. In the front seat sat Olliv, chipper as always.

"What, no meditation this morning?" Nan asked, climbing the rope ladder into the tent.

"Drills first today, today. You will see Bodhi later this afternoon, afternoon." Olliv informed them, giving a slight whistle.

The two chipmunk servers appeared, dishing up savory mushroom and parsnip tarts with lemon crisps in gooseberry jam. The cute critters handed out large acorn caps filled with sweet clover nectar while the Seekers settled into the tent. The grasshopper-man gave another whistle, and the snail lunged forward, slowly but surely working up to a steady crawl.

A blueish mist hung like a skirt around the rows of trees as the snail moved up the path towards the combat fields. Once they crossed through the bridge and into the valley, they spotted Master Kamani, leaning against one end of a massive fallen sequoia tree. Perl took note; Kamani was big, but this tree absolutely dwarfed him in comparison. The diameter was five times taller than Master K, the length was hard to determine, as the mighty timber seemed to continue far off into the distance.

"Seekers! Today is a glorious day! Ha!" Kamani shouted out to the sleepy group as they finished up the last bits of breakfast.

On the ride, Perl had made two fluffy buns out of her hair which she now pulled down over her ears, hoping they would act as cushions to dampen Kamani's booming voice. Sadly, they had little effect.

"You're in luck! We have new *Erethizon dorsatum*...baby quill pigs! Triplets!" Kamani boasted, as they slowly climbed down from the snail, taking in the full scope of the mammoth tree. "The nocturnal newborns have been up all night playing! Now they need fed and tucked in for a good day's sleep!"

"Quill pigs?" Perl wondered to herself. She wasn't exactly sure what Kamani was talking about.

"Time to begin!" On Kamani's command, a trio of ladybugs the size of small tanks hurried in, each of them pulling a crate of red and purple plums as big as beachballs. "The crates must come back empty, and careful once inside, Seekers! They may be babes, but their quills are as sharp as knitting needles! Ha-Ha!" He rubbed a bandaged spot on his arm. "Luckily, they don't shoot the needles, but they'll detach if the barbed ends get caught in you!"

A thick, heavy door had been carved into the end of the tree. Kamani pulled it open, the hinges creaking loudly, revealing the long, hollowed-out inside. Perl and the others tried to peek down the tunnel; it was mostly dark, but for thin subtle shafts of sunlight crisscrossing through it. The smell, unfortunately, was not so subtle.

"Pee-yoo! That's disgusting!" Bear gagged, covering his nose and mouth. "I just ate...I think I'm gonna be sick."

Once Kamani had opened the door, the ladybugs marched in, pulling the heavy crates behind them as they disappeared into the dark log. Perl and the others listened; loud bumps and squeals echoed out as the sequoia tree began rocking back and forth erratically. The Seekers turned and looked at one another.

"Babies, you said, right?" Nan fluttered her wings nervously. "The whole tree is moving."

"You're not afraid, are you?" Corvax joked.

Kamani laughed. "Fear not! Ha-Ha!"

Bear looked at Perl. "Sure. Fear not. Riiight." He rolled his eyes.

Out from the doorway burst an enormous grey and white barn owl, her large black eyes unblinking as she stared at them. From her neck to the top of her claws, she wore armor made of thick, rugged tree bark. The armor was covered in scratches, and had numerous quills stuck in it.

"Whew! Got 'em into their swings for you, but they're getting cranky." The owl yanked a quill from its wing, wincing. "That stings! Remember, their quills will lie flat so long as they are calm. Good luck." She bowed to Kamani and marched off, pulling more of the porcupine's barbs out of her armor.

"Enter, remember to work together, and empty those crates!" They could hear Kamani's muffled belly laugh as the door closed behind them with a heavy thud.

As their eyes adjusted to the dark quarters, the group took in their surroundings; all the way down the passageway, star-shaped holes had been cut into the log to let light in.

"Tars, since you've got the best vision of any of us, why don't you take the lead?" Corvax suggested.

"Um, sure," the monkey-boy replied, "unless anybody else wants to lead?"

Nobody said a word.

"Okay then." Tars shrugged. He headed down the dark passageway, his eight comrades close behind.

"It's cute, isn't it?" Perl smiled, looking around as the starlight danced along the walls.

Javan replied, "it's like a playroom."

The thumping grew louder as the log rocked back and forth. The team tried to keep their footing on the rough, uneven ground. Nan and Lyre found it easier to just fly.

"This is playing?" Bear joked as he leaned on the wall for balance.

The group moved cautiously down the starlit tunnel until they caught up to the ladybugs, who formed a line along the scratched and scraped-up walls. They silently waited for the Seekers to pass, then fell in behind them, dragging the massive plums.

The tree made a slight bend to their right; gurgling sounds could be heard around the corner.

"Sounds like we're close. Get ready," said Opis, who now led, Tars having slipped quietly to the rear. The nine of them cautiously followed the curve, then suddenly came to a halt.

"Well...now we know where the smell was coming from," Flax coughed.

Nestled inside enormous leafy bouncy seats, suspended in the air by thick vines, hung three porcupines roughly the size of small elephants, their fuzzy feet and spiked tails dragging limply along the ground. The floor underneath the three porcupine babies was a crisscross pattern of claw marks, as well as a fair amount of porcupine droppings. Behind them, the ladybugs released their crates and scurried back down the way they came.

"Cowards!" yelled Bear.

Perl did a happy dance. "Oh, I love them! Look at those sweet brown eyes and pudgy noses. They're adorable!"

Javan raised an eyebrow. "Well, that's one word to describe them." He pulled Perl's ivory sword from her backpack, handing it to her. "You're gonna need this."

"What? No." She pushed the sword away.

Frightened at seeing unfamiliar faces, one porcupette let out a squeal. This got its siblings going, and within seconds, all three were crying out, their thirty thousand razor sharp quills standing on end.

"Um...probably couldn't hurt to just have it at the ready." Perl took the sword from Javan.

"Ooga-booga-booga!" Bear started doing a silly dance, waving all of his arms and legs and bouncing up and down. The porcupines looked at Bear confused, their crying softening.

"Hey, that worked! Keep it up, Bear!" Opis directed as the babies watched the strange tardigrade wiggle and wobble, his arms flailing about. Opis pointed to the pile of plums left by the ladybugs. "Let's get going. Perl, use your sword and slice a few of those in half."

"Gotcha!" Perl said, running over to the crates.

Flax and Corvax had already grabbed a plum and were doing their best to tear it into pieces; purple juice squirted and dripped everywhere.

Perl rolled one of the boulder-size plums onto the ground. She gave a small jump in the air for leverage, bringing Fortis down hard and fast, cutting neatly through the entire fruit.

Nan and Lyre each picked up a piece of plum and flew up to the babies, ducking and dodging as the porcupettes shook their prickly coat of quills and squealed, excited by the prospect of breakfast.

"Open wide!" Nan shoved the gooey fruit into one of the porcupine's mouths, squishing it past its two large front teeth. Noticing their sibling getting fed, the other babies lost interest in Bear and started crying again.

Tars broke off a shaft of wood from the wall and speared one of the giant plums. "Javan, hoist me up!" He scampered up onto the platypus-boy's shoulders. Wobbling, Tars awkwardly held the plum up to the first bouncing porcupine. "Easy, Javan! Move slowly towards him...or is it a her? I can't tell!"

"I'm trying! Move your tail!" Javan swatted Tar's fuzzy tail out of his face, as they teetered back and forth in front of the irritated porcupine.

"Here ya' go, little porky-porky!" Tars held up the plum. The baby porcupine lunged forward, gobbling it up in one bite. "Ha! He ate it!" At that moment, the baby's large tail came whipping up, knocking the two boys to the ground.

"Ugh...watch out for their tails." Javan said, pulling a few spikes out of his fur. He reached down and lifted Tars up.

"Good call," Tars winced, rubbing his cheek as a dark purple bruise began to swell.

Bear continued dancing, and after twenty minutes of bounding around in the hot, stuffy log, he was now drenched in sweat. "Hey...can somebody else distract them...for a while? I'm pooped." He lumbered off to the side, huffing and puffing as he leaned on the wall to catch his breath.

"Got my hands full, sorry, B!" Opis hollered over.

"I'm busy, too!" Perl was doing her best to block the thrashing quills with her sword, keeping them away from Nan and Lyre as they ducked and dodged the razor-sharp needles. Perl swung wildly, but the more the porcupines wiggled, the more the quills whipped around, like thousands of swords.

Corvax yelled, "I have an idea. Flax, toss me one of those pinecones!"

Flax picked up a pinecone the size of a barrel, one of the playthings used to distract the porcupettes, and tossed it to Corvax. The pinecone flying through the air caught the attention of all three babies; they pawed at it, giggling with delight.

"Ouch!" Lyre yelled, grabbing her arm, "look out for the tails!"

"Way ahead of ya' there, Lyre!" Javan shouted over.

"Ah!" A quill caught Corvax in the leg, a spot of blood seeped through his pants.

Perl, darting from side to side, noticed the blood. "You okay, Corvax?"

"I'm good. You just keep that sword held high!"

Corvax and Flax juggled in two more pinecones, continuing the performance. Perl looked over at the crates; one was empty, the other two were still about half full.

Opis picked up a chunk of plum, using the empty crate as a stepping stool. Just as one of the porcupettes let out a cry, in went the berry. The irritable baby swallowed the fruit, belching loudly.

"Yes! That's how it's done," Tars cheered.

The other two babies, however, wouldn't open their mouths. They shook their heads from side to side, flailing their arms and legs about. Nan, hovering in front of one of them, held out a piece of berry, then moved sharply, as one of its paws came swinging around.

"Whoa!" The butterfly-girl squeaked, nearly getting her head clipped by a claw. She reached up, checking her antennae. "Phew…still there."

For some reason, amongst all the chaos, Flax raised his hand. "Hey, weren't we supposed to stay calm, so their quills would lie flat?"

"Right. That is what the owl said," Tars agreed.

The Seekers looked at one another; they were hot, exhausted, and filthy. Bear chuckled, "yeah, this isn't exactly *calm*."

Lyre, being a master mimic, began to replicate the soothing sounds of a mother porcupine.

Bear looked over at Lyre. "Well, we tried dancing, might as well try singing."

Hearing the soft melody, the porcupines started to mellow. After a bit more squirming, they finally settled. Too sleepy to fight the feeding anymore, before long, the crates were empty and their bellies were full. The group continued to hum along with Lyre until all three babies were fast asleep. Nan flew up and tucked a pinecone in the arms of each one. A low shuffling could be heard approaching; the ladybugs had returned for the crates.

"Okay, Corvax whispered, "let's go…quickly and quietly."

The nine Seekers were tiptoeing out when Bear sneezed, "Ah-choo!" The sound echoed through the log. Everyone froze. The babies stirred but thankfully didn't wake.

"Sorry about that," he whispered, "plums always make me sneeze."

Perl took one last look at the three porcupines hanging peacefully in their leafy hammocks.

Back outside in the light of day, they now saw how filthy they were; all of them were soaked in sticky purple juice. Quills and chunks of fruit were stuck in their arms, legs, backs, and rears. As if that wasn't bad enough, some of them had not avoided the manure. The group was stinky and drained; the porcupine babies had proven to be worthy opponents.

"The warriors return! The *Erethizon Dorsatum* triplets are fed, yes?!" Kamani chortled, slapping Bear on the back. He pulled a quill from Tars' tail and laughed. "Bravo! You all look as grubby as the day we met, and your smell! Ripe, indeed! Ha-Ha!"

Tars licked his tail. "Yeah, only we didn't start this food fight. Please tell me we don't have to do that ever again?"

"Babies are hard work! They are innocent! Helpless! Children rise or fall to the level that they are nurtured!"

Perl thought of Papa and her beloved monks; how they had cared for her so lovingly. She felt grateful and hoped they were all safe. Perl wiped the plum juice off of her sword and slid it back into its sheath.

Bear elbowed her, "how about I give you a few lessons with that later?"

"Okay, thanks," Perl smiled back.

"Now we march!" Kamani cracked his hooves together.

The tired group left the massive sequoia and porcupines, following their master down a soft dirt road that sloped downhill. As they descended, clusters of tiny saplings rose up on either side of the road's edge like soldiers. The Seekers trudged along silently behind the burly Light Being, too tired for conversation. The saplings grew taller, bending gracefully toward one another, and before long, they found themselves walking under a glorious canopy of intertwined branches. They passed under the shaded archway, dappled sunlight poking through, the only sound was the cheerful conversations of the birds who had gathered overhead. The path leveled off for a bit then started to rise, as bright golden yellow could be seen at the end of the tunnel of trees. The group was starting to lag as they struggled up the hill.

"Any chance we could rest, Master Kamani?" Bear begged, wiping the sweat from his brow.

"No time to slow now! Come, come!" Kamani shouted as he clomped purposefully up the path.

They gave a collective moan but followed their teacher. As the thick line of trees dwindled, eventually disappearing altogether, the Seekers took in the view; all around them were fields of vibrant sunflowers. The flowers, hundreds of thousands of them, swayed back and forth in unison; a soft melody filled the air.

"They're singing!" Perl delighted as she looked around in wonder. She couldn't understand the words, but it was sweet to the ear, like a choir of angels.

"We may pause here!" Kamani shouted, as they stopped in a clearing, surrounded on all sides by the forest of yellow.

"Thank Ever!" Bear was now leaning on Tars and Flax, the two smaller Seekers barely able to hold up their hefty companion.

"Play," Kamani barked out, "play is important! Necessary!"

Reaching into the ground, Kamani ripped out a thick reed twice as tall as he was. Shaking the soil from its base, he bent and tied it into a giant loop. With a loud grunt, Kamani threw the hoop high into the sky; it disappeared into the clouds.

Flax had his arm up. "Why is play so important?"

Opis answered for her teacher. "Play is vital for physical and emotional development. It aids in healthy brain activity, and fuels creativity when facing new challenges."

"Ha! Opis, the Wise! Spot on as ever!" Kamani gave a nod to Opis, who beamed. Kamani lifted his arms to the sky. "And it's fun! Ha!"

At that moment, bursting from a fluffy cloud, came a giant two-headed winged greyhound. As it passed overhead, they were hit with a great gust of air from its enormous wings.

"Look everybody…Quantaa!" said Bear.

The Seekers were familiar with the Light Realm Battle Creature, except for Perl, who stood frozen, staring up in awe at the magnificent beast. Like a giant turbine, it rippled their clothing, blowing off bits of plum. It circled back and came in for a landing. The lean, muscular creature was magnificent up close; one of its heads was ghostly white with a blue eye, the other, brown-eyed and black as night. It towered over the group, its long slender legs like trees, its body a pattern of black and white spots. The greyhound gracefully folded its feathered wings up over its back and peered down at the group. One of the heads, the black one, held the hoop in its mouth, then dropped it, wagging its tail happily.

"What's a…who's a…Quantaa?" Perl asked, as the dog's huge tail whipped over the singing sunflowers, who bent over in unison, the tail just missing them.

"Only the fastest, fiercest, most lovable Light Battle Being there is!" Javan reached his hand up to the dog. Quantaa sniffed, licked his hand, then turned to Kamani, waiting further commands.

"Good boy!" Kamani pulled two small niblets from a nest in his beard, tossing a treat to each of the dog's heads. "There are many, many ancient Beings that exist in the Light and Dark Realms! We all need to call upon trusted friends! Quantaa is not only a watchdog and protector, he fights alongside us in Half-Light Realm!"

"Like that serpent thing we saw at the bottom of the lake?" Perl asked.

Kamani's tone grew more serious, "yes. Battles rage all around the Earth, as the Light and the Dark clash in the Half-Light. Humans don't see the combat. Instead, they see tidal waves! Avalanches! Wildfires! Tornadoes! They hear them in a thunderclap! Feel them in an earthquake!"

Quantaa lowered to all fours, and Perl was reminded of the great Sphinx of ancient Egypt, a stone sculpture she studied in one of Papa Ximu's history books.

Kamani scratched under Quantaa's white chin; the dog's back leg tapped the ground with joy. "Some lose faith in Ever, questioning how and why these natural things occur! Never seeing or knowing that we fight for them!"

Relaxing his expression, Kamani picked up the reed. "But today, today we play!" He flung it at Bear; the hoop landed around the boy's thick neck, spinning, as Bear stood there, a look of surprise on his face. The others laughed. Bear smiled, picking the heavy ring up over his head.

"Go get it, boy!" Bear spun around a few times, then let the ring go. It landed off in the field about fifty feet away. "Go on, Quantaa! Fetch!" Bear encouraged the dog, but Quantaa didn't move a muscle. His two heads looked over at one another; one yawned.

"Respect! Trust! It must be earned! Quantaa...fetch!" Kamani clapped his hooves. Like a bolt of lightning, Quantaa was gone and back in the blink of an eye, dropping the reed at Kamani's feet.

The greyhound started sniffing along the ground, locking on to a peculiar scent. It meandered around the group, stopping in front of Perl. It smelled the air around her small frame with its wet, drippy snout as long as a dolphin. The top of Perl's head came to Quantaa's kneecaps. She thought he looked more like a dragon than a dog. Quantaa reached over, picking up the disc and dropping it at Perl's feet. It then struck a down dog position; front legs flat on the ground, butt high in the air, tail wagging wildly, ready to play.

Everyone stared in awe. Corvax crossed his arms. "Figures...*mankind's best friend.*"

"Don't be a jumble-gut." Bear nudged Corvax.

Nan poked Perl's backpack. "I think he wants you to throw it."

Perl squatted down, not breaking eye contact with the canine, and attempted to pick up the hoop, but it was way too heavy for her to lift alone.

Javan stepped over. "Here, let me help." Together they tossed the large toy. It only went a short distance, but Quantaa didn't seem to mind. The Battle Being joyfully retrieved it, again and again.

The others, happy to take a break, relaxed among the scenic surroundings. Nan and Lyre flitted over the sunflowers, while Bear, Tars and Flax played a card game using leaves. Opis and Corvax simply laid down and closed their eyes, listening to the flowers sing.

Kamani held up his hoof and gave a quick whistle. Quantaa stopped chasing the hoop and went back to its sphinxlike pose.

"I've never seen him imprint on anyone like that! No one, besides me! Ha!" Winking at Perl, Kamani made a series of clicking noises. Quantaa stood, reared up like a stallion, then took off, its great wings flapping; it lifted up into the sky.

"Remember that life is fun! Never cry boredom! Your imagination is limitless!"

The Seekers looked up, squinting to see the last of Quantaa disappear through a rainbow.

The familiar tune of Olliv's cello wings could be heard approaching. "Ah, your buggy awaits!" Kamani met the snail, grabbing hold of its reins and giving a slight nod to Olliv. One by one, the Seekers climbed up the ladder, finding their seats under the tent.

Kamani called up to them. "There will always be battles to fight! Many ways to keep the darkness at bay!" Looking up at Perl, Kamani stroked his beard; his tiny oxpecker beards poked their heads out, fluttering and chirping. "And to protect those who are counting on you!"

"But for now..." Kamani smacked the snail's backside; it jolted forward with a jump, "...see about getting clean, yes?! Ha-Ha!"

Perl watched as Kamani lumbered away, laughing. She thought to herself, *"those counting on me...back home."*

19 RABBIT RABBIT

Bodhi, the ethereal Being, sat cross-legged on the ground with his many peacock eyes closed, as the Seekers reached the Callowhorn meditation valley. Off in the field beyond the rows of lilac bushes, the Master's team of horses quietly nibbled at the grass, the sun reflecting off their curled horns.

"Rest."

The Seekers, feeling restored from the ride after feeding the porcupine triplets, jumped down from the snail and formed their circle around Bodhi. The Being bowed to the group of Seekers, who bowed in return.

"We know Ever is an artist. But Ever is also a master scientist. Let us see."

A different variety of leaf materialized in each of the student's hands; a maple, sycamore, birch, magnolia, oak, elm, hawthorn, cottonwood, and in Perl's, a leaf from an aspen tree.

"Now consider the human hand," Bodhi said, "both have veins. Vessels of nourishment."

Perl looked at the back of her auburn hand, seeing the similarities. All the countless drawings she'd done back on Mont Michel, all the leaves she'd gathered, and still Perl had never noticed this. She marveled at how truly connected she was to the nature she loved so much.

"Magic," Perl whispered to herself.

Bodhi slowly stood. "All has been designed." Bodhi gave a slight wave of its hand, the leaves fade from their palms, and chunky brown walnuts appeared. "The shell has a right and left hemisphere, as does the brain of a human." Bodhi clenched a fist and the shells cracked open, exposing the inside of the nut. "Witness the folds and wrinkles. Eating the walnut nourishes the very organ it resembles. Ever offers humankind clues. Whether they choose to pay attention is up to them, yet we must encourage."

With a deep inhale, Bodhi turned in a circle then stopped, letting out a slow, deep exhale; the walnuts in their hands turned into kidney beans. "The human kidney requires fiber, protein, iron. The bean of the same shape and color provides exactly that. There is no coincidence in nature. All is designed."

Moving back down to its knees, Bodhi lowered its head; the kidney beans vanished from their hands. "Close your eyes. Bring your attention to my voice. Feel the pressure of your body on the ground. Now, inhale."

The Seekers bowed, all of them taking in a deep breath.

Perl tried to remain focused, but as it often had a way of doing, her mind began to wander. As she sat on this familiar ground, surrounded by the people she'd grown to know well, Perl tried to figure out just how long she'd been training. *"Was it three weeks? Ten weeks? How much time have I been in Venusto?"* Time passage was different here, if it existed at all. The sun rose and set, Perl attended her classes and ate her meals regularly, yet she couldn't gauge how long it had been since she arrived with Uriel on the balloon. It felt like forever since she had said goodbye to Papa and the others. *"How many pages have I filled in my journal?"* she pondered, when Bodhi's voice interrupted her thoughts.

"Breathe. In. Out. Feel yourself connect."

Perl cleared her mind, refocusing on the lesson.

"Discover the sacred in ordinary places." Bodhi rose again. "Humans believe their thoughts and actions are separate from the whole of nature. We must widen their circle of compassion to all creatures, all of nature. To the miracles in the folds and the veins."

The nine students remained focused; their breathing synchronized.

"Open." When they opened their eyes, sitting in front of each Seeker was a rabbit.

"Aww…hello," Perl couldn't help breaking the silence when she saw the cute bunny looking straight at her.

"Communicate without words." Bodhi continued, his voice calm and measured, "connect with the hare. Every species has a voice. Each one has a story to tell."

Some of the rabbits hopped away, other stayed close to their assigned Seeker. Perl started to wiggle her nose in unison with her new fuzzy friend. Up, down, up, down, went the peach-colored rabbit's nose. Up, down, up, down, Perl imitated the bunny right back. The two gestured back and forth several times, Perl moved onto her stomach, practically touching noses with the rabbit, their eyes locking. Perl slowly began to hear the rabbit's voice in her head.

You are the net of safety,
with your hand,
I'm always caught...

Perl closed her eyes and could visualize herself through the rabbit's point of view. She scampered through the forest, hopping skillfully over rocks, diving under rough branches. She felt the strength in her hind legs as she thumped the ground, felt her heart beating rapidly. Perl saw the burrow in front of her. She dove into the opening, under a thorny bush down, down, into a tunnel she ran. The smell of wet earth and moss filling her nostrils. At the bottom, baby bunnies nestled, awaiting her return. Perl heard their gentle cooing, felt her warm body pressed in against theirs.

You're my mirror,
my reflection.
Your voice echoes in my soul.

The rabbit spoke its song to Perl and she listened, lost in the melody. She felt a warm fuzziness caress her face, bringing her back to the present. Perl opened her eyes, blinking.

The rabbit had turned, its cotton tail brushed her cheek as it scurried away.

"Mom?" Perl whispered, waking from her trance. Perl realized she was now on all fours, and had hopped into the middle of the circle.

"Looks like this *Lepus* found it's leap!" Corvax teased, as everyone laughed. Perl quickly scooted back into her spot.

Bodhi's hand went up, silencing them. "Even those that house an ancient essence, still have much room to grow. Seeker now, but in time, Seer." With a wave of its arm, the rabbits vanished. "Each must journey away from the expectations of others, to discover their true self. That which you were created to be. Only then can you offer yourself to the world."

Bodhi dismissed the class with a deep bow, then mounted its steed and rode off in a cloud of dust, its pack of horses following. The group stood, waiting as they always did for Olliv to pick them up. Across the white waters from Callowhorn, the laughter and cheers of a crowd could be heard echoing over from the nearby island of Greenheart.

"Wonder what's going on over there?" Flax was on his tiptoes with his hand to his brow, peering out towards the island. "Sounds like a fun time over there today," another rousing cheer went up.

Perl leaned on Flax. "Let's go see. Maybe Quantaa's over there now."

Flax frowned, "Umm…Greenheart is off limits for us. Seers only over there."

"Oh, come on, let's go!"

"We can't. Besides, I'm starving. Let's go eat!" Flax rubbed his smooth, moist belly.

Like clockwork, Olliv strolled up, whistling a tune and waving his buttercup baton in the air. "A plum of a day, I presume, presume?" he asked, a knowing twinkle in his ancient gray eyes. "But you must all be hungry, hungry. Let us be off to Dragon Maw!"

The nine followed Olliv as the skies above faded to a soft lavender. As they walked, Javan was by Perl's side. She glanced over at him; it seemed as though Javan ended up next to her often.

"Javan?" Perl asked.

The boy looked over at her, flipping his dark hair out of his eyes. "Yeah?"

"So…how long have we actually been training? It all seems jumbled up and kind of fuzzy to me." She pulled at her double-bun hairdo, trying to fluff it back up; the plum juice had done a number on it.

"Well, time isn't really a linear concept in the Light Realm." Javan looked down at his feet, trying to find the right words.

"Here we go again," Perl sighed.

Javan continued. "Actually, I take that back. It is and it isn't. I mean, we do age, but not like you do on Earth. It can take many centuries to look as old as say, Tryfon."

"I know that. Uriel explained it to me," Perl replied, a little irritated at not getting a straight answer from the platypus-boy. "So you can't tell me how long it's been since I left Mont Michel? It feels like a long time," Perl paused, "and well, I think maybe I need to return to Earth, to make sure my Papa is okay."

Overhearing this, Opis chimed in, "the ocean calls, Perl. If you are the Chosen One, then you must finish your training here in Callowhorn."

Javan gave Opis a stern look.

Opis corrected herself. "I mean, *you are* the Chosen One. However, you won't be any good to anyone unless you continue to learn and develop."

Perl ignored the part about being The Chosen One; to her that was nonsense. "But if I wait, Papa and Regor and Victr, all of them will be…" Perl stopped and sat down on a stone bench carved into a dove. She lowered her head to her knees. "That thing—Malblud—It's coming…or it's already there, I can feel it." She wrapped her arms around her legs, squeezing tightly.

Javan and Opis stayed back with Perl as the others continued into Dragon Maw. The savory aroma of smoked vegetables lingered in the air.

Opis sat down next to Perl. "You're allowing your impulses to guide you. I know you're worried. It's hard to be so far from home, in a strange land. But you have us…all of us." Opis put her arm around Perl. "Try not to focus on the negative."

Javan laid a reassuring hand on Perl's back.

"Easy for you to say," Perl mumbled, her voice cracking.

Opis shrugged and stood, "I suppose you're right. Venusto and The Light Realm have always been my home. But now we're sisters, you and I." Perl looked up at Opis holding out her hand. "C'mon, let's go get something to eat. You'll feel better." She smiled at Perl. "Dessert first today, whaddya say?"

Somewhat reluctantly, Perl took Opis's hand, "okay."

Pulling herself to her feet, Perl looked at Opis, her long, electrified tentacles making sizzling zaps and pops as they swished around her head. *"Sisters."* Hearing Opis say that made her feel better. Perl hugged the slender, willowy girl. Javan smiled at the pair and the three of them walked into the crowded dining garden, stomachs growling.

Inside Dragon Maw, they found the others sitting at a large *Dracena Cinnabari* tree table next to a group of Awakeners. One of the Beings had a saucer-shaped head full of seedpods that shook like a baby's rattle whenever the Being moved, while long green leaves served as arms. The others at the table were identical, both with long Hope-colored robes. Their heads were carved marble, each with one large unblinking eye, high chiseled cheeks and toothless mouths.

"Hey, over here! We saved you seats," Bear waved all his arms at them.

Javan and Opis made their way over, but Perl, mesmerized by the curious marble Beings, gave Bear a dismissive wave as she continued staring at the strange Awakeners. She finally joined the others only after the seedpod Awakener shook its head at her, suggesting Perl keep walking. Perl pulled out a toadstool chair and sat down next to Bear. Over the hum of the diners, the roar of laughter once again could be heard off in the distance.

"Wow, Greenheart is rocking tonight!" Bear said, gobbling up slice after slice of rainbow-colored bread.

Lyre pecked at a bowl of birdseed. "How do you know it's them and not Natatory?"

Bear wiped his mouth on his sleeve. "I just know things."

"Oh, sure you do." Corvax said, waving his forkful of dark blue noodles at Bear. "The sound is simply reverberating off the lake, from the bottom tip of the Heart Shores. That's how you know it's coming from Greenheart!"

Bear swallowed another whole slice, smiling. "Perhaps."

A flying lemur glided in, placing a warm cherry-soaked dumpling drizzled in edible flowers in front of Perl.

"Thank you." She popped a few orange petals into her mouth.

"How about how we handled those porcupine babies this morning, huh?" Tars poked Nan in the arm with a plantain before chomping it in half.

Nan fluttered her iridescent wings. "It's a good thing I'm such a skilled flier."

Javan grabbed a couple of carrot and cauliflower biscuits off a passing tray, dropping one onto Nan's plate. "You mean, as Perl was protecting you with her sword?!"

"Well sure, that helped too. Thanks, Perl," Nan agreed with a giggle, as another wave of cheers from Greenheart echoed across the water.

"What is going on over there?" Flax asked, instinctively half raising his arm.

Perl looked up from her dumpling. "Well...instead of guessing, why don't go see what's so funny?"

Corvax and Opis answered in unison, "no, Perl, it's off limits."

"Oh, you guys are no fun. Didn't Kamani tell us to have fun?!" Perl argued.

Opis answered, "well yes, but 'follow-the-rules' fun."

Perl dabbed a finger on her plate, picking up a flower petal and eating it. "But you said it yourself...play is vital for a healthy brain and for facing new challenges."

"Not that kind of play...and don't use my words against me." Opis crossed her arms, flipping her tentacles to one side.

"Ha! She's gotcha there, oh wise one!" Bear chuckled so hard it shook the entire table.

"Good one, Per— hey, where are you going?" Javan watched Perl slink out of her seat and quickly step away.

Lyre pointed to Dragon Maw's entrance. "And there she goes."

Perl was already out the front gate and running on the path towards the docks.

Corvax groaned, "ugh...humans. They're just so...impulsive! Too curious for their own good sometimes!"

Javan started to argue back, "she's not all human—never mind, I'll go!" He sprang to his feet.

Opis jumped up after him. "Wait up. This somehow feels like my fault."

Nan started to follow, too, when Corvax grabbed her arm. "Hang on. Let them handle it. No sense in all of us getting in trouble."

A spectacular array of boats was tied up along the shoreline. When Javan and Opis reached the docks, Perl was already inside of one; a beautiful midnight blue rowboat with Earth's constellations painted around the hull.

"Wait!" Javan yelled, as Perl was unfurling the line.

"Geesh, you're fast!" Opis put her hands on her hips, trying to catch her breath. "What are you doing? You can't go to Greenheart. Certainly not alone."

The small boat bobbed up and down gently on the water. Perl pushed it away from the dock. "Then come with me."

Opis looked at Javan, already knowing his answer. "Javan. Don't."

A loud roar rippled from across the water, the setting sun coloring the white seas a bubblegum pink.

Perl clutched the oars with both hands. "You coming?"

Javan looked her in the eyes. "Alright, fine. Someone's gotta keep an eye on you."

Perl held the oars up. "Yes! Hop in!"

Javan grabbed an oar, pulling Perl back to shore. "I'll go...*if* you promise to stay out of trouble, and we go when I say it's time to go."

"Okay, I promise. I promise. Come on!" Perl said excitedly, making room for Javan to sit.

Javan motioned to Opis.

"No," Opis shook her head, her tentacle braids whipping back and forth.

"Come on, Opis. Remember...*sisters?*" Perl said, smiling a big toothy grin.

Rolling her eyes, Opis took Javan's hand and stepped onto the boat. "I just know I'm going to regret this."

Visiting Greenheart was like stepping into the pages of a storybook. Fields of exotic flowers as large as trees grew wild everywhere, painting the island in an array of vibrant colors. All around, flying creatures of every size and shape mingled from blossom to blossom. As the three Seekers coasted up to the shore, an insect perched on top of Opis's head. It had fuchsia butterfly wings, a bumblebee's body, and the long blue beak of a hummingbird.

"She thinks you're a flower!" laughed Javan.

They pulled their boat up onto the bright green sand.

"Wow…Look at this place!" Perl blurted out.

"Shhh, not so loud," Opis hushed, as the trio tiptoed along a pathway of violet moss that was as soft as a blanket under their feet. The cheering sound stopped them in their tracks.

"Did you hear that? It's this way—come on!" Perl rushed ahead.

"Perl, wait up!" Opis gave Javan a look. "Can't you control her?"

Javan smiled. "I don't think anyone can."

They caught up to Perl, who stood leaning against a giant green hedge wall. "Come on, you two!" She quickly scaled up the one-story tall bush like she used to climb the trees back home. Javan shrugged, following the impulsive girl up the leafy wall.

"What, now we're climbing?" Opis sighed and hastily tied back her hair to avoid getting it snagged in the twisted limbs. She grabbed hold of a couple of branches and hoisted herself up.

Once they reached the top, they paused, marveling at the perfectly symmetrical topiary garden that lay before them.

Perl took a deep breath in. "Mmm, it smells like citrus."

Lemon, orange and lime trees were lovingly manicured, quite the opposite of the wild terrain outside the garden walls.

"Those are the living quarters for the Seers," Javan pointed.

At the far end, rows of massive baobab trees overlooked the hedges. Perl noticed dozens of artfully designed tree-houses hanging like giant bird feeders from the trees, complete with winding staircases spiraling down.

Opis chimed in, "okay, so this was fun, right? How about we head back…"

Before she could finish, Perl was halfway down the other side. She leaped off the hedge to the ground below. Javan was right on her heels, landing with a thud.

"You've got to be kidding me!" Opis climbed down slowly, a tentacle got caught on a branch, so she had to hurry to catch up as the two ventured ahead.

The neatly trimmed walkway was flanked with enormous bonsai trees that grew out of heads that looked to be made of glazed terra cotta. Perl stopped and admired the pots; each one was the bust of a woman, her entire face painted with strange symbols. Perl thought it looked like some kind of writing.

Opis caught up to them. "Come on. We really shouldn't be here."

Perl ignored her, pointing up ahead. "Look, up on that hill, a greenhouse! It's so cute, like a smaller version of Palo Santo's!"

The sight of the quaint glass house with heart-shaped windows got Perl's heart skipping. She started up the path towards it, when Javan grabbed hold of her backpack.

"Ahahah. Sure, it's cute…from the outside. But you don't know what you're walking into. That building is a training facility. Inside there's are all kinds of violent, unpredictable weather patterns—tropical rainstorms, arctic blizzards, scorching heat, dust storms, hail—all happening at once."

"Not to mention it's chock full of giant carnivorous plants," Opis added, "trust us, you don't want to meet them."

Perl looked up at the charming glass building. The entire structure was translucent; bright flashes of light--white, then orange, then blue--reflected inside the walls. Perl swallowed. "Okay. Maybe we skip that one."

The three surveyed the massive grounds of the garden, realizing how eerily quiet it was; not even the buzz of the insects could be heard. Javan's highly sensitive nose began to twitch.

"Hm. Strange. There's not a Seer in sight. There should be at least someone here in the garden. Something seems off."

"It's getting dark. We should go," Opis agreed.

"But we just got here," Perl whined.

Just then, the ground trembled violently beneath their feet—*Boom! Boom!*— Followed by a deafening trumpet sound. The pebbles jumped along the pathway; lemons and oranges dropped from trees, rolling across the lawn.

Opis plugged her ears, turning to Javan. "Is that what I think it is?"

The deafening pounding continued, getting louder.

"Hide!" Javan grabbed both girls' arms, pulling them down to a crouching position behind a water fountain with an umbrella-sized tulip in the center. With each loud boom, water splashed over the sides of the fountain. "Mastodon Riders," he muttered.

Pounding through a side gate in the garden lumbered a pair of colossal beasts, their thick black fur draped with heavy cloaks made of woven palm leaves. Perl blinked in disbelief at what she was looking at. Two identical riders, lean and muscular, their fuzzy, bearded faces resembling mandrills, sat atop the great mastodons. The riders bright red nose and lips and electric blue features looked like painted masks. Crystal clear horns protruded from the top of their furry teal heads, with matching horns jutting from their shoulders, poking through openings in their gleaming Humor-colored uniforms. Once the two reached the center of the garden, they stopped. The mastodons loudly trumpeted again, lifting their ten-foot-long tusks to the sky. Like a pair of acrobats, the two Seers hopped up and stood on the backs of the creatures; they lifted their arms, and held their pose, as if about to begin a performance.

From above came the same cackling noise Perl and the others had been hearing since Callowhorn. It was much louder now, and to Perl, it no longer sounded like laughter; it sounded angry.

The riders began gently waving their arms like twin conductors, unaware they were being watched.

"What are they doing?" Perl asked.

Perl looked up and saw an amorphous shape, twisting and undulating hundreds of feet above her. She quickly realized they were birds; tens of thousands of them. The dark birds swirled and twisted in fluid, synchronized motions, swooping together in tight formation, then spreading far apart, then back in again, moving rhythmically through the air, creating beautiful organic patterns.

"They're starlings. The Seers are teaching the flock," Javan whispered.

"Teaching them to what? Fly?" Perl asked.

Opis was quick to answer, "murmuration. Starling flocks use them as defensive movements whenever there's danger."

The Seers set the tempo with waves of their pale blue hands, controlling the birds' pacing and formations. The starlings followed closely, moving effortlessly to the choreography in a synchronized mid-air ballet.

Opis went on, "they're showing the flock how to appear larger, in order to scare away predators."

"What kind of predator? Where?" Perl stood up. Javan yanked her back down.

"That predator!" Opis said, just as a bird the size of a dragon buzzed over their heads, squawking. The mastodons stirred, unsettled by the creature's presence.

"Wow, a Roc!" Javan gasped, taken back by the enormity of the creature.

Perl had never heard of a Roc; to her, it looked like a massive brown eagle, only the creature had two pairs of dark red wings, with gigantic talons large enough to lift a house...or three small Seekers. The Roc swooped towards the starlings. At the Seers' command, the flock collectively twisted out of the way. This angered the beast, who let out an ear-piercing screech, circling back around, this time with its beak opened wide and talons up high. It shrieked again, its pink forked tongue flapping in the wind. Its squawking did sound like the laughter of a crowd, but Perl saw nothing funny about this monstrous beast as she cowered behind the fountain.

The twin Seers' arms moved fluidly and confidently, guiding the starlings into shapes, transitioning from a bear, to a whale, then to a swirling cyclone. The changing shapes confused and unsettled the Roc, sending the creature into a rage of laughing squawks and cackles. The obedient starlings, locked on the Seers and remained in perfect harmony, oblivious to the Roc's proximity.

Perl watched the starlings; as she did, she began to calm, her heartbeat slowed. She marveled at their natural beauty and grace, not realizing that the spots on her arms, legs, and cheeks had begun to glow. The giant flying beast dove repeatedly at the flock, either missing them or simply getting spooked by their strange, unpredictable maneuvering. Growing more frustrated, it hovered briefly in the air as if contemplating just giving up, when the monstrous bird's ruby red eyes caught a glint of light shimmering on the ground below; every barbed feather on its head stood on end. The Roc flapped its pairs of wings, rising high into the air as it let out a deafening screech that shook the trees around them.

"Perl," Javan said, "cover your arms!"

Perl fumbled with her sleeves, pulling them down. She tried to hide her arms at her side, or behind her, but it was no use. Hearing voices, the mastodons turned and looked, along with the Seers.

"Who's there? Show yourself!" the riders shouted.

Unable to abandon the flock, they continued orchestrating commands to the starlings, though somewhat distracted.

Deserting the starlings, the Roc turned its sights on a new prey. It made a beeline straight for Perl's light.

"Run!" Javan grabbed Opis and Perl's hands, lifting them to their feet.

The three bolted down the twisting garden path in the direction of the conservatory.

"Careful...don't slip on the fruit!" Opis yelled out as she hopped over a stray lemon.

Javan, with his platypus-like feet, could only waddle-run. "It's gaining on us! Faster!"

Perl's light was like a beacon, drawing the legendary creature to them like a shiny lure. The Roc's shadow loomed above them, blocking out what little of the sinking sun there was.

"Aaa-ha-ha-haa!" it screeched at them, its hot breath hitting the back of their necks even from forty yards away.

Perl slowed, pulling her narwhal sword from its sheath. She stopped, turning to face the angry bird.

Javan slowed to look back. "Perl, what are you doing?! Are you mad?! Keep running!"

Perl braced herself, holding up her sword with both hands. The Roc's eyes narrowed. It opened its curved, sharp beak wide, its forked tongue dripping saliva as it closed in on Perl, ready to scoop up a delicious snack. Perl ducked to one side, closed her eyes and swung; thousands of razor-sharp snail teeth sliced into the side of the bird's serpent-like tongue. The Roc reared its head in pain, a thin trail of blood spraying from its mouth as it retreated.

Javan stood frozen, half amazed and half horrified. He expected to witness Perl being devoured, but the girl still stood, her white blade now crimson red.

Opis called out, "run! It's coming back!"

The Roc, hurt but not hindered, let out another nightmarish scream, poised for another strike.

"Over there! We need to hide!" Opis pointed to a red speckled flower, its petals opened up in a great bloom. "We can all fit, come on!" She ran over to the jumbo-sized plant, which was taller than her.

Perl turned and ran to her sister, then slowed as she saw where she was; she recognized the flower from her visit to Palo Santos. "Opis, that's *Rafflesia*! You don't want to go in there!"

It was too late; Opis had already stepped inside the corpse flower, too frightened to take notice of the appalling stench.

The Roc circled back, its four wings beating angrily as it nose-dived towards them.

"C'mon, there's no time! Get in!" Opis pulled at Perl's sleeve.

Javan leapt past Perl into the open flower. Perl held her nose and crawled in; the threesome squeezed together tightly in the soft, damp petals.

"We need to camouflage the opening." Javan reached up and gathered the flower petals together, sealing them up like a cocoon. Perl covered her nose; the smell was enough to make her gag.

They heard a loud whooshing sound as the Roc landed with a crash. Its wings stirred up plumes of dust and debris. The three could hear it scavenging around as it scratched and pecked the trees and bushes outside, searching for its victims. With a raspy "caaaw!", it ripped a cherry tree up from its roots, throwing it across the garden in frustration. The Roc eyed the large spotted corpse flower and lumbered over to it, recoiling as the rotting scent burned its eyes, irritating it even more.

With just the soft white glow of Perl's spots lighting the dark, cramped flower, they fell silent. The hot breath of the Roc wafted around them, making the tight, muggy space that much more unbearable. Javan, still holding the petals closed, tried desperately not to move a muscle. Perl looked up at Javan's veiny, webbed hands.

'They really do look like leaves," she thought, remembering what Bodhi had taught them; that everything in nature is connected.

Javan's quick thinking was enough to fool the Roc. They heard a loud

148

ruckus as tree limbs snapped, claws scratched against stone, and several more screeches rang out as the beast finally gave up the hunt. Blasts of wind were felt as the Roc flew off. Opis, Perl and Javan sat, squished together inside the smelly flower, holding their breaths, too afraid to move.

"Is it...gone?" Opis whispered.

Something dragged along the bottom of the flower, tickling Perl. "Hey," she yelled, "watch it!"

Javan couldn't hold still any longer; he threw open the petals of the flower. Perl came up with her sword held high, just in case.

"Easy, easy, brave one!" Looking down at them, laughing, were the two Seers. They had dismounted from their mastodons and now stood next to the flower; one of the mandrills held a silver staff in his hand.

"Good Ever, that is horrid!" declared Seer number one, holding his fuzzy arm up to his face, his bright red nose wrinkling; opening up the corpse flower had unleashed a horrendous odor.

"Get me out of this sewer," Opis gasped for breath.

"Witness. Do my eyes deceive?" Seer number two said to his twin, "is that little Opis we see before us?"

"Why, it is! Greetings, ancient one."

Perl noticed that every movement made by one rider was mirrored by the other. One Seer placed his hands on his hips, the other followed. One threw his head back and laughed, so did his twin. It was like their synchronicity when conducting the starlings, who had since vanished.

Perl turned to Opis, "how does he know you?"

The Seer held out his staff, not wanting to get the strong scent on him. "Allow me to assist you." Opis grabbed the end of the stick and hopped out of the corpse flower. The mandrill looked at her, his close-set eyes a steely gray. "What brings you to Greenheart? Are you lost?"

"You might say that." Opis raised an accusatory eyebrow at Perl.

The other Seer gestured to Perl's weapon, "if I may ask, how did one so small acquire a narwhal sword?"

Perl twirled Fortis around proudly. "My father. He made it for me."

"Behold! Such craftsmanship. You possess something truly rare and beautiful."

"Just like its owner," Javan scrambled out of the flower. Realizing what he'd said, he cleared his throat awkwardly, "uh, we'd better get back to Callowhorn...before we're missed."

"Surly they will smell you coming." The Seer waved his hand in front of his nose. "That said, the three of you should not be here. We are obligated to report this."

Opis looked crossly at the rider. "Do, and I shall be forced to do the same." The mandrills looked at her confused, as Opis circled around them. "I seem to recall an evening, perhaps two, three hundred life-years ago, when a certain pair summoned forth an ancient Air spell. A spell that they were not given clearance to conjure. A spell that unleashed a Zaacotta, one that they needed assistance in containing. Does that ring a bell to anyone, hmm?"

Seer one grinned; his brother did the same. "You've made your point, Opis. Still the taskmaster, I see. Make haste," he waved his staff at them, "before we have a change of heart." The mandrills crossed their arms in unison.

Perl, Javan and Opis smelled so awful, even the mastodons backed away from them as they walked by. On their way out to the hedge wall, Opis tore off several eucalyptus stems. Dirty, irritated, and exhausted, they were relieved to be back in the boat. Javan paddled swiftly, the great greenhouse on the hill lit up the dark island like a strobe.

Opis dipped the eucalyptus leaves into the frothy white water; handing a clump to Perl. "Here, scrub yourself with these."

"What's this for?"

"For our stench!" Opis began rubbing the leaves on her face, neck, and arms. "Eucalyptus acts like a soap...and in our case, a deodorant. It won't get rid of it completely, but at least it will help to mask this deathly scent some."

Perl leaned back, letting her arm hang over the side of the boat; her fingertips skimmed the water as she hummed softly.

Opis looked at the girl; she gave a wry smile. "Well, I hope you had fun."

"I did, and according to the reason *you* gave to Kamani for having fun," Perl mimicked Opis, "my developing brain has been sufficiently stimulated." Perl giggled; Opis flung a handful of soggy leaves at her. Javan shook his head.

"Seriously, we're lucky we didn't end up as a snack for that Roc," Javan said, resting the oars on his knees for a moment, "I mean, what were you thinking?"

"I didn't think. I just did what the—What I thought I should do." Perl didn't want to reveal that she'd heard a voice in her ear telling her to 'fear not.'

Opis sat up. "It was foolish either way, but I'm glad you did. It bought us time, and maybe the Roc will think twice next time he decides to attack."

Perl was feeling quite the adventurer, proud of her actions; Opis wasn't one to hand out compliments. The three fell silent, the only sound was the creaking oars pulling through the calm waters. Javan nudged Opis, gesturing over at Perl. Opis peered over the side of the boat. Perl's arm was halfway in the water, and trailing after it was a large school of neon tetras. They swam up, lightly nibbling her fingers. Perl smiled, moving her fingers over the surface of the water, and like the starlings, the school of fish reacted, following Perl's hand in unison. They reached the shores of Callowhorn just as the sun was setting behind the Natatory mountain range. The three pulled the small boat up to the dock, secured it, and made their way back to their nests.

"Mother of all things smelly!" Bear sprang up in his bed when Perl and Opis entered the nest.

"Sorry, we had a bit of a—" Perl began to say.

Bear cut her off, "a what? A skunk spraying party?! You two reek!"

Opis flopped into her middle bunk bed and rolled towards the wall.

Bear made a face at Perl. "Wait. Did you end up going to Greenheart? We all wondered. Corvax and the others didn't think you'd do it, but I said you would. Did you figure out what all that noise was?"

"We found out alright," Perl climbed up the ladder to her bunk, "and it wasn't anyone laughing…it was a Roc."

"A Roc?" The tardigrade's small eyes grew wide. "You saw a Roc?"

"It attacked us, and I sliced its tongue with my blade….left it for dead, probably," Perl said, embellishing her tale much like she did back home.

Bear eyed the girl suspiciously but played along. "So why do you stink so bad? Did it drop a load on your head as it passed by?" Bear plugged his nose, laughing.

Perl dropped her head over the side of her bed, looking down at Bear. She squinted her eyes. "And after I defeated the mighty beast, all of Greenheart came out to sing our praises!"

Opis chuckled, "the girl can spin a fairytale, that's for sure."

Suddenly, the door of their nest sprang open; rays of bright colors filled the room.

"What now?" Opis moaned, rolling lazily over towards the doorway. "Who is it—?" Seeing the vision in the doorway, she immediately jumped out of bed.

Bear too, slid off his bunk, standing with his head lowered, his multiple sets of hands behind his back. Perl, not sure what was going on, swung her legs around and sat on the edge of the bed, shielding her eyes from the brightness.

Like a glowing beacon stood Master Tryfon, larger than life. Because of his size, he was forced to hunch over, his back nearly grazing the top of the entrance. He seemed to float as he approached the beds.

"You've been on a quest, I see." Tryfon spoke softly as his body swirled and blended from one image to the next. "Or rather, I smell," he smiled.

Perl spoke up, "it's all my fault, Master, I made them go. You can send me home for breaking the rules if you want. I was just…stupid." Perl was overwhelmed by the presence of the great Being; his skin morphed, shifting from a starry night sky to an array of tropical plants and birds.

Tryfon held up his palm, softening the light in the room. "Careful. You become what you believe, dear child."

Opis looked at Perl. "Don't say you're stupid. It isn't true, and you didn't make me go...I made the choice."

"Quite true. No one would ever claim to make Opis do anything that she did not agree upon," Tryfon said, winking at the jellyfish-girl.

The old master rested his grassy bearded chin on his carved walking stick. "Emotions are a force of nature, wired into the human experience. Animals act on instinct. Humans think, and therefore choose their behaviors."

Bear chimed in, "humans are complicated, aren't they, Grand Master?"

Perl reached over and gave Bear a playful poke.

"Emotions can be a motivator for good or evil." Tryfon tapped his walking stick on the ground. "It is through your will that you must choose wisely."

Perl was listening, but the more she looked at Tryfon, the more she became mesmerized by his appearance. She wondered what his beard felt like, with all the pretty pink flowers and stems weaving in and out of it.

"So, I'm not getting kicked out? Thank you, Master."

Perl unconsciously reached out to touch the great Being's ethereal cloak. Tryfon, with his large, soft hands, took hold of Perl's; feelings of warmth and contentment washed over the girl. In that moment, Perl could smell the salty sea air back home. A tear ran down her cheek as she grinned ear to ear; it was heavenly.

"That is now a memory, child, to apply to tomorrow's dream." Perl was confused by Tryfon's cryptic way of communicating, but his presence calmed her immensely, making her feel safe and loved. Stepping back, he reached inside his long, glistening cloak and pulled out a green envelope. "Ever sends us what we need at the moment we need it the most."

Bear put his hands on his belly and rubbed. "Then I really could use some strawberry crumble cakes right now!"

Tryfon handed Perl the envelope; it was folded from an elephant ear leaf, with a beeswax seal closure on the flap.

"Mr. Bear, you do have a voracious appetite," Tryfon said, smiling. Plucking a small, pink flower from his beard, he gently placed it on Perl's pillow. "May your Divine Protectors watch over you all. Sleep well."

As the celestial being turned, the door opened by itself, and he glided out into the twilight, his shimmering glow disappearing with him.

"Ha! Thank you, Master Tryfon!" Bear shouted.

On the table by the door was a plate of cakes. Bear bounded over, scooped up the snacks, handing Opis and Perl each one.

Opis held her hand up. "You can have mine."

Bear gave her a sloppy smooch on the forehead. "This is why I love you!"

Opis wiped his spit from her brow. "Yuck. You're welcome, I guess." She crawled back into her bunk. "Perl, what did Tryfon give you?"

Bear crawled back into bed, squishing a cake into his mouth. "Yeah, I've never heard of The Master coming to a Seeker's nest to visit before."

Perl climbed into bed, the envelope in her hand; no name or address was on it. Perl turned it over, examining the wax seal pressed into the paper. She recognized the image; it was the same Aztec marking on the secret door back home in the library, the one that led to the catacombs. *The Ravine Trapdoor,"* Perl thought, her face lighting up.

"It's from home!" Perl broke the wax seal; her brow furrowed as she noticed first the signature at the bottom.

"Well…what does it say?" Bear bounced impatiently, shaking the bunk beds.

"It's from Brother Victr." Perl read the letter aloud:

"Sweet Perl,

The Root Cellar is so very dull without your shining face and adventurous stories. We all miss you, especially Regor, who is doing double food runs, mostly without complaining. In your spirit, he has continued to leave bits of nature with every delivery drop off.

Papa Ximu is on a special mission, so I am the one writing to you. He said to tell you to remember your whale's song, and to keep believing in the magic and love that binds us all. He is very proud of you, as am I.

We hope you are making new friends and your training is going well. I hear the gardens there are rich with diversity, and that the food is delicious. (But hopefully not as good as mine!) I can't wait to hear all about it.

Be the brave warrior I know you to be.

Much love, Brother Victr"

Bear sniffed the air. "The smell…it's gone! Another gift from Tryfon!"

Opis reached up and tugged on Perl's bed sheet. "See? All is well at home. Let's clear our minds of worry now and get some rest. It's been a long day." She blew out the candle on the shelf above her headboard.

Perl stared at the letter, running her finger over the broken wax seal. "What special mission could Papa be on? Why didn't he write me himself?"

Opis leaned out of her bed. "Don't let your imagination get the better of you. Trust your friend Victr. Would he ever mislead you?"

Perl sat up onto her elbows. "No, but…"

Opis cut her off, "no 'but's'! Goodnight, Perl. Sleep well. Olliv will be at our door before you know it." She pulled the sheets up, folding her tentacles over her eyes like a sleep mask.

Bear yawned loudly. "Goodnight, fellow Water Buddies. Sweet dreams."

Perl sighed, noticing the pink flower on her pillow from Tryfon. She opened her sketchbook, sticking it to a blank page with a drop of strawberry jam filling from her crumble cake. She tucked the letter in as well. *"Opis is right. Victr's never lied to me."*

Perl took out her pencil from Uriel, closed her eyes, and thought for a moment; she jotted down a line from the raindrop's song.

"I quench the willow, in the raspberry field, where children run free."

After sketching a little raspberry next to the verse, Perl closed the book. She quickly drifted off to sleep, and dreamt strange dreams. *Tryfon, his long beard had grown into a dense forest, whose roots and limbs glowed a fiery orange. The branches grew around Perl, who lay trapped in her bed, unable to move. Perl opened her mouth to scream but a host of starlings flew out. High-pitched laughter could be heard, as the branches coiled around her wrists and ankles, pulling her down through the bed and into the dark earth below.*

Fortis → (made by a father I've never met)

The other morning was so fun. We got to feed the baby porcupines. They're newborns but they were ginormous! I got to use my sword a lot, to keep the sharp quills away from everyone. That day really made up for the scary one the other day at the lake. There's something closing in on me and I'm afraid. Everyone thinks I'm brave. I don't feel brave. Guess I have them fooled. Sometimes I do things before I even know it. Like facing the Roc. I got lucky with that.

the stinky Rafflesia flower that saved me and Opis and Javan.

I stacked rocks by the river today. It always clears my head. 13 high— my record is 20.

I can't do self-portraits very good, but thought I'd try one since my hair was extra big. I sure do miss my hood.

in my hair today I found 2 feathers and part of my breakfast biscuit

I ♡ Quantaa so much♡

Sometimes I think I like animals more than people. They're always happy to see you and they never hurt your feelings.

One time I saw some kids playing at night and they were throwing fireflies on the ground and stepping on them and streaking their light across rocks. It was like they didn't even care that they were killing them. Like they didn't have feelings. Like they didn't have families. No. I'd much rather hang out with the bugs. Come to think of it, I'm going to re-name them "hugs" 'cause they never bug me.

"lightning hugs"

155

21 MELEE

"When your weapon is drawn, always be at the ready." Bear stood up like a grizzly on two hind legs, holding six blunt-ended sticks in his numerous paws.

Perl scratched her head. "At the ready?"

After Perl's recent run-in with the Roc at Greenheart, the pair decided it was a good idea to begin to do a little sword training, weapon work being one of Bear's specialties. They agreed to meet every other evening—*after* dinner at the Dragon Maw, Bear was quick to insist—in the open meadow just down from their nest. The large tardigrade needed the extra energy, and thought a full belly might slow the girl down a step or two. Perl was light on her feet and quick, with endless stamina. Patience on the other hand, was not her strong suit.

"Take hold of Fortis with both hands…wait, are you right-handed or left?"

"During my writing lessons back home Basil said I was ambidextrous, so…"

"Even better! You can wield your weapon with either hand. For today, let's start with your right as dominant. Place your right hand on the hilt, your left underneath firmly."

Perl adjusted her grip. "Like this?"

"Perfect. Now pretend I'm attacking…take a step towards me and block my attack. Ready?"

The girl nodded. "Yep. Come at me!"

Bear swung slowly in from his left, Perl met his stick, stopping it inches from her face. He repeated the movement, swinging in from the right, and Perl blocked him. Again and again, over and over, Bear came at her, attacking with one stick at a time, moving at a turtle's pace.

Perl huffed, "come on, I've battled porcupine babies tougher than you!"

The water bear ignored her taunts, keeping the easy, methodical cadence—left, right, left, right, up, down, up, down. Bear brought a stick over Perl's head, she crouched, stopping it in mid-air, both arms held high and firm.

"You sure you're the one giving the lesson here?" Perl, her Harmony boots off, playfully danced a circle around her fellow Seeker, tossing Fortis confidently from hand to hand. "Too much molasses syrup with dessert, eh?"

She pranced like a show horse behind him, slapping him lightly on his shoulders with the side of her sword. Without looking, Bear swung his stick low behind his back, sweeping Perl off her feet.

"Oof!" The girl landed hard on her backside, knocking her sword out of her hand. In a surprising display of quickness, Bear spun, stepping on Fortis and pinning Perl to the ground, all six sticks bearing down on her; he cracked a smile.

Perl struggled to release herself, squirming. "No fair," she whined, "you're twice my size!"

Bear puffed out his chest. "Mm, more like five times, and there's nothing fair in battle! Anyway, size won't matter once you get to the point when you're ready to fight the Dark Realm." He backed away, freeing her sword he'd been stepping on.

Perl did a quick roll, snatching her sword and jumping to her feet. "I am ready! Because you just fell for the oldest trick in the book! The "woe is me" routine...so gullible."

Bear rose up tall once again and slapped down on both of Perl's wrists with his sticks, causing her to drop her blade again.

"Ouch! Hey!"

Before the tip of the blade hit the ground, Bear hooked its handle, flipping the sword into the air and caught it in his teeth. "Tada!" He took a deep bow.

Perl squinted, trying to look angry, but she couldn't; the sight of her roommate posing, his sticks jutting out like porcupine quills, drool dripping from his mouth as he clenched Fortis, was too much not to laugh.

"Ha-ha!" Perl bent over.

"Whath tho funny?" Bear replied, long strands of spittle running down his chin.

"You should see yourself! You are one gooey gladiator!"

"Ptooey," Bear dropped one of his weapons and pulled the sword from his mouth. "That was a masterful move and you know it."

"A gross move, you mean! You're getting slobber all over my handle. Give it here."

Bear held the sword out of Perl's reach. "On one condition...we do this my way, slow and steady. I teach. You listen and learn."

Perl crossed her arms. "Slow is boring."

"*Say it*," Bear waved Fortis above her head.

"Fine. You teach, slow and..." Perl mimed a big yawn, "...steady, and I will listen."

Bear wiped the spit off with his sleeve, handing it to her. "And you will learn. Okay?"

Perl smiled, taking hold of her weapon. "At the ready, Master Bear." She bowed respectfully.

The silhouettes of the towering tardigrade and the tiny girl practicing in the meadow became a common sight at the Callowhorn campground. As days passed, and the two picked up their tempo, training more aggressively, Bear pushing Perl harder each time they met. As time went on, Perl began to anticipate the tardigrade's moves, countering them as she continued to hone her skills, learning how to use her size and quickness to her advantage. She was preparing…for what exactly, she wasn't quite sure.

22 SHAPESHIFTER

"Behold, Earth. So still, it seems." The nine Seekers formed an unbroken circle around Master Yew's tangerine glow, listening closely, their hands interlocked. They stood high on a mountain plateau; in the middle of them, a three-dimensional projection of planet Earth slowly rotated. "Look closely," Yew continued, floating above the projection like a fiery phoenix, "sands blow. Rivers run. Stories are shared. The connection of life is evident."

Perl blinked, astonished at seeing Earth from this point of view. There were no borders; everything was interconnected, one. She saw the endless patterns of clouds, swirling around the great blue sphere like a veil. Perl could make out the tips of mountain ranges, painted deserts, and the angelic glow of the aurora borealis. Her home was so beautiful, so fragile. Perl's heart swelled with pride, and a hint of sadness.

Javan looked over at the small girl, seeing the emotion on her face.

"You okay?" he asked.

Perl nodded, "yeah, just...I dunno...missing my Papa."

"With all living things, there must be a willingness to change, to evolve, to grow," The Master motioned for the class to follow, as the feathery Being floated to the very edge of the cliff. "Accepting change can prove difficult."

As the Seekers let go of one another, the image of the Earth disappeared.

Yew closed its bright tiger eyes, and glided out past the edge of the cliff, hovering weightlessly in the air. The Seekers ventured as close to the edge as they dared; the mountainside dropped off into a bottomless sky.

Tars peered over. "Whoa. That's a long way down."

Yew drifted over to a white fluffy cloud nearby, where it sank down into it like it was a beanbag chair.

"Change," the cloud Yew sat on went from cotton white to coral pink, then to electric blue. "Change is inevitable. The ability to trust in change is not...That must be learned."

Bear took a few steps back. "I don't like where this is going."

Corvax crossed his arms. "Is this a riddle you're asking us to solve?"

Yew's eyes flashed open; it floated closer to the group. "No riddle. To trust is to accept our connection with the universe." It folded its arms. "Now, let us all pair up. Hold hands. Take the leap."

Flax raised his hand, "you mean leap? Like over that bush, or that rock over there?"

"Leap." Yew opened its arms wide, gesturing to the sky below.

"Over the cliff?" Bear said trembling, "nope. No way. Huh-uh!"

Yew's eyes narrowed. "Embrace uncertainty. Trust your connection."

Opis took one of Bear's meaty hands, pairing up with her old friend, then quickly let it go, wiping off the sticky crumbs and sweat, "gross, Bear." She grabbed a different hand. "Come on. We'll go together," she coaxed him.

"I'm going first." Corvax had taken a few steps away from the edge. The others cleared a path. "There's nine of us, someone has to go alone!" The crow-boy took a running leap, launching himself off the mountaintop like a cannonball, vanishing into thin air. "Caw! Caw!" echoed from far below.

Bear yelled after him, "show-off!"

Nan and Lyre flapped their wings and clasped hands. "Master Yew, we'll go next."

Yew nodded. "Yes, but no flying. You must fall."

Nan and Lyre stepped to the very edge, tucked in their wings and did a graceful swan dive through the billowy clouds.

Bear grabbed hold of Opis, wrapping his arms around her. "No fair! Nan and Lyre *could* fly if they wanted to! They have a safety net."

"Trust will give you wings," Yew replied calmly.

"If it's all the same to you, Master, I'd rather have real wings," Bear replied.

"Gah!" Opis gasped for air, "you're choking me, Bear...wh—whoa!" She tried pushing Bear off of her but tripped over one of his feet. The two fell, rolling off the edge in a tangled mess of flailing limbs and long pink locks. Bear's panicked screams could be heard, growing more and more faint.

Four remained. Tars and Flax locked hands. "How bad could it be?" asked Flax.

"Famous last words," chuckled Tars, wrapping his tail around Flax's waist.

"Oh, let's just go!" Tars blurted out, closing his large bulbous eyes as they jumped.

"Look out below!" Flax yelled.

Perl swallowed nervously, watching them disappear over the cliff.

Yew studied the remaining pair. "Like the water, we must fall." The Light Being faded away, leaving only a misty orange vapor that dissipated into the cloud it was sitting on. A single yellow feather appeared, turning cartwheels on the breeze.

Perl and Javan stood alone as the strong mountaintop winds whipped their hair around.

"How about we go get some lunch and meet up with everyone later?" Perl suggested, moving away from the edge.

"Oh no you don't," Javan held out his webbed hand. "Yew said to trust.

Do you trust me?"

Through his thick dark bangs, she saw his warm, brown eyes. "Maybe?"

"Maybe?!" He wiggled his hand at her, urging her to take it.

"Okay, yes. I trust you, but Papa always said, just because your friends jump off a bridge, doesn't mean you should, too."

Javan stepped closer, taking her hand. "I'm still here with you…so not all your friends have jumped."

"You think you always have the right thing to say," Perl smiled at him, "don't you?"

"Mmm, maybe." He shrugged shyly.

They moved to the edge. "Ready?" Javan said, looking down and then back over at Perl.

"Okay. On three?" Perl nodded, biting her bottom lip.

"One, two…three!" They stepped off the edge.

"Oh…my…*Everrrr!*" Perl shrieked, holding tightly onto her backpack with one hand, Javan with the other, as they plunged through the chilly air.

She heard the squawks of birds as she plummeted, the wind screaming in her ears. Perl felt the moisture as they passed through cloud after cloud. She squeezed Javan's hand, smiling at him as she yelled over the rushing wind.

"Look at me! I'm a starling!" Perl released her grip, lifting her arms above her head; her bioluminescent spots glowing a bright white through the hazy clouds.

"Woo! I'm a Roc!" Javan hollered back, echoing her joy.

Strangely, their fall steadily slowed as they neared the ground. Below them, like a huge gaping mouth, they saw a giant open crevasse, ready to swallow them.

"Hold on!" braced Javan, taking Perl's hand again.

They dropped down through the crack in the earth and splashed gently into a crystal-clear pool. The other Seekers stood around them, wet, but no worse for wear.

"Finally! Glad you could join us." Corvax joked, rustling his feathers to shake the water off. He held out his hand to help Javan up.

Perl was surprised to see the water was only waist deep. She looked around; the hole they had fallen through opened up into a vast grotto. The water's light cast shimmering reflections on the surrounding walls. From the pool, a small stream wound its way through an opening in the cave, emptying out into a large body of water.

Master Yew floated above the water, its bright honey-and-carrot plumage reflecting off the surface. "Trust. It is the foundation of all things. But it originates in the heart, not in the eye. Observe." Yew swept an arm gracefully over the water. "The rainforest of the sea."

Perl looked past the water's still, glass-like surface, seeing straight to the bottom. Beneath her feet, covering the entire bed of the shallow pool, was a coral reef. It was bursting with brilliant color; orange, pink, turquoise, and green coral beds blossomed out of the sandy floor, teeming with life. Small tropical fish darted in and around Perl's legs.

"It's amazing," Perl said, "the colors look painted on. It's hard to believe they're natural."

The others took in the lovely sight, all but Tars; something had caught his attention. He turned to face the wall, his large eyes expanding. "Oh wow…"

The others turned to look; the cave walls were crawling with hundreds of fuzzy yellow yeti crabs. They scrambled up and down the walls like a rippling carpet. Perl noticed how similar the crabs' golden feathery claws were to Yew's yellow plumage. *"Everything's connected,"* she thought to herself, smiling.

"Ah! Kiwa hirsuta. Eyeless crabs, yet nature provides other ways to see." Yew redirected the class's attention back to the water, "now. Focus." Yew lightly tapped the surface of the water, causing a tiny ripple that gradually grew into small waves as it reached the pool's edges.

The Seekers watched as the sands swished back and forth to the rhythm of the current. Perl became mesmerized by the gentle sound. She shuffled her bare feet along the soft sandy bottom, squishing the pebbles between her brown toes, the spots on her kneecaps glowed cheerfully. Perl closed her eyes, tasting the salty air on her lips; her mind drifted to the shores of Mont Michel. She thought about how polluted her ocean was back home. Although she loved those waters—it was her "birthplace," as Papa would sometimes say—she'd never been able to see below the surface, to the magical world underneath. Some movement around her feet caught Perl's attention.

"Hey, that coral just turned into a seahorse!" Perl bent down to get a better look. The other Seekers wandered over. "No, wait, now it's a water snake."

Flax reached in, plucking the snake out of the water; it instantly morphed into a lionfish with deadly-looking spikes. "Yikes!" The salamander-boy quickly dropped the fish back into the water.

Yew's tranquil voice vibrated in the cavern, *"Thaumoctopus mimicus.* Mimic octopus. Carnivorous. Without its ability to change, it is defenseless prey. But it adapts. Imitates its predators."

"Like me!" Lyre spoke up.

"Similar. You use sound, it uses color and texture," Yew said.

"A real-life shape-shifter," observed Nan.

"Like all living creatures, one must know when and how to change," the Master added.

Flax nudged Tars, "if I had that gift, I'd be unstoppable."

162

They all watched as the amazing creature stared up at them; in a blink, it changed again to resemble a long jellyfish with tentacles. It glided over to Opis and curled around her feet.

"Opis, I think he likes you," Perl teased.

The girl flipped her braids back. "Careful, little mimicus," she crouched down in the water, looking at the octopus. She touched the creature; a tiny *zap!* emanating from her thin translucent fingertips. At that, the mimic flattened its body and jetted off down the small stream and out of the cavern, leaving a cloud of black ink in its wake.

Master Yew bobbed weightless over the clear surface. "Evil is deceiving. It will imitate good in order to fool. In order to destroy."

"If evil is camouflaged as good," Nan flew next to Yew, "how will we know the difference?"

"Trust from inside, not out," Yew closed its eyes. "Make the leap."

The Being floated up higher above the group so they could all hear. "A leopard blends in tall grass. Stalks gazelle. Kills gazelle. Is the leopard bad?"

Corvax spoke up confidently, "no, it's acting on its Ever-given survival instincts."

"Mm," Yew nodded, "yet is the gazelle good, for its sacrifice?"

Shifting his stance in the water, Corvax looked around, less confident. "No. Yes. Maybe?"

Yew shook its head. "Both pure of heart. Both are following the natural order of life. Therefore, both are innately good. It is only when a living creature becomes corrupted by the Realm of Darkness, when it defies the laws set by nature, that it ceases to be good."

Like a nervous tic, Flax's arm shot up. "Master Yew, if something goes to the Dark Realm, can it ever return to the Light?"

Yew turned, gesturing out of the cave to the bright cerulean sky above the sea. "The sun sets below the horizon. Things go dark. Is it gone forever? Vanished? No. Shines elsewhere. Until it reveals itself again in full."

Perl asked, "so how can something evil turn good again?"

Yew looked at her, its tiger yellow eyes bright. "Through Ever's greatest and most powerful of gifts...love."

"Love?" Bear asked.

Tars playfully slapped Bear. "Yeah, you know...*love*...As in "you *looove* your gooey tarts."

Bear grabbed the skinny monkey-boy in a headlock. "I don't love them...I just, you know, *like* them."

Nan and Flax giggled, while the others wandered around the pool, gazing at the vibrant aquatic life below.

Perl reached into her backpack, pulling out her sketchbook. Tiny spots on her feet glowed faintly as she began jotting down notes. *'Evil can mask itself as good,"* she scribbled. She looked at Yew, who had picked up one of the yeti crabs and was letting it climb along its feathered arm. She wrote more, her pencil moving rapidly, *"Love pulls light from the darkness."* She thought of the times when she had gotten into trouble; Papa would scold her, but it didn't mean he loved her any less.

Javan, who happened to be looking over at Perl as she was writing, suddenly spotted long shadows moving through the water towards the girl. Against the bright clear water, the unsettling streaks of black stood out.

Corvax also noticed the strange shapes. "Perl, watch out!"

One of the snake-like creature's mouths opened, ready to latch on to Perl's calf, its long fangs visible. In one swift motion, Javan reached down and grabbed the eel, ripping it out of the water, its rows of razor-like teeth snapping hungrily at his face. He flung the angry thrashing eel onto the rocks. Instantly, the yeti crabs swarmed at the free meal, their yellow furry claws devouring their prey in seconds.

"Wh—What just happened?" Perl spun around confused, lifting a leg out the water. She saw the scuffle of yeti crabs and Javan and Corvax by her side.

"That lamprey was about to take a bite out of you!" Javan took Perl's arm, pulling her over to him.

"Out. Now." Master Yew commanded to the group; half of them had already scrambled out of the water.

The Light Being eyed one of the remaining lampreys as it slipped between the coral trying to escape the pool. Raising its arms outward, Yew closed its eyes and took a long, deep inhale. The cave waters began to reverse course, the current now flowing from the edges toward the center of the pool. It churned and spun violently, until it began to lift upwards, forming a long, slender cyclone. The funnel pulled like a vacuum, sucking sand and water up out of the basin.

"There!" Lyre pointed to the dark shape entering the funnel.

It wriggled and flopped, desperately trying to escape the pull of the water. Yew floated over, reached in, and plucked out the eel.

"This poor creature. Tainted with darkness," Yew spoke softly, almost as if in prayer. The Light Being held the creature up with one hand and closed its snapping jaws shut with the other. The eel calmed, transforming back to the Light. Yew released it gently into the water whispering, "you are loved."

The last lamprey had escaped the funnel and was swimming out of the cave.

"Master Yew, that one's getting away!" chirped Lyre.

Strapped to its back, Yew pulled out the great longbow. Plucking a feather from its arm, the Being nocked the arrow and let it fly. It cut through the water, narrowly missing the eel as it disappeared below into the open ocean.

"Were those things after Perl?" Tars watched as the crabs finished off the last of the eel, leaving only bones and teeth behind. "Sure seemed like it...but why?"

"Yeah...why?" Perl asked.

"This was..." Yew spoke, almost in a whisper, "...unforeseen." Kamani had advised Master Yew and the other Guides instructing Perl to be extra vigilant; that the thing known as Malblud had awakened, and was now trying to locate the girl. "I will inquire. I need more understanding. The lamprey will return to its Dark Realm host."

"So, Perl is in danger." Javan whispered to Yew so Perl couldn't hear.

Yew reached down and touched Javan's shoulder. "Bravery. In the face of danger. You trusted your instincts. Very good."

Perl gave the platypus-boy a light punch on the back of the arm. "Yeah, thanks. Not that we're keeping score or anything," she said, pretending to count on her fingertips. "Of course, I did save you from the Roc...oh, and those nasty porcupine quills."

"Right, right...no score keeping," Javan gave her backpack a slight shove forward.

"Let us leave the cave to the *Kiwa hirsuta,*" Yew suggested.

As the Being spoke, it drifted upwards, exiting through the gap in the cave ceiling where the group had fallen through. The Seekers looked at one another.

"Guess we'll go this way," Bear shrugged, gesturing over to where the river ended at the mouth of the cave. The group marched out to meet Yew.

Javan studied the bright yellow-orange Being. His platypus senses were tingling; it seemed to him that Yew wasn't necessarily giving them the whole truth.

The class walked to a secluded beach. Like the neighboring waters, the pure white sand was the cleanest Perl had ever seen. It felt like walking on flour, and reminded Perl of days in the kitchen with Victr; how he insisted that the flour be sifted three times to make sure it was as soft and light as spun silk. *"Oh Victr,"* Perl thought, *"I miss you."*

"Circle," Yew directed; the Seekers sat on the soft sand.

Yew gave a quick wave of its arms, as if guiding an aircraft in for a landing. Perl's eyes widened, as a flock of extremely large pelicans swooped in; the enormous birds waddled over to each Seeker and opened their beaks wide. Nestled inside each was a coconut shell bowl and spoon.

"What's this?" Perl asked.

"What's this?" Lyre mimicked Perl, then smiled sheepishly. "Sorry, I can't help myself sometimes."

"Lunch!" Bear said, digging in enthusiastically, "and it's delicious," he added, a strand of wet seaweed hanging out of the corner of his mouth.

"Seekers. Observe. *Phyllobates terribilis*." Yew was holding up a small golden colored frog. "One of the most poisonous creatures on Earth. Nonetheless, only uses as defense." Yew released the frog, allowing it to hop into the middle of their circle. "*Lioohis epinephelus*." Yew held up a grey water snake with a yellow underbelly. "It has evolved in the same ecosystem as the deadly frog." Letting it go, the snake slithered through the sand towards the frog, unhinging its jaws, swallowing it whole.

Perl covered her eyes; she peeked out between her fingers, seeing that the snake was still alive. She watched as it wiggled away into the tall grass with the frog lump in its stomach.

"Ew," Lyre put her hand to her mouth.

Yew slowly rotated, looking at each of the Seekers. "Only this species can prey on this frog. Over time, snake became immune to poison. If not for snake, frogs would cause plague. Other species would die off. Ecosystem destroyed. Balance is critical."

The pelicans took flight as Yew motioned for the class to stand.

"We are finished for today. No battle exercise with Master Kamani."

Perl pulled out her journal, ready to jot down any final thoughts.

Yew looked at them. "Trust your heart, not your eyes. Looks are deceiving." Perl wrote as Yew continued, "where poison has no enemy, it will overwhelm. Nature becomes increasingly unnatural. Follow the way of the *Thaumoctopus mimicus*. Learn to adapt."

Perl put her pencil to her lips, then wrote, *"poison frogs are deadly, snakes are resilient—but they must co-exist. Learn to adapt and change. Be a soldier for good."*

23 CUCKOO

"This will lead you to your next destination," Yew ushered the Seekers off the beach to a wide, rainbow-striped pathway of tightly packed sand. Flanking either side of the pathway were two massive hands carved out of smooth, dark stone, each nearly twenty feet in height. The hands pointed the way home. The path reminded Perl of art she used to make with Brother Jonathan, where she would pour in one color of sand into a jar, then layer on a different color, then another, until the jar was full, making it look like a multi-colored mountain. She smiled.

Bear groaned, "Olliv's not coming? So, we're walking back?"

"Tragic," Opis teased, sidling up to her large roommate and wrapping an arm around him.

After the lamprey drama, none of them were thrilled about having to walk back to their nests, preferring the leisurely crawl, and the snacks, provided by Olliv and his snail.

"This is going to take forever!", "Could those of us with wings fly back?", "We're going to miss lunch!"

As the group aired their complaints, Master Yew halted them. "Together. Nine are one." With that, Yew clapped its feathery arms twice, vanishing into a cloud of peach-colored smoke. Yew left behind its signature parting gift—a single orange and yellow flower; this time, a chrysanthemum. Nan picked up the flower and twisted it around her antenna.

Corvax broke the silence. "Okay, well, it's a long hike back. Let's get going." He headed down the path; the others looked at one another.

"Mr. Personality," Bear joked. The others laughed as they followed Corvax, jogging to catch up with the crow-boy.

At first, they walked quietly, taking in the scenery around them. Flax raised his finger, "anyone want to play a game or something as we walk?"

"I know! How about we tell a story?" Nan chimed in.

"Excellent idea," Opis said, pulling her electrified locks back in a pony tail. "One of us begin a tale, and we'll each add a part as we go. It'll be fun, and might make the walk go faster."

Corvax, who up till now had seemed to be in his own world, suddenly whipped his head back to the group. "Sounds good. I'll start!" Corvax did an about face, and began walking backwards in front of the other eight. To the other's surprise and delight, he began speaking in a very theatrical voice.

"Once upon a time, there was a kind, old woman who lived in a tree house in the woods. She loved children, but had none of her own, only the companionship of a fat lovable cat named Gem, who never left her side…"

Perl smiled. *"I like this Corvax,"* she thought to herself, listening intently as he began the adventurous tale.

"…Her prized possession was a cuckoo clock in the shape of a gilded merry-go-round, complete with a dozen painted horses that turned round and round…" Corvax pointed at Lyre, who was right behind him, "next," he uttered, bowing deeply before stepping to the back of the line.

Lyre mimicked Corvax, spinning around and walking backwards down the road, continuing where he left off.

"…But! It was no ordinary cuckoo clock! The old woman had bought it at an antique store, from a peculiar man whose eyebrows were so long, he tied them to his mustache! What the woman didn't know was this man was a wizard! He took pity on the old woman for being childless, and so he placed a magic spell on the cuckoo clock. Every night, when the clock struck midnight, the ponies would come to life and break free from the carousel! They would gallop around the room, chasing Gem, who would meow in terror as its chubby legs scrambled to get away! The old cat would jump onto tables and chairs, hissing and crying as the old woman giggled with joy…" Lyre curtsied, and fell to the back into line.

"Great job!" Perl said, as Lyre flitted past her.

Opis skipped out to narrate next, "…on four of the ponies, rode four little girls. The old woman named them Bess, Bonnie, Betty, and Beatrice, because she loved names beginning with the letter B, her own name being Bellarose. Oh, how she adored those girls, and they her! Every night at midnight, Bellarose would set out thimbles of hot cocoa and graham cracker pies on doll-sized plates. The girls would sing and play tiny flutes and Bellarose would clap along as she sat in her rocking chair, knitting them all tiny sweaters…"

Flax jumped out, excited. He pulled the skinny girl out of the way. "Hey, watch it!" Opis objected, stumbling back to the rear of the line.

"Okay, okay, my turn…ahh…but this blessing was also a curse! For it would only last one hour each night. After that, the fancy ponies and their riders had to return to their carousel clock on the mantle, and poor Belly-rose would be sad and alone the rest of the hours of the day, waiting and staring at the clock for her one moment of happiness to begin again…"

Lyre yelled out, "it's Bellarose, Flax! You're ruining it!"

Corvax refereed. "Lyre, everyone gets a chance to tell their part. Stories and life can change on a dime, we all know that."

Flax stuck his long tongue out at Lyre. Corvax waved Flax to the back of the line, trying to keep the peace. "Tars, you're next." The monkey-boy somersaulted out, bouncing upright.

Clearing his throat loudly, Tars began, "…But then, one cold winter night, everything changed! The girls' nightly singing drew the interest of an angry, rotten, no-good toad-troll."

Lyre interrupted again, "What? No, no trolls!"

"Lyre, it's Tar's turn. Let him finish." Corvax said. Lyre shook her long tail in frustration.

Tars held a paw up to his large ear, pretending to listen. "...The wart-covered toad-troll had never heard anything so lovely in all his thousand years of existence! One night, under the light of the midnight moon, the toad-troll followed the sweet-sounding tune...wanting a closer look, he climbed up the tree, and peeked into the window. There he saw Bonnie, Beatrice, B-b-b...Beany?"

Lyre interjected, "it's Betty and Bess!"

"Right, right," Tars proceeded, "so the troll saw the girls and thought, 'Yum! What a delicious sweet snack those darling girls would be!'" Tars giggled and ran to the back, his buddy Flax giving him a slap on the shoulder; the two boys were quite pleased with the direction the story was going.

Nan took over, fluttering her butterfly wings as she spoke, "...The adorable song from the beautiful girls took hold of the troll. Deep inside his black, shriveled heart, he felt something he'd never felt before...joy! He cracked a wrinkly smiled for the first time in five hundred years, revealing a row of very yellow teeth! Beatrice, who was the smallest of the four girls, looked out the window and noticed the smiling toad-troll. The tiny girl wasn't afraid at all, seeing his toothy grin. As their eyes met, both of their hearts melted. It was love at first sight!" Lyre squeaked with glee at Nan's clever twist.

"You're up, Perl," Bear called from behind Javan.

Perl shot a worried look back at Bear, and Javan could see she wasn't ready to share, so he stepped out. "I'll go."

Javan brushed back is bangs from his eyes, "...Little Beatrice wanted desperately to go outside and be with her new love, but how? She'd never lived anywhere except inside the carousel clock, inside the safety of the tree house. Beatrice's heart was bursting for adventure, and so she took a leap of faith, jumping onto her pony and bolting for a tiny crack in the door! The toad-troll held out his big green webbed hand, and the girl galloped safely onto it..."

As Javan was continuing the story, Perl had an idea. She gestured frantically to Javan, letting him know she was ready. He politely stepped aside as Perl hopped to the front of the line. She turned and faced the group with her hands behind her back, like a professor.

"...The toad-troll, whose names was Samuel, knew a secret that no one else knew—not Bellarose, or the mustachioed wizard, or the little girls! Only Samuel knew that Bellarose lived in an enchanted forest, and had built her house in a Wishing Tree," Perl exclaimed, seeing the group's faces light up. "Seeing how sad old Bellarose was every time the girls and the ponies had to return to the clock, Samuel took pity on her. Breaking off a prickly limb from a Boojum tree, he waved it into the air and uttered the magical words to make the wish come true—'Abraca-coo-coo! Alla-be-free! You are now real, one, two, three!' And just like that, Bess, Betty, Bonnie, and Beatrice all turned into real girls! They hugged the old woman, who they called their mother, and Bellarose was finally happy, every day, for the rest of her life!" Perl was beaming with pride, as Bear stepped up.

"Excuse me, my turn, Perly," Bear made a grand gesture, stretching out his sets of arms. Perl stepped back, forgetting Bear hadn't gone yet, thinking hers was the perfect ending to the tale.

Bear gave a wry smile, comically raising his eyebrows up and down. "...So, Samuel and this alive but very tiny wife, Beatrice, returned to his cold, smelly toad-troll cave. They spent many happy days together. Beatrice even got use to eating flies and sleeping in the mud, because with each new dawn their love grew stronger. Samuel loved Beatrice so much, he began to worry that perhaps one day she'd want to return to her sisters. On the days she would go out riding on her pony, his toad-troll heart would ache so terribly, it felt like it was breaking. While sipping a cup of warm spider spit, the troll had an idea how they could be together, forever and always. That night, when Samuel held out his webbed palm, and Beatrice road up onto it, he sprinkled some salt on her head like snow...and ate her and her pony whole! The End!" At that, Bear fell on the ground, tickled with his ending. Tars and Flax ran over and jumped on the roly-poly, all of them giddy with delight at the tragic turn of events.

Lyre, Nan and Perl all groaned, while Javan and Opis looked at one another and chuckled, and even Corvax smiled.

Perl shouted at the boys, a little irked at their twisting of her tale, "no, I meant that Beatrice and the girls grew to full size when they came to life, so he couldn't have eaten her, because they all grew big!"

"Sorry, all's fair in storytelling!" Bear laughed as he continued to roll around, quite pleased with himself.

Corvax broke up the disagreement, "and look, just like that, we're back home." He pointed up the road.

Perl saw the silhouettes of their nests. "Wow, that did make the time fly. Race you guys the rest of the way!"

Perl hopped over Bear, Flax, and Tars, and took off in a sprint. None of them chased after her.

"I'm too pooped to run," Tars laid back down in the grass.

"That girl has way too much energy for me," Bear grunted as he rocked back and forth, trying to stand back up.

"Everyone has more energy than you," Opis replied, twirling a tentacle around her finger.

"Wait for me!" Flax jumped up and chased after her; the sun had kept him fully charged.

Perl ran until she reached the blue-pebbled path leading up to their nests, finally stopping to catch her breath. "I win, slow-pokes!"

Perl turned around and realized that no one but Flax had bothered to run. She plopped on the ground next to a small sapling blossoming with little white flowers. Perl recalled that first day in Venusto, and her conversation with Uriel.

"Hello, little friend," Perl said. "You started off as a tiny seed, and look how much you've grown."

24 SPELUNK

Perl rose before the sun some mornings to take walks, always mindful to stay within the confines of Callowhorn, ever since her adventure at Greenheart. As the days and weeks rolled by, Perl was slowly getting to know every inch of her home away from home. Having made friends with Olliv's chipmunks, Perl liked to wander down to their kitchen to keep them company while they prepared the day's breakfast.

"Good morning, Chef Dewdrop," Perl said cheerily to a small critter, who stopped and gave her a quick wave, his tiny rolling pin covered in flour. Perl grabbed a seat on a log chair across from a long row of wood-burning stoves; each was encased in a hearth of stone. "Mmm...Something smells delicious."

The chipmunks didn't speak, but they did make happy, little chirpy noises while they worked, checking the oatmeal bread in the oven and filling flower cups with nectar. They reminded Perl of her beloved spider-monks, scurrying around the root cellar pantry, preparing the island's food for deliveries.

"How about a tune while you work?" Perl asked, pulling out her kalimba from her backpack. She plinked a few times on her turtle-shaped instrument. "Okay, here's one my friend Victr taught me."

"Roll, roll, roll out the dough,
flour your pin, and roll it again!
Cut, cut, cut out the shapes,
pop them in, and do a spin!
Ding, ding, ding goes the bell...
eat up, my good kin, 'til your belly grins!"

The chipmunks moved with the plinking of the instrument, jumping and bobbing to and fro as Perl repeated the song, finishing with a grand bow. Plucking a large shiny fiddle-leaf from a nearby fig tree, a portly chipmunk wrapped up a piece of bread for Perl, tying it up with a long wispy vine; the bread was toasty warm in her hands and smelled delicious.

"Oh, thank you! See you later," Perl said, playfully flicking the chipmunk's fuzzy chin. Through his soft white fur, the chipmunk blushed, his plump cheeks turning a rosy pink.

As Perl casually strolled along, taking in the natural beauty of Callowhorn, a flock of magnificent flying manta rays swooped down, circling around Perl, fully knowing she would toss them a snack.

"Greetings, friends! Ready? Catch!" Perl threw a bit of bread into the sky; a golden ray with blue speckles snatched it out of the air. "Oh, here...have the rest," Perl crumpled the bread into bits. "Open wide!" she yelled, tossing the rest into the air and running. The manta rays swarmed in a frenzy over her head, their fins rippling as they gobbled up the tasty morsels.

Almost skipping now, Perl stopped to say hello to a patch of roses who were just waking up, their bright red petals slowly uncurling. "Wake up, sleepy heads!" The flowers were not quite ready for the sudden greeting; they closed their petals back up and shrunk down, returning to their slumber. Perl shrugged. "Okay, but you're missing the best part of the day."

Perl followed a path down the hill from the kitchen towards the large shimmering white lake, one of her favorite spots in Venusto. This was where she had first docked with Uriel in their webbed balloon boat, floating in through the great bear cloud. Perl liked to come here for some alone time; the peaceful surroundings helped to clear her mind as she filled her trusty sketchbook.

A few boats were on the water, and there wasn't a Being in sight. Perl strolled past the rows of tall wooden pilings that anchored the dock, which had been intricately carved into a variety of animal busts; as she passed each one, she tapped them on the head—there was the lion, then the kangaroo, the llama, the bumblebee, wolf, alligator—on and on. Perl loved seeing what peculiar new vessels might have sailed in overnight. This morning, there was a hollowed-out coconut, large enough that Olliv's enormous snail-taxi could have comfortably rode inside of it with room to spare. Palm trees grew off the bow and stern of the boat, as a rigging of dark green fronds served as sails. Next to the coconut boat was a catamaran built of one giant pair of caribou antlers; every foot or so, a wax candle had been melted onto the antlers; the glow lit up the boat like a Christmas tree.

Perl stepped off the dock, walking along the water's edge toward her private spot. As the flat, sandy ground gently rose into a series of undulating grassy hills, nestled in one of the valleys, stood a single tree. The tree was unlike any Perl had ever seen back on Earth. From thick wide roots it grew, though it wasn't a particularly tall tree; Perl guessed it was about the height of say, Master Kamani. Golden branches with thick, flamingo-pink leaves gently swayed in the breeze. Dotting the tree were cottony white flowers, slender and tube-like, attracting every type of pollinator on Venusto. Perl listened to the music of buzzing insects traveling from flower to flower. She loved this tree and knew that the tree loved her, too. In fact, the tree had become such a friendly companion that Perl had named her.

"Good morning, Lottie. Thanks for saving my seat." Perl settled in between two raised roots at its base, the perfect size for her bottom to rest comfortably on. She took out her sketchbook, leaning back against the tree's smooth, cool trunk; a warm breeze rustled the book's pages.

The nook, just a few short paces from the shoreline, allowed Perl to see across the entire lake all the way to the cave on the far side of the water. To Perl, this was the perfect spot for some quiet time before the day began.

"Whatcha doin'?" Javan plunked down next to her.

"Ahh! Where did you come from?" Perl jumped.

Javan laughed, "Well, that's a long story. Maybe I'll tell you someday." Perl shoved Javan playfully.

"What are you doing here so early? Did you follow me?"

"Pardon me, I live here too, you know," he said, crossing his arms, "I like to come down here once in a while for a morning swim." Perl liked that Javan seemed to love the water as much as she did. Javan raised an eyebrow at Perl. "You know, I could ask you the same question. What brings *you* down here this early?"

"Well, it's usually my *alone* time," Perl said, closing her sketchbook, "but since you're here, how about we do a little exploring?" Perl hopped up and started walking along the lake's edge.

"Oo-kay," Javan chuckled. He trotted after her. "So, where we headed?"

Perl gestured up ahead, "I've seen most of Callowhorn, so I thought I'd check out the caves."

Javan caught up to her. "Those are off limits…at least I think they are," he said, scratching the fur on his tightly-cropped head.

"Says who? Aren't you even a little curious?" Tucking her sketchbook into her backpack, Perl slung it over her arm, stepping up her pace.

"The last time I was curious with you, I ended up stinking like old socks for a week!" Javan tried to keep up with the speedy young girl. "Oh, and almost got killed by a Roc! Remember that?"

Perl hid a smile, ignoring the boy waddling behind her.

As they neared the entrance of the cave, Perl could hear the rushing river echoing inside. She paused to look back across the water at Venusto remembering her excitement at seeing this glistening paradise for the first time. It all sparkled like sunlit jewels.

"C'mon, let's go!" Perl said.

"Alright, but if I get swallowed up by a cave beast, it's on you."

"Haha, very funny,"

It was cool and damp inside; slivers of glistening stalagmites and stalactites lined the floor and ceiling, twinkling like stars.

"It looks like a place that magical fairies would live, doesn't it?" Perl's voice reverberated off the cave walls. Specks of light reflected off her face; her elongated shadow wiggled and danced on the smooth sienna-colored walls. "This is the tunnel Uriel and I came through," Perl pointed up to a crude drawing of a herd of animals. Their black stick legs moved back and forth as they ran along the walls. Perl took a seat on the cool cavern floor and pulled out her journal, sketching out what she saw, her fingers flying.

Javan peered over her shoulder. "You're really good, you know that?"

"These are rough." Perl covered her sketch with her arm. "I'm not really trying."

"Well, just think how great you'd be if ya' did try," he teased. "You have amazing talent, Perl. Truly Ever-given gifts."

"Are we still talking about my art?"

"Sure, but you know—all of your abilities. It takes time to fully learn how to use them.

Perl examined her pencil, her special gift from Uriel, taking in every tiny detail; the girl, arms forward, riding atop the whale, her full head of hair blowing back in the breeze. "I know I need more practice." She shot him a quick side glance, then continued doodling.

Javan leaned back and looked up at the cave drawings. The herd had migrated and were now on the wall behind Perl, huddled together, watching. "Yes, but you clearly have a magic all your own."

"I've always seen and heard strange things." Perl put her pencil down. "People around Mont Michel thought I was a weirdo. I knew that, but I didn't care because I had my monks."

"I'm sorry, humans can be so cruel to one another sometimes."

"Yeah people can be," she stared at the page, "but I never saw anything that wanted to hurt me or anyone I cared about. Not until the day before I had to come here. Out of nowhere, flowers were biting me, the Golden Palace was a nightmare, and we got attacked by Whisper Wisps!"

Javan kneeled down beside her. "Wait. You saw Whisper Wisps on Earth?"

Perl sighed, "yes. Victr killed a few of them."

Javan nodded, biting one of the sharp nails on his webbed hand.

Perl continued in a quieter voice, "when I was little. My Papa would tuck me in at night, and I'd always ask him, 'Do you love me?' It was like a weird habit. I knew he loved me, but I felt like if I didn't hear him say it that something would come from the darkness of my room and get me." She slid her pencil back into its holding place. "It's like my worst fear is coming true. That thing in the darkness. It's after me, even here."

"You're safe here, you know that, right?"

"You saw that creature at the bottom of the lake? It almost killed Bear, and what about those lamprey eels in the reef pool? They were sent here to get me, I know it!"

"By who?"

"Malblud. I have to face it, before it hurts anyone else."

"But Perl, this isn't just your fight, don't you understand that?"

"You...you wouldn't understand." She stood up. "This goes back to my fath—" Perl paused. The sound of muffled voices could be heard coming from farther inside the cave. "Hello? Is someone in here?"

Javan dipped one of his hands into the river, his electroreceptors trying to pick up any distant movement in the water; it was quiet.

Perl took off towards the voices, stuffing her sketchbook into her backpack.

Javan sighed. "See? This is what I'm talking about…safety in numbers!" He hurried after her as the two of them slipped down a side corridor.

Halfway down they stopped. Approximately five feet above their heads were three holes cut into the cave wall.

"Listen. It's coming from up there." Perl looked around the cave; she and Javan spotted a few flat rocks and stacked them into a makeshift ladder. Perl climbed up and was on her tiptoes, straining to see as Javan held her legs for support. The openings were just big enough for one person to see through.

"Well?" Javan asked anxiously.

"What the—? It's the beach. My beach. Back home in Mont Michel. How am I seeing this?!" Perl watched as the seagulls squawked and cried over the dark gray waters.

Javan shook her legs. "What's in the next one?"

Perl peeked in the middle opening; the scene before her was of a yacht out on the water. Perl recognized Count Graves. He was with another man. They had guns and were shooting into the water, laughing as they puffed on cigars.

"What are they shooting at? I don't understand," she mumbled,

"Shooting? Who's shooting? Lemme see," Javan asked.

"Hang on, I have to see what's in the last one." Perl leaned over. "It's two people but they're in the shadows. I can't see who it is…pee-yoo!" She held her nose. "It stinks like rotten fish. Wait. I recognize that voice. It's Uriel! She's got something in her hand. Looks like a small bottle." Perl thought back to her and Uriel's visit to Palo Santo, where she saw Uriel slip a vial into her pocket.

"Come on, let me have a look," Javan pleaded, but Perl was glued to the spot.

"Oh my Ever…it's Malblud," she gasped. "Why is Uriel with Malblud?" She stepped off the rocks, slumping down against the wall.

"What?" Javan climbed up, peering through the hole. "She's with a man."

"It's the Slaughterman." Perl said.

"The who? You know him? But you said it was Malblud," Javan stammered, his head going from Perl, back to the window, back to Perl.

"Don't you see? They're one and the same! He was in Mont Michel all along. But why? Why would Uriel meet with him? I thought she was on our side?" Perl stepped back onto the rocks, squeezing next to Javan. "Move over!"

Javan teetered on the edge as Perl took another look. There was no doubt, it was Uriel, handing the Slaughterman the bottle. She had her arm on the shoulder of his filthy coat; it was covered in blood. A mixture of anger and sadness overcame Perl; she could feel tears welling up.

Javan tried his best to comfort her. "Look at me, Perl. Uriel is on our side." A tear fell from the girl's cheek; it hit the rocks and a tiny green leaf immediately sprouted up. "Don't be so quick to judge. We don't know for sure what's going on."

Perl turned her head towards him; they were nose to nose. "And who's side are you on?"

He gave her a look of surprise. "Yours, of course."

She rubbed her eyes and turned back to have another look.

Javan stepped down off the rocks, "I'm always on your side," he whispered to himself.

"She's saying something to him." Perl was listening intently, trying to read Uriel's lips. She mouthed Uriel's words, "that…should…take care…of her." Perl was in disbelief. She was also certain she saw Uriel utter the word, "poison."

"What's she saying?"

Perl lied, "I'm not sure. It's too far away to hear." She watched as the Slaughterman stuffed the vial into his pocket and scurried off, the rotten smell fading away as he left.

"I bet you anything that's *Gyromitra*," Perl muttered.

"The toxic mushroom? Why would you think that?"

"I saw one when Uriel and I were at Palo Santo's greenhouse, and…"

"…don't jump to conclusions, Perl."

"I saw Uriel take something from there and I didn't say anything." Perl took one more peek into the hole; the two were gone. She hopped off the rock, her brow furrowed. "I just don't get it, Javan. How were we able to see them? Why are these holes even here?"

"I honestly don't know. Come on, we gotta go. Olliv will be coming soon to take everyone to meditation." Javan could see the disappointment on Perl's face. He tried to think of something to change her mood. "Hey, wanna swim back? I'll race ya!" He cannonballed into the river.

Despite how she felt, Perl couldn't resist a challenge, especially when there was a chance to beat a boy. She did her best to tie her backpack to the top of her bushy head, and waded carefully into the river. Javan was doing a leisurely backstroke in front of her.

"This is hardly fair. I can't get my book wet," Perl contended. She bobbed in the water, doing her best to keep her head dry.

"Whaddya call that stroke? The Perl Paddle?" Javan laughed.

177

Perl tried to splash him. Javan went under in a flash, waving his webbed foot at her as he dove. He swam circles around Perl. She couldn't believe how fast he moved through the water. Javan popped up behind her, shaking his furry head. The water droplets beaded up, rolling off him like a duck.

"Show-off!"

"You think that's something? Watch this!"

Perl watched as he swam towards the bottom and then came rocketing out of the water like a torpedo. Tucking into a ball, he flipped twice in the air before hitting the water, splashing Perl in the face.

"Hey! Watch it, platypus!"

His grinning face broke the surface. "Jealous?" Quick as a seal, Javan crossed to the other side of the riverbank, waving back at Perl.

The truth was, Perl was envious. She imagined how awesome it would be able to swim like that; racing along with the whales, launching herself up out of the water and coming down in a mighty *ker-splash!* She grabbed onto a log floating by, letting the current carry her. Perl closed her eyes, picturing the whales, and began to hum their song:

> *"Hmmm, as the rough tides topple*
> *we need your light,*
> *still you don't seem to care,*
> *this is our Earth,*
> *the home we all share.*
> *There's still magic to believe,*
> *some love that binds us…hmmm."*

Out of the water and shaking like a wet dog, Javan watched Perl as she causally kicked, her bioluminescent glow lighting up the water around her. She was singing. Javan smiled, happy her spirits had lifted. Perl casually bumped along the rocky shoreline to a stop. Javan held out his hand.

"Second place is still good," he smiled smugly.

Perl let go of the log and reached up, careful not to drop her backpack. She looked at the boy, the water droplets in his hair sparkling like diamonds.

She squeezed his hand, "I let you win," she joked, giving a yank on the boy, pulling him back into the water.

25 UNDER ONE'S HEEL

Even for the tropical isle of Mont Michel, the day was unnaturally humid; the thick air causing the windows of the Golden Palace to sweat as the condensation formed. Sunken down in her swan-shaped chair, Mik Graves was too hot to move. She sat across from her comatose sister, cooling herself with a fan shaped like a gingko leaf; the handle made of jade. Unfortunately for Mik, her mother, The Countess Sarr, seemed immune to the stifling heat, having endless amounts of nervous energy.

"I cannot believe your father had the audacity to go out with his cronies at a time like this." She flitted about the twin's bedroom, fluffing the piles of pillows around Ivry, reading and re-reading prescription bottles, and hysterically yammering on.

"Honestly, darling, your sister hasn't opened her eyes in three days, and I have asked Zell—No, demanded!— that more doctors be brought here! We need as many minds working on this as we can!" She ran her white gloved finger along the top of one the girl's vanities, staring at the trace amount of dust it revealed, a pained look on her face.

Countess Sarr was not used to taking care of anyone other than herself. Ruby, the twins' governess, had always seen to their every need. However, since Ivry had fallen ill, Sarr had made finding a cure for her sick daughter her full-time job.

"Mother, you're exhausted. Why don't you take a break? I'll watch over Ivry." Mik slowly pushed herself up out of the chair, and stepped into her enormous walk in closet. She snapped a photo of her latest pair of rare python *(Pythonidae)* heels to keep up the daily postings for their rabid Redhot fanbase. "I know, dear mother, why don't you go and have a nice, cool milk and honey bath?" Mik popped out of the closet and over to her mother, prying a pill bottle from her grip while gently guiding her towards the door. Sarr, half in a trance, gazed at her daughter as if she were a stranger.

"Oh? Oh yes. I suppose, just for a while, and it is quite warm, isn't it? What is with these extreme temperatures of late?"

Mik gave her mother a condescending nod. "Yes, it is warm. I'll tell Ruby to lower the temperature in your suite to sixty degrees, alright?" Mik fanned her mother as she escorted her out of the room, giving her a slight push as she angled her down the long hallway. She watched as her mother bumbled halfway down, then seem to regain her bearings, and off she went in a frantic speed walk. Mik breathed a sigh of relief, but no sooner had she closed the door behind her, when there came a light knock. Mik stood, arms crossed.

"What now? Who's there?"

"A friend," said a low, deep, gravelly voice. Mik didn't recognize it.

"We're not expecting any visitors today. Go, or I'll call the guards." She turned and leaned back against the door. There was another thin rap.

"There is a cure, trust me." The man's eerie tone made Mik's skin crawl.

"I said, who are you?!" Mik shouted through the closed door, slowly locking the brass deadbolt. There was a moment of silence. Mik thought the stranger may have left, but then a slip of dirty, stained paper was pushed under the door. It rubbed up against her shoe and Mik gave a slight yip, jumping as if a mouse had scampered underfoot. She ran over to where a gold embroidered rope dangled from the ceiling, and gave two angry tugs on it. A low bell could be heard down the hall, and in less than a minute, a buzz outside the door went off; the door unlocked, and two large, muscular men with guns entered her room.

"What is it, your grace?"

Mik picked up the note and slipped it into her pocket. "There was someone here, knocking at our door. He said he was a friend, but I don't know who he was."

The guards glanced around the hall. "There's no one here, Princess Mik."

The twin pushed past the two brutes, peering down the hallway. To the left, there was nothing. Looking to the right, she gestured at the floor.

"Then what do you call that?" She pointed to dirty footprints on the plush white carpet, running down the hall. "And what is that horrible smell?" She waved a hand in front of her face. "Find this creep, now!" She yelled, slamming the heavy door and locking it behind her. The two guards looked dumbly at one another, shrugged, and began following the footsteps to the servant's staircase.

Mik sat on her bed across from her sister, speaking softly but firmly, "Ivry. Ivry please wake up. I need you." Her sister remained motionless; the only sound was the beeping of the medical equipment hooked up around her. Mik unrolled the crumpled note, careful to touch it with just the tips of her long red manicured fingernails. The message was scrawled in broken, jagged lettering:

"Come to the cave."

Next to the message was a rough sketch of a mushroom. Mik held the grimy note away from her with two fingers. She took a pink perfume bottle from her vanity, and gave the paper a spritz to mask the foul odor. Rolling it back up, she opened one of the drawers of her ivory standing jewelry chest. Retrieving a small silk bag from the drawer, she slipped the rolled-up note into it, closing the drawer with a slam. Mik thought for a moment, twisting a strand of bright red hair around her fingers. *"A cave...?"* For years, she'd heard the servants gossiping about someone named Slaughterman who lived in a cave on an island of trash. *"Probably just a dumb rumor,"* she thought, then looked over at her sister. Her heart sank.

Out at sea, the twins' father, Count Graves was preparing for the arrival of a few members of a private society. This association's constituents had risen to great power in recent years, and through various subversive practices, they now controlled more than half of the free world's resources. Run by representatives from their respective parts of the globe, this shadow group had no official name, but rather, a secret mark they all shared. Inked onto the bottom arch of each member's right foot was a tattoo of Earth. Draped around the globe was a banner, with a phrase in ancient Latin: *'Qui sub plantam fratris tenebat—* 'Under One's Heel'.

Today's meeting was being held on board The Count's mega-yacht, a massive craft the length of a football field, complete with helicopter pad, one hundred state-of-the-art guest suites, an Olympic-size glass bottom infinity pool, and unparalleled custom décor throughout. At cocktail parties, The Count liked to brag that the amount of money and resources needed to maintain his floating "pride and joy" surpassed most country's entire gross domestic product, much to the delight of his peers.

At the helipad, the Crown Prince of the Desertlands stepped down from his private executive chopper. Tall, slender, and sun baked, he strode over to meet The Count.

"Count Zell, this has to be one of the most unnecessary, self-indulgent frills I've ever laid eyes on...I love it!"

Graves shook hands with the rail thin Prince, a proud grin plastered on his face. "Prince Tobias, so glad you could make it."

The Prince patted his stomach, "anything for some of your famous beluga caviar."

A flamboyant character to say the least, the Prince wore a double-headed cobra *(Serpentes)* headdress, tight snakeskin pants, and a cape made of lizard scales. His knee-high black boots came to a curled tip, creating a strange look—part Egyptian pharaoh, part woodland elf.

Graves boastfully showed Prince Tobias around the top deck of his monster yacht. "We have three full chef's kitchens, and I believe the caviar is being chilled as we speak." With a handkerchief, Graves wiped beads of sweat off his brow; he handed it to a servant, who whisked it away. "It's a bit on the warm side today, would you care for a bit of shade?" The Count clapped twice and in an instant, two stewards appeared, carrying giant umbrellas.

The Prince chuckled, waving away the servant. "Hot? Surely you joke. My blood is thinner than a scorpion! This feels like a winter's day compared to the heat of the Desertlands!"

The Count laughed. "If you're comfortable, I'm comfortable," he said, dismissing the umbrella-bearers. "Come, walk with me."

The two strolled over to a small impromptu buffet that had been set up to greet the guests. A portly chef stood at attention behind an impressive ice sculpture of a miniature version of the Count's yacht. An elegant display of caviar was neatly arranged; the dark purple fish eggs daintily scooped into small white half shells, the entire array glistening against the shimmering ice.

"After you, Prince," The Count said, sweeping his arm toward the buffet in a grand gesture. The Prince eyed the chef, who smiled nervously.

Tobias clasped his hands in anticipation as the chef selected a half dozen of the shells, delicately placing them on a small silver plate. He offered the Prince a silk napkin, then handed him the attractive dish, bowing. Before the chef could even come back up, the Prince had scarfed down two of the servings, making loud, obnoxious slurping sounds as he did. He tossed the shells on the ground.

"Mm...delicious," he mumbled, finishing up the rest.

Count Graves smiled. "I'm glad you're pleased. Ah, but I see more guests are arriving. Please accompany me."

The Prince nodded, black caviar dripping out of the corner of his mouth. He swiped a few more as they left the buffet stand. The chef quickly ran around to pick up the broken shells.

Because of the stifling heat, Graves chose not to wear his signature black three-piece suit, but instead opted for a crisp black, short-sleeved dress shirt, knee-length shorts, and his pointed, jet-black boots. Sewn on top of each of his shoulders was a small smoke-gray shark fin *(Carcharodon carcharias)*. Count Graves' exposed arms revealed tattoos inked with liquid gold; ones he was eager to show off. His upper right arm had the Graves family crest—two crowned dolphins with crossed swords. His left arm was a full sleeve of menacing-looking sea creatures—sharks, a killer whale, barracuda, a mythical kraken, various eels— all bearing razor sharp teeth.

"Quite intimidating," Tobias pointed to Grave's arm.

"These creatures," The Count ran his finger along his tattoos. "They rule the ocean...along with yours truly," he laughed. The veins in his sweaty forehead pulsated.

The two men strolled along the immense upper deck toward the helipad, when a loud voice came shouting from behind them.

"Tobias! You dare show your face, knowing I'd be here?!" A heavyset man pointed at them; below the man's hips, a pair of brass prosthetic stallion-legs flashed in the sunlight. It was King Coppice; he'd remained on Mont Michel since attending the twins' birthday ball, and was invited by Graves to join today's meeting. He clomped over to them gruffly.

The Prince, unfazed, responded. "Your Highness still owes me those black diamonds and barrels of fuel I won off you during the Hot Springs Games."

Coppice yelled at the Prince, "you'll get your gems, and your gas...when I get my legs back!" The King stomped his fake horse-leg hard on the deck. The two stood nose to nose, their chests puffed out like gorillas, glaring at one another.

Count Graves looked on nervously. "Uh...gentleman...?"

Slowly, the King's face softened into a huge grin. "Life's a cruel maiden, is she not? Ha! How are you, my friend?"

The Prince smiled. "I am well...and you?" The two men embraced in a bear hug, laughing loudly.

Graves breathed a sigh of relief. Breaking the men's jovial reunion was a loud splash. A small pink, tiger-striped submarine surfaced alongside the massive boat. Immediately, four hydraulic arms emerged from the side of the yacht. They slipped over and under the submarine, clamping it firmly and hoisting it effortlessly out of the water.

"Surprise, surprise. She's on time." The Count motioned to the first mate, who wore a vampire squid *(Vampyroteuthis infernal)* vest over his crisp whites, to lower the staircase.

Stepping out of the sub's hatch and slinking up the stairs was a tall, gorgeous woman in her early 40's, with olive tone skin and long raven hair. She was wearing a skintight bodysuit identical to the pink tiger pattern of her sub.

"Hello, boys." The woman held a pink gem-studded leash in her hand. Giving a slight tug, up came a small cheetah cub *(Acinonyx jubatus)* crawling out of the hatch behind her. "Come, Baby. Come say hello." The small cub gave a snarl.

"Ambassador, welcome aboard." Graves held out his hand.

The woman looked up at him with big blue eyes. "It's just us, honey. Call me Kandy."

Tobias stepped in front of Graves, taking the woman's arm as he gestured to the cub, "I didn't know we could bring dates. I'm a little jealous." The Prince gave a slight wink, reaching down to pet the cat; it swiped at him, hissing angrily.

"Baby never leaves my side, do you, Baby?" Kandy picked up the cheetah, kissing it on the nose as the three men watched.

Kandy Vandenmire was the heiress to her grandfather's steel empire. After a brief but successful stint as a pop singer, she eventually took over the family business after her father's untimely death at the age of just forty-two. Her latest foray, of which she had held for the last nine years, was that of Ambassador to the Southern Archipelago.

"Come inside. We'll have a drink or two...or six." Count Graves directed Prince Tobias, King Coppice, and The Ambassador and her cheetah cub into a lush estate room located on the main deck. The entire room, from the walls to the furniture, was upholstered in a haunting black and crimson palette.

"My, this is…something," the Ambassador turned in a circle, taking in the room, twisting the cub's leash around her legs.

"Thirteenth century, Venice. But of course, I added my own touch." The Count ran his hand along the raised flocked heirloom wallpaper, and in an instant, the whole room changed to a royal blue and gold motif. Swiping his hand across the back of a chair, again the room changed, this time to neon pink and silver. "Sensory Responsive Design…the latest in personal interior optimization. I'm the first to have it."

Kandy clapped, "marvelous! Zell, talk to Sarr…I simply must have your designer's name!" Graves ignored the ill-mannered attempt to pilfer one of his clients; she should know that was in poor taste.

"What sort of host am I? Angels, see to our guests." At the far end of the room, standing at the ready behind a long, curved mahogany table large enough to seat a small village, six young women dressed in angelfish *(Pterophyllum)* outfits glided into the room on hover footwear. They zipped around without saying a word, handing each of the guests a smoky black drink in a crystal skull glass.

"Try it," Graves encouraged, "I discovered it on my recent trip to the Ice Islands. Apparently, it's becoming quite popular…Forty-year-old Scotch, infused with magma from live volcanos…"

One of the servers handed Prince Tobias a plate loaded with caviar. "Lovely! More beluga!" He talked with his mouth full, "so what brings us all here today, Count? Besides your delicious caviar and exotic libations?"

Graves whispered into the tiny mic implanted in his temple, "Snive, bring me the case."

The Count's squirrelly assistant, Snive, scampered into the room, always ready to please. He placed a tortoise shell briefcase on a glass table.

"Gather round, won't you?" Graves downed his drink, taking another cocktail from the server.

The three moguls crowded in, always intrigued by something new and shiny. Graves motioned to Snive to open the case. "Yes sir." Unlatching the case, it appeared to be filled with dark sludge. A harsh odor of sulfur and oil wafted up.

Kandy held her hand up to her face. "Oh my…what is that smell?"

Prince Tobias gave a sarcastic snort, "is this a joke? I came all the way here for…mud? I've got things to do, Graves, and you are costing me time and money."

"Zell, old pal, what is this crap?" King Coppice grunted.

"It's our future, my skeptical colleagues," Graves boasted. The Count stuck his hand into the shell briefcase, pulling out a fistful of oily mud. He waved it in their direction, the pungent smell wafting around them. "This is the most fertile soil in existence, excavated from 5,000 meters below the seafloor. It contains an amalgamate of three of the rarest minerals on Earth—Cassiterite, Coltan, and gold—as well as other minerals the labs have yet to identify."

King Coppice adjusted his monocle, looking at the bluish-brown goop as he scrunched his nose. "It looks like mud to me."

Graves chuckled. "This *mud*, as you call it, is responsible for nearly all the technology we as a race have come to covet! Everything—from communication, to travel, to entertainment and weaponry—relies on this mud." The Count gave a menacing grin, curling his fake tentacled mustache. "It's worth billions…and it's all for the taking. The world will come begging us on their hands and knees!"

Prince Tobias lapped up his second plate of caviar. "You've piqued my interest, Graves. What's next?"

"First of all," with a sudden jerk, The Count flicked the mud off his hand and back into the case, "what I'm telling you stays in this room. No press. I've got enough of those annoying activists at my shores, I don't need more. Seafloor ecosystems are…tricky, so mining them will only rile up those insolent protesters." The Count wiped his hands on Snive's shirt. "Secondly, there's a slight issue we need to be discreet about. When my men retrieved this, trace amounts of unidentifiable radioactive material were apparently released into the waters. Small amounts. Barely noticeable." The Count held up his drink, "are we in agreement…partners?"

The three of them raised their glasses. Prince Tobias placed a hand on Grave's shoulder, careful not to get stabbed by his shark fin epaulet. "So, when do we start drilling?" He said, finishing his cocktail in one gulp.

"Soon, soon. But let's celebrate with a bit of sport, shall we?" Graves walked over to an imposing wall of weaponry, pulling a gold harpoon gun down. "What do you say, gentlemen? And the lady?"

Laying across the red velvet couch, stroking her cheetah cub, Kandy took the last sip of her drink. "I have prior engagements, I'm afraid. You boys have fun and keep me updated on this project." She strolled over, giving Graves a peck on the cheek. "I'll see myself out. Tat-ta!" Graves gave a nod to Snive, who followed the woman and her cheetah back to her pink submarine.

King Coppice pulled a pair of harpoon guns from the wall brackets, handing one to the Prince. "Very well, then. Enough business, time for pleasure."

"Maestro! Some music!" At The Count's command, loud classical music mixed with a techno beat began playing. The three men strolled out of the estate room to the main deck's front railing. The angelfish servants with their flowing white fins floated out to them, dispersing pipes.

Prince Tobias took a deep puff on his pipe; he looked at it—it was carved into a busty mermaid. "Oh, how I do love the high seas!"

Graves nodded genially, then peered over his shoulder at Snive, who, having returned from escorting The Ambassador out, now lurked under one of the deck's many canopies. Eyeing a drone hovering suspiciously about the rear of the ship, he nodded back at Graves.

Snive spoke into his headset, "take it out."

"Roger that." A gunman stationed at the other end of the yacht took aim and shot the buzzing drone out of the sky with a net-gun; it crashed into the water and sank.

Graves watched it go down. Satisfied, he turned, slapping the two men on the back. "Coast is clear, gents. Ah, perfect timing! Here they come now."

A pod of bottlenose dolphins *(Tursiops truncatus)* swam up alongside the fast-moving yacht.

"What's the wager?" Prince Tobias balanced his harpoon gun on his shoulder.

"Whatever it is you still owe me." King Coppice took a long draw off his pipe, blowing a smoke ring around the Prince's face.

Count Graves took aim. "Five for a body shot, ten thousand for a flipper, twenty thousand for a blowhole-in-one." He took a shot and missed. A nearby deckhand quickly reeled in the bobbing golden arrow and re-loaded it.

"You're a bit rusty, I see!" Laughed the King.

The dolphins continued to play, flitting and hopping next to the massive vessel, unaware of any danger. King Coppice shot, hitting a fin, splitting it in half. "Ha! Count it!"

The dolphin's high-pitched whistles rang out to warn the pod.

"Quickly now, they're smart!" said Graves. "They'll start to break off!"

Prince Tobias shot, spearing one's tail. "On the money, boys!" The dolphin cried out.

The pod scattered in the water, jetting in all directions. Count Graves' final shot landed in the center blowhole of an escaping calf. Blood splashed up like a fountain. "Bullseye! Twenty big ones, boys!"

As quick as they had appeared, the dolphins were gone. The King stomped his large stallion legs. "Bah! Well played, Zell!"

Tobias tossed his gun into the water like a spoiled child. "What's the damage?"

"We'll settle up later." Graves handed his gun to the guard. "What's a little money between friends, eh?" The harpooned dolphin wriggled on the deck. "Who needs another drink?"

"Make mine a double," King Coppice said, as the three men left the deck.

The deckhand cut the rope, releasing the calf into the water; the gold harpoon still stuck inside its air supply. The pod of dolphins regrouped; they squeaked and squealed, gently nuzzling the small calf from side to side, trying frantically to dislodge the metal spear. The dolphin thrashed about, gasping for breath, before finally suffocating. The synchronized cries and trills of anguish from the dolphins rippled through the waters. The sorrowful sounds crossed the ocean; from pod to pod, news of their loss spread.

Sitting cross-legged on the grassy field with the morning sun, Perl was deep in meditation with her fellow Seekers. Master Bodhi's soothing voice floated on the breeze, directing the day's lesson, when Perl let out a sharp moan; a great wave of sadness hit her like a punch to the gut. "Oh no. No." Perl murmured under her breath. She had never felt such grief, and it seemed to have come out of nowhere. Tears welled up in her eyes; they ran down her cheeks and fell to the ground. Sprigs of greenery sprang up, forming a small bouquet at her feet.

The rest of the Seekers didn't notice. Bodhi, however, heard Perl's cry and briefly opened one eye, noticing the fresh cluster of plant life growing beneath the sad girl. The Light Being frowned and shook its head, its peacock plumage rustling. Bodhi took a deep breath, closing its eyes, refocusing its energy.

26 RED TIDE

"As Earth's climate changes, changes, so does its weather patterns, patterns," Olliv addressed the Seekers as they stood, sleepy-eyed, outside their Bowerbird nests.

Kamani stood next to Olliv; their contrasting shapes silhouetted against the rising sun. Olliv continued his lecture, "that is why all six of Callowhorn's Seeker training classes, classes, have been summoned this morning to the Half-Light Realm, Realm!"

Rubbing her eyes, Perl stumbled lazily out of her water droplet hut, hair unruly, boots unlaced. She slipped into line next to Bear. "What's going on? Why's Kamani here?"

"Don't know. Something strange is happening with the weather." Bear held a muffin dripping with sticky syrup. He took a big bite, crumbs covering his face.

"Shh!" Corvax hushed the two. "In case you haven't noticed, there's been a lot of strange things happening lately. Pay attention." He turned his back to them.

"Why is he always such a jumble..." Perl didn't get to finish her thought, as Kamani's voice boomed over the group.

"Erratic shifts make predicting the weather hard! Changes are especially confusing for wildlife! They need predictability to migrate! Today, we venture to Yule Island! You will assist the inhabitants! Olliv, if you don't mind?" Kamani gestured for Olliv to step aside.

"They're all yours, Commander Kamani, Kamani," Olliv bowed with his buttercup baton, backing away.

"Circle!" The nine Seekers gathered around their giant Light Protector Guide. "To Yule! Ha-ha!" Kamani bellowed, stomping the ground, stirring up dirt and dust around them, until the air was a thick haze.

Flax shouted, "here we go again!" Locking arms with Tars, everyone shielded their eyes.

As Kamani's thunderous hooves slowed, the clouds dissipated, giving way to a lush rainforest to their one side, a crystal-clear ocean to the other. Whistles and screeches of exotic birds could be heard within the dense, twisted jungle. Between where Perl stood and the water stretched was a busy two-lane road. It ran around the entire island, a ring of black asphalt, separating the rainforest from the beach.

Perl fanned away the last of the dust, coughing, but a quick whiff of the salty air brought a smile to her face. She took in her surroundings; the group was just at the edge of the rainforest, on some sandy, scrubby grassland. The road hummed with traffic, as cars, trucks, and bikes, whizzed by them in a blur. The noise from all the traffic was bad enough, but the veil of thick black smoke that hung over the road was far worse.

Perl put a hand over her nose and mouth. "Ugh! The stench is awful!"

Nan and Lyre tried to fan the polluted air away from the group, but the smog kept wafting back toward them.

"So, what is it we're supposed to be doing here, directing traffic?" Tars said, wrapping his tail over his nose.

Far off in both directions, Perl spotted small groups gathering; the distinct shine off their Harmony clothing a dead giveaway. She gestured to Bear and the others, "look, out there, and over there! The Seekers!"

"And the day just got a bit more interesting," Bear held one of his hands up, squinting through the sun down the coastline.

Kamani stepped into the middle of the group, putting his massive arms around Javan and Flax. "Welcome to Yule Island! You see, you are not alone here! All Seekers share a common goal!"

At that, he made a series of extremely loud whistles and clicking sounds with his tongue, and like a flash of lightning, Quantaa, the mystical two-headed greyhound, rocketed through the sky, cutting clouds in half as he sped towards them. The Seekers delighted at the sight of Quantaa. A loud rumbling sound farther down the beach caught their attention. They heard a faint cheer go up as another team welcomed their own Battle Light Creature.

Perl looked up at Kamani. "What is that?" she asked, watching as a shadow stepped out of the trees. The bird-like Being, its grayish brown feathers perfectly mimicking tree bark, towered above its team. The creature was as tall as a bus standing on end, with cartoonishly large yellow eyes. It let out a loud, raspy cry that carried down the beach.

"Ha! *Nyctibius grandis*! Potoo bird! A master of camouflage!" Kamani answered.

A giant growl could be heard in the other direction about a hundred of yards off, as another Battle Creature rose up out of the sand. Its head was like that of a seal, with the rugged body of a grizzly bear. It reared up on its hide legs and shook violently, throwing sand from its thick fur.

Perl turned to Opis, standing in the high grass between the rainforest and the road. "This must be a pretty big deal to need so many of us."

Opis didn't respond; she was deep in thought, staring off into the rainforest. Perl looked at the traffic, then crinkled her brow as something odd caught her eye; there were hundreds of dark streaks running like tiger stripes down the road.

Opis spoke, almost as if she were hypnotized, "I recall this island now. I know why we're here."

In that moment, a light drizzle began to fall, bouncing off Opis' viscous, translucent dreads. The others took cover under large canopy leaves near the jungle's perimeter.

"There! The *Gecarcoidea natalis*! They come! They'll keep moving as long as the rains continue!" Kamani barked out.

Perl didn't need to ask anyone for the definition of the species. As the rains picked up, hundreds of thousands of fire engine red crabs scuttled out from under the shadowy nooks and crannies of the rainforest. A sea of red crustaceans poured past the nine Seekers in a matter of seconds.

Tars sprang up into the tree, hanging down by his tail. "They're everywhere!"

"Ouch! Careful, they pinch!" Flax yelled out, brushing several off his spotted feet.

Perl watched as waves of crabs surged towards the ocean, and it suddenly became clear to her what all the dark streaks on the road were; dried blood. Perl felt sick to her stomach. She glanced over at Kamani, who was sitting crossed-legged on a boulder, Quantaa by his side. The other Seekers scurried to and fro, looking a lot like the crabs they'd been sent to help.

"How can you just sit there? Help them!" Perl begged Kamani.

"The task is yours! Succeed by any means!" Kamani closed his eyes and folded his arms as the crabs parted then rejoined each other, flowing around the rock like a red river.

Corvax yelled out to the others, "circle up!" The nine closed in around him.

"Hurry! We don't have much time!" Perl yelled out.

Nan and Lyre hovered off the ground as an endless stream of crabs passed by.

"What's the plan?"

"They're headed to the ocean. No way we can stop them all, so we need to keep them off the road. As many as possible." Corvax looked up, seeing long vines hanging down from the trees. "If we can use those vines to make some kind of bridge, maybe we could direct them up the vines and over the road safely."

"The vines are too thin," Opis insisted.

Lyre cut in, "we could braid them together? Make them wider?"

Corvax nodded. "Good! Okay, the rest of us will gather the vines into one area. Nan, Lyre, you start weaving the vines together, and then lift it up over the cars to the other side. Now, go!"

The group started collecting the thick vines. Nan and Lyre frantically twisted them into a makeshift overpass. As the first wave of crabs reached the road, Perl's heart broke as the cars ran them over, killing them instantly. She plugged her ears, shouting to the others, "this isn't working! We need to do something else! They're dying!"

"She's right." Javan tossed a handful of vines aside. "We need to get the people to stop, not the crabs!"

Perl looked up at the trees looming above them. "I have an idea." Pulling Fortis from its sheath, Perl walked over to a banana tree and whispered, "forgive me." She backed up a few steps, and with a mighty swing, brought the sword down, deep into the base of the tree. All eyes turned to Perl.

"Like Kamani said, by any means!" Perl shouted. "For the greater good!" After hacking one side, Perl pushed on the tree. "Help me!"

Bear, Flax, and Javan sprinted over to assist. Nan and Lyre floated above them, their wings flapping furiously as they shoved with all their might. They heard a cracking sound; the tree began to lean.

Bear shouted, "tim-berrr!"

They watched as the tree toppled and hit the road with a thundering crash, as bananas tumbled and bounced like mini acrobats. Tires screeched and horns honked as traffic came to a sudden halt. Most cars were equipped with motion sensors and quickly slowed, while others drivers simply slammed into one another, the crunching sound of metal on metal drowning out the other noise.

Not waiting for the first tree to even hit the ground, Perl ran to the next closest tree, stopping at a Kapok tree nearly one hundred feet tall. The girl gently laid her head against it, careful of its thorny bark. "Thank you," she spoke to the tree. Fortis' blade sank three-quarters of the way through it, but it did not fall. Perl called out louder over the traffic and pounding rain, "your sacrifice will make way for generations!" On her next strike, Fortis sliced clean through. The Kapok fell, landing parallel to the banana tree some fifty feet apart.

"I see what she's doing!" cried Bear.

A gap between the cars had been formed, creating a safe passage for the crabs to cross. Corvax and the others began pulling smaller trees and plants next to the open entryway, trying to create a funnel to help guide the crabs between the two fallen trees. It seemed to work, as more and more crabs scuttled through.

Kamani approached the group. With a series of whistles, the great Bison-Being summoned Quantaa to his side.

"Go! Tell the other Light Battle Creatures!" Quantaa jetted to the sky, reaching the next group of Seekers in seconds.

"You too, Lyre and Nan! Fly! Spread the good word!" The two girls took off, holding hands.

Once Quantaa got the word out, the other groups quickly followed suit, mindful to only take down what was necessary. Trees fell, blocking sections of the road and forming impromptu walkways, as traffic around the island came to a stop.

Once high enough up, Nan and Lyre got a clearer view of the scene below; the dark green center of the island seemed to be bleeding, as tens of thousands of crabs trickled out of the rainforest in meandering lines, branching out, crossing the roads, turning the vast area of white sand a bright crimson.

"Behold!" Kamani raised his hoof. "The humans take note! Miraculous!"

People all around Yule Island stepped out of their vehicles, some even stood on top of their hoods, watching as the tiny crustaceans scuttled past. Now that traffic had stopped, the crabs wandered freely, no longer sticking to just the pathways Perl and the others had made. Islanders balanced on the fallen tree trunks, scratching their heads in amazement, snapping photos, taking videos and marveling at the strange sight. A girl with an umbrella in the shape of a big green frog climbed onto her father's shoulders. She reached up, taking hold of some of the discarded woven vines that were hanging down, comparing them to her braided pigtails. "Daddy, look! It's like my hair!"

Her father laughed, "yes, sweetie, I see that." He looked at the fallen trees. "Wow, that sure was an odd storm. Look at how the trees fell. It almost looks like a pattern."

Of course, the islanders weren't able to see the Seekers, who occupied the Half-Light Realm, hidden to earthly eyes. Master Kamani stood, hooves on hips, beaming with pride.

Nan and Lyre returned. "It's amazing up there," they gushed. "Guys, we did it!"

"Most impressive!" Kamani hollered. The nine Seekers had gathered around him on the white beach, the waves crashing behind them.

Perl held her ears, trying to muffle his booming voice. "Impressive? How was that impressive?" she asked bitterly, "look at all the crabs that died, and they've been dying like this for years!"

Opis took Perl's hand. "But now the humans' eyes have been opened to the migration through your quick thinking, Perl. You saved them."

"Nice job, Perl." Bear dropped a heavy hand on the girl's shoulder. Javan, Flax, and Tars all gave nodding approval.

"But once again, she acted carelessly!" Corvax blurted out, "typical human…you do whatever you want, never pausing to think!"

"I did what had to be done!" Perl shot back, "the braiding was taking too long. Too many of them were dying!"

Quantaa, who had remained next to Kamani, now curled behind Perl. He looked down at Corvax, his two giant black and white heads lowered, four piercing eyes locked in on the dark-headed boy with the wet, ruffled feathers.

Corvax lowered his voice, "you're too impulsive! It was too dangerous."

"And you're full of yourself! You don't know everything!" Perl felt a little bad saying it, but Corvax needed to hear it; she was tired of his attitude and the way he questioned her every move.

"Enough!" Kamani shouted, his beastly roar shaking the trees around them, "make peace! The job is half done! The humans now see what they have not seen! This part is a success! Now, shake!" Kamani leaned down, his large bison head looming between them, his hot breath on their faces.

Corvax and Perl reluctantly shook hands and parted ways.

Flax rose his hand. "Master, what do you mean by 'half done'?"

Tars jumped from a tree branch to the ground, landing next to Nan and Lyre, who had folded their wings back to rest.

Kamani plopped down in the sand and closed his eyes. "We wait!"

"Wait? But we passed the test, what are we waiting for now?" Bear asked, a bit timidly.

Kamani cracked one eye. "For the waning moon, of course! To create the neap! To calm the tide!"

"Oh right, the neap, yeah. I totally knew that," Bear said, shrugging his shoulders at the others. The tardigrade-boy ambled away, curling up into a ball to relax.

Javan gave Bear a pat on the back as he passed. "How long is it until the moon is waning, Kamani?"

"A bit—no more, no less! Eggs take time! Let us set up camp!" Kamani closed his eyes again, opting not to divulge any more information to his confused group of Seekers. The family of oxpecker birds in his massive, tangled beard, disrupted by his voice, now settled back into their nests.

The group looked on, as the male crabs dug dens for the females, then retreated back to the forest, while the mothers remained. The traffic was still stopped because of all the fallen trees. According to locals, the sudden gale-force winds—though nobody really seemed to have felt anything—had knocked over trees all around the island. Surprisingly, nearly all of them had fallen outward onto the road. Because of this, the island's thoroughfare would be shut down until the debris could be cleared. The rain had slowed to a soft warm drizzle, and the rows of cars sat quiet.

"So, Lyre, just how long does it take to incubate a crab egg?" Nan fluttered her wings, tipping her toes on the top of the sandy beach.

"Earth time? About thirteen days, I believe. Obviously, for us, though, it won't feel that long. As the tides calm, the mothers will release their eggs," Lyre turned back towards the forest. "Guess we could rest for a bit. My wings are soaked."

The challenge now half complete, every Seeker group around Yule Island settled in, some taking naps in the tall grass and soft ferns of the rainforest bed, or curling up under makeshift twig and leave canopies. Perl, looking for a bit of friendly shelter, saw Javan by himself, leaning against a tree. She plunked down next to him.

"Can you believe Corvax? I mean, he just seems to have it out for me."

"No. That's just his way. He's a planner and a strategist. Always has been." Javan was clutching his arm.

Perl was about to get angry at Javan for defending Corvax, when she noticed him wincing. "You okay? Let me see. What happened?"

"It's nothing, just a scratch," he insisted. Perl noticed blood seeping into the fur on his forearm, running down to his webbed fingers.

"Nothing, huh? You're bleeding."

"A small branch from one of the falling trees nicked me, that's all."

Perl pulled his hand away. Her stomach turned at the sight of his deep wound. "Javan, you're not fine!" She paused, a look of worry on her face. "Wait, did I do this to you?" She glared at Javan, who looked away. "I wasn't paying attention when I was cutting the trees down. I...I hurt you."

Javan chuckled, "no, it's not your fault. I'm clumsy. I didn't get out of the way in time." Blood spilled out from the wound. Perl could see he was in pain.

"I'm so sorry." Perl yanked off her backpack, searching for something to bandage his arm. "Corvax is right. I am too impulsive. I need to stop—" Perl looked over at Javan, who was turning pale. "Javan...Javan, look at me!"

The boy's eyes fluttered, then shot open wide. "Huh? I'm fine, Perl. Really."

"No, you're not," Perl argued, just as Javan's eyes rolled back white. "Help, over here, quick! Somebody! Anybody! Help!" She grabbed Javan as he started to slump over, placing her backpack under his head. "Somebody, please! Hel—"

Before Perl could finish, she heard the sound of beating wings. A flurry of hummingbirds, in the unmistakable shape of a woman, materialized from out of the trees.

Perl recognized the hummingbirds. "Palo Santo? Is that you? Please help me. It's Javan. He's hurt," Perl glanced back down at her friend, her hands now covered in blood. The tall, ethereal figure waved the hummingbirds away, and Perl saw that it was in fact, the Garden Nurse.

"Hello, youngling," the Light Being's gentle voice was like the strumming of a harp.

"I...I can't stop the bleeding, and it's all my fault."

Palo Santo knelt down; even on her knees, Perl had to look up at the regal woman.

"Let me see, child." Palo Santo's kind sky blue eyes gave Perl comfort.

A few hummingbirds circled above her, giving close watch. The Light Being pulled her enormous wicker basket off her shoulder, placing it next to Javan. When she opened it, a swarm of buzzing bees and orange and violet butterflies fluttered out. Perl watched intently as the Garden Nurse went about her business, humming softly to herself. She dripped a number of sticky saps into a wooden bowl, crushed a variety of aromatic herbs into it, and stirred the concoction together with a thin white branch, a small white stone tied to the end of it.

The others heard Perl's cries for help and bolted over, where they now found her and Palo Santo, kneeling over a pale, bleeding Javan.

"Oh! Javan!" Lyre cried out.

"What's going on?" Corvax asked, looking over at Perl.

Perl could feel her face begin to flush with guilt; she said nothing.

"It's Javan! He's hurt!" Tars called to Bear, who was the last to arrive.

Nan and Lyre fluttered above the group. "Is he going to be okay?"

Opis tapped Perl on the shoulder. "Did you see what happened?"

Perl shrugged. "I...no, I didn't."

"But you were over here with him, weren't you, Perl?" Tars asked.

All of them were looking at her now.

Perl stood up. "It was an accident. I didn't mean to..." Slowly stepping backwards, she stumbled on a fallen log.

"You didn't mean to, what?" Asked Flax.

Palo Santo applied the ointment onto Javan's wound, then wrapped his arm in a palm leaf bandage, securing it with a vine of pink flowers to hold it in place.

"He has lost some blood, but nature is resilient."

The group breathed a collective sigh of relief, all but Corvax, whose silver-gray eyes were locked on Perl. He turned to the group. "What did I tell you? She acts without thinking, and now she's gotten one of us hur—!"

"Corvax!" Kamani, who had followed them, corrected the boy mid-sentence.

Perl sniffled; her fists clenched tight. She stared at each of her fellow Seekers, and wanted to speak, but the words wouldn't come. She turned and ran, disappearing into the forest.

"Someone should go after her...meaning *you*," Opis stared at Corvax.

The crow-boy started to head after Perl, when Kamani interjected.

"Wait. Leave her be. Quantaa is with her...she will return in her own time." He knelt next to Palo Santo, the two enormous Light Beings creating a fortress around Javan.

"He will be fine," Palo said, taking out a soft, glistening blanket from her basket and wrapping it around the boy.

Slowly, Javan's eyes flickered open.

"Welcome back," the Master Garden Nurse whispered softly.

"Powerful platypus!" Kamani's voice boomed. He placed a hoof on the boy's chest. The Seekers gathered around Javan as Palo Santo stood, closing the lid on her wicker basket. "You must rest. This should heal in the

195

passing of two moons."

The soft-spoken woman quietly walked off. She went around a thick cluster of trees and disappeared; a spray of hummingbirds emerged from the other side. Javan, woozy, slowly sat up. He looked around at the faces of his fellow Seekers and frowned; Perl wasn't there.

Perl kept running, deeper and deeper into the forest, her bioluminescent spots in full glow. She ran as fast as her feet could take her—jumping over logs, ducking and weaving in between the thick brush—until finally, she stopped to rest against a large mossy boulder, out of breath and her heart beating like a drum in her chest. Quantaa caught up to Perl quickly but chose to keep his distance. Seeing her take a break, the Being now slowly approached. Perl peered over her shoulder, seeing the great winged dog.

"Oh, Quantaa, what have I done?" she said, her voice catching in her throat, "I've hurt the one person I'd never want to hurt."

The greyhound lowered its white head, nuzzling her arm, as the black one gently licked her cheek, its giant tongue coating Perl's face in saliva. Despite her sadness, Perl giggled softly. She held the dog, wrapping both of her arms around its spotted leg. Perl thought how similar it felt to hugging a tree.

Quantaa circled around Perl three times before lying down. Perl nestled up next to Quantaa's stomach. His fur, she thought, was so much softer than it appeared, and made for a perfect blanket. Quantaa unfurled a spotted wing and draped it over Perl to keep the rain off. The pitter-patter of raindrops soothed Perl. Feeling the warmth and affection from the great greyhound helped ease her mind, and soon she drifted off to sleep. Sighing heavily, the Battle Beast closed three eyes, one remaining open to keep vigil.

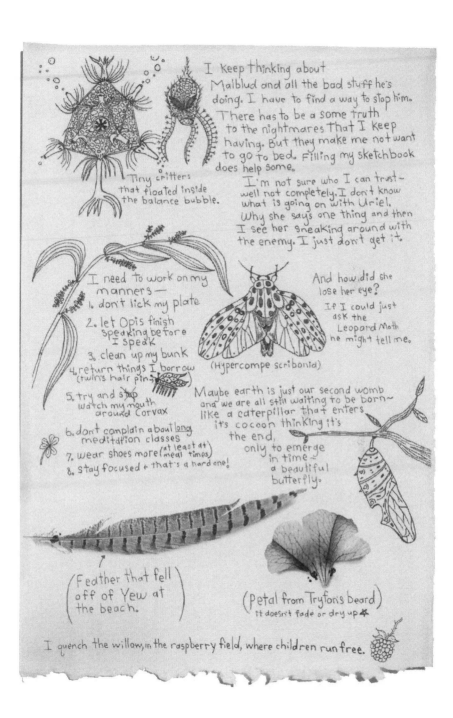

I keep thinking about Maiblud and all the bad stuff he's doing. I have to find a way to stop him. There has to be a some truth to the nightmares that I keep having. But they make me not want to go to bed. Filling my sketchbook does help some.

Tiny critters that floated inside the balance bubble.

I'm not sure who I can trust — well not completely. I don't know what is going on with Uriel. Why she says one thing and then I see her sneaking around with the enemy. I just don't get it.

I need to work on my manners —
1. don't lick my plate
2. let Opis finish speaking before I speak
3. clean up my bunk
4. return things I borrow (twin's hair pins)
5. try and stop watch my mouth around Corvax
6. don't complain about long meditation classes
7. wear shoes more (at least at meal times)
8. stay focused & that's a hard one!

And how did she lose her eye? If I could just ask the Leopard Moth he might tell me.

(Hypercompe scribonia)

Maube earth is just our second womb and we are all still waiting to be born — like a caterpillar that enters its cocoon thinking it's the end, only to emerge in time — a beautiful butterfly.

(Feather that fell off of Yew at the beach.

(Petal from Tryfon's beard) it doesn't fade or dry up

I quench the willow, in the raspberry field, where children run free.

197

27 WILDFLOWER

The dark skies above broke, and shimmering rays of light cascaded through the rainforest, casting a faint light through Quantaa's translucent wings, just enough to rouse Perl from her slumber. She squinted at the annoying brightness, rolling over and burying her face in Quantaa's soft fur. The greyhound grumbled and repositioned himself. Perl was just about back to sleep, when she heard a twig snap and a rustling nearby. She sat up, her head bumping against Quantaa's wing. Another twig snapped. Quantaa bounced up; both heads emitting a low, deep growl. The dog instinctively pulled Perl behind him with his wing, moving her effortlessly.

"Whoa, easy, boy. It's okay." It was a boy's voice.

A thick fog hung in the air; Perl couldn't see a thing. Quantaa stiffened. *"Grrrrr!"*

The voice called out, "Perl?"

The small girl peeked over Quantaa's wing. "Corvax? What do you want?"

"I was looking for you. Kamani said to leave you alone, but I wanted to make sure you were okay." He approached slowly. "I had a hard time finding you." Corvax held up his hand for the dog to sniff. The enormous creature bent its black head down, the white one fixed on the crow-boy.

Perl reached up and stroked the greyhound's belly. "It's okay, Q." Quantaa, still in protective mode, circled around Corvax. "Really, Quantaa, I'm fine. You can go." She patted his nose, and at that, the great dog licked her cheek, once again coating half her face with drool. Perl wiped her cheek on her sleeve as Quantaa gave Corvax one last side glance before galloping off into forest, the thuds of its heavy paws shaking the leaves off the trees. The two Seekers stood awkwardly together in the silence.

"You left this." Corvax handed Perl her backpack.

She strapped on her backpack and marched past him, grazing his sleeve. "I don't need your help."

"I can see that." He followed after her. "Look, Perl, we may not see eye to eye sometimes."

Perl gave him a quick glance over her shoulder. "Understatement of the year."

"Okay, most of the time. But you have to understand, you just can't go off doing things on your own! That's not how it works here!"

Perl didn't respond, picking up her pace to get away from the boy. She brushed past an old log where a rainbow of brightly colored frogs had gathered. Seeing the two, they hopped into hiding. "You're not my parent, you know that?"

"No, but technically, I am much older than you. Haven't you been taught to respect your elders?" He tried to joke, but Perl wasn't having it; she shot him a glare, her piercing green eyes locking in on his.

"I respect my monks. I respect my Masters…but they also respect me." Corvax was about to respond, but decided to keep his mouth shut.

The two made their way back through the jungle towards the Seekers campsite, neither of them saying a word. The canary-yellow sky was dotted with steely gray clouds, and all the leaves on the trees stayed curled over, wary of more rain coming.

Finally, Corvax broke the silence. "I was just trying to help, you know."

Perl kept walking; her arms crossed. "Okay."

"And…I'm sorry for yelling last night, and well, all the other times, too. I have an annoying habit of always wanting to take control of every situation."

Tight-lipped, Perl looked at Corvax; he forced a smile.

"Yeah, I'm sorry, too," was all she could muster as she started to jog.

Corvax ran shoulder to shoulder with her. "You know, you're like a wildflower," he said, "they can pop up in the most unexpected places…on rocky ground, or in open valleys, always stronger than people think."

It was strange hearing Corvax speak so openly, not to mention saying something nice.

"I'm pretty tough, ya' know…for a human."

"But a wildflower can also grow in a garden, where it can flourish, safely and happily…ya' know?" Corvax pushed her shoulder playfully.

That thought made Perl feel better, but she continued to challenge him. "Until they're seen as a weed and get pulled out for being different. And who's to judge what's valuable and what's not? A dandelion is just as magical as a rose! I mean, you can make wishes on a dandelion's seeds. That's magic!"

For someone so new to Venusto, Corvax thought, Perl had a wisdom that seemed to come from a deeper place, one that usually took many cycles to acquire.

"You're right. Humans are quick to judge those that are different from themselves. Some even see diversity as a weakness, something to fear. Instead of trying to understand it, they find it easier to separate from it."

Perl slowed to pick up a walking stick nearly as tall as she was. She ran her hand along it, smoothing off the dirt. "Well that's just dumb. We're all created from the same soil."

Corvax smiled, "right again."

"Thanks, Corvax…I'm glad you're finally seeing things *my* way," Perl joked.

"Sure," Corvax teased back, "whatever you say."

Through the trees, Perl could see the orange glow of a fire. "We're back…race you!" The girl took off, Corvax racing to catch up.

Perl felt better knowing things between her and the crow-boy would be different from now on. Reaching the edge of the forest, Perl saw the Seekers had set up camp. Bear stood over the fire, holding a hot metal kettle in his bare hands; being a tardigrade, the extreme heat didn't bother him at all.

"Hey everybody, look who's back!" Bear called out, "Come and eat, I whipped us up some grub!"

The others crowded around Perl, welcoming her back with open arms.

Javan stood behind the others, still looking a bit pale with his arm bandaged, gave Perl a slight nod. She couldn't tell whether he was glad to see her or not.

Bear walked over with the hot pot in one hand, bowls and spoons in the others. He handed Perl and Javan each a bowl, glopping in a ladle of steaming mush.

"What is this?" Perl asked.

"Walnut and mushroom porridge, one of my personal favorites," he grinned with pride.

"Sounds…yummy," she winked at Javan.

Javan smiled back, lifting his spoon up. They clinked utensils, not saying anything. The two found a place to sit, and after a few minutes of eating in silence, Perl spoke up.

"Glad to see you're okay."

"What, this old thing?" Javan lifted his arm. "You should've seen the other guy."

"Oh yeah?" Perl teased, the weight on her shoulders lightening.

"Yep. Messed him up somethin' good," Javan laughed, taking a mouthful of porridge. "You know, this isn't half bad…it's not half good, either." He and Perl giggled. Everyone ate and joked, and Perl felt good to be back with her family.

While a full two weeks had passed for the islanders, in the Half-Light Realm, barely a day had come and gone for the Seekers-in-training. Despite that, the group began to grow crabby, like children on a long car trip. The group lounged lazily in the soft sand, as the cloudy evening gave way to dark purple skies, twinkling with a million stars.

"Master Kamani, when did you say the crab eggs hatch?" Flax asked.

"Yes, when?" Nan moaned.

"I'm bored," whined Tars.

"Me too," added Lyre, her long plumage wrapped around her neck like a feather boa.

"Ha! Bored? Then let's put you to work!" Kamani laughed.

The Seekers had been told that once the mothers laid their eggs, their final task would be to make sure they returned to the forest safely. Kamani ordered the team to start cutting and gathering trees to make a path back like they did before.

Kamani gazed down the beach's moonlit coast, a long, curved pipe poking out of the corner of his mouth. He gave a little whistle, coaxing the oxpecker birds out of his scraggly beard. Nearly a dozen of them took flight, up and down the coast, carefully scanning the sands. The crescent moon hung like a big glowing smile in the sky above. After a while, the birds returned to Kamani's beard, poking their heads out and squawking their message to him, their tiny red beaks going a mile a minute.

"Ha, fantastic!" Kamani nodded. "Students, look up! She wanes!"

"Finally!" Bear sat up.

"Is it happening?" Tars bounced to his feet.

"Females are ready! The tide is calm!" Kamani called out. "We finish the task at hand!"

The group stood, brushing the sand off their silky Harmony outfits. Before anyone said a word, the nine Seekers watched as the female crabs slowly emerged in masses from their sand burrows like clockwork, carrying their precious cargo. They moved to the shoreline where they performed a tiptoe dance in the shallow surf dropping their eggs into the water's gentle waves. Then the mothers scuttled back up the beach.

"Hatch!" Kamani raised his outstretched arms to the water. "Grow! Survive!"

Perl wasn't quite sure what was happening. "Wait. They're abandoning them?" she whispered to herself.

Millions of tiny larvae floated in the moonlit tide. Seeing all of them in the water, so vulnerable, a twinge of concern gripped Perl.

"Kamani, won't they be eaten by fish if we don't do something?" Perl asked.

"Some will! Predators must eat, too! Remember your teachings!"

Hearing this, Perl's heart started to pound. She waded out into the ocean. Almost instantly, her knees began to glow as cold waves lapped against her goosebumpy legs.

Kamani walked out to Perl, placing a heavy hoof on her shoulder. "It is the way of life! Nature has a plan!"

Perl looked up at him, "so we just do nothing?"

"Not our place to interfere, young Perl! By doing nothing, we are indeed, doing something! The megalops must find their own path!"

Perl didn't like that answer, but she knew Kamani was right. She pulled away from him, crossing her arms as she splashed through the calm waters. Knee deep in the chilly ocean, the spots on Perl's legs intensified, drawing the attention of the morphing baby crabs, who began moving towards her. She took a few steps backwards, not wanting to confuse them.

Kamani mused, "nature is beauty! Nature is wonder! But nature is pitiless." He strode back up to the beach.

The purple night sky gave way to a soft peach color as the rising sun greeted the inhabitants of Yule Island. The empty road slowly began to fill back up with cars, shopkeepers swept their walkways, and the early risers slowly trickled onto the beach. Kamani gathered the Seekers. The enormous gathering of mother crabs, having released their eggs, were now making their way back to the rainforest.

"As they wander, so must they return! We finish our task! Ha! Let us make a safe passageway!"

No sooner had Kamani said this, when Corvax interrupted, pointing to the road. "Master, look! The humans, they're helping the crabs!"

Kamani and the Seekers watched as the traffic around the island slowed to a stop, allowing the waves of mother crabs to cross back safely.

"Ha! Our true duty is done! Because of you, the humans awake!"

After the bizarre storm, and what the locals now called the "Red Tide," daily life resumed on Yule Island. The road was once again busy with the hum of traffic, although signs had been erected, reminding drivers to 'Mind the Crabs!" during the migration period.

Perl looked on as scores of crabs scuttled across the road. "Maybe they are beginning to see," she beamed, feeling proud of her fellow humans.

As the day grew brighter and the group observed the crabs, the calm seas behind them began to churn. Despite the day looking clear and sunny, one very dark, ominous-looking cloud hung over the water; a strange, unnatural shadow in an otherwise perfect powder blue sky.

"Is it me…" Bear turned around, his round face scrunching up, "…or is there something weird going on with the water?"

Flax pointed, "and look at that cloud."

The Seekers and Kamani's attention switched from the crabs to the ocean. The surface of the water stirred intensely, frothy waves crashing at their feet. Perl, who had been squishing wet sand between her toes, saw it too; a large, black, undulating cloud, with a whirlpool forming underneath it.

Javan's nose started to twitch. "Strange…there's no wind, none at all," he said, his eyes darting across the water.

"Kamani, is this still part of our challenge?" asked Opis.

The giant bison-man peered out uneasily, his brow furled. "Step back, Seekers! Away from the water! All of you!"

Just as the Seekers retreated, the water started bubbling up like a cauldron. A sickening screech was heard as a half dozen black tentacles thick as redwood trees wriggled out of the frothy water, dripping black, oily sludge. At first glance, rows of suckers lined each of its flailing arms like an octopus, but upon closer inspection they weren't suction cups but hideous, deformed heads—pale and shrunken; part human, part fish. Their mouths were stretched black holes filled with rotting teeth, opening and closing angrily. They let out an ear-piercing scream, sending icy chills up the Seekers' spines as they scrambled up the beach, all but Perl who stood motionless, waist-deep in the water.

"Get behind me!" Kamani hollered, turning his sights back to the giant creature.

Over the turmoil of crashing waves and creature's shrill cries, Perl yelled to Kamani, "The baby crabs! What do we do?"

The serpent, sensing the girl in the water, raised its great snake-like arms in a horrific display.

"Chiiiillld!"

Its tentacles, like giant black worms, came at her, the rows of hideous faces howling in one high-pitched shriek, shattering lampposts along the beach's boardwalk. As it got closer, the tentacles dipped lower, now just black limbs poking up a few feet. Perl screamed, trying to fight her way back against the pull of the tide.

The Seekers screamed at her from the shoreline. "Get out of the water!", "It's coming!", "Move, Perl, move!"

Hearing the monster speak filled Perl with pure terror. She struggled against the current with all her might, but was going nowhere. The spots on her legs were glowing bright white.

Like a periscope on a submarine, the tentacles slipped through the water, closing in on the girl. Perl, frantic, took a quick peek over her shoulder and locked eyes with one of the faces screaming *"chiiilld,"* its mouth a twisted black gash. Something took hold of her ankle.

Perl's screams were drowned out by a deafening bellow, louder and deeper than a lighthouse foghorn. From the beach charged Kamani, no longer upright but down on all fours like a raging bull, stampeding in Perl's direction; great spouts of white sand sprayed up behind him.

"Arrrrggghh!!" The great bison warrior lowered his head and launched himself at the serpent, one of his razor-sharp horns ripping the open mouth of one of the nasty screamers. The monster shuddered in pain, releasing its grip around Perl's leg. Free of the creature's grasp, Perl staggered up the beach.

"I've got you!" Javan ran down to meet her, helping Perl back to the others, who formed a protective circle around her.

"Gahhhh!" Another deafening roar was heard, as Kamani, now standing up in the water, the tentacle still squirming on his horn, whipped his head back in a violent jerk, ripping it clean off the serpent. Blood and innards sprayed everywhere as the creature's muffled cries of pain could be heard. Its arms slapped the water in agony. Kamani watched as the creature shrank away from him, leaving a trail of red in the water. Far off, black tentacles

resurfaced, the deformed faces screaming, full of rage. The great Light Being whistled, and from inside the rainforest, a response came back in the form of a loud "*woof!*" Kamani pulled the chunk of tentacle off his horn and tossed it aside.

"Is she okay?!" Kamani called to the group before reaching them. The Seekers huddled around Perl, who sat with her arms wrapped tightly around her knees, her head down; one of her legs had a bite mark on it.

"She's okay!" Bear yelled back, giving a thumb's up.

From the forest, branches cracked and leaves scattered as the great greyhound burst from the trees like a flash of lightening, its heads growling, teeth bared.

"Quantaa, attack!" Kamani shouted, pointing to the water.

The Battle Beast took to the air over the group's heads like a jet, scouring the water. Seeing the greyhound, the monster let out a cry. Quantaa dove straight at the target, pressing his wings tightly to his sides. He hit the choppy waves hard, like a pelican diving for a fish. There was a gigantic splash as the two went under.

"Quantaa! No!" Perl jumped up. "Kamani do something!" She grabbed Kamani by the arm, desperately trying to pull him back toward the water, but he held his ground.

"We wait," he said, matter-of-factly.

The Seekers, including Kamani, could do nothing as the underwater battle raged on in front of them. All they could see was a swirling vortex of white foam off in the distance. The Seekers stood at the ready, gathered close to their master. Perl looked at Kamani; he was worried, something she'd never seen before.

"Master? Nan and I could fly out there to—"

"No! Too dangerous!" Kamani said firmly.

"What on Earth *is* that thing?" Tars asked Flax.

"Not of Earth…an ancient beast from the Dark Realm."

Javan leaned over to Corvax, "it spoke to her."

"I know," he sighed, gritting his teeth.

"The Dark One's power is growing," Opis whispered to Kamani, not wanting the others to hear.

"Yes," Kamani replied grimly, wiping the blood from his horn.

They stared out at the ocean, helpless. After several long minutes, the distant thrashing in the water subsided; the dark cloud began to vanish, and the waves, which had been over three feet at the shore, were now barely a ripple.

"Where is he?" Perl wailed.

Kamani ran to the water's edge, the others right behind him. He squinted; perhaps a few hundred yards out, a dark shape bobbed up and down.

"There!" shouted Tars, whose eyes were the keenest of the bunch.

Something burst out of the water like a cannonball; Perl's knees buckled at the sound. She looked up and saw Quantaa in the sky, a tentacle clutched in both of his jaws. The great hound landed on the beach with a heavy thud, dropping the gruesome, seeping appendage at Perl's feet. He wagged his tail happily, as if he'd simply fetched a stick.

"Good boy," Perl, relieved, wrapped her arms around his treelike leg.

The greyhound had fought and won, but not without a struggle; his body was covered in scratches and bloody patches where the serpent had bitten him.

"Are you okay?" Perl asked. The greyhound looked down at her; his white head licked her cheek.

"Warrior, indeed!" shouted Kamani, patting the greyhound's back. He was happy to see his trusted companion alive and well.

"Look out! He's gonna shake!" Shouted Bear, as the greyhound wiggled, spraying salt water everywhere. The Seekers ducked for cover, laughing.

"Did you know that through evolution, animals with fur learned to shake water off their bodies?" Opis stated matter-of-factly.

"Here we go," Bear rolled his eyes.

Opis continued. "By quickly drying their coats, they avoided hypothermia. Also, it uses less energy than sun-drying…"

Bear reached over, playfully covering her mouth. "Okay, we get it, book worm."

Opis pulled his hand off and gave him a slight punch on the shoulder, then smiled sheepishly. "I, uh…tend to recite trivia in stressful situations." She shrugged, twisting a strand of hair.

Perl brought Quantaa's head down to hers, placing her forehead against Quantaa's long nose, "I'm so glad you're safe."

While Quantaa was battling Malblud's serpent, the locals of Yule Island only saw an abnormal thundercloud causing some sort of whirlpool. Weeks later, the fisherman still didn't understand the phenomenon. "How did a storm of that severity happen so fast, and so close to shore?" They asked one another, never able to come up with a reasonable explanation.

"Platypus, if you please?" Kamani gestured for Javan to join him away from the group.

Perl watched them walk over towards the road, now humming with traffic. Her curiosity piqued, she tiptoed behind them, hiding behind a clump of palm trees within earshot of the two. She couldn't make out everything being said, but Kamani's loud voice carried even when he tried to whisper.

"Send word to Uriel…his minions are getting too close…we must deal with this…the sooner the better!"

Perl thought back to the day in Venusto, when she'd spotted Uriel and the Slaughterman in the cave. *"Uriel had given that vial to him for a reason, but why? And what was in it?"* Perl's imagination was running rampant. *"And now Kamani's talking to Javan about Uriel? Are they all working together? Is this about me?"* Perl didn't know what to think, but she realized two things—she had to figure out who Malblud was and destroy him, and two, she wasn't about to be whisked away into hiding again.

She peered back around the palm tree; Javan was gone.

"Quantaa! Praesidio!" Kamani bellowed. The greyhound walked right over to Perl, picking her up by her backpack with his teeth and trotting like a retriever with a chew-toy back to the bison.

"Hey! What are you doing? Put me down!" Perl struggled, her feet dangling.

"Take her home!" Kamani ordered.

Quantaa swung his black head down, whipping Perl up into the air and letting her go. She landed smack in the middle of Quantaa's back.

"Grab on and hold tight! Quantaa will take you back to Callowhorn!" Kamani shouted up to Perl.

"What? Why? I'm fine. I want to stay with everyone!" Perl pleaded.

"The crabs are safe! Now you!" Kamani commanded to the Quantaa, *"Volant!"*

Perl gripped two handfuls of hair. In a short gallop, a few flaps of his wings, and the two of them were airborne, Quantaa slicing through the air like a blade. The chilly air whipped Perl's thick hair straight back, and she had to squint to see through her watery eyes. Looking down at the island as her Seeker friends shrank into tiny dots, reminded Perl of the day she left Mont Michel in the webbed balloon. Homesick, she leaned over and squeezed Quantaa tightly.

The two steadily rose up into the clouds, the air becoming quite cold. Perl shivered. "Quantaa, please slow down!"

To her surprise, the dog obeyed, coasting to an easy glide, wings straight out. Perl was pressed against Quantaa's back, but now sat up as they broke through the clouds, the sun warming her amber skin. She peeked between Quantaa's silky heads; there was nothing but blue skies ahead, fluffy white clouds below, and—*Oh! My! Ever!* She was riding a flying greyhound!

"Woo-hoooo!" she hollered at the top of her lungs, to which Quantaa echoed with a rousing "arooooo!"

A flock of geese flying in V-formation joined in the celebration, honking back at the two of them. Quantaa gently glided down though a butterfly-shaped cloud, taking them into Venusto. He passed over the isle of Greenheart, where Perl saw classes of Seers meditating in the lush garden. Quantaa banked left and looked to be headed towards Natatory's mystical floating mountain range when the greyhound turned, veering them back on course for Callowhorn.

"Hey, I wanna go over there!" Perl pointed to the purple mountain range, now getting smaller by the second. "Let's go see what the Awakeners are doing, okay?" Perl yanked at Quantaa's hair in her tight grip trying to get the hound to turn back. His black head gave a cautionary glare back at her.

"Oh, come on, Q! Just for a little while? I've never been to Natatory!" The dog did not respond. "Oh, so that's how it is? Fine, I'll remember this when you want a treat."

They flew over the various combat fields, animal sculptures, and Tryfon's Garden, circling around the great cloud woman before gently touching down near Dragon Maw.

Several Light Realm Beings, having their mid-day meal, looked on in disbelief. One Awakener, a silver dragonfly, pointed at Perl. "Look! The girl is riding Quantaa!"

"Impossible," declared a rhino beetle sipping nectar out of a flower, "no one has ever ridden Quantaa."

"Well, not for centuries." A Light Being resembling an armadillo, its skin like gleaming armor, stood up for a better look.

Perl swiveled around onto her stomach, feet first, and slowly eased herself down the giant greyhound's side, gripping handfuls of fur on her way down. She turned and was greeted by a small crowd of Light Realm Awakeners and Seers, all staring at her.

"Nice day for a ride," Perl said awkwardly, patting Quantaa's leg.

"Indeed," said a statuesque blue ostrich, nodding respectfully to Perl.

Perl smiled a big toothy grin as she backed away, heading to her nest. Quantaa walked slowly as Perl trotted underneath him until they reached the blue pebbled pathway. She stepped out from under Quantaa. The majestic Being graciously lowered his heads, and Perl gave each of them a kiss on the snout.

"I love you."

Perl climbed up to her top bunk. Still a bit chilly from the flight, she grabbed a blanket, wrapping up in it. She slipped her backpack off, rolled over and closed her eyes. Within minutes, she was sound asleep.

Outside the nest, Quantaa circled three times, dropping with a heavy thud into a ball outside Perl's window. Closing his eyes, the Great Guard Dog of the Light Realm let out a long, heavy sigh; it was now okay to rest.

28 MARMALADE-MALLOWS

Uriel moved briskly, her long strides carrying her through the grounds of Callowhorn in a flash as she approached the Luna Bridge. She paused momentarily to collect both her thoughts and her breath before stepping on to the old oak bridge to meet with Tryfon, who was fond of this location; the view being one of the most breathtaking in all of Venusto.

Sitting at a small bamboo table under a flowering tree that grew up through the middle of the bridge was The Divine Master. He was entertaining two Light Beings of the High Council; both were albino. The first was a tall, angular praying mantis, the other, a short, squatty owl with a pair of twisted horns that curled up between its ears. Each of them was draped in long flowing robes of soft marbled ivory and gold that swirled about their forms like drops of oil in water; this was Hope, the color worn by all Awakeners. A copper teapot sat amongst them as the three leisurely sipped from wooden mugs carved into elegant birds.

The ancient boards creaked beneath Uriel's heavy boots as she lumbered over the bridge, announcing her arrival. The three paused their conversation, turning to see who was approaching. The owl, whose back was to Uriel, simply rotated its head completely around; it stared at her with its large, pink, unblinking eyes. Uriel stopped immediately and bowed; she spoke in a somber tone.

"Your Graces. I'm very sorry to disturb you. However, I must have word with Master Tryfon. It's urgent."

Tryfon's trio of faces all nodded solemnly. "Approach."

The snowy white owl stood from his chair, picking up his mug. "Hoo-we hoo-will continue our story on the hoo-morrow, Master."

Tryfon rose from his seat, touching palms with the white owl, thanking him for the visit, *"Gratias tipi ago."*

The lean, thin mantis levitated from its chair, hovering in a lotus position. It spoke to Tryfon telepathically.

"The pleasure is all mine," the Divine Master chuckled.

The mantis blinked twice, bowed, and at that, the two mystical Beings departed, moving silently down the other side of the emerald green bridge toward the lavish gardens.

Overlooking one side of the bridge was the meandering brook. As it flowed under the bridge, the stream opened up into a small reflecting pond. The bright blue sky cascaded down onto the pond's mirror-like surface, blending the horizon, making it difficult to detect where water ended and sky began.

Tryfon moved to the bridge railing, where he began tossing tiny crumbs to the bright orange koi fish. Uriel walked up and stood by the old Master's side, looking down as the koi jostled over the morsels of food.

"You are not in the moment, Uriel. Your mind is distant." Tryfon handed her some breadcrumbs. She dropped a few bits into the water, watching as the bright sun sparkled off the fish; they glistened like shiny new pennies.

"Yes, and that is why I'm here." Uriel tossed a few more crumbs to the happy fish. "It is Malblud. He draws closer and closer. I need assistance to protect the child."

Tryfon stroked his long floral beard; it changed and morphed minute to minute, going from honeycomb, to dandelions, to a nest of tiny twisted driftwood. "Let us not speak dark names when in the Light. Lophius is lost. He, too, needs assistance."

"But Master, Lophius is too far gone." Uriel looked at Tryfon. "We have been trying for ages to save him—" Tryfon lifted his hand; Uriel bit her lip.

The Master gestured to a patch of peonies. "Every time one enters a garden, it is anew. Each time, Ever grants us with a miracle. Fresh buds. Changing colors. One never sees nature the same way twice." He fed the remaining breadcrumbs to the koi. "Come, Uriel. Walk with me."

The two made their way to the end of the bridge, passing under an archway of wisteria and following a pathway of stepping stones that led them into Tryfon's lush, scenic garden. They strolled past a myriad of wildlife—black deer grazing on clover, wolves drinking from a stream, a pair of lions blissfully napping on a hill, birds and butterflies—an endless array of creatures, all enjoying the surroundings in peace. Tryfon stopped in front of a towering wall of rock; above them, large, furry white mountain goats stared down at them curiously.

"Why does a human child dislike a school day?" Tryfon asked.

Uriel, not expecting the question, shrugged.

The Master smiled, the faces on either side of his human face changed. On his left side, a baboon, on the right, a horse, black as night. "He or she must remain quiet for long periods of time. Unable to run, or play. Energy is pent up. The child grows agitated."

Uriel forced a smile, not in the mood for a lecture. Tryfon pushed on a hidden door in the rock wall. It opened up into a long hallway filled floor to ceiling with portraits of Light Realm Protectors separated by discipline; Water, Land and Air. An iron sconce with a beeswax candle flickered next to every portrait, bathing each Being in a warm golden light. Uriel recognized their faces; she knew their stories, and had even fought shoulder to shoulder with some of them in ages past. At the end of the passage was a doorless opening; rain fell in front of it like a thin silver curtain.

"This way." Tryfon walked straight through the water wall, not bothering to shield himself from the rain. Uriel followed, stepping through and emerging on the other side, completely dry. They were now in a charming little dining nook; the smell of chai and fresh mint filled the air. The walls were a colorful mosaic of hand painted ceramic animal masks, meticulously decorated, all of them dyed a robin's egg blue. Tryfon gestured for Uriel to sit.

"One must always find time for tea," Tryfon gave a little laugh, then went over to the corner of the room, where a kettle was brewing over a small fire.

Uriel took a seat at a table, also painted robin's egg blue. Having a second to ponder Tryfon's earlier comments, she responded.

"Yes, well, *a child* may also grow agitated to the point where *a child* explodes uncontrollably, dealing death and destruction to everyone around them." Uriel dropped her hands heavily onto the tabletop, her chainmail armor rattling. "Besides, we're not talking about a child, Master. He—it, is dangerous. Far more so than we imagined."

The wise Master, his back to Uriel, said nothing. He reached up to a tree branch that held various drinking mugs, and pulled down two powder blue tea cups that looked like woven birds' nests. He inspected them carefully, nodding. "Yes, these will do."

As was his way with all things, Tryfon quietly and patiently took the whistling teapot off the fire, and poured each of them a steaming cup of hot tea, deliberately taking his time, as if the act itself were a small ritual. Tryfon sat, taking a long sip. "Or..." he paused, continuing his previous thought, "...the child ventures out. Discovers something new. Is comforted. Changes." Tryfon tapped Uriel's cup. "Drink while it's hot. Warms the body, mind, and the soul."

Uriel took a sip and set the cup down promptly. She placed her hand on his Tryfon's arm. "Master Tryfon. He is destroying the ocean. He is turning the tide! The girl, Perl, she—" Uriel pulled her hand back, balling into a tight fist. Tryfon did not respond, choosing to listen. After a brief silence, Uriel spoke, calmly and matter-of-factly.

"In my current state— my battle wounds still healing— I need help. There was an incident during a routine training session in the Half-Light Realm, and now Kamani has sent word of an ancient Gaarum sighting. Seekers-in-Training were attacked on Yule Island during the *Gecarcoidea natalis* migration. It was after the girl."

"Was Quantaa not there?" Tryfon stroked his beard.

Uriel shifted her weight. "Thank Ever, yes, but—"

He held up his palm. "It is not yet time to release her light."

Uriel put down her cup. "You're saying there will be no help coming?"

A soft chime sounded. "Ah, they're done," Tryfon uttered with genuine delight. The Ancient One went over to the brick oven and pulled out a tray;

the smell of spice and berries instantly filled the tiny room. He reached in and removed a tray of freshly baked fig and oatmeal cakes.

"Sometimes, the things we need are the things we resist," he said, offering Uriel a warm cake.

She raised an eyebrow at her Master. *"How could he think of treats at a time like this?"* She took one as a courtesy.

"Let us hope I'm enough." The great towering Light Being stood, tossing her flowing cape over one shoulder.

"Worry is a fish out of water." Tryfon placed an arm on her shoulder. "It needs a place to go. Give it over to the brook's babble. Wish it well, and let it swim away."

Uriel nodded. Tryfon picked up his walking stick and tapped it on the floor. The moth that hovered over Uriel's eye began to flutter rapidly.

"I will contemplate the matter further, Protector Uriel. There may be one particular *Thaumoctopus* I could offer you as an aide."

Uriel bowed. "Thank you, your Grace."

He waved his cane. "Go with Ever."

Uriel walked to the rain curtain doorway and hurried through. Tryfon watched her leave, and after hearing the outside stone door open and close, the Divine Master pulled the small table away, revealing a secret hatch. With a firm tug, he opened it; water was rushing below. It was the same waterway that ran under the bridge and around Venusto. Tryfon knelt, reaching down into the water and retrieving a koi fish; its silver eyes looked up at him.

"Hello, my friend. I have a message for you to deliver," Tryfon said softly. He spoke to the koi in a language of bubble-snaps and whistle-pops. The fish popped back twice, and Tryfon gently lowered him back into the current.

Perl slowly woke, wiping drool from the corner of her mouth. She had slept the afternoon away after returning from Yule Island, dreaming of the waves of red crabs. Perl looked around, her eyes slowly adjusting; it was dark, the sky now an orangey-purple, and for a moment she wasn't quite sure where she was. A cool breeze brought the smell of smoky pine into her room.

"What time is it? Papa? Where..." It slowly dawned on her that she wasn't in her quilted bed on Mont Michel, but in her top bunk at Callowhorn. Reaching over to her shelf, she lit a candle. As if on cue, a giant leopard moth flew in through the open window and hovered above her bed.

"Hypercompe Scribonia. Good evening." In her free time between training sessions, Perl had been studying her classifications, learning the Venustoian

terminology for all the different creatures she'd encountered. The moth fluttered its wings, a cloud of sparkling dust gathered, and in a brief moment a crystalized message formed in the air:

My Precious Perl,

I received word of your remarkable day on Yule. I trust you are well. The Gecarcoidea natalis were fortunate you were there. Stay close to dear Quantaa. He is a loyal watcher. Trust in your circle of friends. Remember, no girl is an island.

Much Love in Ever, Uriel

The leopard moth flew out the open window, the dust from the message slowly vanished. Perl yawned, and rolled off her bunk, still groggy. The candlelight threw strange, twisted shadows on the far wall, reminding her of the creature she'd seen in the waters; a slight chill ran up her arms. Perl's stomach moaned like a whale. She hadn't eaten since earlier in the day, and judging by the skies, she knew she had slept past the Dragon Maw dining hours. "Great."

Hearing laughter outside the nest, Perl peeked out the window. There were the other eight Seekers, gathered around a bonfire. Quantaa lay in his Sphinx pose behind the group.

"Hey! Look who's up!" Tars waved, shouting up to Perl, "come out! We're roasting marmalade-mallows and celebrating!" He tossed a gooey glob into the air to catch it, but in a flash the dark head of Quantaa snapped it out of the air. "Hey!" Tars groaned; Flax gave him a hearty slap on the back.

Perl grabbed her trusty backpack and flung open the door to join them. "Celebrating what? Us saving the crabs? Quantaa, slaying that beast?"

"Well, that, and we're excited about tomorrow," beamed Corvax. The dark feathered boy sat cross-legged on a tree stump; Perl thought he looked genuinely happy.

"What's so special about tomorrow?" Perl picked up a stick, wiggling it in Bear's face, requesting a marshmallow.

Opis answered, "tomorrow's the Pompeius Games! Our final training exercise!"

With a free hand, Bear grabbed a marshmallow and dipped it in a jug of thick marmalade. He placed it on the end of Perl's stick.

"Oh, I totally forgot with everything that's happened today." Perl held the marshmallow over the flickering orange flames, watching it brown. "So, fill me in, guys…what are the games like? What are we playing?"

"It's not a game, exactly," Javan pulled his burnt glob from his stick, popping the sticky treat in his mouth.

"We'll be going up against the other five Seeker classes!" Nan fluttered her wings excitedly.

"It's a great honor to win," Opis added, "it shows who can work together best, using our Ever-given gifts. It's all about teamwork." Opis nudged Nan's stick aside, making room for hers over the flame.

"Yes, Opis..." Nan glared at her, flicking one of friend's tentacle strands, "...*teamwork.*"

Tars added, "the Pompeius Games are difficult. They take place inside these giant anthills on the other side of Callowhorn called The Domes."

"The puzzles change with each new Seeker class," Lyre pulled a hand-stitched quilt up over her lap, "so there's no way to study for them."

Perl pulled the scorched outer layer of marshmallow off of her stick, gobbling it up. She stuck the small gooey lump that remained back over the flame. "Sounds fun! I've always wondered what the inside of an anthill looks like."

Corvax stood up, a stick in each hand, toasting two marmalade-mallows. "Fun won't be our focus tomorrow. We'll need to work as a unit—combine our physical talents and utilize all of our intellectual abilities." He held out one of his sticks to Perl, the marshmallow toasted golden brown. She plucked it off and ate it, as marmalade ran down her chin. The crow-boy continued his speech, "we need to observe and collaborate as a team, and avoid letting our emotions get the better of us." He gave Perl a knowing wink.

"Sounds like a plan..." she smiled, licking her fingers, "but it also sounds fun."

Bear held six sticks over the fire pit. "Sure...until you can't solve one of the clues, and you get claustrophobic, or worse...go mad down there!" he said, waving his arms about dramatically, the marshmallows lit up like tiki torches.

"Oh, stop that, Bear," Lyre said, wrapping her quilt up around her winged back. She leaned over to reassure Perl, "it's true. We do stay in the hill for as long as it takes to complete each puzzle. But no one goes insane, Bear."

Perl shook her hair out to a full poof, crossed her eyes, stuffing her mouth full of marshmallows. She tried to speak, giggling, "itsh a good thing I know how to manage my frushtrationsh, right Corvathh?!"

There was a moment of quiet, then Flax, who had been staring dreamily up at the stars, started laughing. Grabbing a handful of mallows, he stuffed his salamander jaws full, rolling his eyes. "Yesth! Me toos!"

"And me!", "And me!" Tars and Javan joined in, their cheeks comically puffed out with marshmallows.

Quantaa sprang up and wagged his tail, fanning the flames, sending tiny

213

embers drifting up into the night sky. Soon, they were all making faces and laughing uncontrollably.

Perl fell backwards on to her backpack, leaves clinging to her mound of dark hair. She looked around at her friends having a good time, the fire casting a warm glow on everyone. For the first time, Perl started to see the group not as individuals, but as a true family; she sat up.

"Hey! Don't we need a team name?" She asked, getting everyone's attention.

"Well, normally they just assign us numbers and we go by that," Opis replied, pushing Bear, who was trying to steal the marshmallow she was toasting.

"*Borrrring!*" Sang Perl, as she reached around to pull her kalimba from her backpack.

"Oo, I got it!" Flax raised his hand. "How about The Super Seekers?"

Perl feigned a yawn, plinking her turtle instrument.

"Wonder Warriors!" Tars whipped his tail in a circle.

"Mmm, better. What else ya got?"

"I got it…" Bear rolled back and forth on his massive frame, tossing a flaming marshmallow into his mouth. "The Callowhorn Commandos!"

Perl shook her head, crinkling her nose.

Lyre chirped, "The Nimble Nine?"

"The Intellect Squad," Opis insisted, flipping her tentacles.

Javan threw out a name, "The Merciful Lions?"

"Mmm, those are…okaaay," Perl teased, "but we gotta have something that…stands out."

"Okay, let's hear your brilliant idea," Corvax insisted.

"First of all, thank you for the compliment. I am ever so brilliant!" Perl stood and bowed to Corvax, her glowing arms stretched outward.

He shook his head. "Well, she doesn't lack confidence," he smirked.

Perl held up her stick, dramatically waving it in the air like a wand. She began writing the letters 'T- F-P-O-N-C-J-L-B' in the dirt, forming a circle.

"Is that a word?" Flax asked.

Javan looked Perl. "How is that a team name?"

"You are correct, wise platypus. It's not *a* name. It is, in fact, *nine* names," Perl said, grinning her big, toothy grin.

Opis stepped up. "Explain, please."

Perl curtsied. "My pleasure." The fire cast a long shadow onto the tree behind her; she looked as large as Uriel. "It's all of our initials…'T-F-P-O-N-C-J-L-B.'
*Tars…Flax…Perl…Opis…Nan…Corvax…Javan…Lyre…Bear…*and, it's also a secret code."

"Again, I'll bite. What's the secret code?" Opis asked, now more intrigued.

Perl pointed her stick at the Seeker whose name went with each word, first to Tars. "The..." then to Flax, "Fearless..." to herself, "Protectors..." to Opis, "Of..." Nan, "Nature's..." Corvax, "Curious..." Javan, "Jewels..." to Lyre, "Little..." and finally to Bear, "... to Big!"

Nan clapped, "I love it!"

"Clever," Javan agreed.

Bear beat his round belly like a drum with his hands, repeating the secret code, "The Fearless Protectors Of Nature's Curious Jewels, Little to Big!"

"You do have an extra 'to' in there," Opis corrected, "but I still like it."

"A minor technicality, sister!" Perl popped another marshmallow into her mouth.

They all started chanting, as Nan and Lyre flew circles around the fire pit. *The Fearless Protectors Of Nature's Curious Jewels, Little to Big! The Fearless Protectors Of Nature's Curious Jewels, Little to Big! The Fearless Protectors Of Nature's Curious Jewels, Little to Big!*" Perl plucked her kalimba to the song; Quantaa howled along.

Corvax looked over at Perl. "Bring that big brain of yours to the games tomorrow...*Wildflower.*"

Javan noticed Corvax smile at Perl; a twinge of jealousy took him. *"Since when does he have a nickname for her?"*

Quantaa, having grown tired of the festivities, turned in a circle and laid back down. Within minutes, he was asleep, the great greyhound's snoring blowing out the fire. Thick smoke wafted up, enveloping everyone.

"Agh...it's like one of Master Kamani's dust clouds," coughed Flax.

"That's my cue. Goodnight, everyone." Opis jumped up and gave a wave. The others followed, retreating to their beds.

Nan, Lyre and Corvax headed back to their Air nest. "Everyone get a good night's sleep!" Corvax shouted. "We're gonna need it!"

"Later!" Bear grabbed the jug, running his finger along the inside for the last little bit of marmalade.

Javan walked with Perl to the end of her path. "I like the team name," he smiled, "and I noticed you gave yourself the name 'Protector'...you know something we don't?"

Perl walked backwards, feeling the pebbles beneath her bare feet. "Maybe..." she grinned. "Goodnight... *Jewel.*" She spun around, and ran up the pathway, quickly opening and closing the door behind her.

Javan's bangs fell over his eyes, hiding his blush.

29 POMPEIUS GAMES

"Welcome! Welcome! To the Pompeius Games, games!" Triumphant horns sounded and there, on a speckled toadstool pavilion, stood Grandmaster Olliv.

The grasshopper-man was dressed head to toe in a gold robe that shimmered in the morning sunlight. He was dwarfed on all sides by six enormous anthills, each of them hundreds of feet tall. A number designating each Seeker team, One through Six, was marked in mud along the side of each hill. Perl stood with her fellow Seekers at the base of Dome Number Four. Looking up, she spotted Masters Kamani, Yew, and Bodhi. Each team's trio of Light-Realm Protector Guides stood at the top of their pupils' anthill.

"These games are the final test, test! Your training will serve you all as you graduate to full-fledged Seekers of the Light Realm, Realm!" The students let out a collective cheer. Olliv raised his baton.

"Armed with your newfound skills, skills, and understanding, you will help to defend Nature by enlightening humans to their world, world! These are unstable times, times, and Earth may appear to be in turmoil, turmoil! But there is always a path to the light, light! Seekers, today is the first step in your journey, to help restore balance, balance!"

Another round of applause went up. Perl straightened her posture, feeling proud to be a part of both the Light Realm and of Earth. Perl thought of Papa Ximu, and how proud he would be to see her here. She glanced around at the other teams; they all had looks of determination on their faces.

Raising his buttercup baton high, Olliv continued, his voice reverberating through the arena, "Seekers! Protector Guides!" He paused slightly for dramatic effect, "I present to you, Commander Marabunta, Marabunta!"

A great rustling from the nearby woods got everyone's attention. All heads turned, as a gigantic female ant emerged from the trees. Nearly fifty feet in length, with mandibles the size of rowing oars, the incredible ant looming above them was a sight to behold.

Perl clapped with the others. "Now I know why the hills are so gigantic," she said to Bear, marveling at the enormous ant.

Wearing bright, gleaming plate mail like a medieval knight, Marabunta crawled over to the toadstool podium, the polished steel flashing bright white in the sun.

"Comrades of the Light Realm," Marabunta spoke, her voice as hard and steely as the armor she wore, "every ant in a colony has a task, from building roads, to gathering food and protecting eggs! Alone we would perish, but as a colony, we thrive! Today, you must do the same! Work as a unit to solve the puzzles three!" Marabunta pointed up to one of the anthills. "As a team, you shall race to the top and enter the domes. Make your way through the chambers. Each anthill has identical challenges within. The first full Seeker team to reach the Queen at the bottom and return to the surface with one flawless egg shall be crowned Champion of the Pompeius Games!"

Perl watched with anticipation as Marabunta pulled a longsword from a sheath on her back. "The Seeker class that finishes last will be forced to re-train their lessons before graduating." There was an audible grown from the Seekers. "The winning team will receive the Queen's patch, and their names shall be engraved for all eternity on the Painted Tree of Ever!" Marabunta pointed her sword at the Protector Guides, who stood alert. "On my command! Seekers, ready? Good luck to you all." Every Seeker got into a racing stance; Marabunta plunged her sword deep into the ground. Let the games…begin!"

Perl was nearly knocked over as her teammates took off, jostling for a position. Behind Marabunta, a herd of white elephants stepped forward. They raised their trucks, letting loose a rousing trumpet fanfare. Behind the anthills, plumes of rainbow-colored smoke and neon fireworks filled the skies. The games had officially begun.

"Here we go!" Shouted Bear.

As the Seekers scrabbled up the treacherous hillside, the Guides shouted words of encouragement down to them. Through all the training, Perl had never once heard Bodhi raise its calm voice, but now the Protector's words were like a clap of thunder, "make haste, Seekers! Together!"

Like a bright orange and yellow cloud, Yew floated down next to the nine as they made their way up the hill, the Light Protector's yellow tiger eyes wild and intense. "Swiftly, now! Rise together!"

"Climb!" At the top of the dome, Kamani's voice boomed, "this is the easy part! Ha-ha!"

His arm still not one hundred percent, Javan was feeling a bit clumsy, but for once, he didn't find himself in last. Behind him, he saw Opis struggling to run up the slippery side, her long tentacles flopping in her face as she stumbled along.

"You okay, Opis?" Javan yelled back.

Opis glanced up, "just keep going!" Her boots were sliding on the loose gravel.

Nan and Lyre were already at the top, having flown up. They hollered back down at the remaining seven, "come on, guys! Team Three is already going into their dome!"

Corvax blew past Perl; not about to let the crow-boy show her up, she dug in and was right behind him when they reached the summit. Bear, breathing heavily and sweating, plunked down next to Kamani, followed by Flax and Tars. Javan grabbed Opis' hand and pulled her up the last few feet.

"Ha! Welcome to the top!" Kamani's shouted. "Now, down you go!"

"Where's the ladder?" Perl asked, peering into the dark hole.

Yew advised, "like the cliff, you must trust. Make the leap."

Bodhi blinked its peacock eyes, gently giving advice to each Seeker as they dropped down through the opening. It placed a hand on Corvax's back, "use your intelligence." The Being patted Flax on the head, "notice details." To Tars it advised, "reach out." Bodhi brushed its hand across Nan's delicate wings, "see the patterns." Fluffing Perl's hair, it said, "adapt."

Kamani was busy heckling his Light Battle friend on the next hill over, "your Seekers will need more than luck on this day! Ha-ha!"

On Dome Three, a towering green iguana Battle Guide with cactus spikes for hair bellowed back, "When was the last time your thick head solved a puzzle, Kamani?!"

"Venture a bet then, my friend?" Kamani blew smoke from his bison snout.

"Quill pig triplet tasks for the loser!" The reptile Being crossed its scaly arms.

Kamani raised his arms. "Ha! *Erethizon dorsatum* triplets it be! It's a wager!"

"A Beetle in a Haystack"

Opis was the last to make the plunge. Sitting down, her legs dangling into the opening, she pushed herself off, letting out a slight scream as she slid down the tunnel. Winding this way and that, it dumped her onto the backs of her Seeker friends, who lay in a pile.

Perl bounced up, brushing the dirt from her legs. "Wow, so this is what it feels like to be an ant. Look at all these passageways!"

In the large round space were five entryways; four tunnels, one with a door. A large leaf dangled from the doorknob.

"That must be the one," Corvax said, racing over to the door. He pulled the leaf off; on it was a message.

"Well?" Nan said.

"Gimme a second, I'm reading."

"Out loud, so we all can hear, please," Lyre insisted.

Corvax cleared his throat:

"Beetle-dee, beetle-do,
Your journey's just begun!

218

For the quickest way out,
Seek the one,
That's by far the shortest route."

Tars had his paw on the doorknob. "Everyone ready?" The others nodded. "Okay then, let's do this," Tars yanked the door open.

"Agh!" Lyre let out a small squeak of disgust.

"What the?" Bear gasped.

"Bugs," muttered Flax.

Inside the damp chamber, a torch on the wall revealed thousands of beetles of every color, pattern, size and shape, crawling and flying in every direction.

"Quick, close the door!" Corvax yelled, "don't let any of them out!"

Once their eyes adjusted to the dimly lit room, they took note of the walls; from floor to ceiling were tiny doors, each one of them only inches tall, and far too many to count.

"The doors are made for beetles..." Bear surveyed the room, "...not even Perl could fit through one of these."

Perl shook her head; a dozen beetles flew out of her hair.

Flax raised his hand. "So, where do we begin?"

"Maybe there's something inside one of the doors we're supposed to find!" Nan offered.

They started opening door after door. Javan peeked inside one. "They're just tiny crawl spaces."

"And you can't even tell where they go." Bear opened six doors at once.

"Look around! It would take days, weeks!— to open all of these," Opis said, grabbing the note from Corvax. "There has to be a clue here. *Beetle-dee, beetle-do.* What do beetles do?"

Perl remember Papa showing her beetles in the garden. "They love to munch on plant leaves and nibble on fruit trees."

"I don't see any plant life in here." Tars waved bugs out of his face with his tail. "Just a billion annoying insects!"

Nan quipped back, fluttering her wings, "watch it, Tars. There's nothing annoying about insects."

Bear, Flax, and Perl continued opening doors. Javan glanced up at the ceiling; it was painted like a starry night.

"We need to focus. Everyone get together," Corvax suggested, waving them in. They huddled up, locking arms, mainly so they could see one another in the shadowy room but also to keep out some of the bugs. "It says to find the one. So, there's only one bug or door in here that we need to find. We just have to figure out which one it is."

"Oh, is that all," Javan joked.

Hundreds of beetles hovered and crawled around them as they

continued their discussion.

Lyre questioned, "but what's *the shortest route?* There are doors everywhere! Which is the closest one?"

Opis recited, "the shortest route between two points is a straight line."

Corvax smiled. "Good! Now which of these buggers is flying in a straight line?"

They looked around; the room was chaos as beetles moved in every direction.

"Well, that narrows it down," Bear said sarcastically.

Perl's gaze went to the ceiling. "That looks like the Milky Way."

"Perl, we need to stay focu—ack!" Corvax accidentally swallowed a bug.

Bear giggled, "let's hope that wasn't the magic beetle!"

Javan agreed with Perl, "she's right, it is the Milky Way. Before I went in, Master Bodhi told me to 'notice the details.' I think Perl's on to something…the constellations have to be a clue."

"I am? I mean…I am," Perl beamed, "but what do you mean, exactly?"

"There's only one beetle in the world that uses astronomy for guidance." Javan said.

Lyre and Tars shouted together, "*Phanaeus vindex MacLachlan!*"

Perl understood them. "The Rainbow scarab?"

Opis spoke up over the buzzing of flapping wings, "we're looking up, when we should look down."

Bear dropped to the dirt floor, careful not to crush any of the bugs scampering underfoot. "Get low, everybody. The one we want will be crawling, not flying."

Perl nudged Javan as they got down on their hands and knees, "I still don't get it."

Javan's head was nearly flat to the ground. "The dung beetle has a photoreceptor in its eyes that can detect a light pattern in the galaxy. They always roll their dung ball in a straight line, in accordance to the stars' alignment."

"Dung ball?" Perl raised an eyebrow.

"Yep, poop."

"Hey, hey! I think I found him!" Tars blinked his giant eyes. Through the swarm, he stood above a little brown beetle rolling a poo-ball twice its size.

Bear scurried over. "Follow that bug!"

They all crowded tightly around the insect, watching as it moved diligently across the floor.

"It looks like he's headed straight for that one," Tars said, drawing a line in the dirt from the beetle to a tiny green door.

"Try it!" Corvax directed. Tars flipped the door open. Inside was an even smaller door with a key already in the keyhole.

"Can you unlock it?" Nan asked.

"No...my paw's too big."

"Let me try." Perl laid down next to the door, grabbing hold of the tiny key with two fingers. She could barely turn it. "I...I think I've got it..." The lock clicked, and a large opening in the wall gave way, revealing a staircase going down. Perl watched as the dung beetle reached the door, rolling his poo ball through the tiny entrance.

"Ha! You did it, tiny hands!" Bear lifted Perl back to her feet in one swift jerk.

Corvax barked orders, "okay let's go...no time to waste."

The nine Seekers scurried down the stairway.

Outside the anthills, the Light Protector Guides were chatting, waiting anxiously for news of their team. On Dome Number Four, an ant sentry crawled up their hill and planted a red flag with a beetle stitched on it next to Kamani. Seeing this, the bison let out a great cry of joy, "success! One down! Two to go! Ha-Ha!" The masters from the other five hillsides looked over.

Seconds later, on Dome Number Three, the same red flag went up. The cactus-spiked iguana grabbed hold of it, waving it vigorously at Kamani. "Right behind you, bison!"

"And that is where you will stay! Ha-Ha!"

"Pillars of Strength"

The stairwell ran down to a small vestibule, the cool, damp walls a mixture of soil, clay, and pine needles. The only thing visible in the room was a large oval-shaped door made of wood, held in place by hinges of thick roots. Writing was carved into the face of it. Javan, being the closest to the door, read the message aloud.

> *"A circle within a circle,*
> *You learn as you teach,*
> *Close of heart, close of mind,*
> *The key's within reach."*

"A circle within a circle. Any guesses?" Lyre asked.

"Um...two circles," Bear joked. Opis looked at him, shaking her head.

Tars laughed. "Nailed it, Bear."

Corvax tugged on the heavy door; chunks of dirt fell away as it slowly opened, revealing an enormous circular chamber, the walls stone, the floor covered in a fine, powdery sand. In the center of the room stood a ring of nine thirty-foot high pillars, a small dais in the center.

"Nine columns," Flax counted. "Nine of us...coincidence? I think

221

not."

On the opposite side of room was a massive door with a bronze heart-shaped lock in the middle of it.

Nan flew over and tried to open it. "Nope. Guess that would've been too easy."

Perl walked up to one of the pillars. "There's steps spiraling up." She didn't hesitate, taking the steps two at a time like she would on her daily deliveries back home.

Lyre looked at Corvax; he shrugged. "Worth a try...everyone choose a pillar."

The Seekers climbed the pedestals. One by one, they reached the top, carefully balancing on the flat slab capping the column.

Bear was the last one up, huffing and puffing. "Okay...okay...I made it."

As soon he stood on the base, a portal opened up in the dais. From it, an arm made of polished white marble rose up; in its open hand it held a silver key.

Tars bounced up and down. "Look!" The moment the monkey-boy leaped into the air the arm started to retract back into the ground.

"Tars, stop jumping!" Javan called over.

Tars froze in place; the arm resurfaced, still holding the key.

Nan asked, "can anyone reach it?"

"No way. Nan or Lyre, why don't one of you try to fly over?" Opis suggested.

Nan fluttered off her perch; once again, the arm began to lower.

"Never mind," the tentacled girl waved her arm at Nan, "come on back."

"What did the riddle say again?" Lyre asked Javan, "something about close to your heart?"

Javan closed his eyes. "Close of heart, close of mind...the key's within reach."

"Maybe we should all jump down at the same time?" Lyre thought for a second. "You know, to close in the circle?"

"It's too far of a drop. We'll break our legs!" Flax shouted across the circle, his voice echoing off the chamber walls.

"Come on! I say we try it!" Tars eyed the others excitedly.

"Easy for you to say! You're used to jumping all over the place," Flax argued back.

Javan spoke up, "no, Flax is right. That's probably not it." He repeated the clue, "a circle within a circle...close...within reach."

Perl left her pedestal; the marble hand slipped back into hiding.

"Where are you going?" Opis asked.

"There's no way to reach the key from where the columns are right now. We need to close the circle somehow" She quickly skipped down the steps. "If we push the pillars over and stand on them, we could reach the key." Perl started leaning against her column, but the heavy stone structure didn't budge.

"What's everyone else think?" Opis started down. "Should we try this?"

"I dunno." Corvax shook his head. "If her hunch turns out to be wrong, and we knock these things over, there's no lifting them back up."

"He's right. Once they're down, they're down," agreed Bear.

Nan flew off the top of her pillar, landing beside Perl. "It's not like anyone else has a better idea. I say we try it."

They got off their pillars and went over to Perl's, crowding in close. The tardigrade-boy was last, wrapping his arms around all of them in a giant bear hug. "Like the riddle said, 'close of mind,' right guys?"

Corvax looked over at Perl. "Let's hope this works."

"Don't worry, it will," Perl said confidently, crossing her fingers. On the count of three, she and the others pushed. The towering structure leaned, then fell, landing with a heavy thud.

"One down, eight to go," Bear flexed his arms, patting his muscles. The Seekers moved around the room, toppling the heavy pillars, growing more exhausted as they went.

"Okay, last one. Come on guys, we can do this," Bear was dripping with sweat.

"I...can't push anymore." Nan wiped her brow, flapping her wings to cool herself.

"Me either." Opis leaned against Nan, "I need a rest." The two girls slid to the ground, sitting back to back.

"You have to get up! We need all of us to move these things," Lyre, out of breath, squawked at them.

Perl held out her hand. "Families stick together." Opis lifted her head, and with a heavy sigh, took hold of Perl's hand. Nan fluttered her wings, lifting herself back up.

The tired group pushed with everything they had. As the last column dropped to the ground, so did the tired group of Seekers. The nine pillars were now pointed at the stone dais.

"I really hope this works," Corvax repeated.

"I can't feel my arms," Flax mumbled.

"Hey! This is still a race!" Tars jumped up, shaking the dust out of his furry head. "Get up! Come on, up ya' go!" He held out his paws, yanking each Seeker to their feet.

Flax struggled to raise his arm. "Okay, what now?"

"Everyone stand on the end of your pillar, as close to the dais as you can," Perl directed. Each Seeker inched out to the very edge, but the marble hand did not return.

Javan wobbled clumsily. "Nothing's happening."

Perl could feel her face going flush. She didn't want to look anyone in the eye, so she just stared at the dais, willing the arm to appear. *"Please, come on, key, where are you?"* Perl stretched her arms out to her sides.

Seeing her do this, Bear said, "hey yeah...why don't we try holding hands?" They all clasped hands and waited.

Corvax sighed. "So now what are we—" Before he could finish, the stone arm rose up, holding the silver key.

Never feeling so relieved, Perl gushed, "it worked!"

"Grab it!" Opis yelled.

"Wait," Corvax halted the excitement, "if we let go of our hands, we'll lose the key again."

Tars wiggled his tail. "I got this!" Twisting his backside, he gingerly lifted the key from the marble hand. "There! Easy! Just like Bodhi told me...'*Reach!*'"

"Who would've thought that tail would come in handy?" teased Flax.

The Seekers jumped off their pillars and headed to the exit. Tars, still holding the key with his tail, undid the heart-shaped lock. They pushed on the door; the heavy masonry creaked and moaned on its iron hinges, as if uttering the word *"onnnwarrrd."*

The group squeezed into a small rectangular room. Covering one wall was a mystical creature with three large eyes, spiraling antennae, and wings that looked like flames. Its open mouth was a wide, gaping hole, large enough to crawl into.

"Well that's unsettling," Bear said, staring at the menacing face.

"Looks like a slide." Javan poked his head into the mouth. "Too dark to see where it goes."

"Thank Ever...no more steps. I can handle a slide." Opis pulled her tentacles back. She walked over to the opening and climbed in.

"Wait a sec," Corvax went to grab her, but the wispy girl was gone, zipping down the shaft. Corvax huffed, "I guess this is the plan. Bear, you go next, and we'll form a train behind you. Everybody hold on!"

He and the others crawled into the hole and grabbed on to one another.

Lyre leaned forward whispering to Corvax, "but what about Opis?"

"Don't worry, she's way ahead of us by now," Corvax assured. "Ready? Go, Bear!"

Using all eight arms, Bear pushed off the sides of the tunnel. Perl was last, behind Tars. She laid on her belly, holding on to his coiled tail; down the slippery slide they went.

Opis heard something behind her. She looked back and saw Bear closing quickly.

"Look out, below!" Bear yelled. Opis was about to be steamrolled when the roly-poly scooped her up. "Care for a ride?" Opis held onto Bear's pudgy neck as the team zipped down the tunnel.

Outside, Yew hovered above the pit, listening to the echoing voices deep below, its piercing eyes glowing golden yellow. Kamani, arms crossed, surveyed the other anthills. Gray flags with images of pillars on them were flying from three of the enormous mounds.

"Master Kamani!" His reptilian friend yelled over. "Enjoy cleaning up after the porcupine babies!"

Moments later, the gray flag on anthill Number Four went up. "Not so fast!" Kamani yelled back. The bison breathed a sigh of relief and glanced at Bodhi. "They're not far behind."

Bodhi placed its powdery white hand on Kamani's broad shoulder, its many eyes blinking thoughtfully. "The girl will surprise. Wait and see."

"Ice-word and Upward"

The slide dumped them onto a wide sheet of ice, their makeshift train pulling apart as they slid across it. The room was otherwise empty, save for a prism jutting up out of the ice. It looked like a pyramid covered in frost, three times as tall as Perl. The contour of a triangular door could be seen on one side, with a smaller window near the top.

The Seekers stood slowly; the footing slippery.

"Last chamber, Seekers!" Bear called out, his voice bouncing off the icy walls.

"Brrr! Let's hurry! I'm not sure how long I can be in here!" Lyre shivered, wrapping her wings around her like a blanket.

"I don't know about you guys, but my arctic blood loves this!" Nan replied.

"I wonder how we're doing compared to the other Seekers?" Javan announced.

"We should probably pick up the pace." Flax was the first to the prism, running and sliding over to it on his slick belly. He walked around the curious structure, looking for a clue. He pushed on the door, nothing happened. He pressed his face to the window but saw nothing, inside. As the others skated over, Flax threw up his hands. "There's no note...there's not even a handle on the door!"

Bear ran his hands up and down the slick, glasslike surface, hoping to discover a knob or switch. Lyre and Nan floated up above the prism, but didn't see anything. They all searched and searched, growing more impatient. Lyre curled up on the ground, trying to keep warm; Tars sat down and wrapped his tail around her. Perl's teeth chattered.

Corvax slapped the side of the prism, frustrated. "This makes no sense!"

Perl, having lived her whole life on a tropical island, had never experienced this type of cold. "I c-c-can see my b-b-breath!"

Opis piped up, "the glass! What if we breathe on the glass?" She walked up to the door and breathed a warm puff of air onto the translucent glass; the word *"Rest"* materialized on the glassy surface.

Bear cheered, "everybody breathe on the glass!" As the group huffed and puffed, bright white letters formed against the frosty gray surface.

"Rest and roost in the light,
None is naught,
One is better,
But in pairs, there is might."

As Opis read the cryptic message out loud, the prism started to crack; tiny fissures spidered their way up the door.

"Step back," Corvax moved the group away. Seconds later, one side of the pyramid shattered into crystallized dust.

"Does anyone remember what the clue said?" Corvax asked the Seekers.

"I do." Perl prided herself on having an excellent memory. She had spent many a late night memorizing all the various bugs and plant life on Mont Michel.

The group crowded inside the hollow prism and once they were all inside, it started to lower, dropping through the ice like a frozen elevator.

"Brace yourself, everybody," Javan urged the group.

The group held on to the walls and each other as the icy carriage descended into the ground, eventually stopping with a crunch.

Lyre poked her head out of the doorway. "It's a cavern!"

"As long as it's warm, I don't care what it is," thought Perl.

The Seekers filed out, looking around. As soon as they left the prism, it melted, seeping into the crevices of the craggy stone floor.

The cavern floor was dotted with stalagmites, shooting up like thick blunt spears. The ceiling of the rocky enclosure was strewn with bats, clinging to the roof with their tiny feet. Long stalactites dangled like icicles, some hanging so low they nearly touched the tips of the stalagmites.

"Acerodon jubatus," Opis recited in her best professorial voice. "Giant golden-crowned bats, also known as flying foxes."

Perl's mouth was agape. "Looks like they're sleeping."

"I hope they stay that way. They always did give me the willies," whispered Lyre.

Perl disagreed. She loved bats. Just like her spider-monks, they were often misunderstood.

Bear nudged Perl, "so what was the first part again?

226

"Rest and roost in the light," Perl replied as if reciting from a textbook.

"Well, that is what bats do," Bear turned to the others. "They return to their roosts during the day."

"True, but that doesn't help us much," answered Nan. "What else do we know about them?"

Corvax climbed up onto a rocky ledge. "They're a vital part of the earth's life cycle. They pollinate. They eat tons and tons of insects every night."

Opis chimed in, "they disperse seeds for new plants to grow."

Corvax crossed his arms, "anything else?"

"Their guano is rich in nutrients," Opis continued, "allowing other organisms to grow and flourish."

Corvax cut her off, "and they use echolocation…"

Opis interrupted, "…to hunt prey."

"I was about to say that," Corvax shot back.

The two Seekers debated, while the others chose instead to go over every word of the riddle. They plopped down on the damp cave floor, resigned to the fact that they could be there awhile. Although it was better than the frigid room above, there was still a clammy chill in the air. Moisture started to form on Nan and Lyre's wings; they shook them off, irritated.

Perl stared at the bats. *The word roost means to rest. We rest our minds when we mediate.* She crossed her legs and closed her eyes.

The others continued their discussion as Perl fell silent, focusing on her breathing. Soon the voices in the room faded, and all she heard were the water droplets trickling off the stalactites.

Perl started tapping on her on right knee with her fingers to the rhythm of the water hitting the stalagmites below—*Drip. Drip. Drip.* On her left knee she tapped once—*Drop.* There seemed to be a pattern. *Drip. Drip. Drip*—Perl tapped again with her right hand. *Drop*—Perl tapped with her left. *Drip. Drip. Drip…Drop.* Back and forth she went, oblivious to everything else in the cave. The others turned and watched Perl as she began to hum.

Javan slapped Corvax on the arm. "It's not about the bats at all, it's the water!" Corvax looked at him, puzzled. Javan explained, "like the riddle said, 'in pairs, there is might.' Stalactites and stalagmites. One drops the water, the other catches it, creating a sound."

Javan sat down next to Perl and closed his eyes. The other Seekers circled around, joining in the meditation. Soon, they began to hear the water droplets' song:

Drip. Drip. Drip…Drop. Drip. Drip. Drip…Drop.

"I speak of…love. In nature…peace," Perl whispered the words aloud.

Once the Seekers heard the pattern and their voices became one, the bats took flight. Hundreds of them escaped, pouring through an opening in the roof. Over the squeaking of the bats, the Seekers heard a deep rumbling sound.

"There!" Bear yelled.

On one side of the cave, an entire section of wall began to crumble; large chunks of rock bounced and careened around them. Jumping to their feet, they backed away from the falling debris. The dust cleared, and sitting in front of them was an enormous white cube, nearly ten feet wide. Behind it, a long, arched tunnel, twice the height of the cube, had opened up. Bear rushed over to the block.

"Careful, Bear," Perl urged.

He looked the massive cube up and down, then ran a finger across it and stuck it in his mouth. "It's sugar!"

"Really?" Flax asked.

"What are we supposed to do with it?" Nan asked.

"Eat it?" Bear proposed, licking the cube once more.

"Stop, Bear!" Opis pulled him away. "I'm pretty sure it's for the Queen," The jellyfish-girl pointed down the hallway; it was lined with decorative banners.

"She's right," Nan agreed.

"Great...so how do we move it?" Javan asked.

Corvax thought aloud, "it's way too heavy to carry...what about those?" He looked at the banners; each of them was hanging from thick dowel rods. "If we take those down, lay those logs under the sugar block, and make a rope out of the banners, we could pull it as we roll it!"

"That could work," Javan said.

"Let's go," Perl followed him.

The group quickly yanked down the pennants, rods and all, tying the banners into long rope. Using the rods, they wedged the massive sugar block up just high enough to place a few dowels underneath it.

"Okay, Nan, Lyre, Tars and Flax...keep rotating the rods from the front to back," Corvax barked orders, "and the rest of us will pull."

Working together, they slowly but steadily moved the sugar cube down the hallway until they reached an immense chamber where a giant ant stood guard. The room itself was quite regal. The walls were adorned with vignettes of everyday ant life; there were ants collecting seeds, carrying leaves, building and tunneling, and guarding eggs. On a massive throne built out of seed casings, twigs and mud, sat the noble Queen Ant, a crown of yellow wildflowers on her head. She was flanked on either side by a row of three armor-clad soldiers.

Seeing Perl and the team enter with the sugar cube, the Queen bowed slightly, tapping her scepter and motioning them forward. Stacked high behind the Queen's throne were hundreds of semi-translucent eggs.

Perl elbowed Bear, "one queen laid all those?"

"That's a lot of babies," Bear chuckled.

"U bonatu, Your Highness," Opis greeted the Queen in her best *Formicidaen* dialect.

The ant blinked her large, shiny black eyes. "U bonatu to you as well."

"We," Opis gestured to the others, "have brought you a gift in exchange for borrowing one of your eggs, which we vow to return with the utmost care."

The Queen summoned one of her soldiers to take an egg from the stack. The ant held it up so she could carefully examine it.

"Very good, present the sugar," The Queen uttered, "and in turn you shall receive the egg."

The soldier scurried over, lifting up the cube effortlessly with its mandibles and carrying it away.

"Okay, get ready," Corvax said. He, Bear, Javan, and Tars made a nest with their interlocked arms, and another soldier delicately placed the egg within it. It was heavier than they thought.

Nan curtsied. "Thank you, your Eminence."

"Everspeed, younglings." The Queen motioned to two guards standing on either side of a great pair of golden doors, the Queen's seal painted on it. The guards opened them, revealing a staircase spiraling upwards.

Bear groaned, "you've got to be kidding me."

"More stairs," sighed Opis.

"I'll lead the way." Corvax adjusted his grip. "Perl, you and the others be the lookouts. We have to keep the egg safe!"

Perl took one last look back, wanting to remember this moment. She and the others began their slow climb upwards with the large, cumbersome egg.

Up above, the final flags were hoisted. Yew, Bodhi and Kamani celebrated as a dark brown flag with an egg symbol on it was planted on their hill.

"Ha! Now, they ascend!" Kamani beat his hooves on the ground with delight, stirring up a thick cloud of dust. Shouting over to his lizard friend, he taunted, "witness our flag! How do you feel about porcupine dung?!"

The iguana master gave a dismissive wave, then began shouting into the hole below. Its cactus-spiked head bobbing up and down frantically, "faster! Faster! Like the desert winds!" he urged his pupils, who lurked somewhere in the dark labyrinth below.

On the staircase, Perl and the others were making progress.

"Easy now, that's precious cargo," Lyre fluttered in the air above them.

"Precious...and really heavy!" Bear grunted, sweat pouring down his reddening cheeks.

"And not exactly calm, either! I can feel it moving," added Javan.

The egg rolled around in the boys' arms as the baby ant inside shifted its weight.

"Whoa, baby." Tars gently rubbed the egg with his tail. "We'll have you back to your mama soon!"

The spiraling steps grew smaller and tighter as the nine climbed. Wanting to help, Perl decided to sing the baby ant a lullaby with the hopes of settling it. It was the same song she sang to keep Regor moving up the endless steps on Mont Michel during deliveries:

> *"Around the corner of my life,*
> *I see a whole new world unfolding,*
> *make it what I wish,*
> *paint it colors fresh and bright,*
> *reds and lavenders,*
> *I see it all blossoming,*
> *I smell the beauty, almost there,*
> *almost there, Almost therrre."*

Nan burst through the opening on anthill Number Four, encouraging her teammates, "a few more steps! You're almost there!"

Cheers rang out on anthill Three just as Perl and the others carefully hoisted their egg out; after being in shadows all day, the late afternoon sun was blinding.

Opis took Yew's feathery hand. "Did we win?"

Yew's yellow eyes blinked at Opis. "Well done, all of you."

Across the way, the Masters on Dome Three—a gorilla, a two-headed swan, and Kamani's rival—the iguana—celebrated with their Seekers.

"Phew!" Bear sighed, flopping onto his back. "That was easy," he panted.

Perl looked over at Team Three. "Wait...*they* won?"

"Impossible," crowed Corvax.

Kamani gathered the group in his arms. "Ha, yet it is! But I am proud, Seekers! Very proud, indeed!" Kamani patted Javan on the back, nearly knocking him into the pit.

Perl saw the other anthill's flags; Team One was still stuck in the beetle room, Team Two had finished the pillar chamber, and Teams Five and Six were making their way up.

"We came so close," she said to Javan.

Commander Marabunta climbed to the summit of Dome Three, escorted by a large soldier. "Step aside," he directed to a zebra-striped boy jumping up and down with excitement. The ant retrieved the egg and held it up to the Commander. Marabunta pulled out a monocle the size of a trash can lid, inspecting the egg like a jeweler as the guard rotated it.

"Stop!" The great ant shook her head. "There is a fracture…tiny, but a fracture, nonetheless!" The Seekers and masters of Team Three gasped. Marabunta raised her sword. "The egg is flawed. Recall the rules, one and all!" she proclaimed loud enough so everyone could hear, "you must bring to the surface…*one flawless egg!* I am sorry, Team Number Three, but you are disqualified."

"What?", "No fair!", "It's just a tiny scratch!" The team aired their grievances.

"I am sorry, but the rules are clear as crystal." As quickly as she had climbed up Team Three's hill, Marabunta and her guard scurried back down, making their way to Dome Number Four.

Perl and the team gently handed their egg over to Marabunta. Tars giggled at Bear as the portly tardigrade bowed gushingly. She meticulously inspected every inch of the pearlescent egg, going over it twice for good measure. The giant ant paused; she looked down at the Seekers, then at Kamani, Yew, and Bodhi. Marabunta turned and faced the crowd, who stared on in anticipation.

"It pleases me to announce that the winners of this year's Pompeius Games…are the Seekers of Dome Number Four!!"

At that, Perl and the others jumped up and down and screamed, squeezing one another tightly. Nan and Lyre turned somersaults in the air.

Kamani stomped his hooves, shaking the anthill. "I knew it! Ha! Ha! Flawless! My Seekers!" He pointed over to his reptile friend, who seethed; the iguana's scales burned bright red, the spikes on its head firing off in frustration. "Easy! You'll need those for protection from the piglets! Ha-Ha!" Kamani boasted, raising his hooves in victory.

Perl watched as the other Seekers brought their eggs out, their tired faces going from hopeful to dejected. The crowd gave each team a large round of applause. *"I'm happy we won, but I feel so bad they lost,"* she thought. Javan and Tars scooped Perl up. "What the—hey!" They carried her down the hillside on their shoulders. Perl laughed, waving at the crowd; she couldn't have been any prouder of her family, and herself.

Later that evening, as the skies turned a pinkish hue, a ceremony was held in Tryfon's lush garden. All of Callowhorn was in attendance, sitting at dining tables on the lawn between the rows of colorful flowerbeds. The nine winners stood at attention in the middle of the emerald green bridge. Master Tryfon walked up to each Seeker, placing the Queen Ant's patch onto each of their sleeves; it magically sealed itself to their uniforms. Perl looked at it; in the center was a portrait of the Queen. Stitched around the perimeter were the letters of each of the Seeker's names— T-F-P-O-N-C-J-

L-B.

Perl beamed; she flashed her patch at Javan. "Look, our secret code name."

The others noticed the initials too, smiling, singing to one another, "The Fearless Protectors Of Nature's Curious Jewels Little to Big."

"I still don't like the extra "to" in there…sister," Opis teased.

Tryfon tapped his walking stick on the bridge; the guests fell silent. "A wellspring of talents, Ever-present in all our Seekers." As he spoke, Tryfon's body and clothing transformed from one natural wonder to the next. "One piece of a puzzle must fall into place so that others may be revealed. To skip a step before another is ready…a solid foundation will not be created. These nine before you walk together, with trusting hearts and minds of one. They are victorious, not just in The Pompeius Games, but beyond."

Everyone cheered; from the flowerbeds erupted thousands of pastel-colored butterflies. They fluttered up into the sky like confetti. From high above, ripping through the lavender clouds, came Quantaa, performing loop-the-loops in the air.

Tryfon folded his three sets of wings and turned to the winners, "follow me." Perl and the others walked behind the Grand Master as he left the bridge, winding past guests to the center of his sprawling garden. "Behold, Seekers, The Painted Tree."

It was the largest, most majestic tree in all of Venusto. Perl had first seen it when she and Uriel had ballooned into the paradise. The tree sprouted like a glorious headless through the top of the great cloud woman's head. Since then, Perl had only seen the tree from a distance; up close it was more spectacular than she could have ever imagined.

"It's like a rainbow grew out of the ground," she whispered to Nan, "look at all those names."

Centuries of past winners were inscribed in colorful rings around the trunk, rising high up into the sky.

"Gather," Tryfon gestured to the nine; the Seekers circled around. The Master knelt down, touching the tree at its base. He spoke softly, "cresco."

The ground rumbled as the great tree stretched, instantly growing a few more inches. Now, at the bottom of the massive trunk, written in violet, were the names of the nine Seekers.

"Behold, you are part of an infinite history," Tryfon announced. He stepped away, allowing the Seekers to approach the ancient tree.

Perl's mouth hung open in awe as she read her name. She took out her sketchbook, wanting to capture it all, though she knew no drawing could ever match the feeling of this moment. While the others celebrated, Perl found a place to sit. She began sketching, starting with the tree's massive trunk. On the drawing, she penciled in all of her friends' names.

"Your father...Noaa...his name is enshrined on the tree."

"Master Tryfon!" Perl jumped up; next to the towering Being, she looked tiny. "He is? Where?"

"Above the clouds by now, I imagine." Tryfon pointed his walking stick to the sky.

Perl gazed up at the mighty wonder before her. "I wish I'd met him."

"In your heart he lives."

Perl squinted slightly at the Master's radiant, dream-like appearance. "He died because of me."

"He died *for* you. There is a difference."

Perl stared at the ground; she watched as a monarch butterfly landed on a blade of grass, gently beating its wings. Tryfon held her chin.

"My child, no other Being in the Light Realm has been blessed by Ever with a human child, not a one. Nor has one surpassed the amount of love Noaa felt being a father to you."

A tear fell from Perl's cheek. Tryfon caught the droplet. In his soft, open palm, it transformed into a perfect white pearl.

Tryfon placed the gem in her hand. "A pearl for Perl."

A peaceful calm washed over Perl. The Master's warm, soothing voice felt like the sun on her face. The Divine Master gently cupped his hand around hers. He looked at her, smiling, his heavenly gaze filled with pure light.

"Love is magic."

Perl opened her hand; endless colors swirled on the pearl's iridescent surface.

"Thank you so mu—" she glanced up, but the celestial Being had vanished; tiny particles of sparkling white light danced on the breeze.

30 PEONY BAKLAVA

"I love it here in Venusto," Perl relaxed in her favorite spot, under her beloved tree, Lottie. Today, she wasn't alone; Javan had decided to come with her. "I mean, it's amazing, more amazing than I ever could have ever imagined." She held up her finger; a tiny green hummingbird with purple butterfly wings landed on it. "But I miss my home, my spider-monks, my room…it just feels like that was another lifetime ago. I've seen and done things that are unbelievable, and I've made friends. Good ones. Forever ones."

Javan sat pulling at the grass around him. "But?" He tossed a handful aside.

Perl leaned back against Lottie's smooth trunk. "I can't keep pretending that that evil isn't out there, destroying the ocean and the people I love along with it. I just wish there was some way to know what's happening with Papa, the twins, everything. My visions have all been so dark lately…like a nightmare I can't seem to shake."

Javan took a leaf-pouch from his pocket. "I get it…I miss my family, too." He unwrapped it and took out a delicate pink flower. Javan plucked a petal off, handing one to Perl. "Try one. It's a gift from my, well, someone you'd call my "mother"…for winning the Pompeius Games."

"Your mother?" She took a small nibble from the corner of the petal. A burst of sweet flavor coursed through her entire body; it was the most delicious thing she'd ever had.

"As pure Beings from the Light Realm, we don't have traditional parents," Javan explained, "we are, however, each given a Light mentor at the moment of our creation. This is our personal guide, given by Ever to watch over us as we grow and develop, forever. They teach us, protect us, and love us. So, in many ways, they are very similar to an Earth parent."

Perl was listening, but the taste of the candied petal was overwhelming. "What *is* this?"

Seeing the euphoria on her face, Javan chuckled, handing her three more petals. "Peony baklava, and nobody makes it better than my…mother," he smiled. Perl placed another petal in her mouth, the sugary yumminess melting on her tongue.

"Tell me more about her." Perl looked out over the water. Dusk was approaching, the sun now an orange fireball against a fuchsia sky.

"Her name is Anaya. She's an elder Land Light Protector. I miss her, but I will join her again when my training is complete."

Hearing this, Perl's stomach twisted into a knot; she'd never considered the fact that Javan and the others might leave her.

"Oh." Perl ate another petal to escape the unpleasant thought.

Javan sensed Perl's unease, so he kept talking, "it's different here. It's not like families on Earth. We're all related, connected…and Tryfon is everyone's Dedo."

"Dedo?" Perl asked.

Javan folded up the leaf pouch, saving the remaining petals for later. "What you'd call a grandfather."

Perl liked the thought of a grandpa. Several spider-monks back home reminded her of grandfathers, but none compared to Tryfon, except maybe Ximu, but he would always be her Papa.

"You know…" Javan stood up, brushing the grass off his legs. "There might be a way to give you some peace of mind about back home."

"Really? How?"

"Well…there is one Light Being in Venusto that might help you, but…"

"But? But what?"

"Not many have ever actually seen this Being. Anyway, I've heard that it's some kind of oracle…maybe it could reveal which path you should take."

"Perfect!" Perl jumped up. "Let's go find it!"

"I've heard that it doesn't want to be found. They say it lives somewhere in the mountains overlooking the Callowhorn Battle Fields."

Perl stashed her last tasty flower petal into a small pocket in her backpack. "But it's exactly what I need, like a fortune teller! Does it have a name?"

"Most just call it the Fawn," Javan began walking back up the hillside towards their Bowerbird nests.

"Well, what are we waiting for?" Perl slung her backpack over her shoulder, catching up to him.

"Nightfall, for starters. Most believe the Fawn is nocturnal. Also, we'd be violating the rules of Venusto by disturbing a Light Protector, *and,* we'd be exploring an area that's strictly off limits." Javan raised an eyebrow at her. "But that doesn't concern you much, does it?"

Perl grinned. "Well, we might not even find this Fawn Being. We could just go and look for a little bit. No one needs to know. We'll say we're on an adventure!"

"If we do this…and that's a big "if," Javan said, knowing full well Perl had already set her mind to it, "we'll need the help of Tars' night vision. Those woods are very old, and very dense."

"Can Tars keep a secret?"

"Yeah, we can trust him. Plus, he owes me a favor from a few life cycles ago."

The two were nearing their nests.

Perl paused. "Um, so speaking of secrets, there's something I've been wondering about."

Javan slowed his pace. "Okay…?"

Perl stopped and faced him. "That day with the crabs on Yule Island, after that monster attacked us. I saw Kamani whisper something to you, and you ran off without saying a word." Perl looked deep into his dark eyes. "What did he say to you? Are they planning on sending me away?"

"Whoa, what?" Javan was taken aback. "No, Perl! No one's sending you anywhere," he chuckled, "your imagination's getting the better of you."

Perl grabbed his arm. "Don't give me that 'it's all your head' stuff, Javan! Not from you. I know what I saw."

"Look, Perl," Javan shook his head, "I don't know what you think you saw, but I was running to tell Uriel so she could let Tryfon know that we were attacked by a Dark Realm beast!"

"Okay then, why you? You're not the fastest in the group!" Perl crossed her arms; she was determined to get a straight answer.

"But I do swim. We were on an island, remember?"

"Yeah, well…" Perl tried to walk away, regretting opening this can of worms, but Javan held onto her backpack.

"And also, that beast was a Gaarum, and it wasn't after all of us, Perl, it was after you…only you." Perl jerked her arm away from Javan as he softened his tone, "I would do anything to protect you, you know that, right?"

"Promise?"

"Promise. I'm on your side."

The two sat back down and watched as the first stars began to twinkle in the sky, the moon chasing the sun back into hiding.

It took some convincing to get Tars to go traipsing around the ancient, mountain forest.

"Are you joking? No way am I going in those woods at night! There's things in there that eat monkeys!" Tars tried to keep his voice down.

In the bed above him, Flax had dozed off early, his arm standing straight up in the air as he slept.

"You owe me, Tars," Javan countered, "plus, if you come with us, you can have the rest of my peony baklava. I know how much you love it." Javan unfolded his leaf pouch and waved it under Tars' nose; the sweet aroma was too good to resist.

"Ohhhh…fine!" Clutching it in his paw, Tars hopped out of the bottom bunk. "But if we get in trouble for this, I'm holding it against you…for eternity!"

"Haha, okay, agreed." Javan patted him on the back.

Tars's large bulbous eyes widened. "And we're not staying there all night!"

"Done. Wouldn't want you to miss your beauty sleep," Javan mocked. Perl already had her hand on the doorknob, whispering, "so, you two ready or what?"

31 FAWN

The crescent moon illuminated the landscape as the three Seekers moved swiftly up the road. They passed under the covered bridge and down the valley to the Callowhorn Combat Fields. The evening dew glistened on the grass like silver. The training grounds were barren except for the occasional rock or tree stump scattered about.

Tars shivered. "This place is kind of creepy when no one's here." He stared out across the patchwork of empty fields. "It's so quiet. Anybody else think it's really quiet?"

"Relax," Javan tried to calm the monkey-boy, whose eyes were as big as saucers.

"I'm relaxed! Totally, totally relaxed," Tars replied anxiously. "You know there's some who say the Fawn breathes fire like a dragon. Is that what we want to run into, a dragon?"

Perl tugged at Javan's shirt. "Is he serious?"

"You know that's just a myth." Javan put a hand on Tars shoulder. "C'mon, let's keep moving. We're almost to the forest."

"If there's one thing I've learned, it's that there's always some truth to myths," Tars insisted.

Reaching the edge of the thick woods, they paused to look up; the deep violet-blue of the mountains loomed above them.

"You two sure about this?" Tars scratched his furry head. "I mean, the Fawn could be anywhere…those woods go on forever."

Perl turned about argue her case with Tars, when she caught a glimpse of something behind him.

"Shh…" Perl whispered, "back there, see it?" Against the dark backdrop, they spotted a tiny white speck fluttering toward them. "It's one of Uriel's moths! It followed us! We can't let her see me!"

The *Hypercompe Scribonia* was coming towards them, quicker than Perl thought a moth could fly.

"See I told you, we're busted," Tars hissed.

Perl pushed past them both. "Just run!"

The three of them ducked into the dense, shadowy forest.

"Over here!" Perl motioned to Javan and Tars to hide with her under a giant yellow mushroom the size of a tent.

The moth entered the woods. It made several loops and passes through the trees searching for them. After a while, it gave up and headed back towards the fields; they watched it disappear.

"Phew, that was close." Perl let out a deep breath.

"And I suppose you think that Uriel won't turn us in?" Tars looked at them nervously.

"Stop your worrying." Javan yanked Tars to his feet. "We have a Fawn to catch."

"Oh yeah, nothing to worry about..." Tars made a face. "I knew I should've stayed in bed."

They walked and walked, Tars leading the way with Perl at the rear as the trio moved silently up the hills and through the dark, sleepy forest. Perl stepped on a twig, the snap causing Tars to leap three feet in the air.

"Easy, we don't want to spook the Fawn," Javan laughed. He looked back at Perl, noticing something tied around her ankle. "What is that? A shell?" He pointed at her foot.

"Mmm, sort of. It was a gift from Master Tryfon."

The night after the Pompeius Games, Perl had woven a small pocket out of twine to hold the pearl, tying up the ends to make an ankle bracelet. To Perl, this magical gem held the memory of her father's love, and she wanted to have it close to her always.

"Wow. No one *else* got a special gift from The Master." Javan lifted up a low-hanging branch so Perl could duck under it. "After you, your Highness," he gave a deep bow.

Perl tossed her head back, batting her green eyes. "I guess I'm just his favorite."

"You probably are." Javan smiled as Perl waltzed past him dramatically.

"Which way now?" Tars threw up his furry arms. In every direction was a tangled mass of trees. They were in the heart of the woods now, the moon's glow barely cutting though the forest's thick canopy.

Perl shrugged. "Well, this is where the path ends."

"We're looking for answers to your path," Javan chuckled, "and you literally just said this is where it ends. Kind of ironic, don't you think?"

"Oh. Hilarious," Perl said sarcastically. "Let's just keep going. There's gotta be a way through this."

"Hold on a sec," Javan said, crouching next to a tree stump. He closed his eyes, and began running his fingertips over the stump, feeling its rings.

"Good idea." Tars leaned over Javan's shoulder to watch.

"What's a good idea?" Perl asked.

"He's asking the tree stump for help."

"Asking it? How?" Perl talked to all kinds of wildlife, but this was new even for her.

"It's sort of like reading braille," Tars whispered to Perl, trying not to disturb Javan's concentration. "Even though most of the tree is gone, its roots run deep underground. The stump remembers everything."

Perl ran her fingers across the ridged grooves and closed her eyes. "I don't hear anything."

"It's a skill particular to Land Beings. We learn the language of the trees at birth. It would take a Water Being decades to master it."

Javan opened his eyes, placing both his webbed hands on the sides of the tree stump. "Thank you." He stood up. "She says the Fawn stays higher up in the mountains where the woods are older. Just keep an eye out for clusters of fireflies."

"You got all that from...her?" Perl asked, looking down at the weathered, mossy stump.

An owl screeched and Tars jumped, wrapping his tail around his legs. "See? I told you, fireflies. *Fire?* Flies?" Tars looked at Perl and Javan. "I don't know, guys, I think this is where my journey ends. I'm not gonna be a woodland goblin's snack. We tried. Honest effort. Truly." Tars spun on his furry heel and started back down the trail.

Perl snatched hold of his tail. "Oh no you don't. You're our guide. We need your eyes."

"Sorry Perl." The girl and the monkey played tug-of-war with his tail.

"But we need your eyesight!"

"Nope! Sorry!"

Perl's hand slipped and she careened backwards, landing on her butt in the middle of a patch of ferns. "Please Tars. I need your help." Tars looked at the girl; he could tell she was serious.

"Fine! But just a little farther, got it?" He reached down to Perl; she looked like a flower blooming in the middle of all the greenery. He yanked her to her feet.

"Just a little farther," she nodded, "promise."

The threesome resumed their trek into the woods. As they walked, Tars picked out a pair of jackalopes hopping hundreds of yards away, then spotted a family of nighthawks, and saw what he thought was a tree-bark yeti, but still no sign of the Fawn. He was about to announce he was done, when he froze in his tracks.

"Up ahead. I think there's a light," Tars shrieked, trying not to be too loud.

"I see it too," Perl agreed, "let's go."

Javan's vision was poor, but his electrolocation was picking up subtle movement. "Hold up a second. Something large is lurking up ahead. Whatever it is, it's got one strong heartbeat," Javan whispered, crouching. He motioned for the other two to get down.

Perl saw a small cluster of *Mimosa Pudica* plants growing off to her right, the same plant Palo Santo had crushed in her bare hand. "Look over there at the Shy Plants. They're curling in their leaves for protection."

Tars opened his eyes as wide as they would go, his black pupils fully dilated, surveying the area. "Something's close."

Perl was afraid to move but her left leg was starting to cramp. She shifted her weight, cracking a branch under her foot. Out of the darkness came a low hiss.

"I knew it," Tars panicked. "Here comes a fireball! Let's get out of here!"

Javan held him in place. "Don't…move…a muscle…*Eunectes murinu.*"

"Anaconda?" Tars whispered under his breath.

From out of the brush slithered the five-hundred-pound nightmare, coming towards them. The snake's natural camouflage kept it well hidden on the forest floor, but Perl and the others could see the ground cover quivering as the serpent slid closer. There was no time to run; the anaconda was fast. Unhinging its enormous jaws, it rose up out of the brush ready to strike. The three cowered as the dark silhouette loomed over them, its long, thorny fangs dripping strands of saliva, olive eyes gleaming in the faint moonlight. Javan threw his arms out in front of Perl and Tars.

Perl saw something moving behind the snake, "wait…what is that?"

It looked as if two trees were uprooting. The trunks bent and moved. One of them came down hard on the snake, pinning the serpent to the ground. The anaconda hissed, trying to work its way out from under whatever was stepping on it. It coiled around one of the trunks with a vice-like grip, its tail thrashing wildly.

"Javan, look out!" Perl screamed; the platypus ducked just as the snake's massive tail whipped over his head.

Tars had scampered to a nearby bush. He poked his head up. "What's happening? Are we dead yet?"

Above their heads was a strange swirling light, so intense they had to shield their eyes. Unable to escape, the anaconda loosened its hold and went limp. Squinting through the glare, Perl noticed that the trees didn't have roots, but rather, shiny hooves.

'Those aren't trees, they're legs.' Tilting her head back, Perl saw that the bark turned into fur.

The bright glow above them dimmed a bit, and they could now see thousands of fireflies swirling about the head of an enormous deer. The dappled, sepia-toned Being was a hundred feet tall. Its enormous rack of antlers looked like branches, covered in needles with pinecones dangling off them.

It lifted its mighty leg off the serpent, allowing the anaconda to scurry back into the shadows.   Javan was the first to find his voice, "thank you!"

The Fawn lowered its massive head down to their level, inspecting the tiny Seekers. "How dare you disturb my solitude?" Its low, scolding voice was that of a very old man's; raspy and hoarse, with a slight crack to it.

Blinking slowly, it studied Perl, whose arms were glowing. Perl stared back into its large, soft brown eyes, and was instantly charmed.

"We are very sorry."

"Yes, we're very sorry." Tars stood, his skinny legs shaking. "We were trying to find you…I mean, that is…she, Perl here…seeks your wisdom."

The deer responded with a loud, "*harrumph!*" shaking the surrounding trees. "You think *you* have found *me?* The girl is the one that is hunted."

The great Light Being opened its mouth wide. Tars shielded himself, waiting for the inevitable blast of fire; instead the Fawn simply yawned, then stomped its hoof.

"Be gone with you all!"

"Please," Javan said, mustering up all his courage, "we came here because Perl needs to know her true path."

The Fawn scoffed, "I am not some crystal ball. What do you have that would benefit I, young platypus?"

Perl stared silently; she wasn't sure if the Fawn was utterly adorable or genuinely scary.

"What is it that you'd like from us?" Javan asked, ever so humbly.

"You possess nothing I desire." It crashed its heavy hoof onto the ground again, rattling the leaves on the trees. "Be gone, I say, and do not disrupt my peace again!" The Fawn turned.

Perl quickly reached into her backpack, pulling out the last peony baklava petal. She held it up to the Fawn. "Wait! You can have this. I was saving it, but it's yours if you help me!"

Swiveling its head, the Fawn drew in a deep breath, so powerful that the petal flew from Perl's grasp. It floated up into the air and stuck to the Fawn's moist, black snout. The deer inhaled, smelling the sweet, mouth-watering scent. It then gave a quick snort, sucking the light petal up into its nose.

"Mmm…ambrosia," it sighed, "very well…I accept your offering."

Standing on all fours, the Fawn was the size of a mature pine tree, but when it suddenly stood on its hind legs, it towered above the treetops.

"Take hold of my legs."

Perl, Javan, and Tars grabbed on to its bark-like hide. The Fawn lumbered effortlessly through the forest, the trees bending out of its way then snapping back upright.

"Are you two alright?" Perl yelled over to Tars and Javan, who rode together on the Fawn's other leg.

"I'm good!" Javan shouted.

"I-I think I'm gonna be sick!" Tars groaned, as the giant legs swung methodically—up and back, up and back.

The ground flattened and the Fawn came to a stop in front of a rocky cliffside teeming with thick moss and ivy.

"We are here," the Fawn's voice boomed down. Perl, Javan, and Tars dropped to the ground.

"I can't feel my arms," cried Tars, shaking his hands.

"That was incredible!" Perl hopped back up.

As the three caught their breath, they watched as the Fawn went down to all fours and slipped through the wall of moss.

"Well," Javan asked, "should we follow it?"

Before he even finished, Perl had already ducked through the vines.

Tars threw his arms up. "Oh, come on!" He turned to Javan. "Maybe she should just go by herself? I mean, we can just wait here. Really, I don't mind."

Javan brushed his bangs back. "Tars."

"What?" Tars slapped the ground with his tail. "I held up my end of the deal...you go if you want."

Javan hooked an arm around Tars. "If the Fawn wanted to fry you to a crisp, he would've by now."

"Thanks. I feel so much better now," Tars tightened his grip as the two slipped through the ivy curtain.

On the other side they were shocked to see a very normal-sized cabin interior, with ceilings no higher than ten-foot tall. The Fawn, upon entering, had shrunk down to fit the size of the cozy lodge. The fireflies, still flitting around its antlers, illuminated the cozy space with a warm glow. The sweet, crisp scent of pine filled the cabin. They saw Perl seated comfortably across the room on a small sofa next to an old stone fireplace.

"Pretty nice, right?" Perl said.

The couch was worn, the dark green fabric thinning. Clumps of mushrooms sprouted from the arms and the top of the cushions, as well as the floor around it.

"There's a chill in the night air. What say we have a fire?" The wooden floorboards creaked as the Fawn walked upright over to the fireplace. Tars and Javan didn't know where to go so they stood awkwardly next to Perl.

"That would be wonderful," Perl replied with a smile, drawing her knees up to her chest.

The Being's guarded demeanor softened. If Perl was on the fence about him earlier, she had no doubt now—she liked the Fawn.

Javan cocked an eye at Tars. "Uh-oh, Tars...a *fire*," he giggled.

Tars dismissed him. "Yeah, yeah."

The three of them watched as the deer raised its front legs in the air gathering up light from the fireflies' glow. The light transformed into a floating ball of fire. The Fawn held the flame, then flung it into the fireplace, igniting the logs inside. At once, the heat could be felt from the crackling blaze.

"That will do fine," the Fawn nodded, taking a seat in a rocking chair opposite Perl. "Legends of long ago spoke of mysterious lights in the water. Humans believed them to be bad omens, perhaps the work of dragons." The Fawn pointed to the wall; behind a convex glass frame was an ancient map of early Earth, the corners of it brittle and torn. "We now know that those lights were bioluminescence, created by the enzymatic compound, Luciferin." The Fawn leaned forward, locking eyes with Perl. "But is it any less supernatural or divine, simply because it can be explained by science?"

Perl felt her face prickling as the spots on her cheeks began to glow. The Fawn leaned back against the mossy cushion and gently rocked.

"Sir, Fawn, sir. I was hoping you could tell me about my future path. How can I help my home island, and also, how do I defeat Malblud?"

"Call me Humboldt, that is my name, not Sir. Formalities are not needed here."

"These are my friends, Tars and Javan." The platypus and monkey nodded politely, then slipped onto the couch next to Perl.

Humboldt continued rocking slowly. "Each tree in the forest is unique. Depending on the season and its soil, there will be ever-so-subtle differences in the color of its leaves."

Perl shook her head. "Sorry?" Her spots were now fully lit.

"You are no different, youngling. You cannot be duplicated. The secrets of life are on Earth, inside every living being."

Perl interrupted, "so, you see, Master Humboldt, I keep having these visions, where my—"

The Fawn cut her off, "you wish to find your path, hm? To do that, you must focus on what you have to offer. What do *you* feel is your true calling, spotted one?"

Perl didn't like being called that. "That's just it, I don't know!" she blurted out. *"Why does every Master in Venusto seem to always speak in riddles?" she thought.*

"It is in the knowing that we do not know, when the knowledge is revealed."

"What?" Perl could feel her patience waning. "Can you please just give me a straight answer?"

Tars raised his eyebrows, "um, Perl?"

Javan stepped in, "I'm sorry, Master Humboldt. She meant no disrespect."

Perl shot Javan a look. "You said he was supposed to be some kind of seer of the future! I thought he could give me answers, not talk about tree growth! I'm running out of time!" Perl stood up, grabbing Tars by the shirt sleeve. "Let's just go.

Tars agreed, "she's right, Javan, we should be getting back."

Humboldt cleared his throat; his voice was calm. "All of nature abides by the rules of the universe. It understands that time is irrelevant, nonexistent. Everything happens precisely when it is supposed to happen. Humankind is the only animal who struggles to appreciate one of Ever's most useful gifts…patience."

Perl glanced over at the mystical Being, then back at her companions; they had sympathetic smiles on their furry faces. A lump like a walnut formed in her throat; she felt lost, and sad.

"Forgive me, Master Humboldt. I'm scared, and I don't know what I'm supposed to do."

"Come to me, young one." Perl walked over to the mystical deer. "Give me your hand." The Fawn examined her tiny hand closely, his nose nearly bumping against it. Perl thought he was about to speak; instead, he ran his tongue along her palm, leaving it dripping with sticky saliva. Her fingers started to tingle.

Perl pulled her hand back, "why did you—?"

Humboldt blinked a few times; his large oval eyes lost their color, going from chestnut brown, to gray, to milky white. Perl stared into the Fawn's dark, hypnotic eyes; she could sense the room blurring around her, then melting away completely. The smell of hollyhock flowers suddenly filled her nose; it was a scent she knew well...from Mont Michel's island garden.

In a low whisper, Humboldt spoke, "Perl of the ocean...your place in this magnificent world is miraculous...much love surrounds you. Close your eyes."

Perl did as the Fawn asked. She smiled dreamily, picturing herself as a little girl, performing for the spider-monks. She could hear them clapping, shouting "bravo, little Bee, bravo!"

Humboldt's melodic voice floated through her subconscious, "...there lies a story within a story," his voice intensifying. The sweet floral aroma faded, replaced by the sickening smell of decay; it burnt Perl's nostrils. "A sickness spreads on land and sea." Perl saw waves of dead fish washing ashore, rotting on the oil-slicked beaches of Mont Michel.

"For so long, a sorrow festers...now turning to hatred!" Humboldt was nearly shouting in Perl's mind. She could see the Graves twins—Ivry, lying unconscious, pale and sickly, her sister Mik, crying at her bedside. She saw Count Graves, screaming, full of rage. Humboldt continued, "you must remove your armor to feel your sameness!" The swarm of fireflies burning brightly around the deer's head stopped glowing, the room went dark. Still in a trance, Perl now saw Ximu, trapped in a dungeon. She had seen this nightmare before.

"Papa! No! No!" Perl began to tremble. She saw the Slaughterman lurking outside Ximu's cell. "What are you doing? Stay away from him!" Perl swung her arms violently in the air.

Javan and Tars ran to Perl, taking hold of her. They looked at the Fawn, uneasy.

Humboldt eyes were two stark white orbs in the darkness. His voice hissed and cracked, "in the bog...face the Many Lost Souls...they protect it...cross over...find what you seek."

Perl was as stiff as a board, her eyes rolled back in her head. Her friends held her upright as Humboldt continued, his voice sounding more like a chant.

"Offer it what it needs to grow…allow your heart to forgive…for if you do not…it will surely return…in another form." All at once, Humboldt fell back into his chair. Perl's body quivered and she went limp, slumping back into Javan and Tars' arms. They dragged her over to the couch and tried to revive her, but she was out cold.

Javan looked at the deer with a mix of fear and concern. "What's wrong with her? Is she alright?"

"Give her a moment…she is returning to this realm," Humboldt reassured the two.

Slowly, eventually, Perl woke, blinking her eyes and mumbling. She struggled to push herself up into a sitting position, then realized she was wedged between Tars and Javan.

"You okay?" Tars asked, his bulbous eyes inches from her face. Perl nodded weakly.

Javan spoke to her softly, "what did you see?"

"My home. It's in trouble."

Humboldt's eyes had returned to a warm chocolate brown; the room was bright again. "Welcome back, youngling," he rocked back and forth in his chair.

Perl took a deep breath as a tear ran down her cheek. Her thoughts hung like a series of grim portraits in her mind. "I know what to do."

Humboldt lifted himself out of the chair, meandering over to a cabinet crowded with hundreds of glass bottles. He took one labeled, *Hippomane Mancinello*. "The Manzanilla de la muerte… Little apple of death. Its sap will kill whatever it touches." He carefully poured some of its milky white liquid into a vial, capping it shut with a cork. "Keep Death before your eyes, so that you live in the moment. Evil can invoke fear, and fascination. Do not let yourself fall victim to either." He handed her the vial.

Without a word, she took off her backpack, tucking it carefully inside. Javan and Tars helped Perl up.

"We are grateful for your guidance, Master Humboldt, but I'm afraid we may need a little more help finding our way home," Javan said.

"Ah, yes…finding our way home," the Fawn mused, then fell silent. Tars and Javan looked at one another; Humboldt added, "look to the trees…they will guide you."

Perl was drawn to the corner of the room, where a baobab tree had grown through the floor. In the thick trunk of the tree were rows of bookshelves. She studied the books, running her fingers along the old tattered bindings, stopping at a small book entitled, *'The Most Curious Life of Sir Chamuel Cureckitycoo'*. Perl pulled it out; it smelled musty. Perl flipped

246

through a few of the curled, discolored pages; it was filled with all sorts of nature drawings and maps.

"May I borrow this?"

Humboldt turned towards her, "you may have it. You and Professor Cureckitycoo have much in common. He, too, was a naturalist, always sketching and collecting. A pioneer of sorts, paving the way for future explorers and dreamers."

Perl tucked the book into her backpack. "Thank you…for everything." She walked over to Humboldt, looking up into his wise old eyes. "Do you think I can do it? Save the oceans? Mont Michel? My Papa?"

The Fawn escorted them to the curtain of vines. "So many expectations. Be who you are, young one. That is enough. You have everything you need inside of you…gifts no one can ever take away."

"Great, more riddles," Perl jokingly thought; but she took Humboldt's response as a yes.

Tars was the last one to leave. Just as he stepped out, he glanced over his shoulder and saw Humboldt pick up a candle and light it with a spark of his breath. "I knew it…fire-breather," he whispered to himself, scurrying out to join the others.

Thin shafts of moonlight filtered through the leafy branches above, but the forest was still a dark place. Javan turned around; the entrance to the cabin was gone, perfectly camouflaged into the surrounding brush. "Well, Humboldt said the trees would show us the way home. I don't see any stumps to help guide us, do either of you?"

"Nope." Tars hopped up onto a branch for a better view. "Not a stump in sight."

Perl took a step, when a loud cracking sound startled her. Two trees on either side of them bent, leaning over as if they were bowing. All three Seekers froze, unsure what to do.

"What in the woods?" Tars uttered

Javan looked over at Perl. "walk a little more."

Looking at her feet, Perl was relieved to see the tiny pouch around her ankle was still firmly attached. She took a few timid steps. *Boom! Crack!* Two more trees bowed, the bioluminescent fungi on their trunks glowing green. She looked up, delighted by this unexpected bit of magic. "The trees are marking our path!"

Tars glanced over at Javan, who smiled and shrugged.

Perl broke into a jog. Rows of trees to the left and right of her bent at their midsections, as if welcoming royalty.

The three ran through the convoy; once they passed by a tree, it straightened back up, its branches creaking. The glowing fungi dimmed, leaving the path behind the Seekers once again in shadow. Perl started walking backwards down the hill. "Wanna play the story game to pass the time?" The trees kept bowing as she stepped.

Javan and Tars looked at one another. "Sure. Why not."

Tars started, "okay, I got one, and it's a doozy," he announced, spinning his tail gleefully. "Once, there was a giant fire-breathing fawn that saved a traveling trio from a monstrous snake. He shrunk down and invited them into his cabin, where he hypnotized the fair maiden, and when they left, the soldiers of the forest lined up to bid them farewell!"

Perl laughed, rubbing the top of Tars' fuzzy head. "I've heard that story. How about one with a mermaid, and a jellyfish, and their forbidden love? Forbidden, because their fathers hated one another." Perl put her hands together, wiggling them like a fish. "The mermaid was so very tired because she had to clean the castle all by herself...See? Because she's a mer-*maid?*"

"Aw, that's terrible! Javan rolled his eyes, brushing his bangs aside."

"I don't get it," Tars looked at the two of them.

Perl kept going, "so, one night, under a full moon, the mermaid ran—well, swam—away from home. That's when she met the handsome merman..."

The whole way through the forest, Perl talked and talked, slaphappy from lack of sleep. She never gave either boy a turn, but prattled on—describing great ocean battles, a curse from a sea witch, and a spell of everlasting love—until finally, the woods thinned, and they saw the combat fields below.

"Wow, that was quicker coming back than going!" Perl started running.

"Was it?" Tars smirked, raising his brow at Javan; the two boys laughed.

Back in front of their nests, the three said their goodbyes. Tars and Javan walked arm in arm up the winding blue pebble path to their pinecone nest.

"Thank you for going with me! I couldn't have done it without you guys," Perl waved. "Good night...I mean, good morning!" The sun was just cresting above the horizon as she ducked into her nest.

The sound of a bow strumming a cello could be heard, as Tars and Javan let out a collective groan.

"You gotta be kidding me," Tars grumbled.

Grandmaster Olliv and his breakfast cart had come to a jingling stop in front of their cabins. The chipmunks bounced out of the basket, chirping loudly.

"It's a new day, day! Rise, Pompeius Game victors! One more day as Seekers! Much to do, do!" Olliv waved his buttercup baton in the air.

Javan rubbed his sleepy eyes.

Tars sat down on the ground, sighing heavily, "you owe me big time."

Javan plopped down next to his friend. "I know...but she really did need our help." He playfully flicked the monkey-boy's large, pointed ear. "And she's definitely going to need it again."

You are the rabbit
To my rabbit,
The reason I don't need luck,
You are the net of safety —
With your hand I'm
Always caught,
You're my mirror,
My reflection —
The world makes sense
As you tell it —
You are the truth
In my words,
As your voice echoes
In my soul.

will find out who did this!

So I left my joural under the maple tree for a few minutes to help a gaggle of turtle geese tip their grandma back over to the right side of her shell, and I find this written inside when I got back!
Mmm, who would do this?? But~ what is even weirder is~ it's the same poem that I heard from the rabbit the one day during class. How could anyone know that?!! Not sure how I feel. This is my private time capsule! Now it's been invaded! On the other hand it's kinda sweet. But I won't be leaving my book out of my sight again.

I have more serious things to worry about, like a plan to get by the Manylostsouls. I'll have to sneak out.

Quantaa will know the way to the bog. I wish I could ask everyone to go with me, but I can't let them risk their lives for me. This is my fight.

Think I'll go outside and play my kalimba for a while to take my mind off of everything.

The killer sap better work.

I never could have imagined that I'd be in this situation. am I this person? How on earth did I get here? To this place where I don't recognize myself.

Ever give me strength.
♡ferl
xo

32 CALM BEFORE THE STORM

Through a small barred window at the top of his cell, Ximu could look out at the blue sky; it gave him comfort. Everything in the cramped, stinking dungeon was charred and gray. Oily water oozed through the cracks and crevices of the cell walls like wounds that wouldn't heal. Brother Ximu, normally a stout and well fed fellow, was now half his size, surviving on bits of moldy bread and tin cups of rusty water the guards deemed to give him. The monk's cheekbones were sunken in; his bloodshot eyes, dark and somber. Ximu grew weaker and more frail with every miserable day that passed in his cold, damp chamber, all for a crime he most certainly did not commit.

Hadza, his feathered friend and garden companion, had located the monk after much searching. The tiny bird landed on the window's stone sill, a bit of honeycomb in her tiny orange beak.

"Good day, my dear Hadza. Is that for me?" Ximu reached through the bars.

The bird dropped the sweet morsel into his hand, chirping a familiar tune; one the two of them often sang together while gathering honey. Ximu pursed his dry, cracked lips and tried to whistled along, but broke into a coughing fit. With a few snapping noises of her tongue, Hadza said goodbye to Ximu and flew off, vowing to return in a few days.

The monk placed the sweet honeycomb in his mouth and closed his eyes to meditate. *"Loamm...Doreaah."* Hearing his chants, the rats, rabid dogs, and other vile creatures that lurked among the garbage outside his cell hissed and snarled, shrinking away from the irritating sound.

Back on Mont Michel, brothers Victr, Basil, along with the servant Regor, stood in the little round chapel room, monitoring the Globus Natura. They watched with concern as the delicate spheres wobbled out of sync.

"This is troubling. Look at the Water Orb. It is greatly off kilter," Basil said, ringing his hands nervously.

The Water Orb was bobbing up and down erratically as it slowly revolved, at moments nearly coming to a full stop. Regor, now a part of the monks' trusted circle, stepped up for a closer look.

"Is it possible one of these could... pop?" No one answered him.

Basil sighed. "I've never seen the water look so murky," he muttered, shaking his head.

Standing in the shadows behind the two, Victr now spoke, quoting a line from The Prophecy, *"...and from the depths of the ocean from which life sprang, so shall the treasure be found."*

Basil and Regor turned to the monk, who stood motionless as a statue, his face etched with worry. "We must continue to trust."

"And pray," Basil agreed. "She will prevail."

Victr stared up at the Globus Natura, his brow furrowing deeper. "She must."

33 APOTHECARY

In the Palace penthouse, Ivry Graves was still unresponsive. Her sister Mik sat at the large bay window, gazing solemnly out at the ocean. It was something she and her sister had loved to do since they were little girls. Mik watched as the surf rolled up the beach and receded, over and over. She noticed how unusually high the tides were today, and for reasons she couldn't explain, it filled her with a sense of uneasiness. She glanced over at her sister. Ivry had been taken off the ventilator, but her breathing was still very shallow, her pulse weak. Mik got up and went to her vanity. From one of her many jewelry boxes, she pulled out the note the stranger had left under the door, reading it once more; *"Come to the cave."* She looked at the crude sketch of the spotted mushroom, thinking back to what he said: *"a cure."*

"Iv, I don't know if I should believe this or if it will even work," Mik said, pinning her bright red hair up into a bun and throwing on a silk crimson poncho, "but I have to try."

Mik pulled the hood up over her head and went into her closet chambers, searching through the rotating shelves of shoes. She selected a pair of spiked boots made from sea urchin (*Enchinoidea*) and sat down on her bed to slip them on. Looking in on the seahorses' tank that rested on a table between the two canopy beds, she noticed that one of them had an extra full belly.

"Go easy on the snacks, Moon, and watch over Ivry for me. She's all I've got."

Mik gave her sister a soft kiss on the forehead and closed the bedroom door behind her. She crept along the white-carpeted hallway, down the black winding staircase towards the foyer. Mik heard her parents talking in the jungle-themed parlor off to her left. They were discussing Ivry's condition with a team of physicians.

"There's nothing more we can do for her now," a doctor reported, his voice somber. "We'll just have to wait and see when or if, she wakes from the coma."

Mik held her breath; she knew her parents would never allow her to run off on some wild goose chase in search of a magic mushroom. Neither Mik nor Ivry had ventured beyond their verandas, their mother putting the fear of Ever in them about the sun's harmful rays on their porcelain skin. On top of that, the twins never went out in public for fear of being swarmed by crazed fans. Mik grew up believing that the bottom of the island was filled with the filthiest and the most dangerous inhabitants, at least according to her mother. But she was desperate.

"Now or never," Mik thought, as she quickly snuck past the doorway, catching a brief glimpse of her father, standing over the doctor, shouting.

Mik hurried by the servant's lounge, where Ruby was gobbling down a bowl of noodles smothered in squid ink. The Governess briefly glanced up. "Hello?" she mumbled, black noodles hanging out of her mouth. Seeing no one, she shrugged and kept eating, slurping her lunch loudly.

Mik tiptoed her way along the gold leaf wall, trying not to make too much noise in her boots. *"Why did I wear these?"* she thought angrily, instantly regretting her choice but refusing to go back.

Her heart was racing as she hurriedly pulled open the Palace's massive slab of a front door. A gentle breeze from the garden wafted in, tossing her straggling strands of red hair into her face. She closed the door and inhaled deeply, the sweet fragrance of roses and lavender calming her. Tightening the drawstring on her hood, the twin hustled down the custom designed marble walkway, bolting through the massive wrought iron gates before reaching a small patio overlook, where the stepping stones began.

Mik gave herself a pep talk as she viewed the seemingly endless stairway zigzagging down the side of Mont Michel. "You're doing this for Ivry…you're doing this for Ivry," she repeated under her breath as she carefully traversed the flights of stairs.

It didn't take long for Mik to curse her shoe choice once again, as the awkward, spiky heels scraped against the rough, uneven rocks. More than a few times she stumbled and nearly fell. Slowly but surely, Mik found her footing, moving from the upper part of Mont Michel down through the crowded Graves District. The various thought projection centers, communal memory vaults, and escape pod arcades were crowded with people, but no one looked up to notice her.

The slope of the steps became less severe as it wound its way to the other side of Mont Michel, where Mik got her very first glimpse of Trash Island. She paused, looking out at the bleak, gray chunk of land. There were no trees, no waterfalls, no pretty brick homes or fancy shops, just great mounds of garbage with a thick cloud of seabirds hovering over it. Perhaps worse than the island was the water surrounding it. It wasn't the bright sparkling blue she'd always known, but an oily green color, the smell palpable even from where she was standing. Mik wondered why she'd never seen trash in the ocean looking out of her window, then got her answer when she noticed the giant floating partitions stretching from Mont Michel over to the island, trapping the garbage in a concentrated area.

"So that's why we don't have any windows facing this side." The twin took a deep breath and continued her descent, trying not to attract any attention as she passed through the mid-apartments and down toward the lower levels. However, one look at the girl's extravagant—and much cleaner—attire, and

the residents began to take notice. Locals did double-takes, catching a glimpse of the strange pale girl in a fancy red cloak. Soon, there was a handful of curious islanders trailing the twin, pestering her with questions.

"Whatcha doin', princess?", "Are you Ivry, or Mik?", "You're a long way from home!"

"Idiots," Mik mumbled under her breath. She pulled her hood down tighter, ignoring their calls. As the path widened, the steps gave way to a dusty footpath that ended at the beach. Mik broke into a slow jog, the gaggle of people still following.

"Hey, you're one of them girls!" A heavyset woman in a matching polka dot swimsuit and visor grabbed at Mik's poncho. "Can I get a pic with you?"

"Please, leave me alone!" Mik twisted away from the woman's grasp. She sprinted across the beach, reaching the floating wooden bridge connecting the main island to Trash Island.

A young girl fishing nearby yelled over to her, "where are you goin'? The tide's rising, ya' know!"

The crowd behind her came to a stop. Seeing the teenage girl getting on the bridge, they went from pestering to shouting warnings; "Don't go out there!", "Come back!", "You'll fall!"

The twin gave a defiant look back then stepped gingerly onto the slippery wooden planks. Mik gripped the wet guide ropes that helped the islanders navigate their way across the wavering footbridge. The spikes on her soles helped her dig into the wood, but the undulating waves and sudden gusts of wind knocked her off balance. Locals watched, gasping when she wobbled, then breathing a sigh of relief when she regained her balance. Although they were worried about the girl, they all had their phones out, snapping pics and posting them. The small crowd of onlookers drew the attention of the activists, who were tethered together in rowboats close to shore, still holding up signs of protest and effigies of Count Graves. Mik lifted her head to see how much farther she had to go. The wind blew back her hood, exposing her red hair that whipped in the wind like a flickering flame.

Gretar, the young boy who had been grazed by one of Palace guards' bullets during the Ball, was in one of the boats; he pointed at Mik. "I don't believe my eyes! It's one of the spoiled brats, out of her golden cage." He chuckled, then watched with concern as the girl slipped and wavered, struggling mightily to cross as the waves picked up. *"What is she doing?"* he thought, pulling up his anchor and grabbing his oars.

Gretar quickly began paddling over to the bridge, trying to reach the Mik. A few others followed the boy, but by the time the small regatta of demonstrators reached Trash Island, it was too late. Mik had already jumped from the muddy bridge and scampered off, disappearing behind the enormous heaps of trash.

"Let's wait. I don't know what she's doing, but there's no way she's gonna stay in there very long," Gretar said. He and the others rowed back a bit to avoid the sour, rotten stench.

"Oh my Ever, this is disgusting." Mik held her silk poncho up to her face, breathing into it, the foul odor making her gag.

She looked around at the tall, dark stacks surrounding her. There were no clear pathways to be seen, only mound after mound of rotting garbage in every direction. A family of rats *(Rattus)* scurried near her feet. "Run!" Mik gasped, momentarily forgetting that her twin, who was always by her side, was not there.

A light mist began to fall; Mik hugged herself. "Why am I here?" she muttered, feeling the panic in her chest. She turned and caught a glimpse of Mont Michel. Somewhere up in that sprawling Palace at the top of the hill was her sister, battling death. Mik gritted her teeth. *"For Ivry...for Ivry."* She ran aimlessly, not sure where she was headed or what she was looking for.

Plastic bags, food wrappers and other bits of shredded paper swirled around her in mini cyclones. In her haste, Mik tripped over an old tire, landing face first into a stagnant puddle. Jumping to her feet with a squeal, Mik looked at her hands and front of her cloak, now coated in a smelly green goo and covered with maggots. She gagged and thought she might pass out, but the feeling passed.

Sitting in an old shopping cart, Mik spotted a bright red teddy bear; its legs had been torn off. She picked it up, noticing stitched on the bear's stomach was a message—*We Luv You Mik & Ivry!* The twin wiped her face and hands on its red fur. "Love you, too, guys," she said, tossing it over her shoulder.

The day was growing warmer in the late afternoon sun. Steam rose from the debris like ghosts, as the sickly hum of buzzing flies *(Diptera)* grew louder.

"Where is this stupid cave?!" Mik looked around, growing angrier by the minute. "It's just garbage, everywhere!"

The piles of trash were too high to see over. Perched atop the mound in front of her lurked three large vultures *(Aegypius Monachus)*. They stared down their crooked beaks at Mik.

"What are you looking at?" Mik yelled up at the creepy birds. She picked up an old soup can and threw it at them, scattering the scavengers.

Mik clenched her fists, steadying herself. "Okay, focus. Just pretend it's not filthy, slimy garbage."

She crawled her way to the top of one of the heaps, her cloak going from red to dark brown, now stained in oil, rotten milk, and Ever-only-knew what else.

"How can there be this much garbage?"

Living in her secluded Palace bubble all these years, Mik had never once thought of where her trash went once the servants removed it from her room.

Mik scanned the area, and there, between the unsightly stacks, like a toothless black mouth, was what appeared to be an opening at the base of one of the piles.

"That's gotta be it!"

Mik started to move, when the pile began to sink inward beneath her. She fell backwards, and was now sliding feet first into the hole in the middle of the trash heap. Frantically, she rolled onto her stomach, grasping at whatever she could get her manicured nails into, kicking with her urchin boots.

"Help! Help me!" She knew if she fell in, she'd be buried alive.

Miraculously, the cave-in slowed to a halt. Mik stopped just short of the gap, her legs dangling out over the pit. She tried to pull herself up, but each time she moved, she slid a little more.

"Help!" Mik screamed out in desperation, "somebody, please help me!"

All she could do was lay there, face down in a vile mixture of black banana peels, oily rags, fish guts, and dirty diapers. The sun was hot now; a yellow steam rose off the trash mounds.

"Ahh!" Milk screamed; at first what she thought was a snake slithering next to her, turned out to be a dirty extension cord.

"Grab hold," a gravelly voice croaked.

Mik glanced up at a dark silhouette against the bright sun. She was frightened, but what choice was there? She reached over, taking hold of the greasy cord, trying pulling herself up. Not used to physical exertion, this was proving to be difficult. Mik kept slipping and her arms were on fire.

"I can't...please help..." Gripping the cord with both hands, Mik put her head down and held on as the man pulled her through the garbage on her belly. Once close enough, he grabbed hold of the girl's hand, yanking her out of harm's way.

"Thank you." Mik rolled over, too tired to stand.

Wiping the sludge from her face, she tried to get a better look at the person who had saved her. Standing before her was an older man in a bloodstained jumpsuit. Slightly hunched over, he had long tangles of dingy white hair springing this way and that, with big gray eyes that darted around nervously. To Mik, he looked feral; like he'd been zapped by lightning, or raised by wolves.

"Decided, I see, to come?" The man held out his bloody, weathered hand, offering to help her up.

"That's okay. I can manage." Not wanting to touch him, Mik instead forced herself to her feet.

Mik reached into a pocket and pulled out the note, now covered in mud and grease. "Did you give this to me?"

"Whispers, whispers, whispers. I hear them. I know what they call me. I slaughter, lest they get their hands dirty." He looked at his own hands and cracked a crooked smile, wiping them on his jumpsuit. "No way north, so south we must go." Turning his back to the girl, he casually slid to the ground, as if he'd done it a thousand times.

"Wait for me," Mik shouted as she half-crawled, half-stumbled down the trash slope, sliding on her butt the last ten feet. She stood up and pulled a long strand of spaghetti out of her hair and flung it. At this point, she was so filthy she didn't care.

"So, what should I call you?" she asked.

"One calls a person their name, isn't that right?" The stranger had a noticeable limp, but he ambled quickly through the maze of trash piles. Once he reached the dark entryway he came to an abrupt stop, turning to Mik, his face a burnt map of intersecting lines. "My name is Dimitri."

"Hello. I'm Mik. Mik Graves, but I think you already know that."

"The difference between someone *thinking* they know something, and *knowing* they know, is as wide as the yawn of a whale," he cackled, his laugh more of a snort. Mik noticed he was missing a front tooth. Dimitri grabbed a lantern off of a nearby hook. "Come, come. Watch your head," he cautioned as he ducked under the overhanging trash, disappearing into the darkness.

"This is crazy," Mik thought, *"what am I doing?"*

The tunnel was pitch black as they descended under the trash heaps. Mik, hearing scurrying noises along the walls, kept close to the man. Dimitri limped over and threw a switch, illuminating the surprisingly large room. Attached to one wall, a giant helicopter blade covered in lavender began to spin slowly, freshening the musty air.

"Dimitri," the old man blurted out, "translates to, Earth-lover."

Looking around at the place, Mik was taken aback; she imagined it would be a dump, crawling with rats. "Well this is...interesting."

There was so much going on, it was hard to know where to look. There were dozens of ornate bird cages hanging from the ceiling, glass terrariums filled with exotic plants, and old sepia-toned portraits covering the walls. Mik walked over to a contraption that looked like a giant brass horn jutting out of a wooden box. "What is this?"

"Sit, sit, a moment," he gestured to a chair constructed out of plastic bottles.

Mik took a better look at the man; he wasn't as scary as she first thought, but he did have an odd twitch that made it look like he was constantly winking at her.

Dimitri stepped behind a floor-to-ceiling assemblage of street signs from ages ago, all riveted together this way and that to form a wall. He shouted from behind the signs, "I did as told…watched and waited, watched and waited…"

"Oh…okay." Mik didn't know how to respond.

The stilted way Dimitri spoke was strange, like a person who'd been alone much of their life and had forgotten how to speak to people.

Mik eyed a long metal table that looked like it belonged in a lab. It was jam packed with glass beakers bubbling with colorful fluids. A heavy oak cabinet in the corner displayed taxidermy, insects pinned in shadow boxes, and lots of jars and vials.

Dimitri reappeared from around the makeshift metal wall dressed in a clear plastic lab coat. On each of his shoulders sat a small white mouse wearing a metal thimble hat strapped to its head.

"Aggh!" Mik jumped. Dimitri raised a hand to calm her.

"What I do is this. A world-renowned hospital lab I ran, before the *Qui sub plantam fratris tenebat* took control. They took, took, took my research for themselves. Sold it to those who could pay. They hid the cures from the world. Let them fall ill. Struggle. Suffer." His eye twitched faster. "Many, many died."

Mik was trying to follow along. "Sorry…the Qui-sub-planta—what now?"

The apothecary pulled a pair of thick Pince-nez style spectacles from his breast pocket, clamping the armless glasses to the brim of his hook nose. "Secret society. *'Under One's Heel.'* Very elite. Very dangerous. Your father is one. *The* one, in fact."

"My father? He would never…you're crazy."

"Am I?" Dimitri leaned in close to Mik, staring at her through his magnified lenses. His eyes were wide, manic. The mice fell forward, clinging to his earlobes. "Crazy is what, after all? Have I gone batty, hiding in this bat cave?" He looked at the girl, his expression pained. "Ah, but-but-but perhaps it is so. Years of toxic fumes would surely corrode anyone's mind."

Mik leaned forward. "I…I'm sorry. It must be dreadful out here in all this garbage. I assure you I had no idea about my father, or any secret society.

"This I know, princess, this I know. I am not mistaken about Graves." Dimitri's face softened. "Yes, graves and graves."

Mik thought the old man looked sad.

Dimitri straightened up, the white mice crawling back onto his shoulders. "Blind, all of you! Blind to the truth." He went over to a small rusted cooler and reached in, pulling out a hunk of smelly cheese. He broke off a pinch for each mouse.

Mik watched him feed the mice. "So why did you leave me the note? Why help us?"

"Tick tock…time to open your eyes. Life is a play and we all have a part.

You included."

"Me? You've got the wrong girl…I'm only here because of my sister! You said I could trust you! You said you had a cure!"

"I said, I said, I said…" Dimitri hobbled over to an armoire. "Mmm, perhaps." He pulled it open, revealing hundreds of small compartments.

"No, you definitely did say you'd help." Mik reached into her pocket. "I have the note right here!"

The apothecary ran his rough, swollen fingers along the rows of drawers. "It's in the finding, that we need to remember the placing, isn't that true?"

Mik watched with growing unease as he searched through the various compartments. "*Is this the person I'm supposed to trust to help Ivry?*" she thought.

"Ah, found you!" Dimitri took out a glass jar, in it was a single mushroom; dry and shriveled, the color of butterscotch, with tiny orange speckles. "No time to waste…instructions. To lead you must follow. Crush to dust. Place in milk. Milk must turn black." He placed the small jar in her hand. "You have the cure. Now, this way." He walked to the back of the chamber, gesturing for her to follow.

Mik frowned. "No, I really must get going, but thank you. Thank you so much."

"Must trust. I have secrets, too." Dimitri pried open a rusty door, its old hinges creaking loudly.

Mik studied the strange man in the plastic coat staring bug-eyed at her. The doorway led to a tunnel lit with a strand of flickering, buzzing lights.

"*This is it, this is how I die,*" she thought. "*If I go in there, no one will ever know what happened to me.*" Mik shook her head. "Um, that's okay…I'll just go out the way I came." She started to back away.

Dimitri motioned to the opening. "Faster this way…cleaner!"

Mik thought of all the garbage she'd have to trudge through, and the awful smell; the mere thought of doing that again repulsed her. "Alright," she took a few timid steps into the entryway, "where does this go?"

"Where you need to go."

Mik took another step, when Dimitri grabbed her arm.

"Hey! Let go of me!"

"Graves! Make him see what you have seen! Open his eyes, or more graves there will be!"

"Okay, okay, I will." Mik sprinted down the tunnel.

She ran through the hot, damp corridor until she thought her legs might give out.

"*How much farther?*" She thought, just as she rounded a corner and spotted a metal door. "Thank Ever!" Needing both hands, she lifted the heavy rusted latch, giving the door a shove. As it swung open, a gust of ocean air hit her in the face.

Mik squinted as she stepped into the sunlight, closing the door behind her. Dimitri's secret passageway had bypassed the labyrinth of garbage, dropping Mik close to the shoreline near the wooden bridge. She pulled her grungy hood down tight over her curls, glancing down at her boots; they were covered in oily mud and bits of debris.

"Ugh, enough of these!" Mik kicked off the spiked heels, feeling the warm sand between her toes for the first time ever. She could taste the ocean's salt on her lips, but also something else; something bitter, chemical-like. Looking out at the green, polluted water, Mik thought of her and Ivry living in their Palace, and realized how incredibly sheltered she'd been her whole life.

Something in the corner of her mind picked at her. *"Could Dimitri be right about my father?"* As that thought lingered, Mik double-checked to make sure the mushroom was tucked safely in her pocket. Feeling the jar, she started across the foot bridge back to the main island.

Gretar and the protesters were still bobbing in their boats. A woman noticed Mik balancing like a tightrope walker as she traversed the muddy planks. "There!" she hollered, "over there! She's coming back across!"

"Row up next to her!" Gretar called out.

A handful of rowboats chased alongside Mik as she slowly but surely inched along the walkway, a death grip on the rope.

"Princess!" Gretar yelled to the girl, "tell Graves that his bullets won't stop us!"

She paused, sneaking a quick peek over at Gretar. "Bullets?" She yelled back, "you don't know what you're talking about!"

"Don't I? How do you think I got this?" Gretar stood up, pointing to a deep purple scar running from his left cheek to his ear.

Mik looked at the boy then back down at her bare feet. The winds had picked up and waves were washing over the bridge. "Shut up! My father would never shoot anyone. Who are all of you people? What are you doing out here?"

A woman sitting in the boat next to Gretar shouted over, "seems as though you don't know your daddy very well! Wake up, child! Open your eyes!"

At once, Dimitri's words hit home; *"Blind. All of you. Blind to the truth."* For a brief second Mik wondered, *"what else besides the trash has Father been hiding from us?"*

The other boats raised their signs at her. "GRAVES = MONSTER!", "EVIL!", "WHO SHOOTS AT HELPLESS DOLPHINS?!?", "FOR EVER'S SAKE!! STOP THE VIOLENCE & GREED!!" The protestors followed in the increasingly choppy waters, shouting and chanting at Mik as she crept along the rollicking footpath.

Mik yelled back at them, her voice cracking, "leave me alone!"

A strong wave crashed over the path, knocking Mik off balance. She tried to regain her footing, but her bare feet slipped on the planks and in seconds she was on her stomach, clinging to the rope. The undulating waves tossed the scared girl around as she desperately struggled to hold on.

"No—"; Mik lost her grip and into the cold, polluted water she splashed.

Some of the protestors got a kick out of seeing the girl flail about.

"Ha! She looks like a cat thrown into a pool, doesn't she?" one person cracked.

Mik panicked, clinging to plastic bottles and garbage, trying to stay afloat. Debris clung to her face and hair as she screamed.

"Help! I can't swim!"

A woman crossed her arms over her sun-faded 'SAVE THE WHALES' t-shirt. "Well, well...that figures. Maybe we should let you drown, girly, as payback for all the damage your family has done!"

Gretar cut the woman off, "take it easy, Thora."

He rowed over to Mik; she locked eyes with the boy.

"Please help me!" She was swallowing mouthfuls of dirty water. "Please...I...I need to get to my sister..."

In the salty, blinding waves, Mik reached up, her thin pale fingers trying to locate the side of Gretar's boat, but she missed and started to sink. He reached down and grabbed her, pulling her to the side of the boat.

"T-thank you!" Mik cried, exhausted. "Pull me in, please!" Her arms quivered as she held Gretar with both hands.

"Will you help us?" Gretar looked down at the girl.

Up close, Mik noticed the dark scar running across his face. Her muddy nails were digging into his arm. "Yes, anything, yes!"

"Promise?" Gretar asked, raising a dark eyebrow.

"Yes, whatever you need!" She felt the waves pulling at her, her grip weakening. "I promise! Please!"

In one movement the muscular boy lifted her up out of the water and into the small, damp rowboat. Mik coughed and gagged, choking as she pulled lettuce, wads of toilet paper, and other bits of gunk from her hair; her arms felt like jelly. "Thank you...w-what's your name?"

The teenage boy plunked down across from Mik, staring at the filthy, exhausted girl. "Gretar...and I'm gonna hold you to your promise." His sea foam green eyes sparkled in the sunlight.

They rowed towards Mount Michel's main dock. The girl had never felt so disgusting in her life.

Gretar asked again, "so you'll talk to the Count? Convince him to stop the dumping and the drilling, and end the senseless murder of innocent creatures?"

Mik swallowed; a part of her still couldn't believe the things they were accusing her father of. "I'll tell him." Mik would have said anything at that moment to be home, next to Ivry.

"What on Earth were you doing, anyway? You could have died." Gretar rubbed his stubbled chin, squinting down at her.

Mik pushed herself up slowly, feeling a bit sea sick. "Nothing. I just needed some adventure."

"Ha! Got more than you bargained for, didn't ya'?" Thora sassed back.

Mik felt her pocket for the jar. *"Thank Ever, it's still there."* She spat off the side of the boat, trying to get the nasty taste out. The rowboat knocked against the side of the dock as Thora roped it to a piling. Without hesitating, Mik jumped out and bolted towards the beach.

Gretar stood up and yelled after her, "remember your promise!"

Without looking back Mik replied, "yeah! sure thing!"

Thora hit Gretar with an oar. "I don't trust her."

The boy sat back down, picking up a sign that read, 'EARTH IS OUR ONLY HOME'. He muttered, "I guess we'll see."

34 MOON AND STARS

The Count was sitting on the veranda, entertaining royalty from the Ice Region, when he heard his loyal servant Snive's whiny voice in his earpiece.

"Your eminence, it's Mik...She was seen down at the beach!"

"What?" Graves blurted out. He turned to the others at the table, "my apologies, Ambassador, your Highness. You'll have to excuse me." As the Count hurried away, Sarr shot him a look for abandoning her with the guests.

The Count barked into his headset, "what in Ever's name are you talking about?"

Snive cleared his throat. "Apparently, sir, Mik was crossing the bridge from Trash Island. The protestors, um...brought her back."

"*From* Trash Island?!" Graves was livid. "Where the hell was security? How did she leave the Palace without you knowing?"

Snive stammered, "I...I don't know sir."

"Where is she now? Is she safe?" There was silence on the other end. "Snive! Is? She? Safe?"

"I don't know that either, sir, but I'm on it."

"Find her now!" The Count knocked a nearby vase to the floor, shattering it.

Back outside, Sarr smiled awkwardly to their guests. "My, such winds we're having today. Things are just flying through the air, haha. More squid ink tea? A salmon crumpet, perhaps?"

Graves returned to the veranda, his face red as a lobster.

"Zell, darling," Sarr smiled through her gritted teeth, "everything alright?"

"Yes, yes, never better, dear. So good in fact, I'm afraid we need to cut our meeting short, as I've just received some exciting news which I feel will benefit us all." Graves gave his wife a knowing stare.

"Oh my, sounds intriguing...do tell," The Ice Queen asked.

"You'll just have to wait and see, and with that, we'll say goodbye...thank you both again for the albino walrus tusks," Graves muttered, practically yanking Sarr out of her chair. "My precious wife and I must be going. Thank you again." The Count tapped his headset; a man in a crisp white nautical uniform appeared at the door. "Please show the Ambassador and the Queen to their helicopter."

In six-inch heels, Sarr hurried down the hallway, trying to keep up with her husband. "What is going on, Zell?" She clapped with delight. "What's the good news?"

263

"Clearly, I was lying, Sarr!" Graves headed to the elevators. "Mik is missing! She was last seen at the beach of all places!" He smashed the diamond button on the panel; the gold doors slid open.

"The beach?! When? How?" The Countess clutched her stomach; she suddenly felt faint.

"I don't know, but Snive said she was seen with those dirty protesters!" He hit the button for the penthouse.

When Mik got to her bedroom she was shocked to see Ivry sitting up and looking at their seahorses. Mik ran to her sister's side, hugging her.

"Ivry! You're awake! I can't believe it. It's a miracle!"

Ivry could barely lift her arms to return the hug. Beneath her silk nightgown, Mik felt her sister's boney back.

Ivry's voice was thin and raspy, "no, Mik. This is the miracle. Look." She pointed to Moon; the male seahorse was giving birth to hundreds of babies.

Mik didn't bother looking at the tank, but hopped up and ran over to the kitchenette in their room. Flinging open the deluxe glass refrigerator, she pulled out a carafe of milk and poured some into a crystal glass.

"I'm going to make you better!" Mik shouted to Ivry from across the grand room, then spoke aloud to herself, "let's see, he said to mix all of the mushroom dust into milk."

With a silver spoon, Mik crushed the dried mushroom into a fine powder. She scraped it off the counter and into the glass, quickly stirring it up. The milk turned a yellowish-brown color.

"C'mon, c'mon, it's supposed to turn black," she pleaded, her heart racing. Slowly, the liquid darkened into a dirty charcoal color. "Close enough."

She brought the glass to her sister's side. Ivry had her forehead and hands pressed against the tank; her skin was as white as a ghost.

"I had a dream, Mik. I was in the ocean with them…it was so peaceful."

"Let's get you back into bed." Mik fluffed up the silk pillows behind her twin, propping her up against the velvet cushioned headboard. "Here. You have to drink this."

Ivry looked up at her sister, dark circles under her eyes. "Look at you…you're filthy."

"I know, I know." Mik held the glass up to her sister's mouth. "It's a long story. Just drink."

"And you stink," Ivry giggled weakly.

"Nice to see you, too. Now sip, please."

Ivry rejected the glass a second time; her voice was barely audible, "do you remember when we were little? Whenever you'd fall and get a bruise, I'd feel the pain, too?"

Mik brushed away a lock of red hair from her sister's eye. "I remember."

Ivry strained to speak, "and when we first discovered that we could finish each other's sentences? We thought we had magical powers."

"I remember..." Mik paused. "Ruby would tell us the story at bedtime about the enchanted star that wanted to become a girl...but just as it was about to be born, the star split into two, sharing the same soul, so the girl would always have a best friend on Earth, never to be alone." Mik held the glass up, swirling the dark contents around. "That's why you have to drink this, Iv. Please."

Mik gently held the glass up to her sister's dry, cracked lips. Ivry pulled back, "I'll drink it, but you first."

"But I'm not even sick anymore. I'm better."

Using what little strength she had left, Ivry pushed herself up. She looked deep into her Mik's eyes. "I can feel the sickness in you, too. You drink, then me."

"Fine, I'll take a sip, but then you finish the rest."

Ivry nodded, a weak smile on her face.

Mik took a sip. The strange potion fizzed like soda pop on her tongue, tickling her throat as it went down. "Well, it's not as bad as it looks."

Ivry wasn't listening. She was watching the tiny, newborn seahorse babies swim around the tank. She reached over, taking hold of Mik's wrist. "Promise me you'll look after them."

"You'll look after them yourself, okay? Now here, your turn."

Ivry turned her head back to the aquarium. "They're so delicate, so vulnerable. Promise to protect them. They're magical, Mik. Truly magical."

"I will. I will. Please now, Ivry, you have to drink this!" Mik held the glass up once again. "Come on, open up. Just a tiny bit, Iv...Iv!"

Ivry's head fell back as she whispered her last words, "I...love you...promise me." Her frail hand slipped from Mik's arm.

"No! No! Don't leave me, Ivry. No!" Mik threw the glass on the ground, grabbing her sister's lifeless body, rocking her in her arms. "Oh, Ivry, no! I promise, Ivry! Come back to me! I promise...I promise I'll take care of them..."

Mik sobbed uncontrollably, not noticing her mother enter the room. The Count was a step behind her as Sarr shouted, "Mik! She's here, Zell, she's fine, safe in her room." She realized Mik was crying. "Mik, darling? Oh Ever. Oh Ever what's happened?" Sarr ran to their bedside.

Mik lay facing her sister, mirroring her pose, just as they had been in the womb.

"No, no, no, my baby! My precious, precious baby girl!" Sarr collapsed on her daughters, crying in hysterics.

The Count stood gripping the edge of the bed; the sight of Ivry's lifeless body was too much from him to bare. Graves reacted in the only way his heart knew how, with anger.

"Curse this wretched world! Curse Ever for this!" He screamed.

Mik's dirty face, soaked in tears, now burned as red as her hair. She stared at her father, hatred in her eye. "This is all your fault! You've poisoned her!"

Sarr looked at Mik then at her husband, her heavily dilated eyes wet with tears, black streaks of mascara running down her face like spider legs. "What is she talking about, Zell?"

Graves pounded his hand against the canopy bedpost. "Mik, what are you saying, honey?! I would never harm your sister! I love her! I love you both!"

"Your father would never hurt either of you girls, Mik! You don't know what you're saying!" Sarr took Mik's face in her hand. "This was just an accident…it wasn't your father's fault!"

Mik pried her mother's hands away. "And you, Mother! You're just as blind!"

"What's all the commotion?" Ruby entered the room carrying a polished silver tray of hot tea and cookies. She looked at the bed, saw Ivry, and screamed. The tray dropped and porcelain cups shattered everywhere. The nanny ran to the girl, hugging her and weeping. "Ivry, no!"

The Count sat down at the foot of the bed; he was sweating, the veins in his forehead throbbing. He placed his hand on Mik's leg. "Mik…I—"

Mik shot up, shoving her father hard in the chest with both hands. "Don't you dare touch me! Get out! Get out of here! Murderer!"

Sarr stared at her husband in horror. "Why is she saying that, Zell?"

Mik stared her mother, teeth gritted. "I'll tell you why. It was the fish, Mother, the fish! The toxic fish we ate at the ball! It came from the polluted waters….and he's responsible!" Mik pointed to the opposite side of their room to the windowless wall. "I know why there aren't any windows facing that way! I've seen it with my own eyes, Father! Ivry suffered, and it's all because of you! You let this happen!"

Ruby took Mik's hand. "You can't believe that, dear."

"I know it, and I don't ever want to see him again!" Mik threw herself on top of her twin, heartbroken.

Graves reached over to rub Mik's back. "Princess."

She flinched. "Go away! Go away!" Mik sobbed harder.

Sarr was confused and filled with despair. She could only shake her head at her husband. The Count got up from the bed, and walked slowly to the door, his mind swirling. Turning back, he watched as his daughters— his most prized possessions—suffered, and for what?

"Could it be?" he thought to himself, looking out the window at the blue, shimmering ocean. "Could I have prevented this somehow?" He slowly closed the bedroom door behind him; the sound echoed through the cold, silent

Palace.

Snive, who had been waiting at the far end of the hallway, ran to the Count. Seeing the graven look on his master's face, he understood what had happened. Snive knelt to one knee. "Your Eminence, there are no words. I am truly sorry."

The Count didn't respond, walking past Snive like a zombie. "What have I done? What have I done?"

Snive looked up. "Sir?"

"Release the monk," he mumbled, dragging his feet down the hallway.

"Sir, are you sure that's wise? You're in shock. That old monk is responsi—"

"He did nothing...release him," Graves waved a dismissive arm. Not a word of this to the press."

"Yes sir."

Graves ripped the shark fins off his jacket, throwing them angrily to the ground. "What have I done?" He fell to his knees, sobbing like a child for the daughter he had lost.

35 BOG

A yellow warbler perched on Perl's shoulder. The bird watched with curiosity as the girl sat curled up reading beneath her favorite tree. Despite a lovely afternoon walkabout around Venusto, Perl still couldn't seem to shake the dark thoughts of Malbud from her mind, so she tried to lose herself in her new book, '*The Most Curious Life of Sir Chamuel Cureckitycoo*'.

Cureckitycoo Field Notes
1 June 1894

I continued my adventure into uncharted lands, farther north than I'd ever traveled before, in the hopes of discovering more new varieties of plant and fungi life.

However, what I happened upon this day of days was of the utmost fascination. As I awoke from my hammock to a hot, humid morn, lying and listening to the trills of the birds, a fluttering of wings appeared before my eyes. A butterfly, periwinkle, with splashes of dazzling coral pink, danced above me. This specimen was ever so peculiar from those I'd encountered in the past. As the butterfly approached, I held out my hoof, feeling obliged to offer it a pleasant "How d'you do." To my bewilderment, upon closer examination, I realized that this creature had not the head of an insect, but a human! Bully, indeed! She landed but for a moment, winked at me, then flittered away! My heart racing with adrenaline, I chased after her, my knapsack of drawing pencils close at hand.

I studied the magnificent Rhopalocera for hours, sketching its inexplicable anatomy- Antenna, Thorax, Wings- all the expected features, but with a Homo sapien head! I thought myself mad from the heat, but no—this was truly a discovery for the ages!

It escaped my sights, mingling with a kaleidoscope of common butterflies, drifting amongst the blazing poppy fields. I filled the pages of my notebook until the long purple shadows of dusk crept over the hills of this magical realm. When I had lost daylight, I packed up and journeyed home, as the golden hour of the day came to an end, and I, forever changed.

I've come to feel strangely at home in these new lands.

"Hey there, whatcha reading?" Javan plunked down next to Perl.

"The book Humboldt gave me."

"You sure have a knack for getting gifts, don't you?" He flicked her pearl anklet from Tryfon with his finger.

Perl placed a blade of grass into the book to save her place. "I only asked to borrow the book. He's the one who said I could have it." She pulled her foot back. "Aren't you late for your morning swim?"

"Geesh, what's with you today?" Javan brushed his wet bangs from his eyes. "I already swam."

Perl stared at the boy intently, the sun reflected in her bright green eyes. "I have to kill him, Javan."

"Whoa, whoa, whoa! Who, Malblud? And how do you think you're gonna do that, Perl?" She shot him a look; Javan put his hands up in a surrender. "Look, I'm not saying you haven't trained...your sword work is good, but you don't even know what that thing is!"

"It has to be stopped." Perl stood, placing the book in her trusty backpack. "I'm going to the bog tonight. Don't try to stop me. I've made up my mind."

"Okay. So, what's your plan? You have one, right?"

Perl nodded. "I'll take Quantaa to the bog, face the Many Lost Souls, then catch Malblud off guard, and end his life...like he did my father's."

From the sheath on her backpack, she pulled out her narwhal sword, Fortis, and stabbed it into the ground.

Javan didn't say a word, but merely stared up at the girl, a look of both respect and worry etched on his face. Perl saw the boy's concern.

"I've completed my Seeker training. I've battled other creatures. I've learned so much in the time I've been here," she paused, "and I know this is what I'm supposed to do, Javan."

"Okay. Sounds simple..." The platypus-boy raised a dubious eyebrow. "A little too simple, though, don't you think? It won't be that easy. You're talking about ancient beasts from the Dark Realm, Perl." He stood up and began pacing around the tree. "This isn't something you just run off and do! And do you even know where the bog is? Exactly how do you see all this happening?"

"I just told you, and I have...this." She unzipped her bag and pulled out the bottle of *Hippomane Mancinello* and waved it at Javan. "Remember? Killer sap. Another *gift*...from Humboldt."

"Easy with that stuff! And I get it, the Fawn took quite a liking to you."

"There's a bog on one of Mont Michel's surrounding islands. It's where the oil and gas pumps are located." Perl carefully tucked the bottle of sap in her backpack.

The two of them left the cool shade of Lottie, heading back up the hill to their final meditation, the midday sun hot on their backs.

"There are thousands of bogs on Earth. What makes you think that's the one?" Javan asked.

"For years growing up on Mont Michel, I heard the villagers' stories about that place. Thousands of years ago, people used it as a gravesite. Their bodies were seen as sacrifices to appease the evil spirits, with the hopes that they'd allow their crops to flourish. They also say it's a gateway to a dark netherworld. Even the people that work on the oil refineries there have talked about hearing weird voices coming from the bog. Plus, there's a black cloud that constantly hangs over the island, even when it's sunny everywhere else. It's gotta be the place."

Javan blinked, "well, that's a lot, and here I thought bogs were for harvesting peat, not people."

Perl stopped. "You don't believe me, do you? Fine, but I know the stories are true."

They reached the edge of the field where Bodhi and the other Seekers were gathering.

"Perl, I didn't say I doubted you, but if that place is really what you say it is, then you can't go alone."

She looked over at her Seeker family forming their circle. "I can do this, Javan. I'm not afraid."

"But you should be!" Javan raised his voice, frustrated at Perl's stubbornness.

Perl chirped back, "I can't risk anyone else getting hurt because of me!"

Javan turned away. "If you could only see yourself as I do."

"What did you say?" Perl looked over at him.

"Never mind…" he flipped his hair. "Come on, we're gonna be late."

The two joined the group and sat down on either side of Bear.

"Almost thought you guys weren't coming," the roly-poly boy's eyes darted back and forth between them, sensing some tension.

Out of the corner of her eye, Perl caught a glimpse of Corvax, staring at her as if he were trying to solve a puzzle.

During the meditation class, Perl simply went through the motions, her mind preoccupied. She left the field without saying a word to anyone.

Master Bodhi's many eyes followed Perl as she walked alone. "So stirs a troubled soul," the Being whispered to the clouds.

Later that evening after supper at Dragon Maw, Perl quickly returned to her nest ahead of Bear and Opis. As she approached, she saw Quantaa curled up in a giant ball against the side of the hut. Not ready to wake the great hound, she tiptoed past him and began hastily filling her backpack with snacks, not knowing how long she would be gone.

As she hurried about, one of Uriel's leopard moths flew in through the partially open window and began to flutter out a message. Perl grabbed a glass jar from the table and quickly trapped the moth, its crystalline dust particles lingering in the air. The moth bounced off the inside of the jar, the sparkling words still forming as it fluttered around. The message was scrambled, undecipherable. Perl poked a few small holes in the lid with the tip of Fortis so the spotted moth could breathe. Leaning down, she whispered to it.

"I'm sorry, but nothing's going to distract me from my mission, not even Uriel." The *Hypercompe Scribonia* filled the entire jar with so much glowing dust that it looked like a snow globe. "Calm down, you're okay. Opis or Bear will be along soon to let you out."

Placing the jar where her roommates would see it, Perl pulled her old, brown robe off the tree branch hook and slipped it on, thinking it was better camouflage than the shimmering Harmony top. Perl stepped out of the teardrop-shaped nest. She looked over at the wooden sign with her and her roommates' names on them, realizing this could be the last time she ever saw this place.

Quantaa was dreaming and making low woofing sounds in his sleep. Perl grabbed hold of some fur and pulled herself up over his wings and onto his warm, broad back. The greyhound woke in a start, instinctively shaking her off. Perl hit the ground with a thud.

"Oof! Quantaa, hey! It's me! Come on, be a good boy."

Perl climbed up again, hunkering down this time to hold her position. The sleepy dog twisted his necks, rolling her off the other side.

"Look, I know you're tired. So am I. But I can't do this without you."

Perl stroked his fur affectionately. The greyhound's eyes were still closed. It lazily opened one eye on his white head, looking down at the girl.

"Pretty please?" Perl smiled.

Letting out a deep, heavy sigh, the hound dipped his spotted wing down so she could use it as a ramp. "Here," she said, pulling an apple out of her backpack and holding it out to him before stepping onto his back for a third time. The massive Being devoured the apple in seconds. "That's my good Q," Perl leaned forward and whispered into his black velvety ear, "okay, time to take me home."

In a few strides the two were airborne, breaking through the butterfly-shaped cloud, leaving Venusto's atmosphere. Once above the clouds, an array of twinkling stars appeared out of the twilight. Perl looked up, trying to make out various constellations.

Perl held on tightly as they soared higher and faster. The steady up and down flap of the dog's massive wings made a rhythmic, whooshing hum around Perl. The air was crisp and Perl ducked down low, wrapping her robe tight around her as she nestled her head into the great beast's furry back. Perl thought about Javan; not telling him or the others that she was leaving was wrong, but so was putting them all in harm's way. The potion Humboldt had given her, along with her powerful sword and fierce Battle creature would be enough to defeat the evil. It had to be.

Quantaa banked left, descending through the thick clouds looming over the world below. Droplets of mist tickled Perl's arms as they rocketed through the dense haze, breaking out into clear skies above Mont Michel. From this height, Perl thought the islands looked like an octopus with tentacles peeking out of the water in all directions, the head of the great beast the main island. As they got closer, Perl could see that much of the

271

rainbow-colored coral reef that surrounded the island had died, having turned white as bone. Perl felt an ache in the pit of her stomach looking down at the ocean, covered in trash. Seeing her home suffering like this broke Perl's heart; it angered her as well, strengthening her resolve even more.

"There, Quantaa, that's the one…take me there." Perl pointed down to a small desolate island with rows of oil pumps bobbing in and out of the ground like huge metal birds searching for worms.

Quantaa landed in the rugged outskirts near the pumps. The weeds and thorny brush were as tall as Perl and sprang up all around them, the air sticky and humid, foul smelling. Sliding down the great Battle Beast, Perl's boots sank into the thick, clammy mud, and she gave a silent thanks to Ever for deciding to wear her boots. The only sound on the island was the sharp, pounding, *clank-clank-clank* of the gas and oil pumps. Metal squeaked and gears squealed. To Perl, it was as if the Earth was being stabbed over and over again. She closed her eyes for a minute, trying to block out the horrible sound. When she opened her eyes, Quantaa was peering down at her, a look of concern on both his faces.

"Okay, Q. Let's go," Perl uttered, stroking the white one's long snout.

With every step forward Perl's boots were suctioned to the mud like glue, at times almost pulling them right off her feet. Quantaa's giant paws left deep sinkholes, and Perl, following closely behind the great dog, was careful not to fall into them. Perl lifted Fortis from her backpack, holding it out in front of her.

The young Seeker and her protector trudged through the desolate terrain, searching for the bog. Even with her loyal Light Creature by her side, fear crawled up Perl's spine; her bioluminescent spots glowed faintly. Gnarly twisted branches, bare of any leaves, were scattered like black bones all around them. Oil leaked from the old, rusty pumps, trickling along the ground like poisoned arteries across the lifeless landscape. Thick veils of moss hung low off the many dead trees. Perl was now walking ahead of Quantaa.

"Don't be scared, Q," Perl said, slowly parting the moldy curtains with her sword. She braced herself for whatever may be lurking on the other side, but it was only more of the same; mud, dead trees, and suffocating heat.

"Are we going in circles?" Perl wondered. The bleak surroundings began to play tricks on her mind. She hallucinated—Papa Ximu, Count Graves, the flower that bit her, the Roc—swirled like gnats in front of her. Feelings of loneliness, sorrow, and abandonment crept into her mind.

"What's happening?" Perl tried to ignore it, but couldn't; the island itself seemed to be taunting her.

Quantaa sensed Perl's distress and dipped a head down, nuzzling her with his soft, wet nose.

"Good boy," Perl mumbled. Her head was throbbing and she was covered in sweat. Sharp wispy ferns slithered up from the ground, seeming to clutch at Perl's legs.

"We're lost, boy," Perl said, her voice thin, "so lost."

Perl leaned against one of Quantaa's tree trunk legs for support. Waves of dread poured over the small girl; she felt like she was drowning. Perl wavered and started to fall forward, but Quantaa lowered his head and caught her small frame. Perl reached out blindly, grasping one of the dog's whiskers as her legs went limp.

Quantaa's nose twitched and his eyes watered as he eased Perl to the ground. "Achoo-oof!" The dog let out a thunderous sneeze. Gobs of sticky mucus splatted across Perl's face.

She smiled up at the Battle Beast. "Bless you…and thank you."

Her head still hurt and her legs were sore, but Quantaa's sneeze had woken her up. Perl pushed herself up with Fortis.

"Let's keep going, boy."

36 GATEKEEPERS

Amongst the clatter of oil pumps, Perl swore she heard someone behind them. She stopped and walked back a few paces with the tip of Fortis leading the way. Quantaa snarled.

"Shh, quiet, boy."

She heard it again—*snap, snap*—the faint sounds of twigs breaking underfoot. Perl took a few bold steps forward, both hands now firmly gripping the hilt of her sword.

"Who's there?!"

Perl noticed a patch of high weeds rustling. She approached it, her weapon above her head, preparing to strike whoever, or whatever, it was. Her Battle Beast was right beside her moving in a low, crouching crawl, ready to pounce.

"Show yourself...*now!*" Perl warned.

She was about to bring Fortis down when out stepped Bear, Opis and Javan, covered up to their knees in sludge. They threw up their hands.

"Hey, hey! It's just us!" Bear yelled.

Perl slid to a stop, lowering her sword but Quantaa kept coming, teeth bared.

"Quantaa, it's okay, boy. Easy." Perl commanded. Javan held out her hand for him to sniff.

"What are you guys doing here? You shouldn't have come," Perl scolded, yet secretly happy to see them.

"Well hello to you, too," Bear said, pulling a centipede off one of his arms and flicking it into the mud. "We're here to help, Perly-Perl."

"Sorry, but you only have yourself to blame...you shouldn't have mentioned which island you were going to," Javan smirked. "We just wanted to be here, if you know...you needed some help. The others are on their way, too."

"How did you get here so fast? I mean, I had Quantaa going at top speed."

"Let's just say..." The platypus-boy smiled. "We *borrowed* a boat. A fast one."

Opis spoke up, "the sphagnan molecules in decaying moss reacts with human organic matter..."

Perl cocked her head. "Huh?"

Opis rambled on, "...the acid from peat creates a bronzed hide."

Javan brushed his bangs aside. "Not sure this is the time for a classroom lecture, Opis...Opis?"

They looked at the jellyfish-girl, who was swaying slightly as she spoke, her eyes glassy, distant. Bear walked over, snapping his fingers in front of her face; the girl didn't flinch, but continued to rattle off information, her voice flat, robotic. Opis' tentacles started to glow, firing off little sparks.

"The bog...it mummifies the dead bodies, preserving them for thousands of years."

Bear chuckled nervously. "Knowledgeable as always, Opis, but seriously—"

She cut him off, "...there is evil among us, surrounding us, watching us..."

Perl gave one of her tentacles a playful tug. "Hey! Opis! Are you alright?"

"...we should not be here...we will not survive..."

"Snap out of it, Opis!" Perl grabbed Opis by her thin shoulders, shaking her. "Snap out of it!"

Roused from her trance, Opis' bright blue eyes suddenly refocused. "Ugh...wow. I don't feel so good." She shook her head trying to clear the fuzziness. "Sorry, I...I don't know what just happened there."

"It's this place. It messes with your mind." Perl hugged Opis tightly. "I'm so glad you're here...sister." Perl took Opis' hand, pulling the wispy, translucent girl forward.

Forming a tight line, the group slowly but surely slogged across the grim terrain. The farther they went, the more difficult the footing became, like walking through sticky tar.

"Somebody tell me when we're there," Bear complained. The portly boy brought up the rear, his short, chunky legs struggling to push through the sloppy mess.

Through the darkness and low hanging mist, Perl made out some sort of dome-like structure. "Look! I think that's it...dead ahead."

The four Seekers and Quantaa picked up their pace, and soon found themselves standing at the edge of a vast swampy bog. The pit itself was quite large; fifty elephants wide and twice as long, its surface pitch black. Above, a latticework of twisted, thorny bramble covered the entire swamp like a cage of barbed wire. Bear reached up and broke off a thorn from a branch close to them. It was as big as his hand and razor sharp.

"It looks like this was put here on purpose..." Opis observed, "...as if to protect it."

"Okay. So, what now?" Javan asked.

They stared through the coiled branches out over the marsh. A yellowish smog hung over it, the stench was unbearable, like rotting garbage and foul chemicals. It gurgled, belching up greasy bubbles as though the ground itself was gasping for air. Quantaa sniffed and whined.

Perl looked up at her Battle Beast; the greyhound was way too big to get through the thorny netting. She patted the dog's black snout.

"It's okay, Q, you wait here…we'll be fine," she said. Quantaa whimpered, pacing back and forth along the edge.

"Hey, what is that?" Bear saw a wooden handle poking out of the marsh. He reached through the brambles pulling out a rusty farming sickle, examining its curved steel blade.

"There's stuff everywhere in here, look." Perl slipped Fortis into her backpack and stepped through the nettles, pulling out a small metal shield from the mud. Scraping off the peat moss, Perl shined it with her sleeve. On the shield in cracked, faded paint were two lions, flanking a castle. "It's a coat of arms. This whole place is like a museum…" She looked around. "Treasures of the dead."

"They're offerings…left here with the lost souls at their burial," Opis spoke. "We probably shouldn't take them." She eyed a small club with spikes on the end. "Then again, we do have to protect ourselves."

The group left Quantaa behind, slipping through the thorny branches and wading into the slimy swamp. Strewn across the muddy pit were all kinds weaponry—swords, helmets, pitchforks, battle axes, as well as personal items, like hairbrushes, jeweled medallions, even boots—poking out of the mud, or embedded in the surface like concrete.

As the group made their way through the sludge, Javan asked the question they were all wondering. "What exactly are we looking for, anyway?"

"I don't know," Perl called back, "but remember Humboldt's warning…evil can come in many forms. It can trick you…everybody just be on guard."

"Agreed," Bear pulled out an iron skillet to accompany his sickle blade.

They did their best to walk in a straight line, Perl in front. Off to their left, about fifty yards away, a thin layer of mist began to funnel, as if being sucked in by a vacuum.

"Look at that," cried Perl, angling towards it.

The smoke thickened, forming a yellow-white cloud that hovered like a ghost in the middle of the swamp. They watched as the vapor spun clockwise, swirling faster and faster. The center of the cloud began to glow red, forming an oval doorway. Its color shifted from dark red to a bright flaming orange, framed by a ring of black smoke. Perl tried to run through the sticky sludge, but the mud was too thick to move quickly.

"Perl, wait! I'm sensing activity!" Javan's electrolocation was on high alert. He stumbled after her. *That's strange…I don't detect a pulse, though.*

"Come on, hurry!" Perl's boots were caked with mud. With each step, they grew heavier and heavier as she made her way to the portal.

Bear and Opis were trailing Javan. Behind them, Quantaa could be heard, barking and growling as he paced nervously at the edge of the bog.

The Seekers were thirty yards from the smoldering portal, when the bog's surface started to heave and undulate, bubbling up like a pot of hot soup.

"What's happening?" shouted Opis; she felt something brush up against her leg.

Before they could react, all around them, ghoulish figures rose up out of the swamp, their rotted bodies splotched with mud and slime. Bear grabbed Opis with one of his free hands, pulling her close to his side. The ancient dead were rising, clawing their way out of their murky graves.

"Hold still!" Javan yelled. The four were surrounded by a horde of specters. Quantaa was barking wildly behind them.

"Ready your weapons!" Perl ordered, holding up her sword and shield.

Opis had the spiked club, Javan a pipe, while Bear held tight to his corroded sickle and frying pan.

Instead of attacking, however, the ghouls simply stood there, motionless. Perl studied them; still flesh and bone, wearing outfits from past centuries, they all had one disturbing feature—the tannins in the swamp had dyed their hair an unnatural red, making them look like gruesome matchsticks, poking up from the earth.

"The Many Lost Souls," Javan said in a hushed tone, breaking the eerie silence.

Bear clung to Opis. "Many, many lost souls." He flicked mud at one; it didn't budge.

Javan waded over to a tall, sinewy figure in a rumpled military jacket.

"Be careful," Perl cautioned.

Javan went right up to the man's chiseled face, nearly touching noses with him. "I don't think they can they see us. Look around…all their eyes are closed."

"Oh, now I feel *so* much better," Bear blurted out. He picked up a hatchet and an old spear close to his feet, equipping two more hands.

"Alright, everybody…" Opis let go of Bear, gripping her spiked club with two hands. "No sudden movement…we need to think."

Perl, several feet away from the others, watched as the orange, swirling portal began to slow its rotation; it also seemed to be shrinking. "I think it's closing…there isn't much time!" she shouted, yanking her feet out of the muck, trying not to lose a boot.

As soon as she took a step, all of the mummies threw back their heads, emitting a collective high-pitched screech. It reminded Perl of a barn owl's piercing cry, only so much more terrifying. The dark souls began to move; they screamed and moaned like banshees, grasping the air blindly. One of them grabbed Opis by the shoulder.

"Get off me!" the jellyfish-girl shrieked, barely holding it off with her club. She pushed forward with all her strength, knocking the mummy backwards into the sticky ooze.

Several of the bog creatures shambled past the Seekers, gathering in front of the portal, blocking the doorway. Perl, Opis, Javan, and Bear closed ranks.

"There's way too many of them, and too few of us! What are we gonna do?!" Javan yelled. He held the metal pipe above his head, ready to bring it down on any that came near him.

Perl held up the iron shield, along with Fortis. She stared at the other three, her spots blazing white in the darkness. "Remember our training! It's time to fight!"

Perl launched herself at the closest fiend, swinging her blade with everything she had; off went the hand of one of the ghouls. It staggered, letting out an ear-shattering shriek as it flailed about erratically. Perl dodged it and kept plodding forward, trying to get to the portal. The severed hand on the ground twitched, then tried crawling after the girl, but sank into the thick mud.

"Keep a tight formation!" Bear commanded.

The four of them struggled to stay together. Bear wielded his four weapons wildly, slashing and cutting whatever was in his way. Javan rammed a creature in the chest with his pipe. It fell backwards, trying to regain its footing. Opis pushed a woman away dressed in a frayed, oil-soaked robe with long scraggly hair.

"Stay back!" Opis yelled, raising her club at the woman. It lunged at her just as Opis swung; the spiked club imbedded itself in the thing's shoulder. Fountains of gray blood and gore sprayed into the air as the creature howled. Opis ripped the club out and the haunted creature dropped to her knees, writhing on the ground.

Javan swung hard at a squatty man, caving in the side of his head. It let out a low moan, falling face first in the mud, its body quivering.

"Rraaaagggh!" Bear was fending off three of them, his arms a flurry of flashing metal.

"They just keep coming!" Perl cried, "I'm making a run for it!" She held the shield up above her head, moving quickly and staying just out of reach of the attackers, her small size an advantage. The creatures seemed to want no part of Fortis, as if somehow aware of the narwhal horn's powerful magic.

The throngs of ghouls weren't stopping. More and more clawed their way up out of the black swamp, emerging with a terrifying scream as if announcing their rebirth, shuffling towards Opis, Javan, and Bear as the three tightened their circle.

Perl's arms were on fire; they shook as she brandished Fortis, cutting down one after another with its razor-sharp teeth. "Quantaa, help us! Quan-taa!"

Above the screeches and groans, the Seekers heard a tremendous howl.

In a flash they felt a great rush of air, as Quantaa came soaring overhead, emitting a deep, rumbling growl the likes Perl had never heard before. The great Battle Beast hovered above them beating its massive wings; the powerful gusts of wind began collapsing sections of the twisted thorny branches, tearing the dry sticks to shreds. Quantaa swooped back and forth over the bog, clawing and crushing mouthfuls of bark in his powerful jaws.

"Watch out!" Javan ducked, as huge chunks of prickly limbs whipped through the air, sticking into the mud like spears.

Bear tried to dodge a falling branch and slipped. He plunged face first into the pudding-like mud, dropping two of his weapons. Bear tried hard to push himself up with his free hands, but the more he moved, the more he sank. A handful of creatures closed in on him.

"Bear! Bear! Get up!" Opis screamed to her friend.

Bear, still with his sickle and skillet, continued battling. The red-haired beasts grasped at him, jaws chomping.

"Agh! Get off of me! *Get off of me!*" Bear twisted and turned in the muck, shaking free of a few of them, knocking a couple down, but they kept coming.

Javan and Opis, seeing Bear in trouble, tried to get to him, but they were cut off by a swarm of undead. Perl and the others watched in horror as an enormous mummy, a full head taller than the others, staggered towards Bear. The thing was wearing a tunic and leather armor, like a gladiator from ancient Rome; it held a broken sword in its hand, a visor helmet covering its face. Dark goo dripped from its eye sockets as it towered above the helpless tardigrade.

"Bear!" was all Javan could say, as the creature raised its sword and brought it down, taking off one of Bear's arms.

"Agghh!!" Bear screamed out in pain.

"Nooo!" Perl looked over; her wide eyes full of fear. She was just a few feet away from the portal now, close enough to step through the opening, when a voice called out to her.

"I am heere, chiiilld…"

Exhausted, scared, and confused, Perl could hardly hold Fortis, which now felt like a tree in her hand. The voice spoke again.

"I am heeere…"

Perl stood, frozen. She looked over at her poor friends; the Many Lost Souls were on top of Bear, dragging him beneath the mud as he screamed and flailed.

"I am heeere…" The voice pounded inside her temple like a drum.

Perl, mustering everything she had, lifted Fortis once again. She took a few plodding steps in the direction of Bear, when suddenly Quantaa burst in through a hole in the prickly branches. Swooping down like a bolt of lightning, the greyhound landed hard in the mud, crushing several of the ghouls. With his massive paws, he knocked the handful of creatures off of Bear and snatched the boy by the shirt, lifting him up like a chew toy.

Bear gasped for air as blood poured out of his open wound. Quantaa flew out of the pit, holding Bear in his teeth, then gently dropping him onto the bank at the edge of the swamp before making a one-eighty back to the group. Bear hit the ground with a soft thump and slumped over, groaning in pain.

The greyhound landed next to Perl, as the menacing voice from inside the portal spoke once more.

"Omnia mors aequat…"

The hairs on Quantaa's back stood on end. He pressed his ears flat against his heads and started whimpering. Perl had never seen him act like this.

"It's okay, Q. It's okay. We can do this. Come." The greyhound did not move, its legs locked in place. "Quantaa, come!"

More mummified corpses continued to rise up out of the swamp, lurching and stumbling over to Perl, their bone-chilling cries like shattering glass.

"Omnia mors aequat….Omnia mors aequat…"

Opis was trying to get to Perl when she heard the voice, recognizing the language. She repeated it to herself, *"Omnia mors aequat*—death makes all things equal." Opis stopped, tossing her weapon aside; she knew what she had to do.

Javan, fighting off two bog beasts, shouted, "Perl, no! Don't go through the portal!" He shot one of them in the face with a few of his darts, then flipped another over his shoulder, hitting it with his pipe. He tried to get to Perl with what little strength he had left.

"You don't have to do this!" he pleaded.

"Yes, I do!" Perl looked at Javan; he was exhausted. She saw her beloved Quantaa, cowering in fear. Opis looked to be in some kind of trance, and Bear…well, she feared the worst for poor, sweet Bear. She glanced at the portal; it was barely swirling, and getting smaller.

"Get out of the bog, Javan," Opis said matter-of-factly. "Go. Now. Perl is crossing over. You can't stop her."

Without saying another word, Opis headed off in the opposite direction. The zaps and pops from her hair were drawing the attention of the Many Lost Souls, who shuffled after the girl, attracted to the sparks. Soon, nearly every creature in the bog was trailing Opis as she moved far away from the portal.

"Opis, what are you doing?" Perl called out to the girl.

"Oh nononono…no!" Javan shouted, "don't do it, Opis!" He started to go after her.

"Stay back, Javan!" Opis shouted back.

The ghouls were all around her now. They didn't attack the girl, but just stared, mesmerized; the light reflecting off their oil-slicked faces. The slender girl took hold of all her tentacles; her braids lighting up like roman candles. Her body began to charge itself. From head to toe, her frame pulsated.

The portal was now just large enough for Perl to slip through. She gave one last look back at her friends; they were her family whom she loved so much, and they were suffering because of her. Perl knew she had no choice; she would go the rest of the way alone. At the far end of the bog, she saw Nan and Lyre flying towards her. On the ground, Corvax, Tars and Flax were sprinting through the mud, shouting at her. It all seemed to be happening in slow motion.

"Goodbye," Perl muttered, "all of you."

Distracted by Opis, Javan spun back just in time to see the back of Perl's head. "No."

Perl stepped into the portal, the orange light swallowing her. The ring of smoke that had been curling around the gateway turned to black soot, falling to the muddy ground.

Quantaa let out a mournful howl. Javan shook his head and turned back to Opis. White light was radiating off of her. Seeing the portal disappear, Corvax and the rest of the group turned their attention to Opis.

"Opis!" Corvax hollered, "what are you doing?"

"Don't come near me, any of you," she ordered as she dropped to her knees, thrusting both arms into the wet swampy soil.

"Opis…" Javan pleaded with the girl; he was physically and emotionally drained.

"I can't hold back much longer! Quantaa, go, and take him!" Opis hollered over the static. She closed her eyes and focused, sending powerful electrical currents surging through the ground, trying to locate the gas and oil deposits that lay below the earth's crust. Nan and Lyre circled above. Flax and Tars slid to a stop, unsure what was happening.

Quantaa stood back up, still shaking. As the white head continued to search the area for Perl, the black head clamped down on the back of Javan's shirt, lifting the boy out of the muck.

"No, Quantaa! Put me down!" Javan begged as they flew off, passing over Opis, her body now a beacon of light.

Just as the greyhound reached the far end of the bog, dropping Javan next to Bear out of harm's way, Opis's electric heat hit the gas streams underground—*KA-BOOM!* The entire center of the bog exploded in a deafening blast. It blew oily mud, chunks of peat and thorny branches high into the air, along with the Many Lost Souls. As their bodies hit the ground, shafts of sparkling light emanated from them. Corvax, Tars and Flax were hurtled backwards into the mud. The shockwaves rippled through the Air

Seekers, nearly knocking them out of the sky. The Seekers gathered around Javan and Bear, checking on their friends.

"Look, Opis is releasing them back to Ever!" Bear, who had rolled up onto his feet, had an arm around Javan. He and the others squinted up at the rays of brilliant light ascending skywards. Hundreds upon hundreds of souls floated up like shooting stars, disappearing through the clouds.

At the same time, the gas and oil pumps at the other end of the island burst into fireballs, one after another, bathing the landscape in an electric orange as the flames crackled and billows of black smoke curled into the air.

A shimmering blue light radiated from the middle of the bog, where Opis's translucent body stood; she swayed as if she were asleep on her feet. The group went to her.

"Opis? Opis?" Corvax called out, but she didn't respond.

"Are you there, Opis?" Tars asked.

"What did you do, you dear, sweet jellyfish," Bear said softly.

Nan and Lyre hugged one another as they wept.

Opis slowly turned to the Seekers and held out her hand. As Javan reached to take it, the girl shattered into a million particles of pink and blue light that swirled up into the night sky like campfire embers before fading away altogether. Like that, their fellow Seeker and companion was gone.

"We will meet again, my friend." Bear lowered his head. He had wrapped a makeshift bandage of leaves around the end of his severed arm. He held his remaining ones up to the sky, palms open to honor his eternal friend. Javan did the same, gritting his teeth, his jaw clenched tight.

After the explosion, the island fell eerily silent; only the low rumble of the fires and the occasional sounds of the metal pumps collapsing could be heard.

Quantaa sniffed and pawed at the spot where the portal had disappeared, whimpering. Seeing that the girl was indeed gone, the great Battle Beast of the Light Realm flapped his wings and rocketed away, vanishing into the clouds.

Javan, his tension building again, picked up a branch and began swinging it angrily at a bush. "How could she?!"

Corvax and Bear walked over to Javan, as the others slowly gathered around.

"Perl's gone, Javan." Bear said. "Opis is gone."

"We need to go, too." The crow-boy added.

"Why didn't I stop her?" Javan continued to batter the bush.

"Because you couldn't have. None of us could." Lyre said softly.

"I could've! *I could've!*" Javan reared back, but Tars caught him mid swing with his tail. He squeezed Javan's wrist, forcing him to drop the stick. Javan looked at his friends. "How will we find her, Bear? How?"

"I don't know," Bear shrugged, pointing at the bush, "but I know attacking another living thing isn't the way."

The platypus-boy blushed, ashamed at his outburst. He looked down at Bear's bandaged arm. "Oh my Ever…are you okay?"

"I'll be fine…but we gotta get moving." Bear gripped his wound.

"He's right," Corvax nodded. "Let's go, everyone. We need to let Tryfon know what's happened."

Nan, and Lyre flew off, while arm in arm, the boys made their way back to the rowboats. Javan and Flax helped Bear in, while Tars and Corvax tied the two boats together. Then the platypus-boy hopped into the water, gripping the stern with his large webbed hands.

Javan looked up at Bear, his eyes full of sorrow. "We were supposed to protect her."

"We did the best we could, brother…" Bear reached back, placing a heavy hand on Javan's shoulder. "This is Perl's journey now."

Javan started kicking, and away they went, slipping through the still waters, away from the burning island, just as the pinkish light of a new day was unfolding.

37 THE MAINLAND

The mighty explosion shook every window on Mont Michel, from bottom dwellers to the Palace elite, rousing them from their beds. News of a fire at the refinery spread quickly; locals wandered out into the streets, setting up chairs to watch the magnificent light display.

Mik was already awake, not having slept a wink since Ivry's death three days ago. The twin was at her desk, composing a message to the protester, Gretar. There was no way to reach him through the various tech devices—she didn't have any information about the boy other than his name—so she decided to write him an old-fashioned letter using paper and ink, and would have Ruby deliver it. Mik wasn't sure if Gretar was the one in charge of the activists, but he'd been the one who saved her from drowning, so she thought she could trust him.

When the explosion shook her bedroom's floor-to-ceiling bay windows, Mik rushed over to see what the commotion was, but everything from her view was serene.

"Maybe something on Trash Island," she wondered out loud to her seahorse companions. "I hope Dimitri is okay."

Just thinking about the old man made Mik's heart sink. If only she'd gone to him sooner, Ivry might have survived. Mik wanted to honor her sister, and so along with caring for the seahorses, she felt that keeping her promise to the ocean protestors was a way to do it. Wiping a tear away, Mik went back to her desk to finish her letter.

Trash Island was not far from the refinery; it had felt the blast and then some. Tremors rippled through the heaps of garbage, toppling them, throwing rubbish into the air.

Chunks of stone and dust crumbled from the walls and ceiling of Ximu's cell. Waves of black, ashy smoke drifted in through his tiny box of a window, reeking of petroleum. Gasping and wheezing, Ximu slid out from under his bunk where he was hiding to avoid the falling debris, pushing his weak, frail body up to peek through the window. He looked up, the nearby inferno casting an orange glow on the clouds, and saw what he thought was the silhouette of giant flying horse with two heads, its wings outstretched. Ximu squinted up at the fantastical creature, and it was at that moment that he heard a voice in his head, telling him that Perl close by.

"My Honeybee," the old monk forced a smile, the first in quite some time.

He stepped down from the concrete ledge, uttering a prayer to Ever.

Just then, the metal lock on his dungeon door clanked. Ximu heard the jingling of keys and assumed it was the wind, when the heavy iron door swung open and a shaft of light cascaded into the cell. There, filling up the doorway, stood Brother Victr; he held up an electric torch, illuminating his wrinkled, worried face.

Ximu chuckled at the sight of his dear friend. He cleared his throat, trying to find his voice in all the swirling dust.

"Brother Victr...are...are you a dream?" The old monk croaked, then doubled over, a coughing fit racking his ailing body.

"No, Brother. It's me." Victr ran and caught the elder monk in his arms. "Time to go home."

38 FALSE LIGHT

Perl stepped through the smoldering orange portal, Fortis drawn, the rusty shield she'd picked up thrown over one shoulder. She was hit with a blast of heat. Stretched out before the girl was a bleak, colorless landscape. Everywhere, hundreds of enormous volcanic chimneys twisted up out of the ground into the thick, gray haze above.

"Giant skeleton fingers," Perl thought, walking up to one. She placed her hand on the rough, pale rock, then pulled it back quickly— "Ow!" The stacks were steam vents; piping hot.

Along the ground were clusters of bleached white coral, some reaching nearly ten feet. Perl heard a low rumbling sound above her. From the tops of the vents she saw hot gas billowing out. Flecks of ash drifted down like snow, clouding the already hazy landscape. Staring up at the vents slack-jawed, Perl closed her mouth to keep from swallowing the soot. Within a few minutes, she was covered head to toe in the powdery embers. Perl looked at the back of her hand. The strange-looking flakes were similar to the ones she had seen floating inside one of the Globus Natura bubbles, the ones Papa Ximu called "the things that make up life." She studied their intricate, multi-faceted patterns.

"What are you all doing *here?*" she asked the tiny specks, scanning her surroundings. *"What am I doing here?"* the voice in her head added.

She glanced back to where the portal had been, and a wave of dread washed over her. The door was gone, as well as her friends. She'd never missed them more than in this very moment.

Perl looked around at the hellish terrain before her; except for the noise from the steam vents, it was quiet. There didn't appear to be another soul in this ill-begotten place.

"This is it..." Perl thought nervously. Remembering her meditation training, she closed her eyes and took a few slow, deep breaths. "Okay, Fortis, it's just you and me."

It was unbelievably hot; the air was dense and sour, as Victr would say to Perl on foggy mornings, "thick as pea soup." Her shield now in front of her, Perl took small careful steps, following one of many snakelike trails that curled around the forest of volcanic stacks. The path she was on was wet, packed sand, dotted here and there with puddles of water. She bent down and dipped her finger into one of the small pools at her feet. The liquid was scalding hot. Perl put her finger in her mouth— "Blecch!" It tasted like highly concentrated salt; way saltier than even the ocean. *"Am I in the Dark Realm?"* Her heart began to race.

The stifling heat was like a weight on Perl's back, pressing down on her, sapping her energy. Perl pulled off her heavy hooded robe, tying it around her waist, slinging her backpack over one shoulder. Her Harmony top was soaking wet; tiny beads of perspiration prickled up over her entire body, and her frizzy hair drooped to one side in the humidity.

Perl's spots began to glow, helping to illuminate her way. Stopping to try to catch her breath in the mugginess, Perl noticed dozens of long, spindly, yellow-gray worms wriggling out from holes in the sand. "Bobbit worms," she frowned, carefully stepping around their hungry, snapping jaws. A worm nearly three feet long came at her, its pincers open to strike. Perl pulled her leg back, knowing that a bite from one of them injected a deadly toxin. *"Not a place to fall deathly ill, Perl,"* she thought to herself, stabbing at the ground with her sword, scaring the menacing worm back into the sand.

Perl picked up her pace, following the labyrinth of trails, albeit with no idea which way to go or what to be looking for. Some of the pathways narrowed when two stacks grew together, nearly closing off the trail. Perl was forced to squeeze sideways through those, careful not to scrape against the hot, craggy rock. She held Fortis up, readying herself for whatever unspeakable thing may come, but still she saw nothing.

As she meandered from trail to trail, Perl felt like she was trapped inside some kind of nightmarish snow globe, all alone, lost forever. She began to softly hum, trying to calm her nerves. An albino crab the size of her backpack scuttled across the path and over the top of her foot. Perl jumped, holding in a slight scream.

"Well, I'm not *totally* by myself," she kidded. Seeing the crab reminded her of Yule Island, and the real reason why she was here in the first place. "I can do this," she told herself, reciting her team's name in her head— "The Fearless Protectors Of Nature's Curious Jewels, Little to Big."

Perl kept going, winding around endless bends, seeking out her enemy. She lifted her voice, singing loudly, no longer caring about whether or not anyone was listening.

"I am of the liiight...I am of the sea...Ever is by my siiide..."

All at once, the already oppressive heat intensified, as if someone had cranked up the thermostat to full blast. Rivulets of sweat dripped down Perl's face. She stopped to wipe her brow when she heard it; through the gray mist came a low-pitched gurgling sound— *"Haaggghh...haaaggghh..."*

"Was that laughter?" Perl gripped Fortis with both hands, knuckles white, waving the narwhal tusk back and forth.

Her eyes darted around, trying to figure out where the noise was coming from. She heard it again, louder this time— *"Haaggghh...haaaggghh..."*

"W-Where are you?" She confronted the grotesque voice, her bioluminescence glowing brighter than ever.

"You ssseek a truth..." the voice teased, *"...you will only find deaaath..."*

Perl's grip on her sword was slipping; she wiped her hands on her pants. "Come out and face me, Slaughterman! I know you're here! Show yourself!"

Her voice reverberated off the volcanic vents. She searched for any signs of movement, but there was nothing but the fall of the gray ashy snow. From the shadows, the thing belched out another laugh. Perl bristled, sensing the thing was mocking her.

"Why are you hiding, Slaughterman? Or should I say, Malblud?" Perl shouted back, her fear shifting to anger.

"Chillld of Noaa."

The hair on the back of Perl's neck stood on end at the sound of her father's name on the monster's tongue. She inched along the path, rounding steaming vent after steaming vent, eyes wide, weapon held high. Perl wiped more sweat from her face. "Where are you, you coward?!"

"I fear nothing…" it growled.

Perl jumped around the next bend ready to strike, but still the path was empty. She called out, "it's easy to hurt a helpless animal, but a lot harder to—". Perl paused; above her, a ball of yellow light could be seen, suspended in the air near one of the smoldering stacks about fifty paces away. Perl inched towards the light, drawn to it like a moth to a flame. She continued talking; the eerie silence being far more unbearable.

"You don't wanna show yourself? Huh?"

"Sssuch ssspirit…" hissed the creature.

"I'm not afraid of you!" Perl realized she was now yelling at the top of her lungs.

"But you ssshould be!" it bellowed back to Perl, its voice seething with hatred.

The bioluminescent spots on Perl's face and arms were like a torch, guiding her along the sandy footpath. Her lights intensified the closer she got to the pale-yellow spotlight. From the darkness, Perl heard the sound of the thing taking in a great wheezing gulp of air.

"Ahh…I sssmell your father'sss blood…the vampire sssquid…" the voice hissed.

"Liar!" Perl was now directly under the orb. It hung several stories above her, clouded by a thick veil of steam.

The chimney Perl was next to was one of the largest she had seen, nearly fifty feet across. Perl wondered if what it had said was true—*Was her father a vampire squid? Was she, too? Or was the creature just taunting her?* Perl gritted her teeth, staring up at the glowing sphere.

Close enough to see now, Perl noticed a dark curved pole like a lamp post jutting out of a large hole about halfway up the side of the volcanic tower, the glowing bulb dangled off the end of it. Perl thought it looked like a mouth holding a lit pipe. She noticed the vent's surface; long streaks of brown, oily liquid ran down its sides. Perl followed the trails back up; the liquid seemed to be coming from the hole where the light pole stuck out.

"Are you up there?" Perl slapped Fortis on the side of the stack.

Up above, a retching sound could be heard as black foam poured out of the hole like vomit. Perl jumped away quickly as globs of the tar-like sludge came splashing down. She watched as the luminous yellow orb wobbled back and forth like a fishing lure.

"A lure big enough to catch a whale!" For some reason, Bear's voice popped into her head.

Perl took a few more steps back, keeping her eyes locked on the light, wondering what to do next. She didn't have to wait long.

An enormous bony claw, more than twice the size of a grizzly bear's paw, reached out of the hole. The rough, scaly hand was covered in barnacles; long black nails gripped the lip of the opening. A second paw appeared. Perl heard an awful scraping sound as the creature inside slowly wrenched itself out from the dark hollow.

Perl stood frozen, staring up in horror. *"What is that? What is that? What is that?"*

Something—a shadow; blacker than a shadow—emerged. The dangling bulb cast a sickly yellow-green light on it as Perl's brain tried to comprehend what she was looking at. It was, by all counts, a nightmare come to life. The thing had an enormous, almost cartoonish mouth, the swollen folds of flesh stretched back to reveal a twisted cage of razor-sharp teeth. The thing's fangs were so long, its lower jaw looked unhinged, locked in a ghastly frown. A sound like nails on a chalkboard could be heard as the ugly beast heaved, freeing itself from the hole, emerging with a roar. It was pinkish-gray in color, like rotting flesh, dark blotches and tumors covered its body. Its lumpy, disproportionately-sized head was covered in barbed quills and spiked fins. Mucus dripped from its many open gashes and sores.

"Oh Ever," Perl gasped, her stomach turning, her hands going ice cold. She could barely hold on to her sword, which hung limply at her side.

The lamppost was the creature's antenna, jutting out from between its two lifeless black eyes. Perl thought it looked like some kind of mutated anglerfish or deformed barracuda, but neither accurately described the beast that hovered above her.

"Not what you expected, I sssee…" The thing's downturned mouth hung wide open as it spoke, its slurring lisp almost comical if it weren't so terrifying.

Perl stumbled backwards as the being pushed the rest of its blubbery torso out of the cavity, the sharp edges of the hole ripping and cutting its body as it squeezed out. Perl had never been so terrified. This thing was not the Slaughterman…this was no man at all.

The beast crouched down, balancing on the lip of the opening like a gargoyle, staring down at Perl. She gazed up at it. It looked ancient, its worn, scaly skin sagging off its bones. Battle scars crisscrossed its leathery sides, and a host of snake-like serpents hung off it like tinsel on a Christmas tree.

Perl recognized the slimy gray eels. *"Lamprey."*

However, unlike the ones that had tried to attack Perl at the cave pool, these were three times bigger. The parasites clung to the monster's torso, suctioned to it by their needle-like teeth.

"Who are you?" Her throat bone dry, Perl strained to talk.

Her bioluminescence pulsed, exposing new rows of spots on her arms; she looked like a glow-in-the-dark leopard. In the vast, foggy emptiness, only the glow of Perl's spots and the thing's antenna light stood out.

"I am darknesss...I am shadowsss..."

Perl re-gripped her sword and slipped behind a stack off to her right, pressing her back up against it. The heat was unbearable; her back was drenched. Perl noticed that the monster was so wall-eyed, it had to continually shift its head back and forth in order to see her.

"Where did you come from?" she yelled up to it.

"Born from fire...as isss all..." Malblud croaked, *"...I watched your miserable kind firssst crawl out of the sssea..."* The evil being coughed up phlegm; tarry liquid leaked from its open sores. *"...the stacks hold the sssecrets of life...secretsss..."* It searched for Perl, the slivers of white in its eyes tinged with red.

"You...little sssecret...you will not leave here..."

Like flinging the reed for Quantaa, Perl flung her shield as far as she could. The creature hissed, twisting its head, scouring the area, its eyes darting here and there. Perl reached around, fumbling through the pockets of her backpack for the vial of *Hippomane Mancinello* poison. She held Fortis out in front of her as she tried to buy more time.

"Why do you hate me? Who am I to you?"

Malblud's eyes narrowed, locating the girl's bio-glow. *"You are a lie..."*

Perl pulled the vial from her backpack. "Oh—!" She squeaked; it slipped out of her sweaty hand, bouncing and landing on the sandy pathway. *"Oh thank Ever...it didn't break."*

"I don't understand." Perl peeked her head out. "What lie?"

Malblud lurched forward, his monstrous head low between his shoulder blades, clutching the ledge with his talons. *"My desiresss were deemed an abomination to the Light...yet you were allowed to live!"* The beast let out a horrible roar— *"Arrggghhh!"* It clung to the side of the chimney, a shadow against the pale, skeletal stack. *"...Ever mussst suffer...for what was denied me..."*

Perl wasn't sure what the creature was talking about, and more importantly, she didn't care. "I don't believe you!"

"Ever's preciousss humanity!" The creature ripped a claw down the side of the vent.

Chunks of rock and debris fell to the ground, bouncing and rolling near Perl. The creature turned, craning upwards at the smoky gray sky. It banged on the vent's wall angrily, the lamprey eels squirming and wiggling to hang on.

Perl's spots blazed and her knees were shaking as she retrieved the poison, sprinting across the path to another large stack. She held the vial and waited as Malblud continued, its fury growing.

"I watched them...protected their world...I was loyal...to what end?? To have a lawless creator disobey its own decree..." Malblud began to crawl down the side of the stack, its jaw quivering in rage, beady eyes darting around, searching for Perl. *"Your exissstence is my pain...you mussst die, so that the Earth diesss...hope diesss..."*

Perl knew she needed to get the creature close to use Humboldt's poison. "You said that you once cared for humans, protected us...then why destroy our oceans?"

Like a panther, Malblud leaped from the volcanic tower, landing with a thunderous crash. Perl cowered as the Dark Realm Being stood just a few feet in front of her, the screeching gray eels scrambling to reattach to their host. The creature was nearly five times Perl's size; it reeked of blood and rot. Perl noted it had wings, like those on a flying fish. However, it looked as though they were too small to ever lift its immense weight.

"I use humanity to dessstoy humanity..." Malblud stomped towards Perl on short, thick reptilian legs, dragging its arms, thrashing its head back and forth. *"To punish Ever..."* Perl's spots were beaming like strobe lights.

"The imposter Ever allowed your father's wantsss to bear fruit...while I was cassst out...my love taken from me!!"

Perl readied her hand on the vial. *"I've gotta get it to swallow the poison."* She thought maybe she could toss it into its gaping mouth, but with its long, jagged teeth, the jar might simply bounce off. She couldn't take that chance. *"Think, Perl..."*

The beast's barbed mouth bobbed up and down as it closed in on Perl. *"In the darkness there is sweet nothingness...I will help humanity to it!"* Long strands of slime dripped from its many wounds.

A light came on in Perl's mind. *"I'll tell him a story!"* She flicked the cork off the top of the vial with her thumb. It popped off, landing next to her foot.

"What isss that?!" it growled.

Shaking like a leaf, Perl answered the beast, "it—it's...a peace offering." She held up the vial of milky white liquid, her hand quivering, trying not to spill any. "It's from an enchanted forest in Venusto. It allows you to go back in time...y-you can find the love you lost!"

Quick as a snake, Malblud lunged forward, snatching it from Perl, leaving sticky green slime and long scratches on her arm.

"Venusssto…?" He held the jar up to his shiny black eye, examining it closely.

"Um, yes…all you have to do is drink it and your wish will be granted." Perl forced a smile; her stomach doing flip-flops. Malblud looked at the vial as Perl held her breath.

The monster unhinged its massive jaws and emptied the milky liquid into its mouth, running a long, greasy purple tongue across its lips. *"Child of Everrr…"* it hissed. Before Perl could react, it seized her by the neck. *"You must dieee—"* The thing's pupils suddenly dilated. It coughed, then spat; white foam bubbled up at the corners of its mouth. Malblud dropped Perl to the ground, clutching at its throat as it tried to scream— *"Sgggrrreeeaagghh!"* Perl heard a fizzy, gurgling sound. She held her nose as the awful smell of burning flesh filled the air.

The girl said a silent thank you to Humboldt as she ran, ducking behind a vent a safe distance away. Holding her sword up, Perl listened, waiting for the creature to draw its last breath. Malblud let out a long, raspy croak as it staggered backwards, leaning against a stack; sticky yellow bile dripped from its mouth.

"It worked," Perl thought, *"I can't believe it."*

Malblud's choking grew louder as it desperately gasped for air. It slumped to the ground, its massive head plopping forward with a heavy thump. Spasms ran through its body as its webbed claws grabbed at the sand in desperation. Several of the lampreys let go, scurrying away from the taste of poison now coursing through their host's veins. Malblud's yellow orb dimmed to a cloudy gray.

The air was eerily calm as thick clouds of dark steam rose off the creature's body. Perl was afraid to move. She peeked around the stack and saw Malblud in a heap, motionless, its black eyes now ghostly white. Gathering up the courage, she slowly approached and poked the monster with her sword. It was still alive, but barely.

Perl lowered Fortis, staring down at the pathetic creature lying before her. The thing's breathing was shallow. "What happened to you?" she asked it, "how did you become this?"

Perl looked around, wondering where to go and what to do now that Malblud had been defeated. Nothing had changed—the stacks continued to blow their steam, filling the sky with ash. It was still hot, and there wasn't an escape portal to be seen. Perl thought about her friends. She wondered where they were, if they were safe. She thought of Quantaa, and Papa Ximu, and—

One of the creature's milky white eyeballs rolled back to black. It reached out to grab Perl; she screamed and ran as the foul beast forced itself upright. It convulsed in a bout of wet coughs, the coughing turning to laughter.

"Ssstupid chillld..." it cackled, stretching its arms and wings out wide. *"Death tree sssap? You dare think that isss enough to dessstroy me?? I sit at the arm of the one who givesss death its venom...The Ullen...The One True Almighty!"*

Perl covered her ears. "No...no...it can't be! The Fawn promised it would work!"

She recalled Papa mentioning The Ullen, but just once, for even the very uttering of its name brought ill omens. This was the most fallen of all Beings—it ruled the Dark Realm, and was the very antithesis of Ever, feeding on pain, and hate, and destruction. Perl ducked behind a vent, her heart fluttered like a bird in her chest and she couldn't stop trembling. *"Why did I think I could do this? Why?"*

A lump formed in her throat and she tried to swallow, but couldn't. A few tears streamed down her amber cheeks, dropping to the warm, ashy sand below, and for the very first time, no tiny green sprouts sprang up. Perl appealed to Ever to protect her in this cursed land of the dead.

39 LOPHIUS

Malblud stretched, the small bones in his neck and vertebrae cracking. It called out to Perl as it staggered down the path, *"now I sssee you for what you really are...a killer...like all humanity..."* It craned its blob of a head, its soulless eyes searching for the glow of Perl's light.

"Chosssen One, indeed...", it mocked, *"...your heart is blacknesss..."* As it limped forward, the eels slithered under its webbed feet, re-attaching to their wicked host. *"If death was your peace offering...than I ssshall offer the sssame in return..."*

Spotting the tip of a sword poking out from behind a chimney, the beast lunged, swiping at it with a loud grunt. At the last second Perl ducked just as the creature's heavy paw smacked against the vent above her head, its blackened claws like giant fish hooks. All Perl could do was run. Darting around the stacks, twisting and turning along the endless pathways, the intense heat pounding her small body, Perl felt as if she were in a bad dream; a hunted animal in a haunted forest.

"I will have my revenge...Ever will sssuffer as I have sssuffered...grieve as I have grieved!"

Perl ran faster than she ever had in her life, the creature not far behind, its ear-piercing shrieks cutting through the silence like an icy scalpel. Bobbit worms, hearing the noise, slithered out of their hiding places, savagely snapping at Perl's ankles as she passed, doing their master's bidding. Without stopping, Perl pulled out Fortis, cutting a few of the grotesque worms in half with the razor-sharp sword.

"There isss nowhere to run, child...I will crush you into dussst! Your ashes will float in the underworld for eternityyy..."

While dodging the gauntlet of wretched worms, Perl stole a quick look back. She didn't see Malblud, but could still hear its voice echoing off the smoke stacks. Perl's dread rose when she noticed she was leaving a trail of footprints in the sand.

"How did you not think of that, Perl?" she chided herself. Slowing a bit, she tried jumping from puddle to puddle to cover her tracks, when the sickening smell of rotten fish suddenly filled her nostrils.

Perl covered her mouth and nose, the stench unbearable. *"It's getting close."* She frantically searched for a place to hide, her heart racing. Perl paused, leaning against a stack to catch her breath.

"Focus, Perl," she urged herself. "You've got to focus." Perl inhaled slowly, trying to clear her mind. She thought back to all of the sessions with her masters. "I can do this..." For some reason, something Papa Ximu often said popped into her head—"When in doubt, Honeybee, look to nature."

Perl's green eyes darted around as Malblud's heavy footsteps grew louder. Not far off, she noticed a large clump of the bleached white coral and sprinted over to it. Using Fortis, Perl broke off pieces of the rocky sediment, enough to create a small opening. She crawled inside, squeezing down into a tight ball. The coral was dry, its edges rough. Untying her robe from around her waist, Perl draped it over herself to hide her spots. She rubbed the heavy wool between her fingers, thinking again of Papa Ximu. *"I wish I could jump into your arms right now."*

Malblud, who had been following the footprints, saw the tracks end. It hissed, *"you cannot hide from me, chiiilld…"* It ran its giant slimy hand along the surface of the nearest vent, gathering up condensation. "There isss no escape from here…"

Perl held her breath, lifting her robe just enough to peek out; the creature was a stone's throw away.

It placed its mangled, scaly foot into a puddle of hot, salty water. *"Perhapsss when I finish you, your preciousss spider monk shall be next, hmm?"* A low, menacing laugh curled from its lips.

Perl watched as Malblud ran its slimy foot back and forth across the water, almost as if it were feeling for something; a chill ran through body. *"Oh, Ever…it's the water…all this time, it's been the water…that's how he's known where I've been…"*

"What if the one you loved mossst was taken?" it peered around; eyes peeled for any sign of movement.

Perl could see his lizard-like feet moving towards her. She knew she had to do something but she was trapped; all she could do was put her head down and hope.

"What then, Chosssen One? Would you kill to sssave what you love? Ahhh, but you have tried that…"

Swallowing hard, sweat running into her eyes, Perl gripped Fortis with both hands, ready to drive it up into its guts as soon as the monster got close enough. She saw the beast stop right in front of the coral, its sour smell nearly making her gag. Malblud stood wheezing above her.

"Now!" the voice in her head ordered. "Do *it now!"* Perl tensed up like a bowstring, seconds from striking, when she heard a high-pitched buzzing sound.

Out of the foggy mist, a swarm of Whisper Wisps appeared; part of Malblud's cursed army of spies. The wretched creatures flitted around, whispering to their dark master. Perl listened, but couldn't make out what they were saying. Malblud grumbled; whatever the Wisps were saying angered it. Perl shivered as the beast bellowed.

"Enough!" Malblud pounded a fist on the vent directly above Perl,

cracking it down the middle. The Wisps scattered. *"Foolish chiiilld…you believe humanity will change over such a meaningless gesssture as a seahorsssse?! Nonsensssse!"* The beast ripped off a huge chunk of the coral, exposing the frightened girl, *"…no one act can make a difference!"* Black saliva dripped on her robe.

Perl huddled there, vulnerable; like a roly-poly bug when the rock is lifted. Holding the piece of coral high over his head, Malblud screamed, *"The children of Everr are unworthy! They are weeeaak!"* Malblud hurled the coral against the stack; it shattered into white powder.

"Seahorse? Perl thought, *"the ones I gave the twins?"* Something deep within Perl stirred; the fire that had always burned in her heart was raging. "I! Am! Not! Weak!!" She leaped out of the coral patch, dragging Fortis across its rough, scaly hide. Blood oozed down its side like spilled paint.

Malblud let out a howl and spun to face Perl, its jagged rows of teeth just feet away from her. *"You were born of the darkesst depthsss of the ocean…void of light!"*

Perl, her adrenaline pumping, screamed back at the creature, "I am nothing like you!" She swung Fortis with all of her might, slashing across its glowing orb.

The creature winced as yellow fluid sprayed from the dangling bulb; its black eye noticed Perl's sword.

"A Monodon monoceros sword…how clever…"

As Perl drew the weapon back for a second blow, Malblud caught the girl by the wrist, squeezing her tiny hand in his mighty talon, forcing her to drop it.

"But not nearly enough, chiiillld…"

The evil beast lifted Perl into the air by her arm like a rag doll. Perl frantically swung her feet, kicking at its bloated torso. She hit a few of the lampreys, who let go of their host, screeching angrily as they slithered away.

"Let go of me!" Perl cried.

The creature ignored her pleas. Perl stared into the creature's cold, dead eye, hoping to find a trace of a soul behind the darkness.

"I have waited centuriesss…" Malblud cracked its jaws open, its teeth shining like wet daggers, ready to devour the girl.

"Nooo!" Perl continued to kick the creature.

Malblud laughed pitilessly, a film of yellow bile from the poison now dry on his lips. Perl tried to pry herself from his grip, but the thing was incredibly strong. She kicked and struggled, but it was no use; she had no options left. The threat of death looming in front of her, Perl stopped fighting and went limp; a strange calmness washed over her. Words she had written in her sketchbook, written not so long ago but now felt like another lifetime, flashed in her mind— *"Love pulls light from the darkness."* Perl closed her eyes.

"Ssso you're prepared to die?" Malblud shook Perl.

Her eyes fluttered but stayed closed. Her voice shaky, she began to sing the whale's song.

"Every day I take a breath and hold it tight,
hoping you see me, but you float on by…"

"—??" Malblud flinched, its eyes narrowing; somewhere, deep within the twisted recesses of its tortured mind, it had heard that melody before…eons ago…*but where? Who?"*

Perl's tone growing steadier;

"…as the tides topple over, we need your light,
still you don't seem to care this is our Earth…"

Malblud, still groggy from the poisonous sap, bristled, confused. It shook the girl violently. *"Ssilence!"*

Instinctively, Perl put her feet against its lumpy, bruised face, bracing herself as she kept singing.

"…There's still magic to believe,
some love that binds us…"

Malblud pulled at her but Perl resisted, her boots sinking into its flesh like wet sand, her notes like daggers. *"Ssstop sssinging!!"*

As Malblud's fury grew, the heat around them became unbearable. Perl fell into an almost trance-like state, the sweat pouring down her face. Her mind drifted back to when she had first heard the whale's song, back home in her little bathtub; she smiled. Both of Perl's legs were sinking farther into Malblud's gray blubber; now up to her shins.

"…just promise not to leave,
I need you to breath…
…please come home…"

Malblud screamed, doubling over in pain; its abdomen was on fire. Jarred by the outburst, Perl woke, blinking her eyes. Malblud still held her. She gazed at the creature staring back at her, pus oozing from its bloodshot eyes and mouth. Its antenna, no longer lit, flopped lifelessly against the creature's side. For an instant, Perl actually felt pity for the pathetic thing.

"The whales," Perl said, a puzzled look on her face, "they weren't singing to me, they were singing to you."

Malblud tugged at the girl, her boots pushing against his scaly hide. The vine holding Perl's anklet snapped, lodging the pearl in its side.

"Aaggghh!" Malblud cried. He flung Perl away. She flew through the falling ash, smacking hard into the side of a chimney.

Malblud's vision went fuzzy. The creature slumped to the ground, moaning, as a blur of images flashed in his mind—*It could see Perl through her own eyes, feel her every thought and emotion, as if becoming the girl. Malblud felt all the anguish inside her—losing a father she had never gotten the chance to know, feeling abandoned, and ostracized, and scared. All this suffering, all by his hand.* Malblud winced, clutching his side as the pain worsened, the visions continuing— *Now he felt all the love Perl had—for her monks, her friends, nature; she had understood the sacrifices her parents had made to keep her safe, and she forgave them.*

Malblud shook his head furiously, screaming, writhing in pain as he tried desperately to escape this fever dream. He called out to Perl, who lay face down in a puddle a few feet away.

"Get out of my head, wretched chiiilld..." Malblud dragged himself over to the girl. A trickle of blood ran down her face. Pulling her upright, the creature mustered what little strength it had left, prying open its tight, aching jaws, ready to devour the girl. *"I...will have...my vengeance..."*

At that moment, another wave of spasms racked the beast; its mind filling with more disturbing visions—*Flashing back to the day it had climbed out of the sea and onto dry land, to the home of Noaa and Dianna, the very day the couple's daughter had been born—Malblud had gone there with one purpose, to murder them. It felt the fear in Dianna's heart as she clutched her newborn baby, watching helplessly— Malblud could taste the despair in Noaa as his life came to an end.*

The visions were unbearable, the pain was excruciating. Malblud wailed, wanting it all to end. It fell over, blacking out.

"Father!" Perl mumbled, clawing at the air.

Like Malblud, she was seeing the visions as well, the watery ground a link between their minds—*Perl watched as her mother ran from the house screaming, holding baby Perl in her arms—Master Tryfon arriving too late to save Noaa—Him yelling at Dianna to head to the sea and find the blue whale near the cliff's ledge— Malblud chasing after Perl's mother but stopped by Tryfon's ethereal light—Tryfon calling to the creature, "Lophius. You have caused enough suffering."—Malblud rejecting the light, fleeing to the ocean depths...*

A wave of pain snapped Perl back to the present. She reached up, feeling a gash on her head; when she looked down, her hand was covered in blood. "Tryfon...help...me..." Perl slipped out of consciousness.

The two Beings lay next to one another in the eerie stillness, flakes of soot and ash falling on them like snow.

Perl woke first, blurry-eyed and confused; her head throbbed. Near her, Malblud began to stir.

"You...you were a Light Protector..." Perl muttered, scooting away from the creature.

Malblud exhaled a wet, heavy sigh. *"Liesss..."*

"Your name...was Lophius...you were a—"

"Enough!" The strange burning in its stomach intensified. *"You...will dieeeuuggghhh..."* Twisting in anguish, the Being ripped and clawed at its scales, drawing blood. *"What did you do to me...wicked...little—"* It coughed and gagged; plumes of yellow gas began to waft out of its body as if its

insides were on fire.

Perl saw her chance to get away. She groped along the sandy floor. *"Fortis, where are you?"* Dark spots danced in her eyes and her arms and legs felt like lead. Perl collapsed. She tried to move but couldn't, as blood seeped into her roots, turning them a deep red.

An unexpected rush of cool air hit Perl, blowing the soot and ash off her. She rolled over and saw a tall figure in shining armor bathed in a soft, violet light.

"...Uriel?"

"Rest, young one. I am here."

Uriel—her Light Protector, her guardian—had come. The warrior picked up Fortis; it was tiny in her hands. She marched over to the creature.

Perl could feel herself fading fast. She squinted, making sure Uriel was truly there, and that's when she saw her wing; one, beautiful, angelic wing.

Perl mumbled, "Uriel...where's your...other..." Her head dropped. The world went black.

Uriel stood over the ancient creature. Malblud, spewing blood and vomit, spat at her.

"Broken One...you are no match for meee..."

"There is mercy for those who seek it." The glow around Uriel intensified, lighting up the entire pathway through the labyrinth of smoking towers.

"It isss far too late for that now..." Malblud looked past Uriel to where Perl lay motionless. *"The Earth diesss...soon they will all be gone...but that one..."* it gestured feebly at Perl, *"that one isss mine..."*

Uriel could see the beast was in great pain. "Lophius!" Uriel called to him, using his real name; the name given to him by Ever.

It sneered at Uriel. Rolling onto all fours, it lowered its head like a bull. Malblud rumbled towards them, teeth bared, eyes locked on the girl.

Uriel leaped forward, grabbing hold of the spindly rod protruding from the beast's head. She climbed up onto its blotchy, scarred back; Malblud snarled.

"Know your truth!" She bellowed, driving Fortis straight down into its spine.

The Dark Realm creature bucked like a wild animal as Uriel plunged the sword deeper into its blubber. With a painful howl, Malblud's legs gave out; it crumpled head first into the sand. Uriel twisted the ivory narwhal tooth. "Remember, Lophius!"

"I feel...nothing..." Malblud uttered. The few remaining lampreys slithered into the shadows.

Uriel leaned over, staring into his wild, bloodied eye. "You are of the Light!"

Malblud lay limp in the sand, its body crippled with pain. *"That sword..."* he cried, *"I...I know him..."*

Its eyes rolled back white as another vision took hold—*A great ocean battle was raging. He was much younger; much stronger, fighting with the Light Realm Protectors against the forces of the Dark Realm. His narwhal companion was by his side, swinging his mighty tusk valiantly. An enemy had snuck up behind Lophius and was about to bring its axe down when the narwhal dove in front of him, taking the fatal blow.*

"...Spero..." Malblud whispered.

Uriel pressed Fortis harder into the evil creature, trying to awaken him, but the malevolent forces that lived in Malblud were powerful, unrelenting. She could feel the Darkness taking hold of the sword, trying to turn its power against her. Uriel yanked the weapon out; the tip of it was charred black.

Oily blood poured from Malblud's wounds, forming a spreading pool in the wet sand. With Malblud subdued, it was time to get Perl to safety. The Light Protector slid off the wretched creature, returning Fortis to Perl's backpack.

"It's time to go," Uriel said, tucking Perl safely under her wing.

Malblud groaned, *"there will alwaysss be darknesss...you cannot...essscape it..."*

Uriel waved her arm in front of her, opening up a diamond-shaped portal. A white, blinding light poured out of it. Uriel looked back at the wounded beast.

"You know your truth, Lophius..." Uriel cradled Perl. "...and that she *is* the Chosen One." The Protector stepped through the glowing portal back into the Realm of Light.

Malblud hissed, *"all of usss cast shadowsss, Broken One...all of usss..."*

It tried to move, but couldn't. Humboldt's tree sap, the teardrop pearl from Master Tryfon, and the enchanted sword, forged from a fallen comrade, had crippled the Dark Right Hand of The Ullen. It stared at the portal, helpless.

Uriel and the child were gone, and sparkling rays now emanated from the other side, cutting through the gray haze. Shafts of light fell upon Malblud's dark, battered body, at once turning his skin from a sickly gray color to a vibrant turquoise. The vile creature—Malblud of the Dark Realm—was dying. His original form, created by Ever—Lophius—was being reborn. His angular skull and lamppost orb remained, yet his features softened, emanating a bright, luminescent glow. His soulless black eyes turned a pale ocean blue. A row of spikes across the top of his head remained, but rather than the tangled array of blackened spikes that had existed, they now gleamed a brilliant silver, almost crown-like. Lophius screamed as his body fought itself, and transformed back to the way he was.

A woman stepped through the portal. She made her way towards Lophius, her forest green gown rippling behind her like waves in the ocean.

Bright, polished beads glistened like diamonds in her long, silky raven hair. A cloud of twinkling, emerald light radiated from her.

Lophius, still too weak to move, tried to focus, but all he could make out was a fuzzy silhouette. His eyelids were heavy, his breathing hollow. *"Back, eh? Come to finish me?"* Lophius grunted; while his body tried to repair itself, his mind still resisted the Light.

The woman did not speak, but simply knelt down beside him.

"Be quick..." he said, squinting at the woman. As she leaned in, the light dimmed around her. Lophius saw her face. *"It...it cannot be."*

"Dear Lophius," the celestial woman smiled sweetly. Her brown almond-shaped eyes were warm and affectionate.

"Is this a trick? Meant to torment me?" Lophius turned his head away, shutting his eyes tightly. *"I will not look..."*

She placed a gentle hand on his rough cheek. "It's no trick, my love."

The warmth of her touch changed Lophius further. His teeth and claws shortened, while his tiny, useless wings grew long and powerful, turning a bright aquamarine. The burning in his chest was gone; he could feel his heart beating once again.

"...Coralena?" he murmured, his voice cracking. "...Coralena?"

"I'm here."

Lophius reached up, caressing the woman's cheek. A memory flashed in his mind—*it was the two of them, walking together along the shore; they were young, so very young.*

"My angel...it is you."

He strained to sit up, grimacing in pain.

"It's alright. You can rest now...rest."

Tears streamed down his face as he gazed into her beautiful dark eyes. "I longed for this day...to see your face...to hold your hand once more...then the darkness came...and I lost you."

"I know, my love," she laced her fingers into his webbed hand, "but you will suffer no more."

Lophius reached over, tenderly stroking her arm. "I don't understand...why...? Why did it have to be this way?"

"It is not for me to say, dear one. But there is still time for you. You heard the whale's song. The sea beckons you home." The tall, thin woman stood, gently freeing her hand from his. She moved towards the light. "I'm afraid I must go now."

"No...stay with me," he begged her.

She smiled. "I hope to, one day."

"Please," Lophius sobbed.

"Goodbye, my love. Goodbye." Coralena stepped back into the portal, the bright light dwindling as it closed.

Overcome with despair, unable to move, Lophius could only yell out,

"Coralena! Nooo!"

Defeated and heartbroken, Lophius gazed blankly into the gray emptiness above him. He clawed at the wet ground, ripping up handfuls of sand, the anguish eating away at his insides. The white stacks towered above him like the pale bones of the dead. Millions of particles of soot danced and swirled

in the sweltering hot air. It reminded Lophius of a starry night sky, much like ones long ago...with her.

"I...am alone..." he muttered under his breath, "there is...nothing..."

Lophius watched as the ashy particles caught fire, the orange embers raining down on him.

"Eternal isss the darknesss...you shall alwaysss be Malllblllud..."

"Ullen...?" Lophius called out weakly.

High above, a shape clung to one of the vents, unseen, its skin blending in to the white, rocky surface. Hearing Lophius' voice, its massive pair of large, ghostly eyes shot open. The shadow launched itself off the chimney, descending silently. As it did, its appearance changed; no longer a chalky white but gold with brown stripes. The massive undulating blob, its enormous tentacles splayed out in all directions, now floated along the ground, mirroring the sandy surface like a giant chameleon. It reached Lophius, hovering over his body.

Lophius unclenched his fists, letting the soft sand leak between his webbed fingers. "Ahhh...the Deceiver..." He cracked a slight smile, surprised to be witnessing an agent not of the Dark Realm, but of the Light.

The great octopus (*Thaumoctopus mimicus*) had been summoned by Master Tryfon to assist Uriel. The Being lowered itself onto Lophius, wrapping its great tentacles around him and lifting him as if he weighed next to nothing. As Lophius rose into the air, the small pearl that had been wedged in the scales of his abdomen dropped to the sand below.

The shapeshifting octopus reached the top of one of the steam vents, and with a puff of cloudy black ink, disappeared down into the hole.

40 HORIZON

They had been home, safe and sound, for many hours. Uriel sat quietly at end of Perl's bed as she slept, softly strumming her gittern—a beautiful instrument, pear shaped, with winged cherubs etched onto the face of the rich mahogany wood. Perl stirred a bit, then rolled onto her back, listening to the gentle sound of the instrument's golden strings, her eyes still closed. She reached up, feeling something strange on her head; a heavy cloth bandage.

"Welcome back, young one."

She stretched, rubbing her eyes to clear the fuzziness. "Uriel?"

Perl realized she wasn't in her bunk bed in Venusto, but back in her cozy little room at the root cellar. "W-what happened? How did I get here?" she said weakly. Her whole body ached.

"Our friend Palo Santo visited you in the night. She treated your wounds."

"My wounds?" Perl licked her lips; her throat burned. "How did you find me?"

"Well, someone was ignoring the messages my *Hypercompe scribonia* were delivering…" Uriel swung the gittern over her shoulder. "So it was a bit trickier than it should have been to locate you." She raised an eyebrow.

"Um yeah, about that…"

"All is forgiven, no need to explain. Just rest."

Perl noticed the bump over Uriel's shoulder; she had wrapped up her wing once again. "Uriel…what happened," Perl's eyes gestured, "to your other wing?"

Uriel adjusted her lavender cape. "That's a story for another time."

"Oh, please? Please tell me. I'm not going anywhere," Perl said, pulling the covers up to her chin and snuggling in.

Uriel held her face in her hand. "When you're feeling better."

Perl frowned. "Okay then, what about Malbuld? Is he dead?"

Uriel placed her hand on Perl's leg, smiling wistfully. "His name is Lophius…and yes, he's gone, for now."

"For now?" A twinge of fear came over Perl. "He's still out there?"

"Only time will tell if the Being Lophius will truly heal, but as for now, he can do no harm to the world." Uriel shifted her weight on the straw mattress. "He's in a place where he cannot hurt you, or anyone you love, anymore."

Perl squinted at her guardian. "What place?"

"Trust me, young one." Uriel gave Perl's leg a gentle squeeze.

"I do," Perl smiled a big toothy grin. "Thank you for saving me, Uriel. I remember you showed up, right before Malbl—"

Uriel quieted the girl. "Perl, it was my duty and honor to be there for you."

Perl forced herself up, pulling her knees into her chest; a panicked look crossed her face as she reached under the covers. "Oh no, where is it?" She felt around the bed. "My pearl, it's gone! Can we go back?"

"There's no going back, Perl. The portal is sealed."

"But it was a gift from Tryfon! I must have lost it in the bog or in that horrible place with Malbl—Lophius."

"I'm so sorry," Uriel replied. "That pearl saved you both."

"What do you mean?"

"It was the magic from your tear that was infused into that pearl. It damaged Lophius immensely, because it was created from pure love. Only love can…"

Perl finished Uriel's sentence, "…pull light from the darkness."

"Yes." Uriel smiled. "It awakened him to his truth. Like you and your father Noaa, Lophius is a Water Light Being."

"I figured out that it was the water that somehow connected us."

Uriel nodded. "And because of your courage, your boundless love, and all that you learned at Callowhorn, the ocean's natural balance will begin to heal."

"I need to see for myself. Can we go see the Globus Natura?" Perl swung her legs over the side of the bed but Uriel pushed them right back up, pulling the blankets over her.

"There will be plenty of time for that. First, there's someone who'd like to say hello…"

Bursting through Perl's heart-shaped door, carrying a tray of freshly baked cinnamon cookies was her dear, sweet Papa Ximu. Seeing the girl awake, the old monk nearly tossed the wooden tray of snacks into the air with joy.

"My Honeybee!" Ximu spun around, hastily handing the tray to Regor, who was right behind the jolly monk.

"Perly!" Regor chuckled as the tray shook in his hands and his cheeks blushed.

"Oh, my sweet, sweet Bee! You're home!" Ximu dropped down on the bed. He bear-hugged the small girl, smothering her with hugs and kisses.

Perl laughed, squeezing him; she noticed how much thinner her beloved spider had become. "Oh, you're so thin, Papa. Look at you! Are you okay? Where's your round belly, my skinny spider?"

"What?" Ximu happily patted his stomach, "this is the new me! Strong as an ox!"

"I saw you in my dreams." Perl's eyes welled up. "You were in chains, and oil was pouring in...I tried but I couldn't get to you. It all felt so real."

"There, there, child. I'm fine, see?" Ximu held her face, wiping away a tear. "I'm right here, and all is well. I am so, so proud of you," he kissed her on her bandaged forehead.

"Um," Regor shyly approached awkwardly, holding out the plate of cookies. "Heh-heh...we all missed you, Perl...want a cookie?"

"I missed you too, Goaty-goat!" Perl swiped two off the tray, poking a finger in Regor's side, forcing a giggle out of him. "I've made so many magical new friends! I know you would love them! They all have such wonderful powers, like night vision, and electrified hair, and—oh! I have so many incredible stories to tell you! We battled a Roc! And solved puzzles inside anthills as big as mountains! And we saved a whole island of crabs, and—"

"Easy now, sweet Bee...you've just woken up." Ximu smiled, the twisted ends of his mustached curling up even more. "You can tell us all about your adventures at suppertime, mm?"

"I can't wait to hear them all, and I have a few to share with you, too!" Regor sat the tray on a side table, grabbing three cookies for himself. He took a bite; crumbs flew everywhere. "After you left, the whole island has been crazy, heh-heh! First, there was all the drama with the Redhots, then the rumors about the Twins, and oh yes, the protesters! And then yesterday, there was a huge explosion over at the gas pumps, and a terrible storm after that! The island shook something awful, and we all thought Mont Michel was gonna sink into the sea, isn't that right Brother Ximu? Heh, heh..."

"An explosion?" she asked, stifling a yawn. As much as Perl wanted to listen to her friend's stories, her eyelids were growing heavy again.

"Come now," Uriel stepped in, "Brother Ximu is right." She wiped the cookie crumbs off the quilt, then rested a heavy arm on Regor's bony shoulder. "Plenty of time to chat and share stories later. Perl, you must rest."

"You've had quite a knock to your noggin," Ximu said, springing to his feet. He cinched up his rope belt, which had much more slack than before, and kissed Perl on the top of the head, giving her unruly hair a fluff.

"But I just got up!" Perl fought the sleepiness, wanting so badly to share more stories. "I don't need to res—" another yawn took her before she could finish.

"Another nap will do you good, Bee. Regor, could you grab the tray, please?" Ximu gestured.

Realizing this was a fight she couldn't win, Perl handed Ximu her cookie, and fell back into the soft, cool pillow. "I suppose I could close my eyes for a minute or two."

At that, Uriel, Ximu, and Regor quietly left Perl's tiny room.

"Sweet dreams...Ever will watch over you." Ximu blew a kiss before closing the wooden door with a click.

A moment later, the door creaked open again; a small candlelight flickered from the hallway.

"Perly-poo? You asleep?" A burly figure lumbered over to her bedside.

Perl let out a small whimper. She lifted her drowsy eyes, slowly realizing who it was standing above her.

"Victr!"

"Shh, not too loud now," he cautioned. "They said you were resting, but I just wanted to welcome you home, dear." Victr pulled a small footstool over, his large frame struggling to balance on it. He set the candle down, the warm glow illuminating the deep creases on his face. "I heard you faced a dragon. A real nasty bugger. What say you, my noble knight?!"

Perl grinned cheek to cheek. How she missed home. It felt so good to be surrounded by family, the ones whose loving faces she knew by heart.

"It was scary, Victr! And exciting! And terrifying! And surprising! It was everything!"

Victr whispered, trying to take her volume down a notch, "such bravery, indeed. Sounds like you learned a library's worth of knowledge, eh?" He said, tucking the heavy wool quilt around her snugly.

"Victr..." Perl reached her hand out and held his fuzzy spider claw. "Nature is even more wondrous and magical than I could have ever imagined."

"More than *you* could imagine?" The stout monk gave her hand a squeeze, grinning; the worry marks on his forehead going away. "Then it must've been truly extraordinary." Victr could see the small girl was trying hard to stay awake. "Now listen, I will see you at supper. I have to go finish giving the potatoes a second rinsing." Placing the stool back into the corner, he watched her roll over, pulling the covers up around her.

"Be sure to make Papa an extra helping, okay?" Perl mumbled.

"I'll do just that, my little warrior." Victr grinned, closing the door behind him.

Inside the secret chapel, Ximu stood with his hands behind his back, inspecting the Globus Natura with his bifocals. He watched as the rotating orbs methodically spun overhead.

Regor, still munching on cookies, stood alongside Ximu. "How does it look? Are they balancing?"

Ximu looked over the top of his glasses at Regor, cookie crumbs stuck to his face. The monk chuckled, stroking his long, graying beard. "The murkiness in the Water Orb does seem to be clearing a bit."

Standing back in the arched doorway, Brother Basil stepped forward. He held open a large leather-bound book and was jotting down notes, the feathery quill dancing in his hand. He repeated Ximu's words back to himself, careful to get the wording right; *"Murkiness...clearing..."*

Ximu climbed up the spider-webbed lace wall. Butterflies, nestled in the delicate lattice fluttered around his head. Ximu adjusted his spectacles for a closer look at one particular orb that was wobbling off kilter.

"What is it, Brother?" Basil asked, ready to record more notes.

"The seeds in this Orb..." Ximu leaned out farther, "they don't look as fresh as they usually do."

Basil flipped through several pages, stopping at an ancient-looking map. He ran his finger along the page. "That would be The Arctic Orb?"

"Mm," mumbled Ximu, nodding. "Make a note of it." He scurried back down the webbing, tightening his robe belt. "But I would say The Water Orb seems to be recovering, praise Ever."

Basil scribbled notes in the margins, then pulled a fern from his robe pocket to mark the page. He closed the textbook, tucking it neatly under his arm.

High above Perl's cozy root cellar bedroom, at the summit of Mont Michel, a meeting was about to take place. Gretar sat twiddling his thumbs, anxiously waiting at a table on the Palace's golden veranda. The table was set for two. Tall crystal glasses with fresh cucumber water and conch shells overflowing with exotic tropical fruit had been placed in front of him. Gretar looked with confusion at the five pieces of silverware neatly resting on a silk napkin, wondering why anyone needed five utensils to eat one meal. Out on the manicured lawn, peacocks, flamingos, and golden pheasants paraded around.

Gretar grabbed a fresh blueberry and popped it into his mouth; it was like an explosion of sweet, juicy goodness. *'I can't remember the last time I had a fresh blueberry,'* he thought. He swiped a fistful of them, shoving them into his front shirt pocket just as Mik Graves emerged though a pair of rose-tinted glass doors. Her nanny stood in the doorway, arms crossed.

"Thank you, Ruby, that will be all," Mik said with a dismissive wave.

"I can stay if it would make you feel more..." Ruby eyed the strange boy in the rumpled clothing, "...comfortable."

"That won't be necessary."

Ruby slowly slid the door closed. The boy watched as the overprotective woman watched him from behind the pink glass.

Both Mik and her governess wore all black, still mourning Ivry's death. Mik's long, tufted gown covered every inch of her; the dark silk shimmering in the sunlight. A stiff, scalloped collar wrapped behind her head like vampire wings. The girl's famous red hair was styled in a row of five tight buns, running from ear to ear. Holding her hair in place were both her and her sister's cherished blue butterfly pins.

Seeing Mik, Gretar stood, suddenly feeling a twinge of nervousness. The twin looked much more beautiful than the day he pulled her out of the polluted seas near Trash Island. He hastily tried tucking in his shirt, but half of it still hung out the back. Mik strolled purposely to the table.

"Thank you for keeping your word," Gretar held out his hand, "and agreeing to see me."

Mik looked at his hand as if it were a bucket of chum.

"Sit," she directed, "and just so we're clear…what we're doing here right now? Why I agreed to see you? This is all for my sister. Just know that."

Gretar stared at the girl's fiery red hair. "Uh, no…I mean yes, of course." His mind briefly went blank. *"What is wrong with me?"* he thought, running a hand through his hair. "I, uh…I have to say, many Earthers are surprised by your sudden change of heart, Miss Graves."

Gretar leaned forward, placing his hands on the crystal table. Realizing they were dirty, he pulled them off immediately, wiping them on his pants.

"And you? What do you think…Gretar?" Mik asked, tapping her elbow-length fingerless gloves on the table. Her nails were painted black; they *click-click-clicked* hypnotically while she spoke.

"If I'm being completely honest, yes," he stammered, taking a drink, then examining the glass carefully. "Wow, this water is crystal clear." Gretar looked over at the girl, who sat staring blankly at him. "Let's just say I was one of the very few that had faith in you…that you'd keep your promise," he said.

"I can't…" Mik swallowed hard; her face softened. "I won't, allow Ivry's death to be without meaning. I made her a promise as well, and it's one I will never, ever break."

"Uh-huh," Gretar was listening, but also found himself staring longingly into her eyes; they were bright blue, like a summer sky—

"Are you even listening to me?" Mik snapped.

Embarrassed, Gretar took a slice of pineapple and shoved it into his mouth. "Hm? Yeah…yes, of course…go on."

"You have to believe me. I had no idea what my father had done, or is currently doing, to the oceans. I never realized how sheltered my world was…starting with the view out my own window. You can see, from this side of the Palace, there isn't a drop of trash as far as the eye can see."

Gretar took another drink, not bothering to look. "I'm more than aware of the ropes they use to keep the filth from coming to this side of the island," he said, now thinking of his fellow demonstrators. "Our boats are forced to float in it every day, which turned out to be lucky for you, didn't it?" He looked into Mik's eyes; she held his gaze, then looked away, her cheeks turning a soft pink.

"I, uh, I've also come to find out that my father reviews all the news feeds coming in, blocking what he doesn't want me to know."

The boy took another drink of water, taking in the lush surroundings;

the perfectly manicured topiary, the fancy gold railing and expensive marble tiles, the teams of servants. It never even crossed Gretar's mind that the twins were unaware of what their father was doing to them or the oceans. In a way, they were victims, too. "Okay, so why am I here? What's the plan?"

"I know why Ivry made me promise to look after the seahorses." Mik looked at the boy, this time holding his gaze. "I'm ready to give a voice to the vulnerable."

"You're willing to join our cause?" Gretar perked up. "What about your father?"

"My father has had his chance, and I'm starting to realize the damage he's done. It's our time now."

"*Our* time?" Gretar couldn't believe what he was hearing; his heart was racing.

"I'll start with the Redhots. They're the most loyal community that Ivry and I have." She paused, her eyes tearing up, "had."

"Yes! Use your power and influence to show the world!" Gretar jumped up out of his seat. "Tell them the truth! They'll believe you! It could be just what we need to make a real change—" He paused, seeing the grief on the girl's face. "I'm very sorry about your sister. I should've said that first. I can't even begin to imagine what you're going through."

"Thank you. I feel like half of me is missing. I keep looking for her, but she...she's not there." Mik sniffled, and quick as a cat, Ruby was out the door and across the veranda, handing the girl a silk handkerchief, a monogrammed 'MG' stitched onto it.

"Thank. You. Ruby," the twin said, more annoyed than grateful.

"Yes, my dear." The nanny scurried back inside.

Without thinking, Gretar reached down and placed his hand on hers.

"Unhand her...now!" A guard who had been lurking behind a tree carved into a swan barked over at him, startling the boy.

Mik looked at the guard. "It's okay, really." She paused, sizing up the short, thick-necked man. "In fact, you are dismissed."

"What? Miss Graves, I'm not allowed to leave my—"

"I said, leave!" Mik jumped up, shooting daggers at the confused sentry. "Now!" The guard, red-faced, turned abruptly and marched off.

Mik pulled her hand free from Gretar. "I've prepared a statement."

She took off her glove and made a series of quick taps on her tattoo. A sequence of tiny red and blue LED lights lit up along her arm.

"You prepared a statement?" Gretar smiled, surprised.

"Do you want to hear it?"

"Please. By all means."

Mik held out her arm; a tiny hologram projected a scrolling text inches above her arm, in bright neon red letters:

309

"My dearest Redhots, and all people of Earth. This is the dawn of a new era, one in which we need to come together. Our oceans, lakes, and rivers have suffered for far too long. My beloved sister Ivry is dead. She is gone from my side because we have turned a blind eye to the poison infecting our waters. Though I could not save her, this tragedy could have been prevented. Today, I am not only joining forces with the Ocean Conservation Coalition of Earthers, I am creating my own foundation which will be known as The Sisters of the
Seahorse Initiative. Stand with me in the fight to save our current and future home!"

Gretar, normally quite the talker, was speechless. Mik glanced over at him. "Well? Say something. What do you think?"

He blinked. "It's perfect."

"Good, then. Ready?" Mik cracked a slight smile. "Here goes everything." She pressed a button on her arm, then put her glove back on. "There. it's sent."

She attached two photos along with the message; one of Ivry beside the aquarium looking happily at their twin seahorses. The other was an image of Mont Michel's enormous trash deposit floating up to its shores.

In an instant, the millions of Redhots, just as loyal as Mik had promised, read her plea, and took action. Within hours, thousands had joined the rowboat protesters, dotting the waters around Mont Michel a bright red as they began a call for worldwide change. Mik had awakened many, but there was really only one person on Earth who needed to open their eyes—her father.

The Count had a dedicated staff of employees that monitored his satellite feeds. Graves current head of tech was a thirteen-year-old hacker who went by the codename Rrat. The gawky teen sprinted to the Spa Room to deliver the news of Mik's outgoing message. Graves was right in the middle of his daily massage when Rrat burst in.

"Uh, Sir, um, Count Graves, sorry to interrupt, but it's an emergency. There's been a breach in security," the young boy's nasally voice cut through the tranquil harp being strummed.

The Count's face was plastered in a neon green exfoliating mask, his eyes covered with two giant squid *(Decapodiformes)* eyeballs. "Who is that? Rrat??" Graves grumbled; he was lounging on a sealskin ottoman, wrapped in a thick, white down robe and matching slippers.

Two servants, one holding a bubbly black drink on a silver platter, the other with a domed serving tray of his world-famous caviar, stood at the ready. Around The Count's neck was his starfish *(Inconaster ilongimanus)* pendant, the tips of it dipped in gold, with a thick, gaudy matching gold chain. Graves sat up; his odd appearance off-putting as the boy inched closer. A third woman in a white leather pantsuit dabbed around Graves' brow with a sea sponge *(Porifera)* soaked in blue whale *(Balaenoptera Musculus)*

310

oil.

"You said a breach? What kind of breach?"

Rrat cleared his throat, "it's your daughter, Sir. She's somehow cleared our firewall and has broadcasted an...ahem...unauthorized message."

"Well, clean it up! Re-direct! Cast shadows! Do. What. I. Pay. You. To. Do!" The Count lowered himself back down, snapping his fingers for his servants to continue.

"It's a little more complicated than that, Sir. She's locked us out. It appears she's on a totally different frequency. I...we...can't locate it in order to scramble the transmission."

Graves sat up again. This time, the giant squid eyes slid off his face and into his lap. "What is this message?"

"You might want to read it for yourself, Count, Sir."

Waving the servants away, Graves jumped up, angrily walking over and stepping on a hidden panel imbedded in the floor. At once, a large six-foot wide screen lit up from beneath the marble. The Count stared down, reading Mik's message, seeing the millions of responses pouring in. "Get out."

"I'm sorry, sir. We'll...that is, I...will keep trying to shut it down." Rrat bowed, backing away nervously, the guards following him out.

"Dammit!" The Count tossed off the feathered robe, switching to a black silk robe, the cuffs circled with shark *(Selachimorpha)* teeth. He made a beeline down the hallway from the spa towards his office, barking into his earpiece, "Snive! I need you...on the double!"

When he passed in front of the twin fawn *(Cervidae)* statues of his daughters, he stopped in his tracks. "Oh...oh, my dear, sweet Ivry," Graves muttered.

"Sir? Sir?" In his earpiece he could hear Snive's squirrely voice. "Tell me what you nee—"

Graves switched off the earpiece and sighed heavily; he suddenly felt very tired. The fire in his belly was waning. Looking down at the heavy starfish pendant hanging around his neck, he casually turned it over, examining the underside of it for the first time. It was breathtaking; there were thousands of tiny, intricate ridges running along each perfectly symmetrical appendage. Graves admired the starfish's rich, subtle colors; far more beautiful than the gold it had been dipped in.

"So fragile...so very fragile," The Count mumbled to himself. He was still looking at it when Mik came up the hallway.

"Daddy, I'm sure by now you've heard."

Initially ready to scream at the girl, to punish her for what she did, The Count found he didn't have the heart. "Mik, honey...what made you say such things? Haven't I always protected you? Made you feel safe?" Count Graves walked up to her, placing a hand on her arm.

311

"That's just the problem, Daddy, you protected me too much. You hid things from me. Horrible things." She pulled her arm away. "Things that you were responsible for."

"Oh, Mik…those are all just rumors—"

"No," Mik interrupted, "I've seen the truth. The garbage, the waste…it was you that supervised that party! You that brought that poisonous fish from Ever-knows-where to our home!" Mik felt bitter tears welling up. "It was you that killed Ivry, and you're killing the oceans, too…but it all stops now!" She was shaking.

Countess Sarr strolled down the stairs, two assistants shadowing her. "Mik, darling, what's the matter?" She looked at her daughter, then The Count; they appeared distraught.

"Leave us!" Sarr turned to her servants. "Go see to that boy on the veranda!" The Countess ran to her daughter, rubbing her back as she glared at her husband. "Did you do something to her?" Her normally cloudy eyes were crystal clear.

The Count crossed his arms, gazing downward. "I suppose I have."

Sarr cocked her head and stared at her husband; she would have had a look of confusion, but years of silicone injections had stiffened her face into a rigid mask. Sarr turned back to Mik, who was crying.

"Oh dear, dear…I know you're still dealing with the loss of your sister…we all are." Sarr tried to hug her daughter, who pushed her away.

"You're to blame, too!" she yelled. "Both of you," Mik jabbed a finger at them, "both of you are responsible for Ivry's death!" Mik ran off, her footsteps echoing down the cold, marble hallway.

All the Count and his wife could do was stare at one another. After what seemed an eternity, The Countess finally spoke.

"She…she was our child, Zell. Our baby." Sarr left Graves standing in the great arched hallway, alone.

There was the clicking of footsteps; around the corner came Graves' puppet, Snive. He was clutching his stomach and panting.

"Sir! Sir! I have the Ambassador…on line three! He'd like to…schedule a day to finalize the drilling contracts….*Sir?*"

The Count looked around his lavish Palace and frowned. One daughter was gone, the other despised him, and his wife? Well…his wife…

"…Line three, Sir?" Snive wheezed.

For the first time in his life, Count Zell Graves, Titan of the Free World, Ruler of Mont Michel, felt utterly, completely lost. Although it seemed as if he had everything he'd ever wanted, he realized, in that miserable moment, he had nothing at all. He held up the starfish again, contemplating the miracle that had to happen for this magnificent creature to have existed. Graves tilted his head toward his devoted aide, who immediately perked up.

"Yessir??"

"Tell the Ambassador we're putting a pin in it for now. I...I need some time to think."

In the months that followed, Gretar's Earthers, side by side with members of the Sisters of the Seahorse Initiative, held rallies throughout Mont Michel. Their numbers grew, as did their voices. A worldwide shift began. Not just an awareness of the damage humans had been causing to the oceans, but also a re-connection to the beauty of nature. More and more people began to leave their homes to venture out, where they could witness firsthand all the magic that had been outside their windows all along.

Perl, still drained from her adventure, slept through the supper hour that first night. She woke just as the sun was beginning to say goodnight, the sky an artist's masterpiece of magentas, golds, and tangerines. Looking over at her nightstand, she saw her old sketchbook right where she had left it, the day she and Uriel had fled in Ximu's spider web balloon. Perl scooped it up, placing it inside her robe pocket, and padded barefoot down the root cellar's main hallway. She was surprised to see all her sketches, which were usually scattered about her bedroom floor, now hanging neatly along the walls.

"My drawings!" she said, pleased that the Brothers of the Quill had been thinking of her when she was away.

In the dining room, Perl saw Uriel, Ximu, and Brothers Victr and Basil seated at the long wooden table, laughing and toasting with mugs of Ximu's famous wild berry ale as a warm fire crackled. Perl tiptoed past them, not quite ready to recount all of her wondrous tales. She needed a moment alone, outside, with nature.

As she wandered down the path leading up to the garden, Perl looked around. *"Everything seems so much smaller,"* she thought. Filling her lungs with the salty ocean air, she let out a long, content sigh; it felt good to be home. Perl took a quick detour over to the beach, wanting to feel the cool sand between her toes, when she saw dozens of people, some curiously dressed all in red, picking up trash.

"Never seen that before," Perl thought, *"maybe there's hope for us humans after all."*

She was turning to head to the garden when she stopped dead in her tracks——there, working off by himself, was Slaughterman. He didn't seem to notice Perl. The old man, his mop of hair blowing wildly in the evening breeze, spoke to no one as he busily cleared the beach of debris. Perl thought back to the cave, when she saw him meeting with Uriel. *"What was he really doing that day?"* She knew he wasn't Malblud after all, but then who was he? Given all that had happened, maybe she was wrong about the stranger. Perl decided she would do something she swore she'd never do— she would look at Slaughterman's essence.

"I'm not afraid anymore. I gotta know," she told herself.

Perl stared at Slaughterman; slowly, his human form faded, and Perl was speechless by what she saw—Standing before her was a large, fuzzy honey bee (*Apis mellifera*). His golden, translucent wings buzzed as he flitted along the sand, picking up garbage with his slender brown legs.

"Of all things? A honey bee?!" Perl giggled; she couldn't believe it.

Hearing the girl, the bee cocked his head at her. The two of them briefly locked eyes. Perl gave a slight wave and the honey bee wiggled his antennae before returning to his task.

Perl left the beach, feeling almost giddy as she meandered up to the garden, humming to herself. Lifting the gate's brass latch, Perl took a moment to breathe in the sweet fragrance. She strolled nonchalantly past the batches of colorful flowers and savory vegetables, running her fingertips along the tops of the hibiscus. Reaching her favorite corner in the garden, Perl squatted down on a tree stump nestled between the orchids and honeysuckles. Opening her sketchbook and taking out the whale pencil Uriel had given her, she wrote in big capital letters, "HOME."

Perl paused, scratching her head. *"Now that Lophius is gone, I wonder if I'll get to see my mom?"*

She began sketching a ladybug *(Coccinellidae)* that was nibbling on a leaf, when she heard the gate's latch open and shut. She ducked down, but the footsteps were coming right towards her.

Perl called out, "guess you found me, huh, Papa?"

Slowly lifting her eyes up from her drawing, Perl was shocked to see Bear and Javan. She sprang to her feet, dropping her sketchbook and bouncing into Bear's arms for a hug.

"Oh my Ever! How are you guys here?!" Perl glanced around, looking to see if anyone was watching.

"Don't worry, only you can see us," Bear chuckled.

Perl looked at the roly-poly boy's bandaged stump. "Oh, your hand! I'm so, so sorry, Bear. It was all my fault."

"It certainly was not," Bear said, wiggling his remaining arms, "and no worries, I've got plenty of spares!"

Perl gave Javan an extra-long squeeze.

The platypus-boy brushed his bangs from his eyes, blushing. "We just wanted to make sure you were alright. The portal closed at the bog and just disappeared. We tried to find a way in, but couldn't."

"It's okay. I made it back. It was awful down there. I was lucky…somehow Uriel found me." Perl looked around, hoping to see the others. "Where's my sister? Opis, where *arrre yooouu?* Lemme guess, she's studying?"

Javan looked at his feet.

"Perl…she's gone." Bear cleared his throat, "Opis sacrificed herself. She blew up the bog, and herself with it."

"What?" Perl cried, pushing Bear. "Stop kidding around!"

"It's okay, really." Bear placed his arms around Perl. "She saved the Many Lost Souls. She helped them find their way home."

"But...she's gone?" Perl bit her lip.

"Don't you worry..." Bear squeezed her. "You haven't seen the last of Opis the ancient." He smiled at Perl as a tear streamed down her cheek. "Remember, we Light Beings always find our way back."

A tiny green leaf sprouted out of the ground. Perl smiled.

"Oh, by the way," Javan added, trying to cheer Perl up, "Kamani said to tell you to enjoy this break, because Seer training will be here before you know it!"

Bear added, "except he didn't *say* it...he yelled it. Very, very loudly."

Perl giggled at Bear; she loved the silly tardigrade.

"Seriously, my ears are still ringing!" Bear stuck his fingers in both ears, pretending to clean them out.

"I'll finally get to see all of Greenheart without having to battle a Roc," Perl said jokingly.

"I can't wait to see what kind of trouble you'll get us into as Seers," Javan smiled. "But for now, we're just glad you're safe."

Bear rubbed his bandaged stump across his belly, sniffing. "I thought I smelled some honey walking in...I just might help myself to a little on my way out." Bear winked. "Ta-ta for now, little Perly-poo." He hugged her one last time, then dropped and crawled away, whistling a little tune to himself.

"Good-bye, Bear!"

Perl sat back down on the tree stump, scooting over to make room for Javan. "Sit for a second?"

"It's nice here." The platypus boy squeezed beside her. "I can see why you like it so much."

Perl rested her elbows on her knees, balled her fists under her chin, and looked out towards the ocean. "Yeah, it's the perfect spot to watch the sun set."

Javan looked into Perl's green eyes. In them he found beauty, kindness, and passion. Most of all, he'd found a true friend. He pulled something out of his pocket, keeping it hidden tightly in his webbed palm.

"The oceans were hurting, and called to you." He took Perl's hand. "Everything in nature holds a secret, one it wants to share, so that everyone will understand its magic."

Perl looked into Javan's dark brown eyes. "Didn't Tryfon say it's only at the end that we see how we should've started?"

"Wise words." Javan nodded, his long bangs falling over one eye.

Perl looked out over the ocean; the red sun sat on the horizon like a ball on a circus tightrope. "I wish I'd known from the start about my parents, about Lophius. I might've done things differently."

"Sometimes you have to go through something in order to learn."

Perl cracked a smile, nudging the boy. "Wise words, indeed."

"Yep, that's me…wisest in all the land." He stood up.

Perl saw Javan was hiding something in his hand. "Whatcha got there?"

"Just a trinket I made, like a souvenir. You've been on quite a trip, and when you return home, it's always nice to bring back a little memento to remember it by."

Perl clapped, "let's see! I love surprises!"

Javan rocked back and forth on his feet. "Okay, close your eyes and hold out your hands, and don't open them until I say to."

Perl shut her eyes, crinkling up her nose. "Oo…so mysterious."

Javan placed a mini wooden sculpture into her hands. He leaned over, whispering into her ear, "with your hand, I'm always caught."

The girl sat there, silenced by his words, trying to recall where she'd heard them. *"The rabbit's verse…from our mediation with Master Bodhi."*

"Javan? Javan, come on. Can I open my eyes now?"

There was no answer. Perl snuck a peek; in her hands was a carving of two wooden rabbits, connected nose to nose.

"It's adorable." She looked around. "Javan?" Perl stood up, scouring the garden, but he was gone. "I love it," she said, placing it on the tree stump next to her.

At that moment, it hit her. *"It was Javan…he wrote the poem in my journal!"* Perl sat back down, whispering, "you're the rabbit to my rabbit, too."

As Perl's bright green eyes scanned the tranquil waters, she spotted in the distance a pod of great blue whales *(Balaenoptera Musculus)*. Like a choreographed ballet, each majestic creature broke through ocean's surface, filling their lungs with fresh air. Misty vapor sprayed up from their blowholes, sending sparkles of shimmering light into the sky.

Planet Earth rolled over ever so slightly, and the sun, now but a faint wink, slipped below the horizon, transforming the heavens into a breathtaking kaleidoscope of color. Perl opened her sketchbook to a blank page and wrote:

Sometimes I feel small,
but never insignificant.

A simple act of love
can change the world.

She closed her book and sat back, gazing up at the stars, and beyond.

LIST of CHARACTERS

Earth - Mont Michel:

~The Root Cellar~

* Perl: The Chosen One. Arrived on a whale to Mont Michel. Adopted by Papa Ximu. Daughter of Noaa and Dianna. Water Seeker. Wielder of Fortis. Brave, curious, impulsive, lover of nature and her sketchbook. Has bioluminescence, can see humans' essences, can communicate with nature.
* Papa Ximu: Head monk of The Brotherhood of the Quill. Guardian of Perl. Kind-hearted, even-tempered, loving, and wise. "Spider-monk."
* Brother Victr: Head cook for the Brotherhood. Dear friend of Perl. Big, strong, worrisome.
* Brothers Simon/ Kirkwood/ Jonathan/ Basil/ Sebastian: Monks of The Brotherhood
* Hadza: Yellow honeyguide bird. Sings with Ximu on their trips to the garden.
* Regor: Perl's delivery partner and good friend on Mont Michel. Older, lanky fellow. Nervous giggle. "Goat-foot."
* Gretar: Teenage boy. Activist. Part of the boaters protesting the destructive policies of Count Graves.
* Thora: Middle-aged female protester. Friend of Gretar.
* The Slaughterman/Dimitri: Mysterious old hermit who lives on Trash Island. Works for Count Graves on occasion. Wild-haired, odd, a scientist and loner. Apothecary. Seen as creepy to some.

~The Palace~

* Count Zell Graves: Chairman of the Oceanic Council/ Worldwide Waterways Committee. Overlord of the Golden Palace. Husband to Sarr. Father to Mik and Ivry. Rich, powerful, ruthless, greedy, cruel.
* Countess Sarr Graves: Wife to Zell Graves. Vain, clueless, nervous, trivial. Adores her daughters but is jealous of them.
* Ivry Graves: Privileged daughter to Zell and Sarr Graves. Twin to Mik. The more amiable of the two. One of two redheads left on Earth. Tech savvy, naive, loves publicity but is guarded. Was named Ivry due to having one less freckle than her sister Mik.
* Mik Graves: Privileged daughter to Zell and Sarr Graves. Twin to Ivry. The more callous of the two. One of two redheads left on Earth. Tech savvy, naive, loves publicity but is guarded. Secretly envious of her sister having one less freckle.
* Ruby: The Graves twins' forever nanny. Buxom blonde. Devoted, loving, protective of the twins.
* Snive: Count Graves' weasely, sycophantic assistant.
* Ms. Kind: The Palace's event coordinator. Gangly, persnickety, stickler for punctuality.
* Gaspar: The twin's personal fashion designer.
* Rrat: Head of the Palace tech surveillance. Thirteen-year-old hacker.
* The Redhots: Nickname for Mik and Ivry's rabid fanbase.

~Under One's Heel Secret Society Members~

* King Coppice: Ruler of the Wetlands. Old friend and business associate of Count Graves. Loud, boisterous, rude. Has prosthetic legs of a horse.
* Prince Tobias: Crown Prince of the Desertlands. Business associate of Count Graves.
* Kandy Vandenmire: Ambassador to the Southern Archipelago. Business associate of Count Graves. Flashy, fiery, ruthless. Ex-rockstar. Has a cheetah cub for a pet.
* Prince Névenoé: Possible future husband to one of the twins. Born into wealth, arrogant, colorful. Rhinoceros racetrack owner.

The Light Realm:

* Ever: Creator of the Universe. Pure Light and Love. Ruler of The Light Realm.

~Venusto~

* *Tryfon:* The Divine Master of Venusto. Magical, ethereal, dreamlike in appearance. Compassionate, enlightened. The voice of Ever's love and light. Always makes time for tea.

* *Uriel:* Light Protector. Eternal guardian of Perl. Chaperone and balloon pilot to Venusto. Stoic, statuesque, celestial, respected by all. From her endless battles, she is missing a wing and an eye. Has telekinetic powers.

* *Master Kamani:* Battle and Strategy Instructor. Great bison head and sturdy body. Large, strong, fearless, with a booming voice and a lust for life. Can transport to other planes through his mighty ground pound.

* *Master Bodhi:* Meditation guru. Tall, graceful, striking. Spiritual guide. Porpoise-like body with fan of feathers containing its numerous eyes. Can conjure up real images and scenes to use in its teaching.

* *Master Yew:* Mystic, thought-provoker. Calm, hypnotic. Pear-shaped with lemon yellow feathers and orange hair. Only distinguishable facial features are two bright yellow tiger eyes. Can levitate.

* *Quantaa:* Two headed flying greyhound. Battle Protector. Powerful, obedient. Unconditional devotion to Perl.

* *Grandmaster Olliv:* Grasshopper-man. Head of Orientation and chaperone for incoming Seekers to Venusto. Joyful, punctual. Says words twice.

* *Palo Santo:* Master Garden Nurse. Lives in a greenhouse in the sky. Ethereal, gentle, gracious. Mother to all nature.

* *Humboldt (The Fawn):* Mysterious Seer of the Future. Ancient, solitary, cryptic. Can alter shape to grow enormous. Lives in a hidden cabin in the heavily forested mountains.

* *Noaa:* Biological father of Perl. Light Realm Being.

* *Dianna:* Biological mother of Perl. Human.

* *Commander Marabunta:* Giant soldier ant. Master of Ceremonies for the Pompeius Games.

* *The Queen:* Giant ant. Queen to all ants. Giver of The Egg.

~The Seekers~

* *Javan:* Platypus-Boy. Land Seeker. Sweet, shy, concerned. Chestnut brown fur, long dark bangs. Clumsy out of water, but excellent swimmer. Electrolocation. Can shoot deadly quills. Of the Seekers, he is the closest to Perl.

* *Tars:* Monkey-Boy. Land Seeker. Fun-loving, nervous, nimble. Large bulbous eyes and a long tail.

* *Flax:* Salamander-Boy. Land Seeker. Cautious, timid, practical, energetic. Reptilian with solar-powered skin. Fond of raising his hand when speaking.

* *Corvax:* Crow-Boy. Air Seeker. Competitive, tall and muscular, serious. Black feathers, mohawk, cool gray eyes. Concerned about the danger Perl's presence is bringing.

* *Lyre:* Bird-Girl. Air Seeker. Thoughtful, entertaining, supportive. Incredible mimic. Lovely plumage.

* *Nan:* Butterfly-Girl. Air Seeker. Sweet, upbeat, excitable. Excellent flyer. Arctic. Beautiful crystalline wings.

* *Bear:* Tardigrade-Boy. Water Seeker. Silly, light-hearted, friendly, resistant to extreme conditions. Caterpillar-like, chunky build, rumpled hair. Roommate to Perl.

* *Opis:* Jellyfish-Girl. Water Seeker. Intelligent, outspoken, sometimes know-it-all. Thin, wispy. Translucent skin. Electrified tentacles for hair. Roommate and self-proclaimed "sister" to Perl.

The Dark Realm:

* *Ullen:* Antithesis of Ever. The Most Fallen. Ruler of the Dark Realm.

* *Malblud/ Lophius:* The Dark One. The Lost One. The Corrupt One. Evil personified. Dwells in the Dark Realm. Ugly, corrupt, grotesque, vengeful. Its twisted, monstrous features resemble an angler fish. Hates Perl and wants her dead. Controls an arsenal of horrific minions.

* *Whisper Wisps:* Foul minions of Malblud. Whisper evil into the ears of humans.

* *Gaarum:* Ancient Dark Realm Water Beast. Tentacles full of hideous, screaming heads and rotting teeth.

MELISSA (Greek for Honeybee) FLESHER
was born hopping from flower to flower,
climbing trees, digging in the mud
and chatting with butterflies.
A wonderer of nature and science,
she draws from both when telling stories
and making art. Pursuing her love for the Earth,
Melissa left her career as a professional greeting
card writer to create her debut novel,
PERL the AWAKENING.

Melissa's home studio is located in Avon, Ohio,
shared with her humor writer husband Erik,
her artist son Noah,
loyal greyhound Merlin, and a cat named Pie.
Follow her on Instagram @melissaflesher.

JACKET DESIGN AND ILLUSTRATIONS
© MELISSA FLESHER

AUTHOR PHOTOGRAPH ©ERIK FLESHER

Made in the USA
Middletown, DE
03 November 2020